PETE ADAMS

Ghost and Ragman Roll

Book Four of

Kind Hearts and Martinets

URBANE
Publications

First published in Great Britain in 2017
by Urbane Publications Ltd
Suite 3, Brown Europe House, 33/34 Gleamingwood Drive, Chatham, Kent
ME5 8RZ

A CIP catalogue record for this book is available
from the British Library.

ISBN 978-1-911583-03-5
MOBI 978-1-911583-05-9
EPUB 978-1-911583-04-2

Design and Typeset by The Invisible Man
Cover design by The Invisible Man

Printed and bound by CPI Group (UK) Ltd, Croydon, CR0 4YY

urbanepublications.com

Dedication

Ghost and Ragman Roll is the fourth book in a now completed, eight book trilogy, *Kind Hearts and Martinets*. As a consequence, *Ghost* was penned sometime ago and I struggle to recall particular support I received from people at that time, other than my family of course, who would often tell me not to bash the keyboard so hard; advice not headed, and the attrition rate of keyboards only appreciated by my IT support chap, Alan East - so thanks there.

Since the aging process limits my memory, I will dedicate this book to my current personified sources of inspiration; all poets, especially those who look upon me in the front row of recitals, the eejit absorbing every word, the cadence, the gut wrenching emotion, the humour. Since I read *Freefall into Us* by Tess Rosa Ruiz, *To the Lions* by Claire Meadows, I have begun a courtship with poetry. I admire how poets capture so much in so few words, achieve such intensity in well metered stanzas, translated also in performance; Sam Cox, Portsmouth Poet laureate, Maggie Sawkins, and in extended works, Stella Bahin in *The Unicorn Skin Drum*; beautiful writing that sends my heart soaring.

By the same author

CAUSE & EFFECT - Kind Hearts and Martinets Book 1

IRONY IN THE SOUL - Kind Hearts and Martinets Book 2

are available as Kindle editions on Amazon.

A BARROW BOY'S CADENZA - Kind Hearts and Martinets Book 3 is available in paperback and ebook editions.

Acknowledgements

My most tolerant Publisher, Urbane; the patience of Mathew Smith who audibly sighs when he receives my frequent emails, sheets of queries and *creative* suggestions. Mathew believes in the *Kind Hearts and Martinets* series, and we both acknowledge and thank the growing following of readers - Jack (Jane) Austin, not over the hill, he's coming over the hill.

The Pyramids Gym, Southsea, mentioned in this book, the staff who support my keep fat regime, contain their titters when I fall off the treadmill, tolerate my moaning about the *wrap* music and changing the TV channels.

"There is no grievance that is a fit object of redress by mob law"

Abraham Lincoln

"And what would he know about the price of fish?"

Pete Adams

Disclaimer

This Novel is entirely a work of fiction. The names, characters and incidents portrayed in it are the work of the author's imagination. Any resemblance to actual persons, living or dead, events and some localities, are entirely coincidental.

The story is principally set in my adopted City of Portsmouth but I have adapted some of the locations, settings and buildings to suit my imagination and the narrative. I love my adopted home town of Portsmouth and Southsea and I apologise to any citizens if they feel that I may have taken one or two diabolical liberties. The same applies to the scenes in Honfleur, an ancient French harbour town that I consider magnificent and have spent many days of peace and relaxation and enjoyed a good few plats de fruits de mer.

Prologue

Four weeks ago

You had to laugh, and people did, since the fight was on a distant beach, the seaward side of Fort Cumberland situated on the barren South-Eastern tip of Portsea Island. It had been a moonless, pitch black, October wintry night. Apparently, Richard the Lionheart, the founder of Portsmouth as England's proud strategic Naval Port, turned in his grave; his heritage defended by the 6, 57, a collection of seedy, fascist, football yobs, from an attack by Lenin's Britain, an equally seedy group of moth eaten, radical, left wing thugs; though not all was as it seemed.

The rip tide probably sucked out many of the protagonists, those few taken by Police, mainly the wounded, were not talking, and those supposed to have survived, just disappeared.

The local paper likened it to the Mods and Rockers, rival fashion gangs that held pitch battles in coastal towns in the nineteen sixties, going on to preach about modern values to a populace that still had yet to recover from being raped and pillaged by greedy Bankers. Many of the ordinary British people were still saturated in debt, and life remained difficult with little prospect of change, despite the pressure supposedly being eased after the Nation's debt had been rescheduled over seventy years, there was still a natural suspicion, a latent anger bubbling below the surface; people suspected the Bankers were at it again and grumbled, and those who knew the British temperament warned, this could be a precursor to something a lot worse; letters of complaint? God, and then what?

Pete Adams

"It'll be a lot worse," Jane Austin said sagely to the newspapers, tapping his nose, "the pressure may be orf, but there's a residua..., linger..., a lot of anger 'anging abowt, and that can be manipulated," and this, ironically, from a man who enjoyed a tin barf (laugh), or so they say.

* * *

Three weeks ago

It was time to turf the fat bastard out, and so they did, unceremoniously dumping him on Eastney beach amongst a gathering of tramps, 'Serve the fucking arse right,' a passing comment as they turned and left.

* * *

Two weeks ago

The financial world was stunned – Banker Jacqueline Parmentier had left her chic Paris apartment, tipped her hand to her eyes to deflect the gusting rain saturated wind, so she never saw the gunman. She bumped into him; "Ecusez-moi" bystanders reported her saying, just before she was shot, twice, in the head.

* * *

Now

'Av a bleedin' egg and bacon sarnie for Christ's sake and let's get going, you can eat it in the car on the way.'

They were getting breakfast at the cabbie cafe in Charing Cross, a quintessential London greasy spoon and Delores loved it. She didn't like her company though, the hideously fat misogynist oaf who will almost certainly end up in Portsmouth with egg yolk down his round the houses (trousers).

He did, and he tried to wipe it up with his grubby index finger elbowing Delores in the process, causing her to drive all over the place, 'Oi, watch what yer bleedin' doing tosspot!' She rebuked in her spiky cockney accent.

'You wouldn't let me stay and eat this in the cafe so how am I supposed eat wiv you all over the fucking show?'

'Shut it bozo.'

So he shut it, and she continued weaving down the A3 to Portsmouth.

Pete Adams

Chapter 1

The fat bastard hotel manager Brian Pinchfist was no longer fat. Whether he was still a bastard remained to be seen? He claimed to police he'd been kidnapped and held, underground for sure, and by people unknown to him who disguised their appearance and voices. He had been found by a Portsmouth Ranger, Jet (John Edward Thomas) Norris, having been unceremoniously dumped beside the incongruously garish, pastel coloured holiday huts on Eastney beach; the third one in, the pink one. Frozen, soaking wet and filthy, his almost skeletal body lost in his baggy shabby rags, he had shivered uncontrollably on a foul, early November morning. He had only a motley crew of noxious smelling tramps for company, if you excluded or could see, the equally skeletal Ghost, who was hauntingly showing concern for Pinchfist's welfare. Standing off from the toxic collection of human detritus was Jet, who, although more aromatically agreeable, had an equally comparable toxic personality.

The street people were too polite to mention that Pinchfist, this skinny, raggedy bastard, smelt pretty much as they did, except for maybe the meths and Special Brew. Jet was not so circumspect in his verbal exchanges to Fat Bastard or to the tramps. He was often on the receiving end of critical denigration, not least his colleagues calling him *Knob-head* when he wanted people to call him Jet; a cool name. So, he enjoyed any opportunity to pass on some vitriol, in equal measure, in the manner of all good bullies.

Apparently, during his near three months of captivity, the fat bastard was made to negotiate every scrap of food, frequently unsuccessfully, and had to learn to go without or so he claimed. The Doctors said he was in reasonable shape considering, saying it was as though he had been on a well-controlled emergency diet; quite remarkable. There appeared to be no ill effects if you ignored the pong, they said, ignoring the pong and Pinchfist himself, who cowered, cartoon like, behind a drip stand.

Pinchfist was unaware he had been missing for so long and looked forward to being reunited with his family and thus was amazed when, after hospital discharge, he was immediately arrested and within a short time incarcerated again, although this room did have a window, even if it had evident bars and the police were moderately polite. His confusion was exacerbated when it was explained to him that the cell's *Teasmade* was on the blink, though they did give him a sausage sandwich, but that sense of temporary rapture was spoiled when the Chief Inspector, a man called Jane Austin, said he would like to shove the sausages up his arse, meteorologically he said, but probably meant metaphorically?

Prior to his disappearance, the obese manager had huffed and puffed his way through his hotel remedial and refurbishment works, had manipulated all of the payments to suppliers and reneged on the final account so the builder lost a considerable sum of money. He had excuses of course, and all the builder could do was watch as everyone believed the fat bastard. The Builder and his family suffered, they cut back. People gave him time to pay the incurred debts as he was a good man, but enough is enough and other people had their own bills to pay, didn't they? A deal was offered, but it would go nowhere near what was owed, although it was acknowledged that a good job had been done; small comfort. "What goes around comes around", more small comfort also, and offered by comfortably well off people who knew only square meals. Even if it came around and visited itself upon Brian Pinchfist, what would it achieve? Everybody believed the fat bastard, he was making a profit for the hotel for the first time and the owners turned their own blind eye. So Pinchfist was arrogantly immune, and snuffled his piggish way around the hotel, bullying, stuffing and gorging, uncaring of the pain he caused other people.

"Penny-pinching, that's how you make money in this business", is what he would proudly say as he would negotiate and renegotiate on previously agreed bargains, until he had bled people dry. If you refused to negotiate or to accept his offers, "So sue me", he would stutter, not through any speech defect but because his words had difficulty in passing the layers of facial fat that constituted corpulent chops.

The builder fretted; what could he do? Then, out of the blue, the hotel settled the debt plus a bonus and a letter; a full apology. It saved the builder and enabled him to pay everyone else and the back payments on his mortgage, but where was Brian Pinchfist? It seemed he had disappeared with not a word of leave-taking; a last magnanimous gesture? People said if it was, it had been his only one and it had been a Brahma at that. The Pinchfist family were equally mystified, fat and mystified, but unmoved emotionally and physically as they stuffed their faces around the telly and looked upon the unrecognisable image of their dad, mum's husband, like a pencil on the TV screen. *Found, but where has he been? Please contact...* the kids changed the channel; *Sponge Bob* was on the other side.

The Portsmouth Community Police Department were equally mystified, not so plump, though some thought that Detective Chief Inspector Austin could maybe shed a few pounds. Ironically, it was Austin who had suggested the hotel owners appoint an auditor, to see if Pinchfist had enabled the hotel to shift a few pounds of their own, which he had of course, the irony being, the shedding of the fiscal had enabled the growth of the manager's larded pounds and his family's combined blubber. It became apparent that over a long period of time Pinchfist had sifted and sorted, small amounts here and little bits there, of cash, DCI Austin called it sausage and mash; he was from the East End of London. "An irony that", he told people, who were themselves then mystified. Jack liked being an irony, it made a change from being an enema, by which he meant an enigma. DCI Jack (Jane) Austin was known as the

Mr. Malacopperism of the Portsmouth Community Police Force, getting words and expressions wrong and often inappropriately used at the most inappropriate times and places. This is what made him so funny people said. He couldn't see it himself, but then he only had one eye.

"There were probably more funds missing than could be interpolated through the books and through those suppliers who were prepared to turn the Queens Shilling", Austin had said, meaning Queens Evidence but then maybe he didn't? They were in the naval port of Portsmouth, where in the not too distant past, men were *pressed* into naval service, forced to take the *Kings shilling.* "The navy was after all a sausage and mash business, like hotels", Austin also said knowledgably, checking to see if his nose grew. "Money over the bar and dealing with suppliers, backhanders, greased palms, know what I mean, nudge, nudge", he had said, fluttering his hand under his arm pit which caused a slightly malodorous (he called it manly) breeze downwind.

Following the arrest, interrogation, and charging of the equally fat accountant, Gertrude Git (she had German origins – "probably the Gestapo" Jack Austin had commented and had later been rebuked for), and if Pinchfist had been around at the time, he would also be well and truly banged to rights.

Later on it was concluded that in total a very large sum had been taken over a long period and clearly Fat Bastard had done a runner, albeit everyone agreed that this was a highly inappropriate use of the term, to infer he could run anywhere. The local Evening Newspaper suggested he had done a "Wobbler" with the money, and reported that the owner of the hotel group, who had turned a blind eye, had suffered an extraordinary accident that left him blind in one eye; ironically, not unlike Chief Inspector Austin of the Community Police Unit, who seemed oddly proud of that particular Irony! But then again, he was a drinking pal of Bernie LeBolt, crime reporter for the local Evening News; and now the fat bastard had been found.

Chapter 2

The honeymoon - Honfleur, France, a few weeks after the fat bastard had been found.

Sunday was market day in the historic square in Honfleur and Jack was in amongst the throngs, clearly, or evidently not so clearly, speaking his pigeon French; not to pigeons-francais but to the confused market stall holders-francais. Mandy could see the Gallic shrugs from the window of their hotel room in the Hostelerie Le Chat, although the hotel is now known by another name, Jack insisted on calling the hotel by its *"proper"* title; he couldn't pronounce the new name anyway. What you call a *"Jack-no-say-quoi"* he had said laughing. Jack Austin was not the sort of person who took change all that well, or speaking another language and that was obvious to Mandy even from this far away. She reflected, and then smiled to herself watching him, secretly admiring his confidence in amongst the *old enemy* as he called the French. She thought she would nip out and join him; maybe they could have a coffee on the square together.

Waltzing out through the swishing, former Le Chat's, electric glider doors she managed to catch up to him as he was regaling a trader about selling pets from a stall. He was preparing to buy all of the mangy kittens just before Mandy stopped him, 'Jack, we'll not be able to take them back with us; let's have a coffee on the square, eh?'

The magic word coffee, a bit like fish or seafood, all words that got his attention and the kittens were immediately forgotten; some *Dr Doolittle*. He changed her mind about coffee on the square and suggested they would prefer the harbour front. She was okay with that even though it was quite chilly, the rain was holding off, but the French had it sorted of course, the outside seats had clear plastic enclosures ready to roll down should it rain or if the wind picked up, so yes, she would do that; that would be nice.

They were enjoying a wonderful honeymoon and were not about to let the November weather distract from the pleasure they were having in each other's company, entering their second week away and they had visited many places in Normandy. Mandy, practiced in the art of living with Jack, had listened with a great deal of patience and not a little amusement as he made like he knew the history of everything and insisted on telling her. In Bayeux he had explained parts of the tapestry and when she pointed out that the card describing the exhibit said something else altogether, she had to stop him going up to the assistants and pointing out their error. But this was the Jack she fell in love with, and he loved her, and this made her feel amazing inside.

She stood patiently watching her *eejit* trying to organise the best seat by the harbour of the particular cafe that currently took his fancy. While he argued incomprehensibly with other patrons she reflected on their, what seemed like a long and incident filled journey over, what was in reality, a short period of intimacy that had brought them to this point in their lives. She was a successful police officer Detective Superintendent Amanda Bruce, now Mrs Austin, as she had married Detective Chief Inspector Jack (nicknamed Jane) Austin. She smiled to herself as he was not really much of a copper, and little by little she had found out over this short time, that seemed like ages, that he had probably never solved a crime in his life. He was though a very good spy, not action man spook, but the cerebral kind. In fact you had to keep the inept, clumsy, gigantic oaf of a bloke, definitely out of the front line or he endangered not only himself but anyone in the vicinity, and that included the bad guys.

It had come as a surprise to Mandy to learn, eventually, that he had never actually retired from MI5, although he did pick up his gong, a CBE, for pretending to do so, and a lot of people, those that knew anyway, would say that about summed up Jack. Typical of the man though, he had surrounded himself with an entourage of amazingly clever but cowboy misfits, and it was this bunch of loyal monkey spanners that did all the solving for him. What he was good at was piecing things together, assembling and dissembling, thinking laterally, seeing the overall picture, and that is what he had always done in MI5 and still did, only in the guise of a community policeman. The fact that this cockney, jumped up barrow boy, spiv of a bloke had settled himself in the Southern England coastal City of Portsmouth was also no coincidence. He had left London, he says, because he wanted to be beside the sea, which was in part the truth. However, in reality, he was charged to set up a benign, low level police unit that could investigate anything that worried MI5 in Portsmouth, a strategically important naval and commercial port.

He had recently been instrumental in resolving a conspiracy that caused the country to be submerged into chaos and saturating debt, and if Mandy knew anything about the price of fish, and living with Jack the renowned seafood nut, she obviously did, there would be repercussions. But for her, she was fifty-four and for Jack, who was now sixty and suffering from Post-Traumatic Stress Disorder, it was time to slow down and look to retirement, which she also knew scared the bajeezers out of him. Still, this was good, a holiday and he had handed the reigns over to Jo Jums, Detective Inspector Josephine Wild, who had a good control of the spook operation known as the Community Policing Squad, which occasionally, and for good form, did what it said on the can.

She thought she would like to continue taking her ease and muse more this morning but the Patron was signalling for her to do something about Jack. So she stepped in, 'Jack, please, this seat is the one I would prefer. I can see the old carousel and I like to look at the mediaeval buildings,' she said, heading for the new table.

'Well why didn't you say? Only I thought as we sat at this table last night...' he had a confused, hang-dog look.

'I'm not like you and have to have the same place all the time, I like a change, prefer a change even,' and she expertly disguised her exasperated look. He wasn't listening; naturally, he was busy directing the waiting staff away from the other table, much to the relief of the woman and the amusement of the man already sitting there.

'Cafe espress et un Americano seal vous plate mate,' and Jack wobbled his head as clearly the waiter understood his order, 'Douze points je pense,' the waiter understood these words also, but not the rhyme nor the reason, nevertheless he toddled off to get the beverages.

'Oui Jack, tres bon,' and Mandy relaxed into her seat and looked around her whilst acknowledging his twelve points; she knew what was important to her husband. Honfleur was truly a magical place, an ancient harbour that Jack insisted William the Conqueror sailed from in 1066, but the man at the museum had told her, quietly, it had in fact been Barfleur. She thought she would not disillusion him, he was so excited and she was sure William the Bastard wouldn't mind. Leaning back in her chair and drifting, she said, 'It's truly divine here Jack, I'm glad we ...' she was brought back to reality as Jack interrupted her discourse and ducked under the table, '...Jack, I was talking to you.'

'Shush look away love,' he whispered, so naturally everyone heard as he was, as he says, a bit Mutt and Jeff (deaf) and consequently shouted everything. He wouldn't wear hearing aids, arguing that he didn't want to look daft, so she was having this so called hushed conversation with him under the table and the both of them looked daft. Then she saw him crawling away and halt at the feet of a man who had parked himself beside their table and then sidled to intercept Jack.

The man looked down, amused, but with no appearance of surprise, 'Bonjour Jacques, comment allez vous?'

'Custard, you old tart,' and Jack began the slow and rambunctious exercise of standing up and pretending he'd just found a franc.

'Jack, please come and sit down and introduce me to your friend, and its Euros now.'

'But we're on honeymoon love and I was talking about a mate

of mine, Frank.'

Used to her man and his face saving inanities, she gestured her head to this rather suave, intelligent looking, forty something swarthy Frenchman; tall, even if he was slightly stooping with more than a hint of a hunch. He had the look of a warped *George Clooney* she thought, and with synonymous confidence and flare, the man took a seat from an empty adjacent table and sat down next to Mandy. Jack eventually joined them, two puddle stains on the knees of what he called his cream holiday round the houses (trousers). He didn't notice, but if the chuckling from the other customers was anything to go by, they all did.

The deformed *George Clooney* took Mandy's hand and kissed the back of it and introduced himself, 'Henri Cousteau, Direction Centrale du Renseignement Intérieur, to you ma cheri; French intelligence.'

'Yeah, yeah Custard now Renard pied Oscar,' apparently French for foxtrot Oscar, fuck off; Monsieur Malacopperism, 'we're on our honeymoon as I'm sure you know.'

'Custard Jack?'

Henri explained for Mandy, 'Jacque mixes Cousteau up with custard for which we French have no word, apart from crème anglais, but what do I know, they all call me Custard in the office now and even my kids do; my wife thankfully sticks to Henri.'

Mandy laughed, recognising the effect that Jack and his nicknames seemed to have everywhere, which clearly extended into mainland Europe as well, then pulled herself up, 'Why are you stalking us, I saw you yesterday evening?'

'You did?' Jack looked surprised.

'Yes Brains, but don't worry, I'm a real police officer.'

Custard laughed, stifled it when he saw the look on Jack's face and stopped completely when he caught the menacing stare from Mandy.

'Okay Custard spill the feckin' flageolets ami, and then feck off, seal vous bleedin' plate.'

Custard laughed at Mandy's use of Jack's famed Cod Irish,

cockney and Franglais, but her face indicated that it was not intended to be amusing.

'I am so sorry Mandy, Jack can take care of himself, certainment, but for you, I am truly sorry. So I will be quick,' he signalled for an espress.

Mandy told the waiter to feck off, but nicely, and in her perfect French, and then to Henri, 'Parlais frog, maintenant!' not so nice, or perfect.

Jack wobbled his head in French and sent the gesture that said *let that be a lesson to you*, over to Custard adding a few knobs de brass, but Custard ignored it and opened up, focusing on Madam Sensible.

'We have intelligence that there is an extreme right wing faction working from our port of Caens and your own of Portsmouth. The reasons, we do not know, but Jacqueline Parmentier, a senior banker who was instrumental in the deal that changed the financial map for Britain and then Europe, the deal you were involved in Jack...' Henri's was a face scrawled with sadness, '...well...' and he wobbled his head, and then said, with clearly a heavy heart, '...she has been killed.'

'Jacqueline, she's dead?'

He nodded, 'Oui Jacque, murdered. We suspect these right-wing individuals and we are worried that this is not just reprisals, but another conspiracy. They want to continue to disrupt society further, still rocking from the knock-on effects of the credit crunch and subsequent recessions, and someone is using right wing factions to achieve this. How, we are not sure, but we think it is being driven from your side.' Henri accompanied all of this with the manual Gallic flourishes that so amused Jack and mesmerized Mandy, doubly so as *George Clooney's* hump was not so evident as he sat facing her; this was a handsome Frog.

But Mandy noticed Jack looked care worn, in significant contrast to the joyous face he had put on especially for the holiday; his *visage vacation* as he called it, was shattered.

'Oh merde on it Custard,' he sighed in French, a token Gallic shrug and he vibrated his lips like a satisfied horse. 'We expected years of social unrest following on from the deal, of course, people were seriously unsettled by recent events but Jacqueline, she was a lovely woman. I knew she was scared. It was mainly her idea to spread the debt over seventy years, did you know that?'

Custard nodded, he understood, 'We do not know what is happening but something is. I thought I would, err, how you say, tip you the wink.'

Mandy stepped in, 'You do know we are thinking of retiring don't you Henri?'

'I do and I wish you well, but you should tip your guys in the field. You know how it is Jacque, it takes time for *les grunts* to find out what is really happening, and sometimes...' he shrugged and pursed his lips, '...it's too late.'

Jack nodded, acknowledging this sad fact, looked up and waved and shouted 'Garden.'

Custard corrected him, 'Garcon.'

'That's what I parled diddli?'

Mandy laughed with Henri and they sat with coffee and Jack ordered three glasses of Armagnac, it was nearly lunchtime and he fancied it and Custard did too; it took the chill off, both physically and emotionally. Custard drank his Armagnac and espresso then excused himself, kissed Mandy three times. Jack noted this and knew he'd got the old European kissing off Pat, she didn't seem to mind, and so if anyone asked he could say that Custard does three, and how could they argue against that, and if they had a problem they could ask Custard or even Patricia?

'A good point Jack, I will remember to support you also on that,' Mandy said. Jack was known for his propensity to speak his thoughts, some saying this contributed greatly to the difficulty people saw he had in life, a picture of life that eluded him, but nobody else.

'Did I...?'

Mandy nodded smiling, 'You did. Shall we go back to the hotel and have lunch? They had some lamb I wanted to try. You can have fish, of course, and then an afternoon in bed eh?' she raised her curvy eyebrows that he thought were gloriously lush on her beautiful, if aging, Sophia Loren boatrace (face). He stood and took her hand and as she raised herself so he pecked her cheeks three times. He looked around to see if everyone noticed, but all he saw was a Patron seemingly pleased to see the back of him, which didn't worry Jack as the bloke was French, so what would he know, apart for the price of fish.

Chapter 3

As they strolled back, hand in hand, Mandy gently enquired about Custard, 'I suppose we have to expect a bit of this eh?'

'Not really, I told Del Boy to get the word out I was winding down, but some of these blokes, and Custard probably, thought if he told me to my face I would get the message through to the right people...' He held his hands out in supplication as he paused and she looked at his face, etched with sadness. '...Aaaah shit on it... Jacqueline. John Sexton was close to her as well, and, well, I liked her; she had balls.'

Mandy stayed looking at his face which, if you could get past the ugly and brutal scarring, always magically portrayed his emotions. It was not what you would call a poker face, although she often thought it looked like it had been hit with a poker, the dustpan and brush plus a few lumps of coal. He was not a good looking fella in any classic sense, especially compared to the humpbacked George Clooney, and she tittered to herself. Glimpsing looks as they continued walking, she saw what she always saw, his face lined almost as a chronicle of his emotional life. You saw this if you got past the empty eye socket, the sunken puckered skin and horrendous scarring that he, of course, saw as a minor blemish and never even thought of covering up.

They reached the square. The market traders were packing up their stalls and the street cleaners were out, the thrum of vacuum lorries killing stone dead the tranquillity of an emptying market square. Jack noticed the kittens had been discarded and left to fend for themselves, hanging around, scavenging scraps of food that had yet to be swept up. He resolved not to think about it but felt oddly *triste* for the plight of the *enfant chats*; he always insisted he was like a comedian and could blend in anywhere, and France was *un piece de gateau*.

Mandy noticed again the animation on his face and the direction of his gaze to the kittens and slipped her arm into the crook of his chameleon elbow, and squashed him to her. He felt the comfort trickle and titillate his body and turned to face her, 'Shall we put lunch back a bit?'

She smiled, a radiantly beautiful smile. Mandy's face in contrast to his, was beautiful, 'Yes, let's do that,' and as they trotted toward the hotel entrance, deliberately plunging in the puddles and avoiding the stares of the people who tried to avoid their splashing, so their good humour returned and they laughed as they ran for the stairs and their bedroom. Jack thought it was a bit like running slow-mo through the cornfields they show in the Rom Com films he liked so much, but he rapidly dismissed that as nonsense; Jack Austin was a town man and was distinctly unnerved in the countryside.

'Jane.' The call halted their progress just as they swept through the hotel reception and were about to put their feet on the lower steps of the broad staircase. They turned in unison to face a man, about five foot eight, stocky, charcoal five o'clock shadow and an immense nose, not unlike Mandy's in shape, which was full-size and Roman, but this was bigger; this man was from Nose City.

'So what can I tell you Abe my boy?'

'Oh no Jack please...' Mandy said despairingly.

The nose pointed at Mandy as Jack made to explain, at the same time mock dodging the gigantic fireman's hose as it swept past him, 'I'm sorry love, this is Abe Hyman, probably not his real name; he's a Tin Lid (Jew).'

Abe rather airily tripped his way across reception to Mandy who was backing up the stair and he pecked her three times. Mandy said, 'Please, let me guess … Mossad?' A little of her good mood had faded.

'Oui cherry douze points, eh Abe my boy,' Jack said in a

remarkably cod French accent.

In fairness, Abe looked embarrassed and a little guilty at the obvious intrusion, 'I am sorry Mandy, and even for you Jack. I was going to leave this until your last day but I noticed Custard talking to you just now and thought I had better intervene. He thinks this is a right wing fascist faction in Caen and Portsmouth, and to a certain extent we are always worried about the rise of Fascism in Europe again, but my government think this is more Middle Eastern; Al Qaeda, who knows?'

Mandy said what Jack was thinking, 'Abe, should we not be talking somewhere more discreet?'

Abe shrugged, 'I've said what I needed to, and so I will leave you to have a wonderful honeymoon, and please accept the congratulations of my government. They are always grateful for past services Jack, you should know that. We never forget and we will always look out for your welfare, and now you of course Mandy, you can rely on that.' And Abe turned on his heel and Mandy watched his bum in tight jeans disappear, aware of the swish of the doors as well as Abe's arse. She thought, apart from Abe's backside, whatever happened to the really good looking spies, or was that only in films, but then she thought Henri was a bit tasty, even if he had a wonky back.

She turned back to Jack, 'Jack, stop playing with your face, and what have you done for Mossad? I suppose all we need is the CIA and then we'll have had a full set,' and she laughed but noticed Jack didn't. 'What is it Jack, are you not diverted?' it was Jack's favourite *Pride and Prejudice* quote.

'Oh yes sweet'art I am exceedingly diverted,' he replied in his best *Pride and Prejudice* accent, 'can I introduce you to Felix Lighter of the CIA.'

She laughed and pushed him gently, lovingly, 'Oh Jack stop messing about,' a poor *Kenneth Williams* impression. 'Let's go to bed, pretty please with brass injuns on pleeeeease,' she tipped her head down from the steps, kissed him on his monk's spot and tugged his arm. He didn't move, and returning to the first step she looked around his shoulder to see a stodgy unattractive man, making an equally diabolical fashion statement; checked jacket and ill matching window pane checked trousers, Hawaiian shirt and a pork pie hat. The man was tall but portly, not unlike Jack but with no style, very much not like Jack, and this man appeared almost bloated, not like Jack either who had the hint of the muscular but you had to be determined to look. Okay, so I'm in love with him she thought; so kill me.

Felix Lighter was clearly a Septic, as Jack would say (Septic Tank – Yank). She exhaled a long held in breath and speaking as she did so, 'For fecks sake, a Frog, Tin Lid and a now a Septic,' and looking around and through clenched teeth, 'let's have lunch. Felix or whatever your name is, you say your piece then I want you to Foxtrot Oscar, comprend?'

The man nodded but not knowingly, then he followed and as Mandy strode deliberately past and ignoring the Maitre d'Hôtel, and she heard Felix asking Jack what Foxtrot Oscar meant and Jack relaying that it was "Strictly come dancing, only instead of the 'come' its 'fuck off' dancing".

Mandy sat down at a corner window table, permitting herself the tiniest of titters, especially as Jack had gone to the table they normally sat at. He saw her sit and decided that maybe the corner table was nicer. The waiters also thought better than to challenge the decision, and started to set the recently cleared table for three places, but Mandy, in her superb French, told the waiter to set for two. She beckoned Felix to sit, Jack had taken his seat opposite her and Felix went to sit next to Mandy. She gave him the look, and he sat next to Jack.

'It's not Felix Lighter, it's Bubba French; please don't laugh.'

She didn't, she was not in the mood for laughing, 'Talk then Bubba,' it was the famed Mandy impatience and even the CIA must know of this by now.

He turned to face Jack but had to look at his blind eye, Jack's good one was preoccupied looking at Mandy. 'Jack, Mandy, we know what has been happening and what people think is happening, here in France and in your country, but to us the perception is wrong. We're worried about your Government Jack.'

Jack became politically animated, 'Well that makes two of us, feckin Tories and Lib Dems, what a load of shysters.'

Bubba seemed unaffected by Jack's reaction, 'Jack, you miss the point. We are seriously worried. You hood-winked them with the financial deal and we think there are some serious dudes upset, not best pleased when the Lib Dems were taken in as part of a coalition; this was not what was supposed to happen. These people are going to do something and it is going to be serious payback,' and as if to accentuate his point, Bubba made a wrinkled face that did nothing to improve his sourpuss look, although Mandy thought it was amusing how his pug nose seemed to move independently of the rubbery cheeks.

Jack swung his head to look at Bubba, smoothed his own recently shaved chin and thought he would like Mandy to rub her hands on it; he liked it when she stroked his face.

'Thankyou Jack, I like stroking your face as well,' she said, melting a little.

He accepted he'd spoken his thoughts, and speaking to Bubba, 'Felix, I think you're saying even Mackeroon and Blogg are at risk. Is it the Civil Service Mandarins what've been nobbled?' Bubba nodded, as if this was all too much for him. 'Well, we're getting more like you Sceptics' every day then. So you think I should pass this up the line do you, to those I can trust?' Bubba nodded again and after the jowls had settled, he made to stand.

'Hold your horses,' not Jack but Mandy. 'You do know we'll look like right tarts unless we can name names and back it up with proof?' She looked at Jack quizzically as if to say, did I just say tarts?

Bubba allowed her a moment of reflection with perceived amusement, not guaranteed to endear him to Mandy, but he seemed oblivious of the danger. 'I do Mandy and I do not have names or any proof, other than we are convinced something is happening. So I suggest you let Jack tell them; they already know he's a tart,' and he laughed and for the first time Mandy thought it was better.

Laughing, he had a pleasant face for a shite dressed advert for why you should avoid McDonalds. He stood, 'So there you have it, I was going to tell you as you left but since you had been disturbed so much today, I thought, what the hell.'

Mandy calmed, 'Okay Bubba, thanks for that and if you will excuse us I want to order, then I'm taking Jack to bed, and then we need to be up in time for six o'clock mass.'

Bubba looked a little bemused at the reference to mass, shook Jack's hand and kissed Mandy, just the once, and Jack thought they've got no class the Sceptics. Turning back to Jack, 'No, maybe we haven't Jack, but I can never get this European kissing thing.' It was the poor Bubba boatrace.

Jack knew how to make him feel better, 'Bubba my old china, you only needed to ask me and I could've squared you on it. See you when you get into London; Tate Modern?' and Jack waved Bubba away, after agreeing to meet at the art gallery that Jack pretended to hate but really liked, and a waiter sashayed and presented them with some complementary drinks; Pastisse for Jack and a Kir Royale for Mandy.

Jack looked up and they were now attended by the Maitre D'hôtel. 'Madame, Monsieur, please accept my apologies for your disturbance, we tried to prevent those men from approaching you; it is not what we like to see at our hotel.'

Jack stood and shook the man's hand, 'Ne pas perspiration mate.'

Mandy's eyes joined the waiter's at the ceiling and she thought Jack had clearly also forgotten that they promised Father Mike they would go to Sunday mass at the church in the square.

* * *

They had a beautiful lunch. Mandy marvelled at how Jack seemed content with the relatively small portions when he was in France. He said it was because it took so feckin' long to get on the table, and then you felt you had to eat slowly because everyone else did, and savour the food, or get a frog cleaver in your tete so, obviously, your appetite went. But of course all he really wanted was his huge Plat de Fruits de Mer, which he ironically took about two hours to eat. He'd had several Plats already and she enjoyed watching the pleasure he got from it, even if he always took one of the whelks out when he thought she wasn't looking and pretended to take it out of his sightless eye socket, and then eat it. It was funny, well it was the first time, and despite all of his moaning he clearly loved it in France, and ironically, liked the French, and would never change a thing. Strange, when he frequently railed about the frogs, but then he would explain that it was all about ancient enmity and how you had to persevere to keep things like that going. "Tradition you see, especially in the rugby. The French did the same only the English were better at it of course".

Chapter 4

They had a passionate afternoon in bed, not fizzing, but intense, and rose to the bells summoning the faithful and Jack to church. The bonging reminded them of Exeter, their first dirty weekend away, but this time the bells were not a Cathedral but a local church, being more or less in the centre of the square and virtually outside their bedroom window. It was safe to say they were awake.

'Darling,' Mandy turned Jack's face to her, 'Father Mike suggested we go to this church, you don't mind going to mass do you?'

He spluttered a laugh then summoned it back as he saw she was serious, not confident he was quick enough though. 'Mike asked?' (Father Mike O'Brien was the eccentric priest who was also a long-time MI5 colleague of Jack).

She put the face on that said she would spill the beans on him when they got home, but continued whispering in his ear; it was actually near on shouting as, of course, he was famously deaf and then add bongs. 'I also would like to say a prayer in thanks for all that we have; you and me. I never would have thought I could be this happy, even with the spook interruptions, whatever nationality. And well, if Father Mike wanted us to go, how can we go home and say we didn't?'

'I will go with you love. Religion leaves me cold but I enjoy the sense of the spiritual and I do get that sense in this church, but it's my own internal thoughts that provide my sustenance; and you of course.' Nice save he thought.

'Thank you love, nothing to do with the fact you're frightened of Mike then?' she let that sink in as he steadfastly refused to change his face; it was his Blow-tox look (meaning Botox), he always said. "Shite-box face more like", she always said. 'Come on, Mass is in twenty-five minutes,' and they made a dash for the shower.

They were ready in time. It helped that Jack loved to see Mandy with her damp hair and minimal make up; she was a glorious beauty to him, "au natural" as they say en France.

'Merci Jack, I wish I could say the same about you, nevertheless I love you dearly, but maybe I should have gone to *Specsavers?*'

They rushed down the stairs giggling and skittered across the polished wooden floor and through the swishing portal, to the shock and horror of reflective patrons partaking of "a pair of teef", as Jack would say; meaning aperitif. They were watched as they flew hand in hand across the square, splashing in the same puddles and shocked more than one person when they went inside the church. Mandy's heels clacked across the stone floor and they managed to get seated just as the priest was commencing, he paused, looked up and acknowledged them. Odd Jack thought, but dismissed it as French, which of course was his explanation of most inexplicable and daft things, even back in England.

The thing about France of course, is that it is a Catholic country and the churches are generally well attended. This one was, and Jack felt warmth from the congregation, even if the air was decidedly chilled. He grabbed Mandy's hand, which she withdrew as she bowed her head for a personal prayer.

'What's that one love?'

'Shusssh Jack, it's personal.'

He nudged her, she swayed, 'Oh go on, tell me, is it about me?' but he did respond to the Shusssh from the congregation; not so warm now, and the stare from the priest was positively frigid. Jack harrumphed but got le giste de le massage. The service proceeded in a melodic way that was so Catholic, Jack didn't understand the French or the Latin; Mandy seemed to. She went up for communion and came back with a piece of paper. She looked up to the heavens that Jack thought was another prayer for him, as she stuffed the message in his hand; it was from Father Mike, he recognised the writing. She told him to put it in his pocket and gave him the stare as he tried to read it first. Alright he thought, I might look at that after, but his head rose from the paper and his hand missed his pocket, as the priest spoke in English and mentioned Mandy's and his name.

'Today I pass on a blessing from the Holy Father, to Monsieur Jack Austin and his wife Amanda, in our congregation this evening. It is a Papal blessing for their recent marriage and to say thank you for their services to all of us in Europe. I cannot say much about what they have done, indeed I do not know what they have done, but I understand it was dangerous and they succeeded and we are all to be very grateful. The priest repeated this in French and the congregation stood, turned and faced Jack and Mandy, and applauded.

Mandy looked at Jack, typically he would be up on his feet, bowing, or hunched and crying, but he just appeared to be embarrassed, was this progress? Jack was an inveterate weeper and she was determined to help him, and weaning him off Rom Com films was to be his starter for ten. He was to be even more embarrassed as the priest stood in front of them and Mandy stood, he kissed her three times and then he grabbed Jacks ugly and wrinkled cheeks, tugged and kissed him, three times on the cheek and finally, a smacker on the lips, standing back afterwards admiring his priestly kissing with Jack's unsightly cheeks still in his hands.

Better not tell Mike of that he thought, as he pretended to spit feathers out of his mouth. But now he was really confused and started to ask the priest what the feckin' hell number of kisses was it, and in England you were lucky to get one kiss and a raspberry tart, but the priest did not really understand feckin' and clearly, contextually, misunderstood raspberry tart (fart).

'Maybe they don't get *Father Ted* over here?' Jack said to Mandy, still bemused that the Priest did not understand him.

Mandy smiled warmly and thanked the priest for the honour, in French, and explained that Jack quoted all kinds of films, *Mary Poppins, It's a Wonderful Life* and TV shows, *Pride and Prejudice* of course, but one of his favourite sitcoms was *Father Ted* and he quoted all of the Cod Irish he could, and whenever he could, the feckin' eejit, she said and she flicked her eyes heavenward, and gave the priest her best exasperated grin that the priest seemed to understand and reciprocate.

Jack nudged Mandy, 'Ask him if he wants a cup of tea? Say, aah go on, go on, go on, go on – go on love.' She shushed him, but he was so proud of his wife conversing in French to the frog priest he looked around, wobbled his head and said to anyone listening, 'C'est ma Oiseau' and got a full on, and in unison, Gallic shrug with the traditional "uuh" in response. Jack made a mental note to add the "uuh" to his Gallic shrug when he got home. He had the pouting lips right though; he was a stickler for detail.

'Yes you are love, and the lips are indeed very good.'

Spoke his thoughts again – le der!

The service ended and Jack and Mandy found themselves as minor celebrities, hugged, kissed and feted as they left the church. The whisper went rapidly around the small square and the Maitre D'hôtel of what was once Le Chat, came out and dragged them back into the restaurant. He stood them by a table and busied himself while they cultivated their Gallic confused look, which Jack reckoned he had off pat now and he had even added the "uuh" , but wondered as a waiter went "phhtt" in reply to Jack's attempt to ask what was happening, in cod French.

'Phhtt, what the feck was that?' he looked for an explanation from Mandy but she was busy being sensible, so he worked it out for himself and added it to his French armoury.

Mandy exchanged some words in French which the waiters ignored as they continued dragging more tables. Soon, Jack and Mandy were drinking champagne with French people they had never met before and this went on for about a half an hour, when Jack's pigeon French and Franglais was brought to an abrupt halt. A man ahemmed in French, and stood to attention in French, with people moving away to give him space; moving as the French did, shuffling, and Jack pointed this out so Mandy would know in the future when he shuffled, in French. Jack whispered to Mandy that the bloke needed the space, as he reckoned it was the *Fat Controller* out of *Thomas the Tank Engine*, minus the top hat; although Jack thought he looked a right top hat (Pratt).

Mandy smiled politely at Jack's cockney rhyming slang as the man commanded the floor for a speech. She whispered quickly, 'He's the Mayor, the red, white and blue sash around his belly is the giveaway bit, dinlo,' and she shushed his anticipated retort, which he resented as he hadn't even thought of one.

The Mayor made his speech, thankfully for Jack it was short and there was energetic applause, 'What'd he say, love?'

'I'll tell you later, hang on,' and Mandy left him and went to the Mayor, kissed him three times. Jack could be heard to say, "C'est trios" and then stood, mouth agape, as his wife made a speech to the assembled melee in perfect French. There was a responding appreciative applause and Jack, proud of his wife, stood in front of her, anxious to bathe in as much reflected glory as possible. He bowed and then bowed again, and as his head returned to its starting point, the Mayor was in front of him. Jack stepped back and bumped into several people, the Fat Controller was trying to kiss him and he was obviously wary following the priest snog. But, standing on tip toes, the Mayor succeeded with three and then dragged Jack to the front.

Mandy was laughing almost uncontrollably, a beautiful face Jack thought as he glanced back at his wife, but the face morphed to a look of horror as the Mayor indicated a speech was required from Jack.

Mandy whispered, 'Jack you don't have to do this,' but he dismissed her with one of his very best Gallic shrugs, managing also to fit in a "pffter", and, assuming a true Gallic posture that resembled his pregnant Swan Lake donkey, he made to start, waving his arms demonstrably. She left him to it, and tried to relax. With Jack you have to take the relaxation where you can find it. So she started relaxing as he started talking.

'Bonjour, bonjour,' so far so good, though he seemed stuck, it was more a perplexed look, not sure why the accent had not been received with energetic applause and then a light bulb came on, which confused Mandy as he was being particularly dim, but he continued with much more confidence, even gusto, 'La plume de ma tante et sur le pont D'avignon avec mon frère Jacques...' and he smiled to himself while the French audience looked for his aunt's pen which they knew was silly as it was with his brother, strangely also called Jack, on a bridge in Paris. They swivelled their collective French gaze back and forth, shrugging their shoulders and going "haaahh".

But Jack had thought of something else to say in the meantime; you see, it's all about buying time he wanted to say to Mandy but thought he'd better get on with it while he was fluent. 'Je suis un pop etoile et un supporter de Millwall, un cloobe de football de Londres.' He stood back to take the anticipated applause but there was none, just une mer de bewildered visages francais. So he continued, thinking they may think he's a football hooligan, the reputation of Millwall extending back to where "Le Conqueror" departed, and this may be the beginning of some sort of revenge.

Mandy heard his spoken thoughts and whispered, 'Revenge on the language, oui.'

But he was off again, seeking to repair any possible damage, 'Je ne suis pas, un nutter extraordinaire, et nous somme tres pleased avec le blessing de papa et nous will be hanging et sur le mantelpiece, dans nous salon de maison.'

There was a cheer for that, whatever it was? Must have been acknowledgement that they had a mantelpiece in their house he thought, and he felt charged with more French words and some of them were verbs. Mandy noticed him set to continue and stepped in, patted him on the back and cleared things up for the French, assured them they were not all Millwall fans and nutters, and they were indeed honoured with the papal blessing. The applause was energetic but polite and Jack stood in front of Mandy again to accept this on their behalf, exaggerating a bow as if he was a concert soloist and muttering, 'Are my shoelaces undone,' and as he came up, 'oh yes they are.' He explained to Mandy that he'd had bowing lessons for when he met the Queen, which he had done several times now. Mandy rolled her eyes along with the Mayor, but they were through it and it seemed they were now to have dinner with the Mayor, his family and entourage, heaven help us she thought to herself.

'Heaven will help us love, we have a papal blessing, der.'

'Did I...?'

'You did love and tolerably well, what's happening now?' and he swung his Gallic gaze back to the Mayor.

The Mayor had stood still, erect, with his hand over his heart but it should have been his ears as the local band, that had appeared from nowhere, played the French National Anthem; La Marseillaise, and to the horror of Mandy, Jack sang his made-up rugby words that ended as, "Marchon, Marchon vous etes un couchon, oooh est le pouf célèbre" (march on, march on, you are a pig and where's the celebrated homosexual? Least this was what Jack said it was). Mandy thought they had gotten away with it and Jack felt he had sufficiently avenged King Harold who probably finished the battle of Hastings with an eye not unlike Jack's, except he was dead, and Mandy was thinking she just might settle for that right now.

* * *

Apart from the fact they were, annoyingly for Mandy but not quite so much for Jack, minor celebrities around town for the rest of the week, the honeymoon went off smoothly and romantically; unmolested by spooks or any other significant interruptions. Their new-found status did have its perks, especially as to where Jack wanted to sit in restaurants and, as he explained to Mandy, she was getting a very good view of his "derriere" when he took bows. Mike's note had said that he loved them both and hoped they have an undisturbed honeymoon, apologised for the papal blessing, but the Holy Father had insisted, "So what can I tell yer, d 'you think it's easy". Nice touch Jack thought, finishing up with a bit of Hebrew; did Jack Austin know languages or did he know languages?

They just had the ferry to get through and they would be home, though Mandy worried, Jack was not known for his seamanship not that he would admit to it. He had mentioned to a couple on the way over that he could have been a Captain if he didn't have, "Un petit bit of mal de mer every now and then". They got a cabin so he could be sick without losing his masculinity in front of the rest of the passengers, and Mandy had a good book to read, as he spent most of the crossing in le bog; he was being sick in French.

The honeymoon had been great but like a lot of good things, it was soon over and it was also very nice to be home, even if the foul weather had followed them; they were back in their own bed. William the Conqueror safely back in Barfleur.

'Honfleur love.'

'Did I...?'

Chapter 5

Monday morning and Mandy was up, dressed, and ready to go into work, feeling remarkably energised. Jack of course was still off sick, the powers that be insistent, finally, that he be treated for his Post Traumatic Stress Disorder (PTSD). She had watched him and wondered if he was keen to get back? Clearly he had energy but it was difficult to know with Jack what he was truly thinking, or how he really felt. A slow slide into retirement she had imagined or even dared hoped, but realistically never expected; was this ever really on the cards? She tried to summon up the words that would describe what it was she actually expected, did she even know what she wanted? Carry on in the next level of MI5 with Jack, or just stop? Then what?

They had shared a languorous Sunday, never straying far from their bed and listening to the weather outside pounding against the windows and walls. They talked about the visits from Henri, Abe and Bubba; Fascists, Al Qaeda or Civil Service, or all three? Should they do anything? Jack dismissed this all as typical paranoiac spook talk and the desire to "big" themselves up in front of a good-looking bird. Mandy took him up on the expression *Big themselves up*, deciding to tackle him on the *bird* reference later. It was another of Jack's traits, using what he thought were modern expressions to make himself appear younger. He reassured her that all the youngsters were using that term now, but did mollify her by saying he thought it was charming having an old-fashioned wife, and she gave him an old fashioned look in response, which he liked. He liked most of her looks, although some were clearly on the danger list and sometimes came out of the blue and when he had done absolutely nothing wrong.

Whatever he said, Mandy had a feeling that all was not well in Jack's state of Denmark and she could tell he was uncomfortable. She knew also he would pass the messages onto Father Mike, so he in turn, could pass the information onto the right people in MI5. She knew Jack well enough to know also, he would do something about it and that he would tell her in his own time, and for now she was okay with that; he needed time to "gurgitate", his term, suspecting he probably meant cogitate but then again, you never knew. So they slipped smoothly back into it, Mandy at work, Jack apparently "recoopering", getting better in the way only he could, gurgitating and being a bleedin' nuisance; maybe even making a few barrels.

They had talked about Christmas, their first Christmas together as a married couple, but Jack's mind went a decided blank, and so she decided to leave that till a bit later herself and settled back into work, which was a lot less stressful without Jack, though she missed being with him and even working with him. Jo Jums had completely taken over the Community Policing (CP) Unit, as Jack had encouraged, and it was ticking over like clockwork, as he had also predicted it would. It was all Mandy could do not to face the fact that she was virtually redundant.

Chapter 6

Late November often threw up foul weather and this morning was no exception. The Solent was full and the prevailing south-westerly, gusting to gale force, was hurling the waves at Southsea's sea walls, and a foaming tidal wave crashed over, then washed across the promenade and even the road.

Jack had left this magically energetic and hypnotically intimidating wave action behind, as his morning walk followed the paved promenade eastwards and now skirted the expansive and desolate beach at Eastney seafront. Sweeping tracts of shingle, interspersed with tufts of sward clinging desperately to some sort of purchase that enabled it to survive, symbolised the barrenness of this eastern Portsmouth coastal landscape. The grey, churning and turbulent sea was dramatically electrified by voluminous black and agitated cloud formations and tantalisingly distant lightning. Jack walked and mused, he liked the barrenness, the lonely landscape that he often likened to his soul. There was nobody else in view, just Snail beside Jack's pastel marker beacon, a lemon beach hut in the distance.

The sounds of the pounding waves were less fearful at this distance, the crashing surf and hissing of sucked and dragged shingle, just a whisper, lost in the sound of a multitude of splashing pin pricks as the swirling wind drove the rain into Jack's face. The mesmerising allure of the turbulent depths eased as his distance from the sea increased, and correspondingly the consequent bubbles in Jack's stomach soothed from boiling to a gentle simmer. The predominant sound was the whistling of the wind and the shushing of the rain, as it hit the pavement in bursts and was picked up and then thrown at his face by the gusting and eddying, gale force wind. Jack's not so good ears rattled and sang with the wind, his music was useless in these conditions, the sound of wind and rain seemingly amplified by the bud ear phones when he squashed them in. This was good though, because on a day like this Jack did not have to decide if he wanted to listen to Sibelius or Mozart, Mother Nature won out on this morning; well Mother Nature and his own churning thoughts, every bit as vigorous and intimidating as the distant tidal action.

Although he missed Amanda being beside him, it felt good to walk on his own. It was also comforting that the powers that be trusted that his sense of self-preservation was such that he could be allowed to go out on his own, that he would not be tempted to throw himself under a bus or into the churning waves, though, given the choice of ending it all, and the trick cyclists (psychiatrists) had never asked, he would choose the waves every time. He always sensed he had a destiny with the sea. Amazing to think a Londoner should feel he had an appointment with the distant sea. Why? He could remember when he was probably around twelve, nearly drowning on a family outing to Hastings. He could clearly recall the mixed sensations of panic and yet an accompanying sense of serenity. He never told anyone. His Aunt looking for him on the beach just asked how he had cut and scratched his feet and legs, which had happened as he scrabbled over submerged rocks, seeking any purchase that would give him time to breathe, before he went under again.

Some thirteen years ago, Jack had been involved in a fight trying to arrest a suspected serial rapist on the Camber fishing quay. This lead to Jack and the suspect falling off the quay onto the deck of a trawler, where the rapist gouged out Jack's eye with a boat hook leaving him blind in that eye and the right side of his face scarred and grotesquely disfigured. He was awarded the Queen's Gallantry Medal; most people were not aware of that or of his CBE. They were aware of his George medal of course, as the fiasco of his receiving this from the Queen was televised and frequently called up on TV Favourites programmes. Mandy, bless her, tried never to be embarrassed but he supposed there are only so many times she can watch the repeats, though he was sure that she thought his arse looked good as he bowed to the Monarch.

It was interesting that the trick cyclists focused on the loss of his eye and the patent trauma suffered to his face as the probable commencement of his post traumatic events. They even saw the fact that he never covered up the resultant vacant socket, with its all too evident sunken wrinkled skin and the vertical white scar that ran from his forehead down to about an inch onto his cheek, as evidence of his disturbed mental condition. They never asked about how he felt when the adrenaline and his well-known berserking nature took the fight over the edge of the boat and into the harbour, how he was hardly aware of the eye injury. They hadn't asked and so Jack hadn't told them. Why?

In truth, the serious disfigurement, the excruciating pain and the blinding, was not what he viewed as the trauma. It was the panic he felt falling into the harbour, which was ironically viewed by people later as Jack selflessly diving in to save the rapist, but in truth, he had stumbled and fallen over some coiled cables; the floundering, the splashing and intermittent disappearances beneath the murky harbour depths, interpreted as Jack trying to save the evil assailant, was in fact panic and again ironically, blind terror, looking and feeling for the rocks from Hastings.

The assailant had drowned, he couldn't swim; more fucking irony. Jack always supposed that as you grew older you could see irony in just about everything, as his sense of it increased; "Irony in the Soul" he called it, to anyone who was willing to listen. He had mentioned this to the trick cyclists and they just said "Very interesting, but also quite stupid". Jack was reminded of the German soldier on *Rowan and Martin's Laugh-in*, a TV programme from the sixties. They thought that was very interesting as well, and Jack felt stupid.

Just recently, as the Head of the Community Policing unit in Portsmouth, he had been investigating the occurrence of dead dogs in the harbour and whilst looking over the quay in the naval base, he had been shot by a sniper. A high velocity bullet thankfully only hit and passed through his shoulder, but it caused him to fall into the water. A strong undertow at this part of the harbour immediately sucked him under and out, sweeping him some fifty metres into the shipping lane, to be eventually rescued by the MOD police harbour patrol; very lucky, but also quite stupid, least he thought so.

The trick cyclists had interpreted his subsequent PTSD event outside Southsea Castle as a consequence of his association of the conditions of the shooting and the cold of the harbour waters. He had been walking with Mandy and their MI5 minder in weather, not too dissimilar to this morning, and his mind had just switched off. Leastways this is what Jackie Philips, psychiatrist and the consultant trick cyclist Dr Jim Samuels of Harley Street, who was also coincidentally head of Jack's MI5 division, had said. The fact is that it wasn't the pain in his shoulder, nor the intense cold of the wind and rain that caused him to collapse; it was the water in the castle fountain pool. As shallow as it was, he had been spellbound by the coursing mini waves, picked up and driven by the wind, and he saw this as a vast ocean in a hazy dream that he could not touch and he felt like drowning himself. He felt the desire to regain that sense of serenity or was it a release of responsibility? He'd never quite worked that one out.

The experts of course pronounced he had switched all his senses off, to go into an infant like state as a sense of self preservation, and of course he would have no recall. He hadn't of course, he just kept a little of what he knew to himself, didn't even tell Amanda and he felt bad about that. He had actually lost his conscious state of awareness, they were right about that, but he could recall why it happened. They didn't know that and he didn't tell them, and he could not say why.

'Snail, how are you my old son?'

Snail was Jack's nickname for Brian, a name after Brian the Snail in *The Magic Roundabout*, a children's TV programme that Professor Brian Mayhew only vaguely recalled. Snail regularly sat on this part of the promenade edge, dangling his legs over and wiggling his feet, looking out to sea as if it was a glorious summer's day, which he did daily, especially if it was a glorious summer's day. He looked out to where, in the distance, the Solent met the notoriously treacherous rushing waters, sucking in and spewing out from Langstone Harbour. He looks to see if his daughter will return. She won't of course, having fallen off a jet ski and been swept out and never seen again.

'Snail my old son, my old mucker?'

No response from this man Jack called old mucker or old son but was actually almost twenty years younger than him; everyone was son to Jack, and often old son or old mucker, never viewing himself as sixty, and many people thought this was the source of a lot of his problems. When Jack Austin supposedly retired from MI5, he emigrated from London to Portsmouth. Emigrated, because this is what you do if you are a Londoner. How anyone could even think of leaving the Capital City is beyond belief for most long-standing London families, not least it was beyond comprehension or acceptance of Kate, Jack's first wife. They separated, she could not understand his fascination with the sea when he hated sailing and was sea sick on ferries, but Jack responded to the call, his destiny to be beside the sea and he joined the Portsmouth CID where his berserking nature and often cavalier attitude, caused him constant difficulties with the bureaucracy to top all bureaucracies.

For a so called inquisitorial service, nobody, except for Detective Superintendent Amanda Bruce that is, questioned where he had come from. How Jack Austin had just walked into the rank of Detective Inspector and, how he got off all of the disciplinary charges that trailed in his wake. Amanda Bruce, the new Mrs Austin, was also the only one to wonder just how this rather inept man kept miraculously coming up with solutions to crimes, both minor and serious, without any evidence of a normal investigative or deductive trail. Most people said Jane Austin was a natural born copper, but Mandy had noticed that many, as they declared this, had their fingers crossed behind their backs. As Jack and Mandy became close, so he had slowly revealed to her his involvement still in MI5, the sometimes dangerous situations he, and now she, found themselves in. The fact is that Amanda Bruce joined Jack in MI5, running the benign Community Policing team whose task was to monitor and investigate events in Portsmouth, a key naval base and commercial port, a modest island City that contained so many overt and discreet services and facilities essential to the security and prosperity of Great Britain.

Jack sat down next to Snail, mimicked the professor and wiggled his feet, although Jack's were inside his sea boots. He was in his trawler gear, sea boots, hi-viz yellow waterproof trousers and a slick coat and sowester, all given to him by Fatso and Maisie the trawler owners with whom he had become fast friends. It was Fatso and Maisie's trawler he had fallen onto and it was their daughter, Dottie, he had saved from the rapist. The waterproofs kept the storm out but it could not stop the interstitial sweat. Despite the cold outside, Jack was bathed in perspiration from the energetic walk and the nervous sweat that accompanied his disturbing daydreams; currently, fear of retirement and incongruously, fear of going back to work and synonymously the fear of being old and washed up. Another irony that "washed up" and that is what he would be if he threw himself into the sea. He needed only to slide down the slippery, sloping, Southsea sea wall, but he had to think of Amanda, he always thought of his kids, Alana and Michael, Martin his dog, Meesh the orphaned waif he had rescued from paedophiles, and now the recently discovered daughter, Alice.

He needed especially to be there for Alice as she, also ironically and tragically, had to deal with a ravaged face. The previously radiantly beautiful (she had taken after her mother) police woman, had been attacked by fighting dogs. You saw them all over Portsmouth, aggressive, arrogant slobbering animals and that was just the owners. Jack vowed he would do something about that some time, and he would. A myriad of missions that kept circling and building up in his head, and this stopped him throwing himself into his sea; that and his children, and now Amanda.

However, his most important daydream was of course, a return to a more caring socialist government. How could he die and not leave that sorted? He saw and hated the prevailing discarding of the moral compass, the reckless abandonment of care for fellow man in the name of wealth and power or even personal survival, and often off the broken back of the ordinary working man and woman. Bastards that trod humankind into the dirt, ground to pulp the human spirit, and he would have that lot as well; just needed to stay away from the sea he supposed.

'Jack, you okay?' Snail seemed to have become aware of Jack's presence.

'Sorry Snail did I just speak my thoughts?'

Snail nodded, but he was well aware that this man, a kindred spirit of sorts, often spoke out loud his thoughts. Many put it down to the onset of dementia but he had always done this, and this was currently also perplexing the trick cyclists who saw the mix of berserking, daydreaming and the speaking of his thoughts, as some sort of psychological key that would unlock the torment of Jack Austin's mind and return him to a semblance of peace and serenity. A peace that a man who had achieved so much in his life, deserved; a peaceful retirement, a slow and gentle slide off the mortal coil, not unlike sliding into the sea, only that was likely to be less painful; euphoric even.

'That's what I feel Jack.'

'Did I...?'

'You did Jack and I know you feel what I feel.'

DCI Jack Austin and Professor Brian Mayhew – founder members of the suicide club, or was it the survivors club, Solent division, and they sat dangling their legs and encouraged the onset of pneumonia. They'd talked about this. You see, if you die of pneumonia, then the loved ones left behind can grieve and move on. Only marginally better than slipping into retirement where you are of course ignored and left to rot above ground. If you committed suicide then you leave behind a screwed-up family, and that was not acceptable, and so the two men, the founder members of this club, followed a philosophy known only to them, well them and the three other men and one woman in the cemetery chapel, and Ghost, and of course the people who were currently observing and listening to them from the adjacent lemon beach hut.

Chapter 7

Jack and Snail sat just along from the pastel coloured timber beach huts, sentinel, lined up as if they were the Realm's first line of defence, on the edge of Eastney beach; defence for modesty at least, and a nice cup of tea in more accommodating weather. If Snail sat too close to the huts, the stretch of water that had swept his daughter Beth away was obscured. Ironically, if Snail had sat closer to the lemon beach hut, then, and in more clement weather conditions, he might have been able to hear his daughter reporting what she was seeing and hearing, back to her colleagues stationed in a nearby cemetery mausoleum. These confederates had turned her away from her father, so much so that she felt no emotion looking upon the suffering of her shell of a parent, once upon a time a man so important in her childhood, a man she had loved and with whom she had shared her life. Beth no longer reflected on how she had arrived in the situation she was in, such was the intensity and success of her induction. In the Seventies Jack would have called it brain washing, but would have known that for the technique to succeed there had to be an underlying desire in the individual for the eventual outcome.

Beth had been studying politics at the University of Portsmouth when she disappeared, to all appearances enjoying the beautiful weather after the exams, sail boarding and jet skiing on the Solent, enjoying the choppy tidal sea conditions at the mouth of Langstone Harbour. She was an activist, but not one with whom Jack would empathise, well not on a doctrinal basis. Beth held, and had energetically espoused, right wing fascist views that had found a welcome home as the British people railed and fought, tussled and demonstrated against greedy bankers, a coalition government of politics and policies that were forced through as the only way out of the economic dilemma. It was the five-year target to address the debt, the symptom of the banking system that had caused so much grief and hardship, as the *austerity* and resultant cutbacks bit into the lives of ordinary people who could see no rhyme nor reason why they should suffer, and lent even mild mannered people a fierce anger that could be taken advantage of. Very much as the Nazis did in the thirties and Snail's daughter and her colleagues encouraged anew.

Like for like, redress? Yes I suppose, Jack would say it was, but social fairness? No.

Jack Austin and his myriad anonymous colleagues who did the behind the scenes clever stuff for Jack, had exposed the credit crunch and the subsequent recessions as a conspiracy. A plot to drive the western world into the ground, to be later rebuilt by self-interested and extreme organisations and individuals who, as a consequence, would have gained control of the big companies and in some instances the assets of nations; even the country's themselves. This was a logical extension of that thought, and isn't that exactly what the Nazis had tried, Jack had argued. Jack had also argued that these new perpetrators had patience and would encourage their insidious philosophy of life to seep into the psyche of the British people, as it would, and it would work, unless it was checked and rooted out.

Following the rescheduling of the nation's debt, the government had pronounced the recession was over; the economy will re-establish itself and grow again, and the perpetrators of the diabolical conspiracy were to be identified and rounded up. Not all of course, and it had been pointed out to Jack that some had to be left in place, to keep the systems going – a big toe rag of an irony that was, and definitely not lost on Jack. "How can you leave even the hint of a rotten apple in the barrel, and wasn't the barrel rotten?" he had said, and this was his big worry. This was a worry that prevented him from fully handing over the reins or even slipping into the churning Solent. He could not discharge his sense of responsibility, he had always had a burgeoning sense of responsibility, and this had dogged his heels since a boy.

For the ordinary man and woman, the country would appear to be no longer under financial pressure, and growth and social investment could return; for the time being at least. Here of course, and ironically again, Jack was the source of the mature thought process, because he knew this would not, could not, be the end of it. Almost hypocritically, he knew the desire for revenge ran deep in the sorts of people that could contrive to destroy a society by taking advantage of an artificially created culture for personal greed, wealth and power, the additional and never ending irony being that by incentivising the ordinary man to seek wealth and power, it played into the hands of those very few people who would eventually, solely, achieve it.

Hypocritically, as Jack never had a problem with his own hypocrisy, he supposed to beat these people you had to identify the individuals and corporations, weed them out and get rid of them, even if the powers that be said to leave some in place! So Jack did not see himself sinking beneath the waves just yet, there were people that needed to be got rid of and this sense of urgency continually rose to the surface of the bile in his stomach.

That was it, and Jack could do no more, well not officially as he was officially on sick leave, but he could keep his radar twitching, he could still sift and sort, still keep in touch with his various contacts. He knew this type of person, this type of organisation, and they called him a jumped-up barrow boy, which actually and again ironically, he liked, because he was. Still he had set things in motion and so...

'Werzer guntle yer.'

'Werzle an gert Ghost.' Jack replied.

'Was that Ghost you were talking to Jack?' Snail asked looking around and seeing nothing, just Jack nodding; Jack was fluent in frontier gibberish as well as Pigeon French.

Chapter 8

Detective Superintendent Amanda Bruce was in her office with Jo Jums and Jackie Phillips. Jo Jums was the nickname given to Detective Inspector Josephine Wild, also known as Ma'amsie, a derivation of Mumsey, which described the appearance and nature of this short, middle aged and comfortably plump, astute and very intelligent police officer. Jo Jums had been a *police* colleague of Jack Austin for more years than she cared to recollect, so of course accepted her co-opting into MI5, as well as her nickname, all as a matter of course. With Jack Austin if you didn't have a nickname then you just felt out of it, though only the special few were co-opted into the secret services. Some people even looked relieved when they received their epithet. Amanda Bruce was variously known as Mandy Pumps, Mandy lifeboats but more often than not just called Mandy; she was after all a Superintendent.

Jackie Philips was the rare exception, a child psychologist and also Jack's MI5 personally attached trick cyclist. She was a tall, slim, mid-fortyish elegant black woman and wore her straightened hair in a French bun that Jack called a croissant. Jack had previously called her Lips (Phil*Lips*- see there was logic) and then Phil. Jackie had tolerated this while she was a friend of Jack's first wife Kate before she died and even for a short time while they investigated a paedophile ring, with Jackie supporting some of the rescued children. But as she grew closer to Mandy and Jack, looking after a young rescued girl, Meesh, she had asserted that she would tolerate "Jacks" but would prefer it if Jack restrained from calling her Lips or Phil. It was a testament to the high esteem with which Jack held Jackie that he agreed, and with only the occasional slip, had maintained.

Jo Jums, Jackie and Mandy, all newly inducted into the parallel world of MI5 courtesy of their various relationships to Jack Austin, were talking about the man now; so no change there then. Austin was the sort of individual who had a larger than life presence, and for your own self-preservation you had to take him in small doses. Mandy, having recently married Jack, was the exception, but she'd also absorbed a lot of Jack's C of E, Church of Egypt philosophy of De Nile (Denial), that and she had a veritable female support system around her, well, all women if you didn't count the gay catholic priest Father Mike O'Brien, a long-standing friend of Jack's and also his conduit, and now theirs, in MI5.

'He thinks we don't know Mandy. He's made progress but is way off returning to work, whatever guise that takes, and I've still not got to the core of his difficulties,' it was Jackie.

Mandy sighed, although working with Jack had its stressful moments, she felt alive just being beside him, at home and at work. He talked about how she'd rescued him from his seemingly unending grief after the death of Kate, but Mandy felt it was more than a mutual thing.

'I've been speaking to Del Boy this morning,' Jackie continued, (Del Boy was the MI5 Field Officer attached to Jack's unit) 'and whilst it is all quiet on our own western front, apart from the stories you learned on honeymoon...' and Jackie broke off to allow a little giggle that Mandy clearly did not appreciate, '...he was asking about Jack, what was he doing?' Mandy was not really listening.

'Mandy.'

'Yes?'

'What is Jack doing?' It was Jo Jums pushing her Superintendent whom she had initially hoped would calm Jack down, be a more mature influence and take over from her own matriarchal caring role, but as it had transpired, the Superintendent had virtually succumbed to the childlike behaviour of her now husband. Jo would ordinarily be irritated, her matriarchal and maternal wing now having to extend to both Jack and Mandy, but she found herself envious. Mandy had found a new lease of life with Jack Austin and had recently told Jo that she felt in her professional life she was finally doing something positive, pro-active even, not just clearing up the mess created by other people. In her private life, as chaotic and worrying as that seemed to Jo as a steady Eddie type of person, Mandy radiated happiness, as did Jack when she saw them together.

'Mandy?'

'Sorry Jo, I was drifting, thinking what he might be up to. I'm not so naive to expect him to share every thought, and he needs time to relax and shake off his intensive eejit, secret squirrel background, and I'm patient, but I do know he's galvanised, but what with, who knows?' She shrugged her shoulders, 'The honeymoon messages were so contradictory I cannot see how anyone can make sense of that information.' She shook her head and looked to her window, large and south-west facing, that afforded a view to a magnificent leafy tree that currently was energetically swaying and resisting the prevailing gale and bursts of intensive rain that machine gunned onto the glazing. Mandy saw this tree as her and Jack's own metaphor, bending and swaying in response to elemental pressure, hoping it could resist the powerful elements and in turn radiate positive energy when more benign conditions prevailed.

'Do you know where he is now?' Jo asked.

Mandy felt a dreadful sense of déjà vue, 'At the gym?' This elicited a knee jerk guffaw from Jo and Jackie. 'What?'

'Jack, going to the gym?' Jo squeezed out between rolls of laughter.

Still in distant thought about where he could be, Mandy matter-of-fact replied, 'Yeah, he wanted something to do and like an eejit I threw that one into the ring. Of course he took the ball and ran with it like a kid,' she sighed and smiled, recalling his enthusiasm.

Jackie sensed some revealing facts coming and if not, then certainly a laugh, and so pursued the sigh, 'Come on, tell all Mandy.'

Mandy looked back from the window, sighed again, returned her gaze to the window and spoke to their tree. 'Where do I start? The clothing, his behaviour at the gym, the phone calls, how they would prefer it if I was with him when he's there, especially during the busy times.' Mandy continued tree watching, blissfully unaware of the giggling from the high ranking professional women sat in front of her desk.

'Well, tell us about the clothing first,' Jackie said, with her fist in her mouth stifling her almost out of control mirth.

Trancelike, Mandy spilled her thoughts, 'We joined, and straight away he wanted to get some spandex, trendy gym kit, but I managed to steer him away from that one.'

Jackie and Jo Jums had to release the pent-up hilarity, picturing Jack, a full six foot four, and a humongous heavy man, in spandex or Lycra.

'Mandy, what does he wear?' a more restrained titter from Jackie.

Mandy turned to face her giggling audience and showed a little of her famed irritability, 'It's not funny, he now wears his old rugby kit that he's not worn for twenty odd years and so of course, in effect, has all the semblance of skin tight Lycra, bar the stretchy material. Plus, he apparently used to do decorating in it when Kate finally trapped him into doing some domestic chores, so it's covered in paint splashes.' Mandy smiled, succumbing herself to the picture that was her husband and the man she loved. Conventionally you might say Jack was big and ugly but in fact, and in a most unconventional way, he was attractive and to many women. Mandy knew this, saw this, and often thought he had that playful personality and acceptable overweight appearance and boyish charm that is *Jack Nicholson*, but with a face that was more of a cross between *Geoffrey Rush*, the actor, and a slapped arse. She laughed to herself as the thought flitted across her mind, but she continued to tell of the trials and tribulations of Jack Austin at the gym, the Pyramids, that he called the Pyramints; an Uncle Josh (posh) set-up, Jack had said.

'He actually goes quite often, and I know this because they will call me if he's fallen off the treadmill,' and Mandy looked up from her thoughts at the almost hysterical Jo Jums and Jackie. 'Yes, he falls off when he has a young woman next to him, actually looking the part in her Lycra, and he tries to look at her without being obvious, even more difficult if the woman's on his blind side. The women love him of course, but the supervising staff worry and try to keep him off the treadmill unless I'm there. They know he'd never look at another woman if I'm there you see.'

They did, but kept it to themselves because Mandy was on a roll.

'Then, in front of the treadmills they have TV's and he fell off once when they were advertising bras and other women's underwear, and the men apparently get fed up as he shouts out woolly woofter to the ads that display men's cosmetic products. He compounds this, laughing at these blokes who could all manalise him anytime they wanted, when they contest him and say they're not averse to a bit of Nivea on the boatrace.'

More chortling but Mandy hadn't finished.

'And at home he's always body popping and singing these modern songs that they play in the gym, which of course he gets wrong, and would you believe it, he wants to go to a *Gig* at the Guildhall, where some rapping band is playing. He looked so disappointed when I suggested he might look a bit stupid in amongst loads of young people and that I didn't really want to go. But, as you would expect with Jack, he put that to one side and he now wants to go to something called Zumba, said you can do this in old clothes with rips in, he'd seen them on the Telly, and of course he has lots of old ripped clothes that he will not throw out because they have juice, and may miraculously repair themselves in the magical wardrobe when he's not looking.' Mandy felt drained and looked up, the laughter subsided as Jackie and Jo Jums reacted to Mandy's look of concern as her inquisitorial skills kicked in, 'I take it he's not at the gym or at home then?' Jo Jums shook her head and Mandy groaned, 'Are you following him?'

Jo Jums nodded and gestured her head to Jackie whilst producing an A4 photograph and slapping it on the desktop. Jackie spoke, 'I'm worried about him Mandy. I know you say he's like normal at home, the gym aside that is...' and she allowed herself a therapeutic nervous laugh, '...but when you leave for work it's as if he takes on a different persona. He thinks I can't see through him. He thinks, I think, I have worked out what disturbs him and although we have identified some of his PTSD buttons, which will help him deal with his episodes, it's not as simple as that. I've spoken to Seb about the core of Jack's problems and I think he knows, and I suppose soon I will know. They're alike those two, you have seen that haven't you? I sometimes wonder if Jack is not a little holistic himself,' and here Jackie allowed a big laugh at what Malacopperism Jack calls autistic.

Mandy still looked shocked that they were following Jack, and then to have obviously discussed her husband's problems with Sebastian Sexton, the autistic lad who lived in a shed, in a cemetery, 'You have, Seb, you do?'

Jackie nodded, 'Let's see what Seb comes up with, I wouldn't underestimate that lad. In the meantime, it's not unusual for someone suffering from this syndrome to compartmentalise their life, and I'm only worried if he cannot differentiate or cannot see it.'

Jo Jums filled the subsequent silence, 'What else?'

Jackie responded, Mandy still appeared to be in shock, 'Samuels, who has more respect for Jack than maybe anyone else in MI5, thinks he's got a sniff of something and you know this can mean trouble. He also thinks he is manipulating something, but what?'

More silence that Mandy filled this time, 'And you want me to find out what this is, and is this why you're both here?' Mandy picked up the photo, apparently taken just thirty minutes ago. She saw Jack in his stupid trawler gear that he insisted he wear in foul weather conditions, whilst simultaneously speaking *fisherman* that was more like *Pirate Pete* talk. Staying in was never an option, he just had to see the sea and could rarely let a day go by. She at first thought it was charming, especially as he talked about all that he saw in the motion of the waters, the depth beyond the surface, its allure, but now it seemed to her a dangerous obsession, but this was the character of her man; a man who developed obsessions and she also knew that these were often for the greater good. She had seen all this but still she worried. 'You think he's sniffed something out?' She carried on looking at the photo, curious as to who the wreck of a man was next to her own eejit, and both of them dangling their legs over the promenade edge like they were on their summer holidays, but in a howling gale and driving rain.

'Well Samuels does, and I want to keep a closer eye on Jack. What're you doing tonight?'

Mandy was alert, not knowing whether to be angry that they were following Jack, relieved that they were, worried that they felt this was necessary or curious as to what he was up to. 'We have of course been staying in a lot, as you probably already know...' and she gave Jo Jums a sideways look, '...but oddly, Jack wanted to go to the Gravediggers tonight. He wanted to see Seb and his dad; its Wednesday you see.' Jackie was not sure that she did see, but had decided some time ago that with Jack it is often wise to have a little bit of his Church of Egypt, and she was starting to apply this to his wife as well. 'Oh, and its quiz night, Jack likes quiz night.'

Chapter 9

Whenever the tide complied, Jack and Snail would leave their wall and stomp their way in the deep shingle to the seas edge where they found the relief of footing on the wet compacted sand. Jack often thought of the marines' yomping on the Falklands, no firm sand, just muck and bullets. There was a statue of a yomping marine by the old barracks nearby and Jack was moved by it, saw this as another irony. People believed Jack was not a great fan of the military, which was unmerited as it was just the martinet, up their own arses, wanker types, as *Mary Poppins* would say, who got up his fireman's hose. So you see Jack was, if nothing else, quite balanced in his views.

When the tide was midway or out completely, Snail and Jack would yomp to the end of the eastern extremity of the beach, and by negotiating rocks, old concrete and sloping battements, they would make their way around the Eastney point. For Snail, this gave him an opportunity to see close up the tidal race, surging in and out of the restricted mouth to Langstone harbour, to stare at the rip-tide that had reportedly ripped his daughter out of his life. For Jack, it gave him the opportunity to walk the seaward perimeter of the old Fort Cumberland and the Ministry of Defence (MOD) stations that were, to all intents and purposes, crumbling and redundant. Known sometimes to locals as the *Glory Hole*, there had been many opportunist developers trying to grab the precious sea view land for housing, but the MOD had steadfastly refused to let it go. Even more curious and frustrating for the slippery money makers, since the Government were currently selling off as much of the family silver as they could. Jack often thought, how feckin' stupid, to sell your best assets in the middle of a recession when property values are at their lowest, but he assumed vested interests were at play somewhere and he did not have the energy to fight that one as well, but knew he should, and eventually probably would.

The *Glory Hole* however, was not for sale, and for those that knew, also knew it will never be up for sale. It held in the deep protected basements, sensitive monitoring equipment as well as command bases; a contingency in the event of something happening to the exposed naval base on the opposite, extreme west of the Island of Portsea. Above the basements were vacant buildings and rusting antennae arrays, an exquisite display of redundancy. Jack had been into the basements many times and knew what was there; sophisticated equipment maintained though rarely manned, kept in readiness, just in case.

This late foul morning, two depressed men yomped in the shingle beach which returned soon after turning the point, even deeper here, and every now and then they would adjust their footing to safety as the violent water sizzled and sucked at the beach; Jack looked inland and Snail looked to sea, for his daughter. Ironically, the lifeboat station was positioned just here at the mouth to the harbour, but it was never able to recover Beth.

Snail was mad of course; Jack knew this, although he was able to see past the scrawny Jesus like appearance, ragged clothes and the all-pervading stench of body odour, foul, soured alcohol breath and whisky scorched vocal chords, and occasionally make contact with an exceptional intelligence. Snail was tall like Jack, six three or so, but much leaner, he had the body that many male models would kill for, skin and bone, but achieved by a diet mainly consisting of methylated spirits, special brew and the vital basic sustenance offered at the cemetery. He had lost his middle class, middle age, pudginess, his symbol of a former comfortable lifestyle that had meant he could afford to send his daughter to Portsmouth University without incurring exorbitant and crippling student loans. The daughter, who had left him and joined Neptune beneath the waves, had had everything, and according to Snail had been doing extraordinarily well on her course.

Jack looked at Snail as he trudged deliberately in front of him. This was a man whose life had been turned upside down and wrecked for the love of a child, and Jack also knew that the man only survived thanks to the charity of food and shelter he received from Pansy and Angel, and the ministrations from the cemetery ghost as well he supposed.

* * *

Having completed the Jack Austin bulletins, Jackie left Mandy's office. Jo Jums shuffled forward in her seat and Mandy reciprocated the conspiratorial gesture. In a hushed tone, Jo reported that officers in Cosham, acting on information received, had raided a vacant warehouse to find eleven men locked in with fifteen savage pit bull terriers. The fighting dogs had systematically torn their human company to shreds. The men were all alive, some only just. Written in red paint on the warehouse wall was the message, *Like for Like*.

'Mandy, the men are those who were on our list from the dog fight that caused Alice to be scarred,' Jo said, then resumed her relaxed posture; message conveyed.

Mandy felt her heart thumping, 'I can't say I have much sympathy, can you?' Mandy said, still leaning, still speaking confidentially.

'No Mandy, maybe some for the dogs; they were all put down. The RSPCA said they were past saving, trained since puppies to fight but that is not what preoccupies my thoughts.'

'No?' Mandy replied, her own thoughts preoccupied.

'No, it's Jack.'

'You don't think?'

Jo Jums stood, gestured with her head which seemed to morph from yes to a defensive no, 'Shall you brief the Commander or would you like me to do it?' Jo asked, but knew the answer; it was a skill of Jo's, mind reading. Mandy was harder, but Jack's mind was a piece of cake, even if it proved jumbled and in a mess.

'No, you do it Jo.' It was a skill of Mandy's that she knew of Jo's mind reading capabilities; had a few of her own. 'I take it you have the follow ups in place?' Mandy was suddenly ashen.

Jo nodded she did, then left.

Mandy picked up the phone and called Bernie Thompson, Crime reporter at the Evening News, tipped him and hung up; now the paranoia. Jack had vowed to do something about the dogs and their owners, and she saw it in his face every time he looked at Alice.

Chapter 10

In the cemetery there were several mausoleums that had iron gates securing steps that lead down and into underground burial chambers. There was also the new drainage system that Sebastian Sexton had built as part of the contract to refurbish and maintain the old cemetery. People said they saw wraiths, disembodied souls, vague and shadowy evanescent forms, whisping in and out of the cemetery. Those who lived in the houses that backed onto the cemetery were convinced the spirits had been disturbed following the civil engineering works; a necessity they understood, but sacrilege just the same. Neighbouring houses would go onto the market and not sell. The rumours were dismissed as scaremongering nonsense and Sebastian Sexton was amused, as much as he was ever outwardly amused, at the superstitious paranoia of those that lived close to the old cemetery; he knew there was only the one ghost.

However, in one of these mausoleums, the one reserved for the now defunct Barnes family, three men met. Over the past few months they had set up equipment which enabled them to listen to the goings on in Sexton House and the shed, not the chapel, they did not have much interest in an unofficial hostel for local tramps. The men changed shifts over the night time periods and monitored events in the house, shed, fort and the lemon beach hut. They gathered intelligence and relayed it to London. The similarly defunct Sidney family vault was host to a modest but deadly arms cache of semi-automatic guns and assault rifles, watched over by the Barnes men and held in readiness. The stock was slowly being replenished after the disastrous assault in Southsea and the loss from the rusty hulk in the north harbour. The Southsea attack was viewed as disastrous by the Barnes team, as they had lost seven men, but the people in London viewed the attack as singularly successful; the loss of the arms in the harbour though was not.

The Southsea target, a whistle blowing merchant banker, was assassinated and any likely survivors of the assault team had all been killed in the attack by the retained marksman. The Merchant banker was due to propose a radical plan for rescheduling the world debt, and to spill the beans on the credit and banking crisis, revealing how a minority of powerful financiers and Corporations had made fortunes at the expense of the British and World economies, and even now, continued to accumulate personal wealth whilst the populace struggled; it was supposed to end there. It eventually did at least temporarily end, but the financial lead had to be taken on by the recently murdered Jacqueline Parmentier, and John Sexton, steered closely and anonymously by Jack Austin and his MI5 team.

John Sexton was the new Head of Cedric James, a small but influential merchant bank in the City of London, and when he was in Southsea he lived in Sexton House. He had purchased the old Sexton's house, chapel and substantial gravediggers shed, along with the responsibility for the cemetery, at the request of his youngest son Sebastian. It was no problem to him, he could afford it, but he did worry about his son who nagged and cajoled that it was fate because it was already called *The Sexton House*. The fact that it was called this because it historically accommodated the caretaker and gravedigger of this ancient and redundant Portsmouth cemetery, only added a frisson of excitement for all of his family, including himself if he was honest.

Sexton House was a modest Victorian two / three storey house, cold in appearance, stone facings and grey-blue brick trims to a flint facade. John Sexton had arranged for the house, the substantial chapel and the old tool and storage shed to be restored and refurbished. In any other setting the property would be called desirable. As it was, it was viewed by locals as macabre, eerie, but all agreed, it did suit the family.

* * *

The wind and rain lashed the tired old Saab, parked on the road opposite the cemetery. This parking position afforded the occupants a fair view of Sexton House and the shed, albeit the hedgerows were moderately robust behind the old and still wonky, green painted iron railings (Sebastian Sexton had still to fix these). The Chapel was completely concealed, but they were not interested in that.

'I'm cold; can't we put the heater on?'

She looked at him, 'Don't be a daft bugger, d'you want to draw attention?'

'Well can we go into that pub and have something to warm us up, a pint and some lunch; we can go one at a time. Surely that'll be okay,' and he wiped the condensation off the passenger door window with his hand.

'Don't do that.'

'Well I've gotta be able to see, 'aven't I?'

'Yeah but that will smear me windah, 'ere, use this clorfe and get yer finger marks off before they dry.'

Reluctantly, the tired, irritable and dishevelled, thuggish man, took the old duster and wiped the window free of his greasy hand marks, revealing a clearer view of the shed that he knew would disappear again shortly as the condensation returned, 'Shall I stop breathing?'

She secretly wished he would, 'Just don't breeve on me windah.'

The man looked at the woman aghast, 'Don't breathe?'

'Just on the windah you prairie 'at (pratt),' she had an edginess in her voice, a distinct East End of London, spiky though lyrical, cockney accent.

'You sure we have the right place?' the man asked irritably. His accent was more Essex, estuarine, forced, and she suspected it covered up for being Uncle Josh; middle class, which was posh to her. She shoved a sheaf of papers under his nose, 'Sexton 'Ouse; says so 'ere, twat.' She waved the computer printout of an AA route map from London, a Google street map and aerial photo, all of which she was tempted to roll up and shove up his arse. The papers were creased and had egg and bacon, greasy finger marks on it from their breakfast sandwich bought at the cabbie café in Charing Cross, London, at five thirty that morning. They had eaten them as they drove out of London and down the A3 to Portsmouth, in torrential rain and gusting wind. He still had egg yolk on his trousers; she was revolted.

'I hate the country,' the man said.

'What, the country or this country?'

The man humphed, he was on a hiding to nothing with his Guvnor and resented it.

'This is a City. We drove frew the country, not that we could see any of it in this filfy wevver. Now, if you said I 'ate this country with its filfy wevver then I would understand.'

She was bored of this bloke, would rather work on her own as she so often did; nobody really wanted to work with her and that suited her fine. She had to agree with him though, this cold and wet, end of November day, was eating into her bones. She hated the damp, just the smell of it reminded her of when she was a kid growing up in an equally cold, damp, East End of London terraced house, they had no central heating in those days, her dad, whom she loved to pieces, Gawd bless his soul, had been a tight bastard. Her mates had central heating and she loved going to their gaff (home).

She rested her chin in the cup of her hand and leaned her elbows on the steering wheel, and puffing, she looked out to the shed, steaming up her own window. She turned her gaze to the pub, that she called the "rubbadub", and then back to the Uncle Ted (shed), took the duster and wiped the misty windscreen, flicked the wipers and the fat raindrops began to consume the glass immediately, but she was able to briefly glimpse their subject premises.

'It's just a fucking shed,' he said, taking a break at looking as she was doing it for them.

'Big fucking shed though,' she said, and it was big as sheds went, although they could only see the top half as the bottom was obscured by a low brick wall that held the wonky green, spiked cemetery railings and bushes. 'He must be in there, you can see the smoke from the stovepipe,' she said, distracted.

The man agreed, disinterested, hungry now as well as cold. It was half-past-twelve and it had been a long time since the egg and bacon sandwich, 'Think we could see the shed from the pub?' he asked.

She returned her gaze to the rubbadub. It was just like the three-storey terrace house where she'd been born and grew up in Stepney, only just two stuck together. It was painted cream with powder blue highlights to the rendered window surrounds and a slightly uneven plinth, well maintained, but the lower half of the building looked like it had been splashed by a lorry driving through a big puddle, the spray reaching beyond the small forecourt garden.

The old sash windows, painted white, faced onto the tiny excuse for a front garden, then onto the street and across to the railings, and then the shed, which was close to the perimeter of the cemetery. Over the entrance door the pub sign, fixed flat to the front wall, was partially obscured by a bundle of privet hedge that swung in the wind from a rusty gallows bracket. The rust residue streaked down the cream façade and tainted the small porch and the powder blue door surround, to compound the grimy facade.

'The bottom half of the glazing is frosted, but we ought to be able to see the shed if we stand occasionally,' he said, pleading to his cold bitch of a guvnor.

She screwed her eyes and wiped the side door window with her hand, 'It's the sort of glass they had in Victorian pubs, acid etched with the pub name,' she looked closer, ignoring the snorting ignorant laugh from the pig ignorant bloke sitting next to her, '*The Gravediggers*, charming, must be the name of the pub, and what you larfing at?'

'You, you wiped the windah with your hand.'

She looked and felt exasperated, but well and truly banged to rights. 'Come on, let's go and get some lunch, though I'm not convinced that I really want to eat in there, are you?'

But he was already out of the car and stamping around like an idiot. She looked at him as he made strides, akin to a constipated stork, to the pavement and to the railings that edged the pub excuse for a front garden, doing the okey-cokey and shaking his legs all about. Bozo she thought as she got out herself and stepped into the same huge puddle, and also stork like, commenced the okey-cokey herself. Subconsciously she went onto her toes, even though this would achieve nothing as the water was halfway up her calf's, and so she waded, swishing the water, to join her dozy colleague by the rubbadub Roger Moore (door).

Chapter 11

The back door of the old house opened a chink; a slice of weak orangey yellow electric light struggled to penetrate the gloom of the porch. The crack of light revealed the toe of a bulbous and flowery Wellington boot struggling to get a purchase on the door's leading edge. After a short while the boot succeeded and was joined by an elbow in an old and grubby, tent like, rubberised trench coat. The elbow flipped the door open in a practiced manner. The previous gloom of the aged timber porch was now mellowed orange as a greater quantity of the insipid light spilled from the hallway. The figure, completely encapsulated in the stiff dirty, formerly cream coat, eased into the porch like a *Dalek*, the boots just visible as it made a floating forward movement; the door was allowed to gently close behind.

The wind and rain hit the plastic Tesco bag on the woman's head, the two looped handles tied loosely in a granny knot under her chin, tight wisps of curly blond hair batting backwards and forwards as she stepped out into the foul elements. She carefully placed her flowery Wellingtons onto the patterned quarry tile path, and tentatively made her way to the shed, holding the tray in front of her, the tea towel cover flapping at the edges in time with her hair and the plastic bag. She could only hear the noise from the crackly bag; the passing cars that usually sprayed past the end of the garden were quiet; the police had parked in the puddle opposite and the traffic was forced across to the higher side of the road. Shame really, because she liked the sound of the splashing, even if it did dirty Jonas's pub front. She hated this path though, it was so impractical, the old tiles were slippery in the wet, a death trap, but Sebastian had insisted in everything being as it should or as it used to be. If it was as it should be, there would be a modern non-slip finish and Seb would come in for his lunch. Bloody kids she thought as she directed one of her flowery Wellingtons and rhythmically kicked the shed door. The woman focused on keeping the tea towel down around the tray, and spat out some stray hair that had flicked itself into her mouth as she cursed.

A deep and ponderous voice called from within; "Yes" the yes dragged out, long and slow and then followed up with, "Sexton's Detective Agency, how may I help you?"

'Well you could open the fucking door that would help, and take this tray off me.'

'Oh, alright Mum,' and she could hear shuffling from inside, the mechanical whirring of locks and the door swung open, smoothly and silently, well oiled, perfectly hung, and looking perfect as was the interior of the old Sexton's shed.

'Wipe your feet Mum,' her son called from inside the perfect interior, as if the woman was a bozo and didn't know the rules. She wiped, but only as a token, knowing he would follow her up on hands and knees with a cloth to wipe the marks off the highly-polished hardwood floor. She placed the tray on her son's desk, on the place reserved for food and beverages and turned, looking down to where she knew her son would be. He looked up from the floor, finishing up on the last non-existent mark waiting to see if she would move her feet again. She nodded that he could stand and she would not move yet awhile.

Slowly he rose to his five foot seven-inch height and looked on his Mum in his dad's old coat; they were pretty much the same height. Sebastian got his height and delicate features from his Mum, Beryl. His brother and sister took after Dad, John Sexton, who was tall and powerfully put together; Mum was the diminutive form of the Sexton powerhouse. Dad was the breadwinner in the City of London where he was the powerhouse, until he got home. Seb often wondered if he was a powerhouse on the train, to and from London, and assumed he was, not that he himself ever went on trains or even outside, except from the shed to the house, the catacombs and occasionally across to his brother's pub.

Beryl Sexton lifted the tea towel off the tray to reveal her son's November lunch, tinned Heinz Tomato soup, doorstep white bread with lashings of butter. As she folded the tea towel, she momentarily thought that it would soon be December and he wouldn't want tomato until February or was it March. She made a mental note to check her son's dining schedule. 'Mmmm lovely Mum, my November favourite,' and his Goofy style slippered feet, padded to his large executive office chair.

'Shall I stay with you while you eat son?' she asked.

He nodded a yes please as he pulled the finely starched linen napkin out of its sterling silver ring, unfolded it, and laid it precisely on his lap and set aside the paper napkin for dabbing his mouth, so as not to stain the pristine and stiff lap cloth. He adjusted the soup spoon to its correct position, a brief admonishing look to his mother, which she ignored and stuck two fingers up in response when his back was turned, and he addressed the bread, which he lined up in size order. He always started with the big lump in November but in December (with a different soup of course) it was the other way around. His dad used to say you could tell what month it was by the order in which he ate his bread, but railed when he adjusted everyone else's bread before they sat down to a family dinner. This was okay for Mum and Dad but when they had guests it sometimes caused a stir, but Seb's stare usually sorted that, along with the piece of pre-printed paper that set out the current month's dining rules.

'Jenny was over again; she's so upset and wants your help, the police have found nothing.' She didn't expect an immediate answer because he was eating, so keeping her Wellingtons where they were, she swivelled her trunk to look at the huge comfy, authentic brown leather, nineteen thirties, curvilinear armchair. She slipped her size five feet out of the size twelve Wellingtons with ease, and stepped out of the Mac that was so stiff, it stood on its own. This was good because she didn't want her son to have to get up and to clean up after her while he was eating. She snuggled back into the overstuffed, organically curvy armchair. It even swallowed up her colossal older son and she had to practically jump backwards onto it and then wiggle and slide to reach the back. She settled and watched her son eat whilst twiddling her toes, suspended at the edge of the armchair, comfortable with herself; she hardly ever thought about the murders she had carried out recently.

Sebastian Sexton was precise in his eating style, almost mechanical, and Beryl settled in because she knew he would chew each mouthful thirty-three times, and the soup was swirled in his mouth twenty one times. Her son rarely rushed anything and this gave Beryl time to think.

Sebastian was relatively short of course, slim and classically good looking with fine blond hair, like her own, except Beryl's curled. He kept it trimmed, she did it for him because he would not consider going out to a barber. She thought he looked like Trevor Howard out of the film *Brief Encounter* and remembered her husband looked like that when he was younger, except he was a lot taller and broader and had thick black hair. She used to rib him about it, thought he was flattered but he never really talked about how he felt. She didn't really care anymore because he was a good father, provided well for his family and was a fucking demon in bed. Seb was very much like his father, except in build, he kept himself to himself, preferring to stay in his shed, whereas Jonas, her eldest, did look like his dad and thankfully was more outward going, across the road running the Gravediggers pub his dad had bought; it went with the cemetery, least this is what Seb had argued and so his dad bought it, the soft sap she thought.

* * *

If she thought things were weird outside the pub, then things got even more bizarre for Detective Inspector Delores Lovington as she entered the rubbadub. She forgot her cold wet feet and the rudeness of her Detective Sergeant, as he barged past her to get into the pub first, because just inside he had stood stock still and she bumped into his back causing him to humph. He stood there stunned by the image that she shared by looking around his not insubstantial, and turning to seed frame.

'Out the way dipstick and let me in,' she said.

The Detective Sergeant stood aside, his mouth still agape, and he turned to look at his guvnor who shared the look. It was like they had stepped back in time, to what period she was not sure, because it had the feeling of a Mediaeval Victorian, and she shook her head at that crazy notion, as she took in the look of the very tall and burly man behind a highly-polished bar. It was the only thing that was polished and it reflected the image of the barman in the depth of that shine. Everything else was spit and sawdust, rough hewn timber with candle wax stains, and she recalled her dad saying this was what pubs in the East End used to be like; she missed her dad, even if he was an arse and a tight wad.

Delores sniffed a hint of gas from the gas mantle lamps on the wall, the only real illumination, some thick candles on the bar added to the atmosphere but not particularly to the lighting levels. It made the pub seem gloomy but it wasn't, it was cosy and especially welcoming in these atrocious weather conditions, though all of these thoughts amounted to nothing as she could not take her eyes off the barman. He had to be at least six foot six. Her sergeant, Barry Richards, was six four and appeared dwarfed as he shuffled, hunched shoulders and dragging cold wet feet to the bar, scraping the toes of his wet leather shoes through the sawdust and making patterns. She watched him, and childlike, she couldn't resist doing the same with her own wet shoes, and as she looked up from her swirly patterns, the barman smiled at her and she felt a bubbling in her stomach which she put down to being hungry; the last thing she needed at the moment was a tosspot bloke in her life, and this bloke looked a definite tosspot, gorgeous, but nevertheless, a tosspot. He had to be, because most blokes were, and here they were out in the bleedin' country; it was a no-brainer.

Delores joined her sergeant at the bar and leaned on the perfectly polished side of what had to be half a tree trunk. She gazed deep into the diamond surface, examining her reflection, allowing her trailing hand to feel the roughness of tree bark below and then looked up and around the pub interior. It was like two substantial, low ceilinged living rooms joined together with fireplaces centrally at each end; the visual appearance suggested an atmosphere that should be fetid but it wasn't, it was floral; the sawdust maybe, but there was more. The grates of the fireplaces glowed red and yellow, an intense fire radiated heat and a scent she could not place.

She was drawn to one end sniffing, and as she approached the fireplace she could feel the radiant heat on her cold damp face, could sense the rain drops dripping from her hair and drying instantly on her cheeks. She rubbed her face and felt the tingle, sensed the glow, and it made her feel good. She had to stop herself from turning, lifting her skirt and warming her bum by the fire. She remembered back to her childhood, her Mum would do this and she only thought it wasn't normal when she brought her first boyfriend home. Her dad would stand by the fire in his string vest, rubbing his big bum in his huge pants. It was actually a competition to get to the fire first. Mum and dad always won because they frightened the kids away with warnings of chilblains, whatever they were, but it was enough to frighten the hell out of the six kids, and as she was the oldest and couldn't offer any explanation to her younger siblings, she perpetuated the myth in the certain and knowledgeable way expected of her.

Barry called out, asked what she wanted to drink and she noticed the barman looking at her, black eyes piercing, like he imagined her with her skirt around her waist and his hands rubbing her toasted bum; she noticed it was her doing the imagining.

'I'll 'av 'arf a daft lager and bring the menu over to the windah,' she replied to her sergeant but still looking at the barman. She was mesmerised by the intensity of his stare, his eyes reflected the pinpoint glow of the fire and she melted when he smiled. Blowing out her cheeks, she made her way to one of the tables by a sash window, tipped her toes to look out and saw the shed with the smoke trailing from the stove pipe chimney. It felt warm and cosy in the bar as the wind drove the rain into the glass. She felt the stiff stream of cold air hit her nostrils as it pierced the crack between the two sashes, and she snorted the air back and adjusted her head. She was cast back to her childhood again, nose pressed against the glass when it rained and they couldn't go out for fear of pneumonia and had to stay in and avoid chilblains. In the summer it was, don't sit on the cold stone or you'll get Farmer Giles, (piles – haemorrhoids). Turning, she sniffed the bar air again. It had a beautiful perfumed smell and as she thought this she tried not to look at the barman.

'They ain't got no bloody lager, what sort of gaff is this anyway?'

'Well what do they 'ave?' she said to her irritated sergeant.

'Just bitter,' he replied, irritated.

'Alright then, I'll 'ave 'arf of *London Pride*,' and she turned to look out the window again and slipped her raincoat off. Barry was still there, 'What?'

'They only have one beer, what he makes himself. He said it's a new batch, hence the bush hanging outside. He looked at me like I was a dipstick for not realising.'

She looked quizzically at her arse of a sergeant, and only then became aware that the bar had no pumps, just two full-size wooden barrels set on the back bar, well not so much a back bar as another lump of wood spanning between two more barrels. 'Well you are a dipstick,' she said and went with him to the bar where the barman greeted her approach by spreading his bared forearms, like a pair of hams, and placing his massive hands on the shiny bar surface; as she neared he locked his elbows. Delores sensed her movement slow as she approached the bar, and the barman leaned to meet her, bent his neck and stretched so his head crossed the bar surface, and before Delores realised it, his face was right beside hers.

'Peat' he said, a gravelly voice synchronised with the rugged look of the man.

'Well Pete, you've no lager, I'll 'ave a drop of cry and tonic please.' He looked at her confused, so she explained for the benefit of the country yokel, 'A drop of cry is gin Pete.'

'I know that, but what makes you think my name is Pete; it's Jonas.'

'You just said Pete,' she retorted, never one to be made a fool of.

He laughed and Delores saw two rows of pearly whites from behind soft full lips that she couldn't stop looking at; she squashed her legs together and wondered what on earth she was doing as she peered deep into his mouth, like she was a dental hygienist. The explanation was of course, that she was out of her comfort zone. Just leaving London was enough to put her on edge, it was like emigrating, and then you had to deal with the bleedin' hayseeds. Jonas moved closer, if that was possible, and she could not avoid inspecting his tanned, leathery, imperfect skin; she imagined he maybe had some acne issues as a teenager. She could smell a masculine sweat that on anyone else would revolt her, but this smelled like her dad when he came in from work.

'It's peat, I have it shipped in from Ireland, it adds to the atmosphere and that is what you can smell,' he said, almost a whisper into her ear; his breath made her shiver.

Delores sniffed Jonas's armpits before she realised he was talking about the fire, aware then that she had been correspondingly leaning into him. 'Well give us a gin and tonic then Jonas sweet'art,' now that told him.

'Sorry, we only have ale, my ale, Gravediggers.'

'What?'

'You heard,' and he stood back and she noticed his big hands smoothing down his full tan leather apron. He folded his exposed *Popeye* forearms across his chest, and she looked for an anchor tattoo; a challenge was forthcoming. 'There are a number of pubs down the road that can accommodate your tastes,' and he turned and poured a dribble of a deep rich brown liquid into a miniature glass tumbler, put it up to a gas mantle and the liquid refracted amber. She involuntarily leaned towards his armpit again as he returned and she savoured his masculine bouquet. He smiled, 'Here,' gesturing with the glass.

Delores took the glass and sniffed. It was flowery, fresh, a hint of mustiness or was that Jonas's armpit. She only tolerated beer if it was ice cold lager and when she was out with the Neanderthal men from the Met (London Metropolitan Police), but they were committed to this pub because they had to stay and watch the shed, which she realised they had not done for at least a quarter of an hour. She sipped from the small glass and there was a blossoming on her tongue, sweet but bitter beneath and to the side of her tongue and cheeks. She smiled and Jonas revealed his teeth again and the flavour seemed enhanced, 'Mmmm rubbery,' she said, 'I'll 'ave 'arf.'

Barry ordered a pint. 'Got a menu mate?'

'No.' Jonas the barman replied, matter of fact.

Barry looked out of his depth and more than a tad fed up. He stamped his cold wet feet and asserted his presumed London superiority, 'Shut-up mate, I can smell food.'

Jonas replied, still matter of fact, 'Indeed you can, it is fish stew or beef stew, what would you like? I can recommend the fish; it's about three days old and just getting good.'

Delores could barely contain a giggle and noticed this elicited another smile from Jonas, which coincidentally she was aware, warmed her cockles. She knew Barry was more of a fish out of water than her when out of London, even worse dealing with country folk.

'Would you recommend the fish or the beef?' she asked Jonas.

He looked long and hard at Delores, deep into her green eyes, and she thought fuck off mate you're not Raymond bleedin' Blanc, but contained her thoughts as the country bozo reflected.

'They are both good but I think you will like the fish,' he eventually replied.

'What about me then, what do you recommend for me?' Barry asserted aggressively.

She looked at Barry and saw he was miffed. He liked to be the centre of attention, always thought his faux Essex, pretend cockney wit, endeared him to everyone; it didn't.

'You, I couldn't give a shit what you wanted,' Jonas replied not taking his eyes off Delores.

This was good enough for Barry, and he ordered the beef and they took their drinks to the table where Delores sat and Barry looked out of the top sash and feigned an interest, as if he was looking at something fascinating, not a fucking shed in a fucking cemetery.

Chapter 12

Seb saved the final crust, from the smaller piece of bread, for the ceremonial wiping of the bowl, performed with his accustomed aplomb that his Mum, now a tad tired of waiting, assumed was the way he wiped his arse, and he managed to collect the entire soup residue and sat back as he chewed; the plate appeared polished. Beryl folded the starched napkin, perfectly, into the ironed creases, rolled and inserted it into the sterling silver ring and handed it to her son. Seb turned the ring so the engraving of the man digging the grave was astride the fold of the napkin, and with his perfect handkerchief, he polished the last residues of fingerprint from the ring and placed it on the tray, in its correct position. He picked up his floor cloth and spoke to his mum as he wiped the soles of his sisters Wellingtons, 'What did Jenny want?'

His Mum sighed, he hadn't been listening, but then he was very much like his father in that respect. Jonas was a talker and she liked it when he came over from the pub and they talked. Pansy, her daughter and the owner of the size twelve flowery Wellingtons, was a talker also but she only really saw her when her Dad was not there, which thankfully was often. Pansy was a lesbian and Beryl's husband was a little uncomfortable with that, but she did approve, her daughter finally happy with her partner Angel, whom she also liked; often thought she might fancy a bash at sex with a woman herself sometime, and so she flirted with women, just in case.

'Chrissie is missing. It was in the paper last night, I brought it over to you,' and she saw the evening news folded on a table beside the armchair, untouched.

'It must have been on a creased bit so I didn't read it,' Seb said, dismissively.

'Must have been on a creased bit so I didn't read it,' she irritatingly mimicked him, 'I fucking ironed it for you,' and she picked up the paper, flicked the pages and watched him wince as the paper rustled and became even more creased. She laid it on his desk and smoothed it with her hand. He looked at it from a distance, as if it was radioactive, the headline read, '*TODDLER MISSING*'.

He read no more, it was indeed crumpled, 'Read it for me,' he asked.

She let out an exasperated sigh, picked her glasses from her apron pocket, polished them on her cardigan, put them on the end of her nose and sifted the article for the salient points; she knew her son had no time for florid journalism, it had to be succinct and to the point.

'Four-year-old Chrissie James went missing whilst playing in the back garden of her mother's terraced Eastney house. Jenny James was making lunch at the time. Police are baffled as the rear garden is enclosed with no access to the outside streets. The neighbours are being questioned but there is still no clue as to the girl's whereabouts.'

Beryl stopped and waited to see if the intrigue of the article and the plight of a family friend interested her son. Seb knew Jenny and there was a time when Beryl harboured hopes of a relationship, but Beryl knew that anyone who had a relationship with her son had to be exceptional, almost a saint. Jenny had had a baby with a chap who immediately deserted her. Beryl liked Jenny and the child, and they visited often, Chrissie played in the bit of the garden that Seb had allocated for those who, for some peculiar reason, wished recreation.

The garden surrounded the house and had several zones; recreation, with part lawn and terrace, which faced south and west and abutted the allotment and vegetable patch, laid out in its regimented rows of crops beside the old chapel. There was the perfectly square pond, the perfectly rectangular chicken run and of course the huge ancient and sprawling cemetery, which gradually Seb was straightening up; the headstones, the paths between, he was getting them to all look right. Part of the terms of the house was that they kept an eye on the cemetery, not that anyone cared but Seb did, arranging also for the network of underground tunnels that he calls his catacombs. He had always wanted some of them, and now he had them; the daft bugger Beryl thought.

Seb turned to his computer and took the dust cover off, wiped his hands and pressed *On*, the screen illuminated whilst he folded the cover and put it in the allocated drawer. Beryl got up and padded to pick up Pansy's Wellingtons, stepped into the coat that was still standing there, went to the door and put her Tesco bag on her head and tied the handles. She looked back at her son who was now busy and completely unaware she was leaving, save for a glance to check the floor was okay. She picked up the tray, shuffled the spoon and napkin as her son wasn't looking, stepped outside and gently snapped the door shut with just a little chuckle; she liked the frisson of excitement she got transgressing his unwritten rules, and even some of the written ones.

The wind whipped across her face as she stepped out onto the path, and she enjoyed the chill and the stinging wetness from the driving rain after the hot, dry, claustrophobic atmosphere of her son's shed. She loved her son but sometimes he got on her fucking nerves, just like his fucking dad. She went down the slippery fucking Victorian path to phone Jenny to say that the Sexton Detective fucking Agency was on the case.

Chapter 13

Delores sipped her half of Gravediggers and Barry drained his pint, 'Bloody lovely drop of beer that,' he said, smacking his lips. She had to agree and was looking forward with just a little less trepidation to the fish stew as a beautiful smell of food pervaded the bar, over and above the scented radiant shimmering peat and the floral sawdust.

Barry was up and down looking out the window. She allowed him this as at Five foot six, eight if she lied, she couldn't see out the top sash without tip toeing, and she knew Barry would leer at her legs. It revolted her, he was revolting, and she often thought he only looked at her legs because it was expected of a chauvinistic, arsehole copper; he made her skin crawl. She sat back in her wooden wheel back chair, smooth from wear and deceptively comfortable; she felt relaxed, more so than Barry who appeared agitated. She listened to the wind and rain outside and glanced across to the only other customer, a bony, grey haired, shell of an old man who clearly was once tall and probably lean and muscular, but all that had faded. He sat beside the opposite fireplace playing dominoes with himself, looked like he was winning as well if the toothless grin was anything to go by.

Delores watched Jonas bring the old man another pint, collecting the empty glass at the same time and affectionately rubbing the old man's back, allowing the huge hand to glide across the wizen face and scratch at the white whiskers; she saw sensitivity in the warm exchange between the giant and skeletal venerable man. Her eyes followed Jonas as he returned to the bar, a man with a full and powerful figure. The shape of the man, whom she thought to be in his late twenties, was only slightly spoiled by the makings of a beer belly, which she also thought was probably to be expected of a pub landlord; the man was attractive, even with his belly, which was probably bigger than she imagined, disguised as it was by the stiff leather apron. Delores liked the contrast of the tan leather with the landlord's thick black and curly hair, he had the hint of a gypsy, which frankly ruled him out of any chance with her; she didn't like travellers. She felt the grab of her breath as he glanced back at her whilst tending a barrel on the back bar. She immediately looked elsewhere. He smiled and disappeared into the back rooms and appeared shortly after with large steaming bowls and hunks of bread on a lump of wood. 'Here we go' he said, as he placed the bowls on the table with what turned out to be a half loaf of crusty bread on a wooden platter, a wooden bowl of golden butter impaled by a broad spreading knife. He put two overly large spoons on the table and wished them a good appetite.

'Got a napkin mate?' Delores asked, and Jonas laughed at the request, shook his head and walked away. She looked at Barry who had his head only an inch or two from his beef stew, smelling it and Mmmming. She wanted to push his head in but resisted, they used to do that as kids, what a tin barf (laugh). She didn't like her sergeant. He was a misogynist when she wasn't around, she knew because people told her. He resented her rank over him and thought she was shit at her job, which she wasn't. He was a tall man and big bodied, running to fat, with a double chin at what must be forty-five, not much more, and a shaved head which frankly she hated on men. He wore tired suits that looked like they'd never seen a dry cleaner and stunk of fag ash. She would not let him smoke in the car, and he'd not had a cigarette since before they left London, and this clearly contributed to his agitation, and Delores took delight in her part in that, but marvelled at the pacifying effects the aromatic beef stew had on the arsehole sergeant.

He looked up at her, 'This smells great,' and dropped his pock marked, snub nose down again and snorted, as if to demonstrate the veracity of his statement, or to suck the gravy into his fireman's hose; she chuckled and thought about pushing his head in again, but resisted again, and took a sip of the fish stew liquor.

She had been distracted and felt something on the top of her thighs and reacted, 'Oi mush, what d' yer fink yer doing?'

Jonas reacted with a laconic and lazy smile, and carried on spreading an old tea towel across her skirt. Paralysed, she watched his hands. The tea towel had a faded picture of an old boat, HMS Victory she imagined, being the only thing she thought worth knowing about Portsmouth, as Jonas smoothed Nelsons ship into the tops of her thighs and she noticed she had not stopped him; aware also of warm sensations in her rigging.

'There you go, get you another drink?'

She'd lost her voice; all of her brain energy was focused on the tingling between her legs. Barry ordered another pint, looked at his Guvnor and ordered a half for her, she nodded and returned to the stew which she marvelled at. It was creamy and thick with all manner of fish and shellfish. She broke off a hunk of bread and slapped some butter on; it was as if she had a get out of jail free card from dieting. Barry was taken aback, used only to seeing his slim and elegant, bordering on bird like, petit boss, peck at salads, but here she was diving in with hunks of bread, loaded up with butter that complimented her golden blond, bobbed hair; dipping, sucking and slurping and thoroughly enjoying her stew.

* * *

The blended smell of methylated spirit (meths) and special brew was just tolerable if you were accustomed to it. The old pews had been gathered around the battered but serviceable iron stove that sat in the corner of the chapel. It was raw cold away from the heat source, but these three men and one woman were used to that. They blew steam through their filthy mouths and even squeezed some out of their congested noses. They were dressed for winter with an assortment of ragged clothes, padded with the quintessential thermal lining of old newspapers and, as they moved for the occasional sip of meths, to accompany their light lunch of more meths, special brew and a side plate of thick crusty bread, ham sandwiches and pease pudding, so the newspapers would crinkle. But here in the Chapel they were safe from the controlling ire of Sebastian, who would want to iron the papers and dress them in clean and pressed clothes. Seb stayed out of the chapel, stuck mainly to his shed and let these people of the street enjoy the space and sustenance that the Sexton's made available to them.

Next to the stove was a pile of wooden logs and this would be replenished when needed by the giant woman and the delicate angel, who were kind to them and rarely spoke, never criticised, only looked on with the look that said, *there but for the grace of God.* They were there now and even if the two women did have what many thought an unnatural relationship to one another, who were they to criticise? Pansy and Angel were cleaning the chapel. They came every day, cleaned, replenished the wood from the house store and served breakfast, lunch and dinner to whomever was there. It was rarely more than four or five and invariably the same four men and one woman; Snail was expected back for lunch.

Pansy seemed to be the comfortable one of the Sexton siblings, sharing between her two brothers, Seb's desire for the neat and orderly but not nearly so obsessively, and she had much of her older brother Jonas's bonhomie and love of people. All three children were however, singular in that they wanted not to stray from the family home; Seb his shed, Jonas his pub and micro-brewery and Pansy wanted only to be with Angel, who lived with her in the apartment above the pub, and together they ran the small bed and breakfast business.

* * *

Beryl Sexton busied herself with the household chores. She was relaxed now that Seb was looking for Chrissie and when she had phoned Jenny with the news, the girl seemed comforted. She'd had a nice coffee and a chat with Pansy and Angel whilst they made chapel sandwiches, but they would have to cook for themselves tonight because John was home from the City, it was Wednesday, and they would probably all meet up in the pub later for quiz night. John stayed up in London most week nights. He had a flat in the City; it was too much to expect him to commute every day, though he came home every Wednesday evening, so it broke the week up and he spent every weekend with the family; she didn't know how his mistress tolerated it? Probably the same way she did, Beryl reflected, a good bit of rumpy-pumpy in the bed department then he can bugger off back to her. So long as he paid the bills, had loads of dosh left for her and the kids, she no longer gave a toss.

She telephoned her husband to say the filth had been outside watching, and were now in the pub. 'It's the nice woman that Jack mentioned, and a horrible tosspot of a bloke I don't know,' and she laughed along with John when she told him they'd parked where it always flooded and she related how they had stepped out into the growing puddle, which was now more of a lake.

John always asked after everyone, 'Jonas has three customers, granddad and the filth. Seb solved the missing jewellery case and the vandalism in the precinct. I passed the information on, only Jack's still off, Mandy was in meetings so Jo Jums used the information, seems she is in with Jack and his spook mates now, so quite cosy, and Pansy and Angel have just left with lunch for the Chapel Club.'

He was always silent when she mentioned Pansy and Angel. She knew it made him feel uncomfortable and she did it all the more because of it, but still looked forward to bedtime tonight.

'Seb is working on Chrissie, she went missing yesterday morning, you knew that didn't you, I told you?' He was still silent on the end of the phone, it often took him five, ten minutes to recover from the mention of Pansy and Angel, not that he had a problem with lesbian relationships in general, he was just uncomfortable in its close proximity but more especially with his daughter, and more importantly with Angel, whom he considered too dominant. Beryl admitted that often, if she wanted a bit of peace and quiet, she would mention their names and then got on with her own thoughts, but he was coming around slowly, very slowly.

Beryl was getting on with her own thoughts, along with some ironing. She had a nice little number to wear tonight and was feeling quite titillated by the look of the garment and the thought of it. She wasn't tall compared with her husband, Jonas and Pansy, but she was a handsome woman for fifty, a slim but shapely figure, sensual John always said and that was how she felt. Medium length, fine golden hair that curled naturally and was thin enough to bounce and swirl, and she dressed to look good and wasn't shy in flaunting it, and delighted in the looks she got from other men; even enjoyed her dalliances, "Goose for the gander" she would say. Still, John was the one, and she knew she was the one for him and so it will always be.

The phone went and she picked it up, listened and replaced the receiver. Packed up the iron, took one last glance at her garment for tonight, laid it aside and went to get her Sexton's Detective Agency trench coat and trilby.

Chapter 14

Seb had Googled the aerial view of Jenny's house and filtered this through his enhancement programme; he only used his hack into the MOD and the Yank systems when he had to. He decoded the image so he could zoom in to examine the close detail, surveying Jenny's garden, the neighbouring gardens and what options the child had to wander off, or for a potential abductor to take his prey. The neighbours and Jenny were a logical thought and he left that line of enquiry to the police. Seb followed the perimeter in close up vision and then it occurred to him. He picked up the phone and called his Mum, she said she would inform the police and go to see Jenny; Beryl liked it when she was on a mission for the Sexton Detective Agency, had even got herself a trench coat and trilby; the women would fancy her in that she, and coincidentally, Seb had thought.

Seb went back to the other cases his Mum had picked out for him in the newspaper. There was a young blind woman and her house had been burgled, her precious possessions, such as they were, stolen. Seb had been monitoring a local group of Herbert's, as Jack Austin called them, and he had them fingered for this. There had been a youngster beaten up on Southsea seafront, and a woman had been raped at the back of the shops in Commercial Road. These were easy and he would use his hack into the satellite surveillance the Americans had on Portsmouth, which he recorded, and then he would pass the details onto Jack, Mandy or Jo Jums.

The Hotel manager had been recovered and charged with fraud, the dog handlers had been found, badly mauled by their own dogs, and Seb appreciated the sense of justice; it redressed the balance, if only a little. He was though currently more intrigued by the melee which had occurred at Eastney beach. Jack Austin had suggested that it may have been some illegal's trying to beach at the mouth of Langstone harbour and had not allowed for the rip tide. They would be lucky to find the bodies, but it was the fact that someone was there to repel that intrigued Jack Austin, and now Ghost had left a message; never to be ignored.

* * *

Jonas was collecting the empty bowls, enjoying the warmth of response from his new customers to his ale and the stew. Delores Lovington was half up from her seat and looking around.

'Lost something?' he asked.

'The loo?'

'Follow me,' Jonas said and he flicked his head.

She stood fully, bristling, resenting being told what to do and having a head flicked at her. She rolled up HMS Victory and thought about flicking the tea towel at him, but instead found herself following Jonas to the bar. He stopped, had a thought, changed direction and walked over to the old man. She followed, wondering if he had all of a sudden remembered that the toilets were over the other side of the rubbadub. They stood and waited beside the old man whose hand shook as he pondered over laying a particular domino down. Jonas nudged him and he laid a six and a three. She noticed that it joined onto a four, looked closer and all of the dominoes were jumbled, no coordination at all; no wonder he was winning she thought.

'Granddad this is Detective Inspector Delores Lovington; Della,' Jonas said to the old man.

While Delores wondered how he knew her name and then her shortened version, only for use by those people whom she liked, two rheumy eyes turned to look up at her. She noticed not just his white whiskers but also an abundance of white nostril and ear hair.

The old man squinted and took a while to focus, 'Hmmm, filth eh?'

'Yeah granddad, and a really beautiful one; Dad's down tonight, its Wednesday,' and he smiled at Delores as he shouted his information to granddad, whom she concluded must be hard of hearing as well as half blind and fully doolahly. 'Just taking her to the toilet and I'll be back, keep an eye on that one will you,' Jonas said, gesturing his head towards Barry who was oblivious and stood looking out the window, using his hands to rub away the condensation then scratching his backside, like he had a bit of dirt in his eye.

'I can go to the bog on me own you know, it's somfing what's encouraged in the filf.'

'Oh, sorry, off you go,' Jonas said pointing, 'through that door, down the end of the corridor and across the yard. Watch out for the dog, he won't hurt you but could give you a serious lick.'

He laughed as she harrumphed and stomped in the direction he had pointed, and the door, which he had assured her resided in the gloom of a corner, became apparent as she approached it. She looked around, trying to appear casual; Barry was still looking out the window, looked back at Jonas who stood with his hands on his hips, and he raised his thick black eyebrows which irritated her, and was then immediately mollified when he smiled his bleedin' gypsy smile. She made a mental note not to be so easily mollified in future, and went through the door with a cavalier, devil may care attitude, just to show him.

The corridor beyond was lit by just one gas mantle which cast disturbing shadows from her arms and legs as she slowly wafted them, testing the environment. As she left the comparative safety of the bar door, shadows from cemetery artefacts that hung from the corridor wall, added to the Edgar Alan Poe atmosphere which she decided would be better if she did not dwell upon. She almost had to feel her way to the end of the corridor, to reach a small sash window and a door beside it. The window panes were smoked, evoking a Dickensian appearance; they let in only diffuse daylight and allowed no visibility. Opening the door cautiously she peered out, it was still pouring with rain and the cobbles appeared slick and uneven. The scent of brewing pervaded the enclosed yard and it took her back to Stepney, the nearby Maltings and huge Brewery, the similar scent casting her mind roistering back to when she was a kid.

Hand over her head affording no protection from the rain, Delores dashed across the yard to one of three doors, opened it and was confronted by large copper and stainless steel tuns and was instantly knocked back by the fumes and the familiar smell, her childhood spinning in front of her eyes. She ducked back from the brewery out into the yard, looked up for a breath of fresh air and got a mouthful of rain which she found refreshing. Then she dashed for the centre door, slipped and fell backwards, and arching herself with her outstretched hands behind her, she was able to stop a full-on fall but the jolt through her arms hurt. The shock of pain did not prevent her from trying to keep her bum off the cobbles though, which puddled in this part of the yard, but in vain, as her posterior hit the ground when she brought her hands round to fend off a large red and steamy, sloppy, hound tongue. She was already wet from the rain and now saturated, as the puddle water soaked through her skirt to her Alan Wickers, and to compound this, a scruffy mongrel, looking like a rain sodden and bedraggled Lassie, was licking her boatrace.

Suddenly the rain seemed to stop and what minimal daylight there had been previously, was occluded. She looked up and Jonas hovered with a black city boy umbrella covering her, offering an outstretched hand. He called the dog off, shouted something like "Cabbage", the dog retreated and she took his hand. Jonas hoisted her as if she weighed nothing, and she found herself looking up directly into his eyes; he stooped and kissed her. The breath was taken from Delores as she felt riveted to the spot. He kissed her again, and despite all of her good sense, she responded, telling herself just this one and then she will tear him off a strip. She felt his arm go around her waist and pull her soggy bottom towards him, and she went, she could feel his firm body. He'd taken his apron off and there was no beer belly. They stayed with their mouths bonded and he breathed and talked into her mouth.

'Would you like me to take you to the toilet?'

She nodded, speaking back into his mouth, 'Yeth pleath,' she responded, enjoying the feeling of his massive hands on her drenched bum, his fingers subtly probing. She could do nothing about it, well she could have but she didn't, and thought why should she? Jonas turned her and with his hand now firmly cupping her backside, guided her to the next door along, took her inside and pointed to a door that said *Ladies* if you were only two inches away.

'I'll wait for you outside, will you be okay? Bit of a tumble that.'

She regained her composure and natural irritability, 'I can go to the bog by meself fankyou,' but she hoped he would wait outside and then worried if he would be able to hear her, so she shoved a few reams of loo paper into the bowl. The loo was clean but cold and she prepared herself for the shock of the cold seat, the thought of which was only marginally more uncomfortable than her now cold and sopping underwear. She thought of Jonas and what had just happened, dismissed it as foolish and then thought cabbage? Finishing her acoustically attenuated business and wiggling back into her wet drawers, she went back outside.

He was dutifully waiting and she was determined to get back to the bar and to talk through what to do next with Barry. He held the umbrella up for her and she stepped under; Jonas didn't move.

'Wot?' she tetchily said to him.

'I would like to kiss you again and I wondered if you would like that too?'

He didn't wait for her answer but gathered her up in his free arm and pulled her to him, he was strong but gentle and she opened her mouth for him. Her hands that had been pressed at her sides like she was in bleedin' Riverdance, slowly moved around his body and she felt his strong back as she pulled herself completely to him, and then, as soon as it had started so it stopped. 'Your Sergeant will be getting antsy.'

'Yeah he will,' she replied breathily, 'I'd like to go back now please,' she said, and he started to lead her and she stopped him and said, 'Cabbage?' wondering where her Uncle Josh voice came from.

'Well the dog's a collie really,' he replied, and guided her into the corridor and back to the bar.

Barry looked at her curiously, 'I took a tumble; the cobbles are slippery.' She could see him trying to contain a laugh and she shut him up with a frigid stare that made her look manic with her rat-tailed hair stuck to her scalp and forehead. She turned to say goodbye to Jonas but he was right behind her, almost squashed into her back, he leaned down and breathed a question right into her nose.

'Where are you staying tonight?'

She sniffed his breath, it was sweet with just the hint of ale, as she recovered her police persona, 'We've gotta go back to London,' she said, defensively leaning back.

'We have a couple of rooms here. My sister can sort them for you, if you would like that? You may need to get your car towed anyway,' and he looked out of the window and nodded affirmation.

Barry, who had been following the soap opera, followed Jonas's example and looked outside to the ground and saw the water up and over the top of the tyres of the Saab, 'Christ what 'appened there?' he said.

'It always floods here, which is why you managed to get a parking spot for your surveillance, the locals know not to park there when it's raining. If you like, I can sort you a room that looks over Sexton House and the shed, they are comfortable and if you want, we have fish or beef stew for dinner, oh, and its quiz night tonight.'

'Oh quiz bleedin' night,' Delores said with more irritation than she truly felt, 'wot more could a girl ask for,' she said, again with more vehemence than she actually felt.

'Fish stew?' Jonas chortled and waggled his head and smiled at her and Delores laughed back and sighed, mollified again.

She looked at Barry, 'What d'you fink?'

Barry was all for it, he clearly loved the beer and the stew, and it was quiz night.

'Barry be a pet? Get the bags,' her best uncle josh, patronise an eejit bloke, voice.

Jonas produced some Wellingtons that looked like they belonged to Hagrid and had flowers on. Barry looked at them, looked at the lake forming and took his already wet shoes off. Delores sat back down, ignoring her patent wet bottom, and ordered another half, laughing at DS Richards in huge flowery Roger Melly's (Wellies – wellington boots).

* * *

Jack had walked back through the cemetery with Snail and left him at the old chapel to get his lunch and a top up of special brew. He thought about some fish stew and maybe talking with Della, but decided not to push just yet and moved on out of the cemetery, waving to Beryl who seemed to be off on a mission, 'See you tonight Burial,' (this is how Jack pronounced her name). She waved and acknowledged him. He thought he saw Ghost but it was heavy rain and visibility was not good. He would head for home via the seafront, he liked to see the waves on Canoe Lake and how the wind tugged at the boats tethered in the centre of the expansive ornamental water, awaiting the return of clement weather and the kids. Then, walking on along the promenade, the real waves and the sense of hypnotic foreboding he always felt, looking into the depths and power of the Solent, a lot like standing on the edge of a railway platform, a train coming. He remembered the sensation as a kid, the hot and smelly steam engines – maybe he will get some fish and chips.

* * *

Alice had finished her latest session of reconstructive surgery, was back from London and she lay down on the settee in the small living room of her and Nobby's Southsea terraced house. She was sore, the pain killers had worn off and it was still a couple of hours to go before she could take more. Detective Constable Alice Herring had grown up as a part of the notorious Herring crime family, but unusually, she had always wanted to be in the police, and even more incongruously had always wanted to work beside Jack Austin. That became no longer a mystery after she had recently revealed that she was in fact Jack Austin's daughter. Jack had separated from Kate, his first wife, who did not want to leave London when he came down to Portsmouth. In the three years they were apart Jack had had a brief relationship with Alice's mum, Jolene Herring. When she fell pregnant Jolene broke off with Jack, saying when he enquired, "As he was about to become a serious filf, he could no longer be seen with her". He had no idea Jolene was pregnant and saw no conflict in the relationship, even liked the family run by Alfie Herring whom he called Kipper; he saw them as charming rogues. That was Jack Austin, a romantic, clip-em around the ear sort of copper, but if you were violent or into serious stuff which included drugs or dropping litter, then he would nick you hard.

Mandy liked this about Jack, but could also see how this had caused him so much trouble over his past as a copper. How he got off all the charges had been a mystery to her and everyone else, but Mandy knew now that it was his spook friends who had stepped in, regularly, to save his hide. She had even known the Home Secretary occasionally telephone and intervene.

So Alice was now a permanent feature in the Jack and Mandy fold. She had resolutely refused to marry Nobby, Detective Constable David Manners, the Commander's son, until the end of her treatment. She could not countenance that Nobby loved her for who she was. She was scarred, and worried if she would ever return to her previous glorious beauty, and could not conceive that any man would want a scarred woman. She had even gone through a phase of wanting to keep her scars, caused by a savaging of fighting dogs, so she could be like her Dad.

Although he shared ownership of the house with Alice, Nobby gave her, her space, but visited regularly the home they had prepared to be their marital home, where they were going to have their baby. In the dog fight Alice had not only been badly mauled, she'd also lost the baby. Nobby was a good lad, Jack approved, and he was patient, though the sleep over's were getting more regular. Nobby was there now and had shared a light lunch with Alice.

'Have you seen Jack, err, your dad lately?'

'Are you kidding, I struggle to get rid of him. I sometimes wonder if I might have been better off not telling him I was his daughter,' Alice said, and Nobby laughed knowing she was kidding.

He looked at her bandaged face and wanted to lift the gauze and kiss her wounds. When he stayed over with her they made love, but she would not let him kiss her or even dwell on her face. The famous Herring temper manifested itself if she caught him gazing upon her face. His reassurances fell on deaf ears, not unlike her dads, so Nobby trod neutral territory and talked about work, 'Mandy, Jo, Frankie and Jackie Philips have been regularly ensconced, so something is happening, I can tell.'

'Well he's said nothing to me,' she was taciturn and he understood why.

'Yeah, well he wouldn't would he, but you can tell if he is up to something, I know, so tell me love.' She winced at the love; he thought it was her face. 'You okay, does it hurt?'

'Yes Nobby it does feckin' hurt.' Alice used feckin' because her dad did. He used loads of expressions, quotes from old films, TV programmes, adverts, just about anything really, but he did like *Father Ted* and he always used cod Irish, and she did as well, because she loved her dad, adored him, idolised him, and as she had trailed after her unsuspecting dad for so long, she had learned all about him. 'Yes Nobby, he is up to something, I can see and so can Mandy; she's told me.'

Nobby jumped up, excited, 'I knew it. I knew it. When is he here next, because I want to talk to him?'

Alice sighed, contained her frustration but recognised the excitement that energised Nobby. Alice, now being a part of the Austin family knew also of her dad's spook background and continuing involvement. Nobby didn't, and she could not tell him, not until her dad said it was okay. Nobby just liked the excitement of the policing, which he thought Jack did, the bozo, also like her dad.

'He'll be here in a minute,' she said, 'he's bringing fish and chips, so stay, you can eat mine. I'm not hungry, obviously, and he would not accept that I had already eaten and he always gets way too much.'

* * *

Mandy's phone rang, 'Amanda Bruce.'

'Austin, Amanda Austin.'

'Jack you tosser, you know I'm keeping my professional name at work,' he was quiet, 'what is it? Jack, where are you?'

'I'm just getting to the fish and chip shop and was going to get some for you and Alice.'

'Me Jack?'

'Yeah we can have lunch together at Alice's.'

'You want a lift, do you?'

'Yeah, cheers babes, that and I want to talk to you both.'

Mandy was intrigued and looked at the photo that had lain on her desk since Jackie and Jo Jums had left, over an hour ago, 'Okay, order up and I will collect you in a minute.'

She jumped up, collected her coat from the back of the door and all in one movement swished into and along the corridor, opened the door to the Community policing room and shouted to Jo Jums, 'Just off for a spot of lunch with tosspot and Alice, be back later,' and then she dashed away before anyone could suggest a reason not to go.

Chapter 15

John Sexton had his arm all the way around her narrow waist, inside of her raincoat which flapped in time with their running. He allowed his hand to frequently slip, to fondle the buttocks of his secretary and they mutually enjoyed the excitement and even the heavy rain; she giggled, she liked it when he paid this sort of attention to her. He was taking her to Pomerol's old place for a liquid lunch and she was looking forward to it. It was tipping it down but it was just a short distance along Cheapside and just up from the Thames. They ran and giggled and jiggled as they skittered and splashed in the City of London streets, eventually reaching the door of the wine bar, only to find it was closed.

'Oh,' she said.

'That's unusual,' he said, and picked his phone from his pocket and speed dialled, got through, 'Seb.' He went on to say that he could not get into Pomerol's wine bar, and he listened for some time, looked up at the sky and the rain drenched his face, and then he looked at his secretary who was stamping her feet, cold, wet and expressing a deal of impatience. He closed the call, 'We have to go back; someone has called in the Receiver.' She looked shocked but more annoyed, this was her time and she was looking forward to getting a room in the afternoon. She enjoyed the fringe benefits of a relationship with her boss but most of all she enjoyed sex with him. He frowned and she stopped her moaning, 'Get back to the office, we'd kept my diary free anyway, I will not be back, and call my wife and tell her I may be a little late home tonight.'

Becky petulantly stamped her foot again, she hated calling his wife. She was sure she knew about her, as well as his mistress and had even mentioned it to John apparently, and he did not seem at all bothered, but she was. She was determined to have her man. She was not happy with third or even second in line.

* * *

Seb had activated the broadcast interference device, it was not reasonable the snoopers should hear stuff that he considered private. It was a simple device; Jack had got it for him from the spook electronics guys, who had in fact supplied most of his kit, although he let his dad think he had bought it.

He took the scrambled computer call from his dad who seemed more agitated than he usually did if he missed sex. Seb didn't understand what all the fuss was about. To Seb, sex was overrated and messy, and although he did find Jenny attractive, he was not prepared to put the effort in. He was convinced he had found Chrissie though, and so moved on.

'Yes dad, I did hear about Pomerol's closing. It was an inevitable consequence of the Star Chamber breaking up and Pomerol's death...' he paused and his dad waited, '...it sends a signal Dad, you do understand that don't you?'

He listened to his dad say he understood and that he may need to stay up in London a little longer, to shuffle a few things, but would be there for quiz night, and Seb said he understood and would explain to Mum. She only wanted the sex anyway, and he told his dad so, who flustered a goodbye.

* * *

Pansy and Angel had finished in the chapel, stocked the wood pile and the lunch plates were cleared. The guests were looking like they might get forty winks, sleeping on the truckle beds, old settee and armchairs distributed around the cast iron stove. Angel stepped high on her toes and Pansy met her halfway for a kiss. Pansy was like Jonas her brother, tall for a woman, six foot three, dark honey blond hair like her mother and Seb, not the black curls of her dad and older brother. She wore her hair long and just over her shoulders. She was not fat, quite lean in fact, but large limbed. When she was younger and had thought about boys and then men, few had taken an interest as she towered over them and they clearly felt intimidated, and sometimes exacerbated, especially if they got on her nerves, when she would bat them one; she had her Mum's temperament. But to Angel, Pansy was divine, and slowly she had ingratiated herself into Pansy's life by just being there, and courting her.

Angel was twenty-five, the same age as Pansy, short by comparison, five foot five, slight, a delicate frame, similar blond coloured hair but thicker, a round and dishy face, with a cherub's nose. Anyone looking at the couple and realising that they were a couple, would never have guessed that the dominant one was Angel, but she was, by very dint of the fact that Pansy loved and adored her partner. Angel reciprocated that love but guided Pansy. She also knew that this is what irritated Pansy's dad, and not because they were from the Isle of Lesbos as Jack always said, but she was determined that John Sexton would eventually accept them and she knew she was close.

They left the chapel, both wrapped up warm and dry in waterproof sailing jackets, leggings and flowery boots and made a quick reconnoitre of the cemetery, as requested by Seb. They noticed the gate to the Barnes mausoleum snap shut quickly, smiled and then came back. They passed the shed and tapped the window; Seb looked up, the closest he got to acknowledgement, and they made their way to the pedestrian gate that opened onto the road they would cross to get to the pub. They saw Sergeant Richards in Pansy's spare flowery Wellingtons, wading into the lake, water spilling over the brim; he was en-route, back to the pub from the boot of the marooned car, carrying two overnight bags. They had heard from Beryl that Jonas was going to get them to stay the night at the pub.

The wind and rain was worsening and the noise from that and the passing traffic, made it impossible to warn the sergeant of the obscured pothole he was about to step in. The two women laughed together as the disgruntled Sergeant climbed out, having fallen over and was, as a consequence, completely drenched, and his embarrassed, angry face, looked up into the pale blue eyes of a blond giant; which one was the creature from the deep was debateable.

'Here Sergeant, give me your bags and we will get you straight to your room,' Pansy said, grinning, 'you can have a hot bath; it might make you feel better. I'm Pansy and this is Angel, quiz night tonight, did Jonas tell you?'

'Yes he fucking did.'

The sergeant not only looked like a drowned rat, he appeared to have acquired a dampened sense of humour. They later confessed to taking some pleasure in the sight and reaction but not so much as Delores, as she saw the bane of her professional life walk through the door, soaked through to the skin.

'Cats and dogs Baz?' Delores commented benignly, sloping her head in an overtly feminine and understanding way. Barry stood rigid, his eyes boring a hole into his Guvnor, but took the proffered pint, grimacing as he thanked Jonas. It was good strong ale and Barry could feel his senses dulling, but the ale could not assuage his annoyance with Delores Lovington for laughing.

Angel gestured with her head and Pansy picked up the cases like they were two feathers, and Delores and Barry followed the two unlikely women to the staircase door, in the opposite corner of the bar to the toilet corridor. They climbed a steep timber stair and clunked along the bare floor-boarded landing and corridor. Angel unlocked a door that opened onto a beautiful, relatively large room, and indicated this was for Delores. Pansy put the case inside and nudged Barry to move on, like she was a jail warder, herding a reluctant prisoner; Barry fell in line.

Delores took in the sight of Barry being ushered, and with a pleasurable smile on her face, she disappeared into the room and immediately noticed a remarkable contrast to the pub below; it was modern, light and airy, or would have been if the wintry weather had not been so foul outside. She felt warmed by radiators, not a fire, a tad disappointed at that. She plumped the bed and then pressed it with both hands, it felt good. She stripped her damp skirt and suit top off, draped the discarded clothing carefully over a radiator and went into the bathroom, it was small, utilitarian but attractively decorated, and she leaned to the taps to run the bath and removed the rest of her clothes and slipped on the fluffy white towelling dressing gown that hung on the back of the bathroom door. She sighed, looking into the mirror over the basin as it slowly steamed up, obscuring her fading image and she worried her looks might be fading almost as a consequence.

Delores admitted to herself that, apart from rinsing through her Alan Wickers, she was standing at the basin looking into the mirror to see what Jonas saw. She was in her mid-thirties, actually just turned thirty-four and she pegged Jonas for late twenties. Well that was okay wasn't it? She firmly moved the skin of her face around with a pinched thumb and forefinger, it was still tight and she was fit. She'd made Detective Inspector on the fast track graduate programme and taken advantage of every course and facility going; this included the Met's central police gym. Despite all of her obvious achievements and even physical attributes, she was not as confident as she liked to portray, or her manner suggested. She did not think she was beautiful and admitted this was probably why she focused on a career track. Men saw something in her but she could never keep a bloke for very long, and reassuring herself, she put this down to the difficult police hours, plus she clearly intimidated most of her boyfriends with her job, rank and strong presence.

She continued looking at herself until the mirror completely fogged. In her mind's eye she saw the visage of Jonas and momentarily enjoyed the tingling feeling that came with the associated image; he had the look of Heathcliffe from Wuthering Heights, she thought. This satisfied her, and so all was well with the world. She stepped into the bath and allowed her tired limbs to submerge. She soaked and felt the worries dissolve into the hot

Pete Adams

water, submerged her head and allowed her thoughts free rein. The fraud squad had been keeping close tabs on the Sexton family for some time. It was her job as a specialist graduate to monitor the comings and goings of John Sexton in the City, to link in with the Met murder squad as John Sexton's finger prints had been all over the Pall Mall room where the PM's cabinet secretary, a man they called Pomerol, the government chief whip and the head of the military had been sprayed with bullets and left brown bread (dead) across the highly-polished conference room floor.

Lifting her head from the water, she said aloud through the cloud of steam, 'But John Sexton had a perfect excuse. At the time of the slaughter he had been meeting with international bankers, funds and institutions, concluding the deal that spread the British debt over seventy years.' She brought herself upright thinking she had better not speak out loud, so carried on her thoughts silently. The bankers' deal had been put to the government as a fait accompli. It was a plan started by a very brave friend of Sexton who had paid the ultimate price, gunned down in a "safe house" and here in Southsea, a district of Portsmouth; the link was not lost on Delores.

Perplexing that, and she had learned also that Jacqueline Parmentier had now also been killed. All this stuff Delores, known as Della to her close friends, was briefed to monitor but it was the activity of the young son Sebastian that was truly on her radar. It would be understating it to say that the father listened to Sebastian. If she did not know the capabilities of John Sexton she would say Seb ran the show, whatever that was, and this was also her brief, although Sergeant Barry tosspot Richards thought it was the Pall Mall slaughter they were investigating. He was not high enough on the intellectual pay scale to even comprehend the fraud and conspiracy possibilities.

She lifted herself up with a start and the ensuing tidal wave swamped the bathroom floor, 'Christ we've not looked at the shed for ages. Shit-a-brick, what has happened to me, and bloody Barry?' Delores said to herself as she threw one of the big bath towels onto the floor to soak up the puddle, stood on the towel and rubbed the mirror with her hands and then laughed to her reflection; she'd smeared the mirror with her finger tips. 'Hypocrite Della Lovington,' she said to her reflection, as she wiped the mirror with a dry hand towel and inexplicably laughed as she formed a turban with another towel for her hair, slipped on the robe and stepped into the bedroom to get ready; quiz night, was she excited?

She went to the bedroom window, tugged the curtains aside and tried to look out, but mainly saw her reflection in the black glass. As her eyes adjusted to the night, she saw a light glowing from the shed, the chapel stained glass twinkled like Christmas lights, and there was a light from a ground floor rear room of Sexton House, which gave a nominal glow to a patch of grass, but that was not what attracted her attention. A police car had pulled up in the cemetery drive, what was that all about? But that was not what really attracted her attention, it was the reflection of Jonas, but not so much that as the feel of his hard hands gently slipping inside her robe, his sandpaper fingertips grazing her nipples causing her to drift into an inescapable sexual reverie before she could think of what to do. But that was not what totally amazed her; it was the fact that she relished the embrace and covered his rough hands on her breasts, sighed and abandoned her vigil of the fucking shed, to fuck a bleedin pikey.

'Seb will be in the pub tonight,' he whispered into her ear causing her body to shudder. He gently turned her and she felt his eyes do even more devastating work to her body and then he kissed her hard, almost roughly, and she responded, what the hell was happening to her?

She inexplicably laughed and spoke into his mouth, 'Cabbage, collie, cauliflower,' Jonas acknowledged her eventual realisation, slipped her robe off and lifted her naked and lowered her to the bed.

Chapter 16

Seb stepped toward the door and into his perfect green wellingtons, shrugged into his perfect slick coat and clicked the remote that automatically put all of his equipment on stand-by and into secure mode. He went out and the shed door swung shut behind him, the automatic locks whirred and clicked perfectly behind him, and he strode surefooted down the path which, in the pouring rain, offered an attractive reflective sheen from the porch light, and he was very soon in the rear hallway of Sexton House, shaking himself down.

He could hear his Mum's high pitched voice in the kitchen, arguing with the policemen. He hung up his coat, lined up his Wellingtons along with all the other shoes and boots that were crooked, straightened the other coats, slipped his Sexton House slippers on, and went to the kitchen. Gently, he opened the door and blinked as the contrast of lighting hit him.

The policeman watching the door read this facial gesture as one of simpering weakness. He must be new, Seb thought.

'Sebastian Sexton?' The policeman asked, and Seb nodded as he stepped fully into the room, 'we would like to ask how you knew the whereabouts of Chrissie James?'

'I take it she is safe then?' Seb questioned back, hovering, momentarily distracted, the kitchen chairs were misaligned.

'She is, and she was found where you directed us to look, in a manhole, cold, tired, exhausted, filthy, but essentially okay,' the policeman responded with a grin that suggested he had his man.

Seb allowed a rare semblance of emotion to run across his stony face, to portray his inner feelings as he sorted the chairs. 'Good' and he sat down and asked his Mum for a Girl Grey tea, as Jack would say. 'Officers would you like some tea?' he offered, gesturing to his mum. The policemen seemed confused, but decided to have some tea as Seb had that sort of posh voice that you complied with; they could have a cup of tea and then press home their argument with this weird lad, who maintained eye contact and followed the line of their unspoken thoughts. 'I assume you are thinking that because you could not find the girl and I could, obviously I must have placed the child in the manhole. Am I correct?'

'Did you Mr Sexton?' the copper drove home his misconceived advantage.

Seb sighed into a rare titter, 'Don't be so daft constable, I used deductive powers and divined what was the bleedin' obvious (he loved it when he used Jack Austin terminology). If she was not abducted by a neighbour, if she didn't scale the house walls and go over the roof herself, and you had already reported no ladders were present, and I know the mother and know she would do nothing to harm her child, therefore she must still be there, but where? That was the question.'

The constable looked up from his notebook to Seb, the logic was powerful, but his sergeant had asked him to haul Sebastian Sexton into the station for questioning, he was a known local weirdo and had to be up to something. Trying to decide what to do, PC Plod was halted by a loud echoing report from the hallway; a gothic echoing, a rhythmic pounding resounding from the heavy iron gothic knocker to the main gothic entrance door, which gave way to the gothic entrance hall; all in all it was quite gothic. Beryl stepped into the gothic hall to open the gothic door.

From the modern kitchen, Seb and the policemen could hear muffled exclamations and squeals of pleasure from Beryl Sexton and she returned with Detective Chief Inspector Austin and Detective Superintendent Bruce, now Mrs Austin.

'Seb my old china (china plate – mate), your family, they are well?' Jack never entered a room silently, unlike leaving, which was often a contrast; he was after all a consommé enema. Jack shuffled around the kitchen giving the patrol officers only a cursory glance and a quick, 'Consternoon afterbules, your families they are well?' they did not appreciate *Pride and Prejudice* and Jack raised his one working eyebrow to Seb.

Having arrived and seen the patrol car, Amanda had phoned Central Station and learned the reason for the visit. Jack was aware that the local wooden tops thought Sebastian weird and therefore a candidate for anything they could not logically explain, a convenience really. To the uninitiated, Seb displayed no reaction but Jack detected a hint of a smile that grew as he focused on Amanda. Seb had grown to like Mandy and he stepped toward her and gave her a hug, something rare; Sebastian Sexton was aspergers, on the autism scale and as such had difficulty in socialising, understanding the social norms. The hug for Mandy had been taught by Mandy, and he performed it as taught.

Jack had gotten to know Seb when his first wife Kate had been his allocated social worker. The boy had difficulties in all of the mainstream schools and Kate had found him a special needs unit, and there he had flourished. As Seb's dad was away most of the week in the City, Kate asked Jack to become a mentor to Seb, and so it was Jack built a relationship with the child, as much as anyone could, and had encouraged the boy's analytical mind and his ability to solve mysteries. Jack slowly fed him local crime projects and had been allowed to take the credit for the results. He also arranged with the boy's dad to set him up with computers that gradually became more sophisticated as the supplier became MI5, obviously worked out by Seb, but if anyone could keep his counsel it was Sebastian Sexton of the Sexton Detective Agency. Jack had thought of the name, and he was right proud of it too; well he had to do something didn't he? It was about all he had contributed Mandy had said when she found out how Jack, all of a sudden, out of the blue, came up with solutions to crimes. Ordinarily Seb would have passed on the information for the missing Chrissie to Jack or Mandy, but as Jack was out and of course had forgotten his phone, and Mandy and Jo Jums had been ensconced in meetings all day, Seb had arranged for his Mum to tell the local police.

'Right officers just as soon as you can Foxtrot Oscar please.' It wasn't a question from Jack, it was an order and the officers looked unsure. 'What part of feck off do you not understand, is it the fox bit?' Jack pushed, rather wittily he thought' he'd used his *David Attenborough* voice that Mandy thought was more like *Wendy* out of *Bob the builder*.

'And if you have a problem, get your station sergeant to call me; Paddy Mulligan is it not?' Mandy said, not quite so polite or wittily as Jack, but then politeness and certainly not the wit, was one of Jack's trade mark characteristics and not necessarily hers. The officers backed to the door and then were gone. Mandy made a mental note to follow this up, she knew Paddy Mulligan and he was a nasty piece of work. This was bordering on persecution and she would not allow that to happen to Seb, not on her watch anyway.

'Good love I am pleased to hear it, and Paddy Mulligan, do I know him?' Jack said.

Mandy let her eyes hit the ceiling just as Burial gave a guffaw that defied the size of the woman. Mandy had, heaven help her, somehow or other, caught the Jack Austin trait of speaking her thoughts; must be sharing the bath water she thought. She also thought he knows Paddy, so why is he saying that? Seb just smiled and wondered if he should hug her again and Mandy made his mind up for him, and hugged the lad saying, 'I will not let them harass you Seb.' The boy did smile and it was worth it, it was angelic a bit like Trevor Howard in '*Gone with the Wind*.'

'Farted has he darling?'

Mandy looked at Jack and cottoned on, spoken her thoughts again.

'Burial Sweetart where's John?'

'Something cropped up Jack, but his tart phoned to say he would be home probably by nine, so in time for the quiz.'

'Sorry to hear that luv anything we can help with...'

Mandy interrupted Jack, 'We already know darling, I just haven't had the time to tell you.'

Jack shrugged and moved on, 'Got the questions all worked out then Seb, sunshine?'

Seb nodded; knew enough about Jack to know he was trying to get a sneak preview, 'Yes Jack, would you like to see them?' Burial laughed, shortly followed up by Mandy and Jack; this was the closest Seb had ever gotten to a spontaneous joke.

'Let's get over to the pub; I'm in need of fish stew and a pint of Gravediggers, come on Burial, Alice and Nobby are coming tonight as well as Liz and Curly. Liz is as big as a feckin' house now, I reckon it has to be triplets and that will make me a number one triple Grandfevvers.'

Liz was Mandy's eldest and Mandy had now settled her misgivings about her daughter being a lesbian and in a permanent relationship with Carla, whom Jack called Curly. Liz was also pregnant, and the couple were staying in Mandy's flat as Mandy had moved in permanently with Jack in his house. She shook herself, their house; she still had difficulty with that one.

Jack however, was a tour de force and everyone here knew it. He was headed for the Gravediggers for some fish stew and a pint, and this is what everyone else did as well, no time for personal thoughts or reflection; "naturellament", as Jack would say.

Chapter 17

Snail had eaten a dinner of doorstep bread and beef stew, and sobered sufficiently to totter back to his spot on the promenade for an evening vigil. The weather had calmed, just a fine spray of rain driven by a blustery wind, and that didn't bother him. He'd heard Jack Austin arrive at Sexton House and noisily make his way over to the pub. He recalled how it was when he could visit a pub when he wanted, could drink modestly without wishing to drown his emotions and seek oblivion. There were times when he thought he was okay, but then the special brew called.

As he stumbled through the cemetery, he thought he saw a light from a grave but dismissed this as an alcoholic mirage, waved to Ghost and continued his determined trudge to the seafront. He took the circuitous route because he tried to make everything in his life hard. He thought if he passed these tests he set for himself God would grant him his daughter back. That morning, before Jack had arrived, he had stripped off, gone to the seas edge and allowed the freezing waves to hit his disgusting body. He had dressed himself afterwards and felt, in the haze that followed, he saw his daughter step out of the lemon beach hut. Maybe the test was not hard enough, because the vision didn't recognise him before disappearing. What could he do that would be harder? This is what he said to himself as he sat on the promenade edge, his legs dangling and his feet twitching, freezing cold, surely he would get pneumonia; would that be a good test?

The occupants of the lemon beach hut heard the raving

mumblings of this tramp and thought they could set him a test, and then set about working out how to set it.

* * *

Jack pulled three tables together and gathered chairs. Nobby and Alice were there, Jack making himself irritating trying to make Alice laugh. Jackie Philips, the trick cyclist, and her partner Gill and the very pregnant Liz and her partner Carla, and they all stood back and talked amongst themselves while Jack created chaos, being very experienced Jack people, knowing they could change anything back later.

Mandy told Jack to sit down, 'And stop trying to organise everybody, and bring your chair over here,' and she pointed, 'where you will not be tempted to look at Seb's questions.'

Jack was a clown, and after that he was a famed cheat, using his humour and madcap actions to cover his cheating, but he did not fool Mandy, she knew he considered cheating as a part of the game. "Never play monopoly with him", she would say, and if you do, "make sure the bank is miles away from his light fingers", similarly the houses and hotels that miraculously appear on the Old Kent Road, where his Mum was born, and Whitechapel, where his dad was born. He never bought, nor stole, Bond Street, Regent Street, Park Lane or Mayfair, that was for Uncle Josh twats. He even refused to pay rent quoting *Groucho Marx, "All property is fucking feft"*, and moving on, as if this was all the explanation that was needed.

Angel glided over to their table and asked if they were ready to order food, Mandy pressed Jack's hand, an indication to curb the rejoinders and order. 'Beef stew for you Jack?'

He looked horrified and Angel laughed as did everyone else, she scribbled fish stew and noted the orders of the others.

'Where's Jonas Angel?' Jack had noticed that Pansy was running the bar, which was filling with more and more locals, all challenged by the prospect of the very challenging Sebastian Sexton quizzes, as well as the opportunity to savour the ale and stews.

'He'll be here in a minute, I think he is settling a guest,' and she tittered to herself as she wafted away, heading for the kitchen.

Jack's tables had split into three teams and the other patrons, in the steadily filling pub, had established their own battle lines. From Jack's other local, C&A's (the Crown and Anchor) there was Brainiac the college lecturer and Bernie LeBolt the local news crime reporter. Another separation was made for Pin head, who bounced here and there courtesy of his St Vitus dance and he was joined by John Bob and Mary Bob the evangelistic couple, also known as the Von Trapp family; Jack looked around, no puppet theatre or flowery curtains for play clothes, so they were safe.

Jonas's granddad had been joined by a few of his mates from the local loony bin, and together they were filling out the answers already on their blank sheet of paper, anxious to get the quiz over and get on with a game of dominos with the pack of playing cards they had brought with them. As they pencilled in the answers on the quiz sheet, so they shouted snap. It looked like granddad was winning, of course; it was his grandson's pub and Jonas supplied them free beer all night. They hogged one fireplace and some other bloke had grabbed a table by the other fireplace, not realising it was Jack's fireplace. Jack explained this to him but somehow or other the anticipated altercation had not transpired but a friendly banter had ensued about Millwall football club. It turned out that Sergeant Barry Richards was one of those rare fellows, a Millwall supporter; as was Jack of course.

Millwall is a London football club which has a dubious pedigree, "Nobody likes us and we don't care", that was their chant, and Mandy knew Jack would likely sing the Millwall song, *Molly Malone* later tonight, along with *If you were the only girl in the world*, all alcohol fuelled and directed to her. It was okay, provided he was far enough away so the beery fumes missed her not insubstantial nose. He actually sung this last song quite well and certainly with a passion, and it touched her as his one pissed eye would attempt to zero into her soul. He had always said he loved Mandy's face; that he loved the look of her, even though she knew she was not a beauty and had her fair share of wrinkles at fifty-four. But he would touch her face and smooth her wrinkles with gentle fingers and say she radiated the full beauty that was womanhood. He said he saw her as his Sophia Loren of Portsea Island. It was all bollocks of course but she knew he meant it and she liked it, finally he would say that he loved her fireman's hose, which was large and roman and had been the bane of her life until she got together with Jack that is, who loved her "Schnozz", as he called it.

The food arrived and Jack returned and sat down, generously allowing Barry Richards to sit at his table, 'Millwall supporter love,' he said to Mandy.

'Oh really,' she replied as if it was the most interesting thing in the world, 'what's he doing down here then?'

'Oh, I forgot to ask.'

Her eyes rolled and she whispered, 'Super sleuth,' and Alice and Nobby tittered but Carly guffawed. Carly really liked Jack and had almost become his doppelganger, and frustratingly for Mandy, Mandy's daughter, who had previously dubbed Jack Austin as a *knobhead of the first order*, liked it when Carly did Jackisms. Liz even laughed when Jack said she was from the Isle of Lesbos. But still he was settled now, and Mandy knew she would hear nothing until he finished his stew. Well nothing intelligible that is, as she did know to expect the mmmm's and aaaah's and the lubbly jubblys, as he *quietly* savoured the fish stew, which is why Mandy jumped in shock when he shouted in her earole, "Oi Della" and her reaction made everyone else jump.

Della was patently surprised, but retained a modicum of coolness as she sashayed across the room, intimately followed by Jonas, and Mandy knew, looked at the other women and they also all knew; this was a post-coital meeting for the woman whom Jack clearly knew. Della looked into the eyes of the women seated with Jack, and she also knew that they knew, and the consequent blush compounded the evident, to the women at least, sexual bloom.

'Jack you fucking geriatric arsehole, I knew you worked down 'ere but never fort I'd bump inta yer,' Della struck back.

Mandy thought, oh no, another feckin' cockney, but Jack was up now and he smothered and hugged the startled and embarrassed petit woman, and Mandy knew what that felt like. Jack was one of those blokes that things happened around, and just as you thought you were squirreled away from anyone you knew, safe in any covert assignations or private thoughts even, Jack would pop up and that was it; everything out in the open. Well out in the open to anyone who cared to observe and Jack was not noted for his observational skills, which is why in actual fact he was a crap copper. A well-connected copper it has to be said, and indeed astute enough to know when to take information he could use, but Mandy knew now that he was primarily a strategist and his skill was assimilating information, processing, and then coming up with a game plan. Now this he was good at, but coppering? He was feckin' useless. Mandy's swearing and cod Irish had also blossomed since becoming close to Jack. She tried to stop, but it had almost became as much a part of her as it was him, as was the speaking of her thoughts; testament of which was her daughter and Curly laughing and confirming she had spoken these very thoughts.

Jack was back to the table having muscled Della to join him, 'Amanda sweet'art this is Detective Inspector Delores Lovington of the Met, I imagine she's down to look over the Sextons,' and he turned to the shocked Della. 'Della babes this is Detective Superintendent Amanda Bruce; now, and more importantly,' he flicked his one eyebrow and wobbled his head, 'Mrs Austin,' and he beamed with pride and patent adoration for Mandy, and she forgave his crassness immediately.

Della turned to Mandy and expressed her most sincere sympathies and Mandy immediately liked the woman.

'Della, pleased to meet you,' Mandy stood and shook the woman's hand.

Jonas squashed closer and put his arm around Della's waist and pulled her to him. She blushed but did not resist. Jack shouted his immediate understanding, 'Ah undercover eh Della?' and guffawed as did the rest of the Austin table, except for Mandy who looked shocked at the comment. Jack went to whisper in Della's ear and the woman responded with a warm smile that turned to a sneer as the other Millwall fan joined them.

Della slipped from Jonas's grasp, 'Jack, Amanda, this is Detective Sergeant Barry Richards, Met murder squad and 'ed of the misogynist brigade.'

Mandy spluttered a laugh but took Barry's hand to shake, and laughed some more because clearly Barry would need to ask Della what that word meant later.

Jack was oblivious, well not oblivious, but was on another mission to change all of the tables around, shifting everybody, their soups and drinks, and spilling copious quantities of both in the process, and with the back of his hand, brushing aside the complaints as well as the soup and beer, onto the floor. He looked around to see if anyone noticed and wiped his hand on his jumper, on the back so he couldn't see the stain. Mandy knew that *out of sight, out of mind*, was another maxim of the Church of Egypt.

Eventually everybody settled. Barry and Della now had the table nearest the door and Jack had wangled his table beside the fireplace. Granddad barked his approval of Jack's move, in a tourettes manner, and the other elderly loony's shouted "Bingo" and granddad, a nanosecond later shouted "House". The crowd reacted shouting back "Flat" and there were great laughs all round, except for Barry, who didn't like his new seat by the draughty door, and Jack took pleasure in the Sergeants discomfort, until he noticed Mandy had noticed. He quietly harrumphed to himself, sent up a silent prayer that they would not have to talk about this before they went to bed tonight, then forgot all about it. For a non-religious man, he relied a lot on the compassion of God while he got on with other things.

Della had eyes only for Jonas as he made a brief trip to the bar, returning with a bottle of chilled Chablis and a glass. He poured for Della, kissed her and she blushed as he whispered into her ear. The whole pub watched silently on as Jonas then returned with a bowl of fish stew, a couple of bread vans and a pure white, starched napkin, which he unfurled with a flourish and made a fuss of laying on her lap. Mandy watched on as Jonas stroked the cloth into Della's lap and was reminded of her own dirty old man, whom she had just married; she approved. She loved the overt sexual attention she got from Jack, even though with the PTSD he was certifiable loony bin material, and not for the first time, wondered if she should sit him with granddad.

They settled and went back to their meals and drinks, Mandy just a tad miffed that she did not get a glass of wine, and noticing that at the bar, seated on a stool that also had appeared from nowhere, was Seb looking eager to get on with the quiz.

Chapter 18

Snail sat on the freezing stone paving, dangling his feet over the rolled concrete promenade edge, looking out to where he knew the sea to be; it was dark, the invisible sea could be heard crashing, sucking and pushing at the shingle, an infinite inky black aural tableau. The raw cold penetrated his bones and he enjoyed the sensation. He sensed a presence, heard a clank, and looked to his side; saw only an image of his daughter placing a four pack of special brew beside him. He reached out and the vision disappeared as quickly as it had materialised. It was God taunting him, his pal Joe Moss had said as much. Joe always said that God was here and now, in us and around us. Well what the fucking hell did he know and Joe was dead now.

Psssst, Snail lifted the ring pull and tucked it into one of his pockets, it might be worth something. He didn't even like the smell of the beer anymore, but he drank it because it gave him a buzz and dulled the pain. Psssst, he opened another and that disappeared as fast as the previous one. He looked, wanting his daughter to appear again, even if only in apparition. Maybe if he drank all of the cans as fast as he could, God would approve and bring his daughter to him? Psssst, Psssst, and the remaining two cans disappeared. He tried to crush the emptied cans to fit in his pockets but he had lost what little strength he had. Fucking God, what did he know of suffering, what did he know of passing tests, had he not done the most difficult of things, 'Where are you then?' he shouted, 'where are you?'

'I'm here dad.'

'Shite!'

Snail looked, and his daughter was there and she looked real, but he was pissed and mad, he knew that much, but what the hell, he would enjoy the moment, enjoy the alcohol hazed vision.

'Come on dad let's get you in out of the cold eh?' And Snail rose up, assisted and held by his daughter's spirit. At first he was amazed his hand did not pass through her hand, it felt solid; as apparitions went this was a good one, he must remember, four cans of special brew drunk very fast. After all of the tests he had performed, this was by far the easiest and had produced the result he had sought, even if he knew it would disappear and probably soon; in the meantime he would follow.

Beth beckoned him to the lemon beach hut. He followed, feeling a tad sick but that was normal; Ghost had said that his stomach lining was going and he should expect to be sick more often unless he stopped drinking, but Ghost couldn't suggest any other way to dull the pain he felt, so he kept on drinking, and voila, here was Beth. He knew he was right to keep on, then thought that maybe he was about to die and she was here to take him. But why the beach hut? Was it a portal? He went in and immediately was hit hard in the stomach, was spun around by a man now holding his arms from behind and he found himself hanging out of the hut door, spewing. All he could think was Beth will likely not be there when he stopped being sick.

He felt himself being lifted upright, spun again and he saw Beth, she was still there and he smiled as a hard fist struck his mouth; he felt teeth disintegrate and the cartilage in his nose crack. He wavered to look past the man and thought, oh good she's still there, I deserve this beating, I've been a bastard, I must have been; he knew he had. If I pass this test then maybe I can be with Beth. The rock-hard fist struck again, and he felt his cheekbone crack; funny, because he couldn't feel any pain, he just swayed and Beth was still there.

Spluttering blood and teeth, 'Hallo love am I dead, am I with you now? I have missed you so much, you look lovely,' and as he smiled a broken smile; the pain began to register.

Beth seemed unmoved at her father's discomfort. 'Hit him again,' she instructed, coldly, and the man did, warming to his task

Pete Adams

as would any good bully. Snail folded but remained on his feet, the other man held his arms and metaphorically his nose; Snail stank and had clearly shat himself. 'You are a filthy communist bastard but you are my dad,' Beth carried on, a gentle stroke of her dad's weather beaten cheek, 'do you want to keep on seeing me?' Snail looked up through his eyelids, which were beginning to crust over, coughed an affirmative and admired his daughter with whom he had talked socialism as she grew up; he felt proud. As a professor of political science he had discussed how Socialism should never be confused with Communism. He had talked about compassionate socialism and a balance in doctrines and he knew she got it. She must have, because here she was railing against communism and that was good, but her vehemence startled his fuzzed-up brain. 'We want Jack Austin and we want you to bring him to us, do you understand,' she asked, even more aggressively.

Snail's eyes were closing and his thoughts spun; he could taste blood and began heaving. The man with the vice like grip of his arms, whisked Snail around to allow him to spew some more onto the shingle beach; finished, he was rocked back upright. 'Dad, tell Jack Austin to come and see us, he can get us into the Glory Hole and tell nobody else; do you understand?' Snail nodded and felt his toes crack, he hadn't even noticed that his boots were missing, but the man who had punched him was hitting each toe with a hammer. The alcohol could not dull this pain, it was excruciating, as was the rhyme, *this little piggy,* but why was Beth laughing; it must all be a dream Snail thought, but it hurt so much; so vivid, so real.

* * *

Seb was ready and Jack had subtly pulled Mandy's chair away from the others and was covering their answer sheet with his arm, like he was in the school exam hall.

'Grow up Jack, it's just a game,' she said, but smiling.

He looked at her confused, as if she didn't know what was really

108

happening here.

Della, looking right royally pissed off that she had ended up paired with Barry, kept looking up at Jonas. Her preoccupation was not missed by her sergeant who was already dreaming up schemes to embarrass her when they got back to London. This could be the moment he had been waiting for since Delores Lovington had strolled in from her fast track, postgraduate programme and taken his promotion to DI.

'I'll take the sport, you do the general knowledge and women's stuff okay,' he said.

'What?'

'I'll take the sport...'

'I 'erd yer, just didn't unerstan' the Neander-fucking-fal finking,' and she followed this up with what was presumably Neanderthal face gestures augmented with extended, dragging arms. She was prepared to continue her vehement diatribe into Barry's face when Seb started, and she was here to watch Sebastian Sexton, although she was beginning to doubt her conviction; *help*, she thought.

Seb was calling out to the bar for order, simultaneously looking for reassurance from his big brother, 'Okay first question,' he said, and seemed to derive courage from somewhere that elicited a broad grin from Jonas, *'If it took a man a week to walk a fortnight, how many apples in a bunch of grapes?'*

'Oh, oh I know this,' Jack said pulling the answer sheet to him, grinning victory to the opposition, whilst nervously fidgeting as if he had ants in his pants.

'Jack sit still, please,' Mandy said with no conviction, she was laughing along with the rest of the party. Della was not sure what to think, she looked at Jack and he returned her gaze but not before covering his arm over the answer he had written; nice to see yer Della but...

Jonas gestured with his head and Della looked to Barry, 'You do the sport and the rest you bleedin' arse,' and she got up and joined Jonas at the bar. He greeted her with a kiss.

'Ooh err matron' shouted Jack, who had inadvertently raised his arm in order to cup his hands to make the call, he was after all a perfectionist, and was now regaling Mandy, 'Cover it up, Curly can see.' This caused everyone to laugh more, except Barry, who was confused by the question and Jack let him know that this had been the easy starter; thought about throwing in a few brass knobs but decided to be mature.

'Mature?' Mandy had caught him! God, Jack thought, must be busy sorting out the other thing for him, not that Jack could remember what it was; he presumed that God will have written it down or something.

Della snuggled into the arms of Jonas and looked across to granddad and noticed that the three 'de'-Mensa candidates were now playing dominoes with the playing cards and shouting snap. She smiled, and Jonas smiled at her when she returned his gaze. She looked at the answer he had written – *NONE.*

'Next question' and Carla had caught Jack's ants and struggled to contain her giggles, '*The Elephant is a Pretty Bird and it swings from bough to bough. It builds its nest in a Rhubarb Tree and whistles like a cow – what is it?*'

Jack jumped again 'Ooh Ooooh, I know this.'

'You do?' Mandy replied, completely stumped, and she watched him write the answer, while Carla tried to cheat. Jackie and Gill had completely lost it, Jackie thinking is there actually an answer, amazed as she watched Jack scrawl using his doctors' handwriting. Mandy leaned over to look at Jack's scribble. He made to cover up, difficult as his hands were on his mouth being careful with what he said; God was busy at the moment, but Mandy wasn't. Mandy dragged the sheet away and read *An elephant bird* and, making a funny noise with her mouth that Jack thought might confuse God, she threw it back down on the table. Carla and Jackie tried to get a quick look. Some hope, Jack's writing was almost indecipherable, a bit like his frontier gibberish. When she had previously tackled him on this, he just said he wanted to be a doctor but couldn't stand the sight of blood, but he'd managed the handwriting.

Seb was calling out again, 'Next question - *I went round a straight crooked corner and saw a dead donkey die. I took out my knife and shot it; it got up, and spat in my eye; where was that?'*

'Oooh, Oooooooh,' Jack again, and he scribbled with his pencil and shouted, 'Seb let's get to the hard ones.'

The De-Mensa crowd shouted "Bingo" and a nanosecond later "Horse" from Granddad. Everyone shouted "Donkey" in reply. Mandy leaned over to look at what Jack had written and was even more confused, but saw Jack was on a roll, really enjoying himself, and she was happy for him, touched his hand and he looked up and smiled at her. Distracted, he missed the start of the next question, leapt up.

'Whoa Neddy, I missed the start of that one Seb,' a look of real worry on his face.

'For the benefit of Jack I will start again,' and Jonas shocked Della by leaping away from her as he went up to Seb. He took the sheet and held his finger on the next question, blanked out the previous ones by folding the paper behind itself. The next question was now on top. Seb read on, like this was completely normal behaviour, *'One Night, Upon a Stair, I saw a man who wasn't there. He wasn't there again today, I do so wish he'd go away; who was he?'*

Mandy grabbed Jack's sleeve and stopped him from jumping up again, and in a hushed rebuke, that fooled nobody as she said it with a grin, 'Just write the feckin' answer.'

Della let Jonas engulf her with his huge frame as she backed into him. She noticed Barry observing, taking mental notes, but decided to let it go and looked at the answer that Jonas had written and wrinkled her face. Jonas responded with a face that said, *obvious Der*, but this is not what Della was looking for. Seb's stare bore into Della appearing to seek a response and then, like a light bulb blinking on, she knew, and conveyed this awareness. With a tight smile that somehow radiated from his fixed face, Seb swung his look to Jack. Jack saw all of this and nodded to Della, Mandy noticed, looked at Jack whilst incorporating her best frown.

Della whispered to herself, 'Fucking Jack.'

Jonas looked at her quizzically; Della flicked her head, Seb was about to ask another question.

'Next question and this is especially for Jack – *A deaf policeman...'* and he waited while the laughter faded, *'...a deaf policeman heard the noise and came to arrest the two dead boys, if you don't believe this story's true, ask the blind man, he saw it too! Who was he; who doesn't see but sees everything?'*

Jack didn't jump up but hemmed, rubbed his chin and Mandy noticed it needed shaving. Jack wrote, she looked then leaned back, looked at Jack again from further away, he nodded. Jackie looked over. Mandy saw a flicker of recognition pass between Jack and Jackie, noticed Granddad had stopped playing dominoes with the cards and was standing.

Seb pursued the next question, transfixed with Jack, pushing and determined, *'Next - A paralysed donkey passing by, kicked the blind man in the eye, knocked him through a nine-inch wall, into a dry ditch and drowned them all – the question is, should you fear drowning or fear the guilt that drowning would be a joyful release?'*

Mandy looked at Seb, who was looking intensely at Jack who reciprocated the look. Seb swung his stare to Della and Jonas, looked to Jackie and then to Granddad, who had shuffled over to Jack. Jack was crying, his one eye riveted on Seb, before he swung his watery gaze to Jackie, his trick cyclist. Oh Christ Mandy thought, bloody waterworks, here we go again and then felt immediately guilty, a Roman candle moment and then thought, why the feck not she counselled herself, she was Roman Catholic after all wasn't she, even got married in a feckin' cathedral, with feckin' father O'Brien officiating didn't she, and now had a Papal feckin' blessing.

The pub was quiet and Carla nodded, Mandy had spoken out loud, but nobody laughed. Mandy looked back to granddad who was holding out his hands for Jack, the madness gone, just rheumy grey eyes, white stubble on sunken cheeks and hair sprouting from his nose and ears, like a caring President of the Tufty club. 'It's okay Jack we know,' Granddad said, 'you're among friends and we will not let you drown; Seb figured it out of course.'

Jackie brought a chair over and sat down in front of Jack, easing granddad and Mandy to one side, 'Water Jack, that's it isn't it?' Mandy looked to say something but got the Jackie stare in return. Jackie readdressed Jack, 'Jack,' a firm voice, but hushed in tone, 'tell me; it's the water, it's always the water isn't it? When did it start?'

Jack stared past Jackie, saw Della looking at him and Seb shrink behind the bar, scared, as he eased Della from Jonas and nudged his way into the protective embrace of his bigger brother. Jack looked into the vacant stare from Seb, shook his head and waved the concern from the boy's face. Seb immediately relaxed and so did Jack.

'Yes Jackie, it's the water, the sea, and it started in Hastings. I was a lad of maybe twelve and nearly drowned in the sea. It wasn't fear and panic that stuck in my mind, but a sense of almost pleasurable release that struck me, the only time I felt really okay, when I had no control and had no need for control; I could give up and let go. I have always felt responsible, responsible for everything. I'm always holding on.'

Jackie gripped Jack's hand tighter, 'Okay Jack, thank you for that,' and she turned to Seb and mouthed a thank you, was about to ask about the quiz questions when the pub door banged open and Snail stood there shouting, 'Pansy, Angel, Pansy, Angel...' Blood dripped from his mouth, nose and cuts to his cheeks and above his eyes. He hobbled and Mandy could see the filthy exposed toes, crooked, black and blue, bleeding and clearly smashed, the smell was indescribable but it mattered not a jot as the concern for this poor man was on the faces of all in the pub.

Angel ran from behind the bar as Jack, who had immediately jumped up, held Snail and carefully lowered him to the floor, 'Who did this Snail?'

'Beth Jack, can you believe it, it was Beth and a few of her friends. Nice chaps really and they would like to see you; can you get them into the Glory Hole? Oh, I'm not supposed to tell anyone else or she will disappear again. I'm sorry Jack, I can't remember much more.'

Jack stepped back, Pansy and Angel eased in, ministering. Jonas called for an ambulance and asked Mandy if he should call the police. 'I think we will take this from here Jonas,' Jack answered. 'Mandy, call Jo Jums eh, and tell her to let father Mike know, I think we have something to follow now.'

The ambulance men took Snail away just as John Sexton and Beryl were entering the pub. They stepped aside as Angel floated by, saying she would accompany Snail to the hospital; she kissed Pansy goodbye in front of John Sexton, and it was all Beryl could do to control her laughter at the obvious discomfort of her husband, deliberately generated, but her good humour disappeared rapidly as she became aware of the disturbed atmosphere in the pub and the state of Brian Mayhew as he went by.

Jack was sitting and looking out into any middle distance he could find. He couldn't stand the sight of blood and was likely to faint anytime. Jackie tried to grasp his attention but it was Alice speaking that he responded to, 'It's okay dad, go home with Mandy. Nobby will run the investigation from here, he has already asked for some follow up down at the beach. I can help until we get Jo Jums to steer it.'

'Are you sure love?' he saw Nobby nodding from behind his new daughter.

Mandy stepped in, 'Nobby leave the beach hut alone, let them think we do not know about it, and Jack and I will see you both in work tomorrow; okay Alice?'

'Okay Amanda?' Alice said, looking at her dad.

Jack turned to Jackie, 'Will that be okay Jackie?'

'I think so, I will be close by.'

'Thanks Jackie, hang on a mo love,' and Jack left Mandy's side and went across the bar to a nervous Seb. 'Good questions Seb, thank you. We have some work to do starting tomorrow, are you okay about that?' Seb nodded, the momentary hint of fear disappeared to be replaced by a pallid expression of subliminal excitement.

Jack sidled to Della and Mandy followed close behind, 'Della sweet'art, I have a few confessions.' He shrugged. 'I know why you're here and will tell you tomorrow; can you trust me?' She nodded and

Jack turned to Jonas. Mandy watched Jack firmly grip Della's hands and they both swung their gaze back from Jonas. Mandy leaned in, to listen. 'Remember when I met you at university?' Jack enquired softly of Della.

Della nodded again and Mandy could see her recollecting, a poke from her memory bank, and she spoke as if reading from her mind's eye, '*Not all is as it seems, not every decision is black and white, if it takes a man a week to walk a fortnight. Who swings from bough to bough, take my knife and shoot him now. Ask the blind man, he saw it too; but is the ditch dry or full? And will it drown us all?* You're still in, aren't you? You fucking arseole.' Jack nodded. Della took some time to smooth her metaphorical feathers, 'Then I trust you. I will send Barry home tomorrow, can you get the Gnome office to contact my boss and square it?'

'Already 'ave Della,' and Jack looked at Jonas, 'I don't know what this is Jonas, but do not hurt this woman; she is special to me. I don't need to say that though, do I?'

Jonas put his hand on Della's cheek, looked her in the eye but spoke to Jack, 'No Jack, you don't need to say.'

Chapter 19

'Not all is as it seems, not every decision is black and feckin' white... if it takes a man a week to walk a fortnight... who swings from bough to feckin' bough...'

Jack detected a certain irritation in Mandy's questioning voice.

'...take my knife and shoot, ask the blind man, he saw it too, is the ditch dry or full?' she paused and Jack thought that was it; he was wrong. 'Jack what is all that bollocks, and who is Della?'

The taxi was pulling up at their house. It was Jack's house but slowly it was feeling like her home too. Mandy had struggled at first but she was pretty much there now, and she allowed herself a wry smile as she noted the dread on Jack's face; he knew they would continue this conversation inside and could see him desperately racking his memory banks for answers.

Inside their home, removing their coats, Mandy reminded him that there were unanswered questions, and prompted him on one, 'Jack, Della?'

With a resigned look, he answered, 'The good one that got away love.' Mandy nodded okay, but that was not enough, a more detailed explanation was required. He couldn't see why, but carried on, 'About ten years ago I was asked to help out with some MI5 recruitment, remember Aisha? I got a secondment to the Met ostensibly, and resided temporarily in London. You can imagine how well that went down with Kate.' Jack mused and Mandy thought he was thinking back to Kate and how she did not want to leave London but eventually joined him some three years later. He continued, 'I recruited Della, she was brilliant, but in the end she hated all the shite that went with the job; did you notice the jaundiced way she quoted the rhyme?' He nodded, as if to himself, recalling some history. 'It was something I conjured for my recruits; don't ask me why, I just did. Anyway, she up and quit. I got her into the Met on a rapid graduate programme, and she's done really well, but even so, she'd be better off in the service.'

'You think, do you?' Mandy was stern, fed up with his constant manipulating of people's lives, not least her own.

'I do sweet'art,' Jack replied, not stern, but conciliatory or was that scared – my money's on scared.

'And what is she doing down here, that have something to do with you as well?' Mandy asked, looking sterner. Jack had noticed that sometimes Mandy could wind herself up, not realising that it was often him that wound her up. Jack erroneously thought that he was a calming influence on Mandy, a bit like Buddha. 'Well you look like feckin' Buddha...' Mandy said, her stern face fracturing into a smile as he spoke his thoughts.

Jack decided to ignore Mandy's barbed comment, preferring to focus on her smile, perceiving it as his wife starting to relax and enjoy the conversation, 'Yes, well, the Met had to investigate the Pall Mall deaths; John Sexton's finger prints were all over the place, but he couldn't be nailed as he was clearly in the meeting with the bankers at the time of the slaughter. Then he was shot at himself if you recall, walking down St James's.' She did recall, Jack had talked her through the whole affair, after she had nailed his feet to the floor and beaten him about the head with a metaphorical soggy haddock. 'The Met got a bee in their bonnet about the Sextons and have been looking a bit too hard at them.'

Mandy leaned back in her chair and gave him her serious old fashioned look and Jack thought it was a lot better than stern, he hadn't seen that in a while and he liked that one, could do it himself. 'I know you can do it, but what else is happening?' Mandy asked again, 'I suppose you got her transferred to the Sexton enquiry and then also to the murder enquiry; did you?'

He nodded yes, and put his arms out as if to say, of course, what else could he do? Or it could have been Julie Andrews on top of the feckin' mountain – sometimes you never knew, and it didn't do to dwell. 'The Hills are alive with the...' Jack sang - there you go, it was Julie Andrews. Mandy stopped him before he could run back to the Nuns and hide, and he answered her, a tad agitated as he liked that song and he knew he could sing it really well and loved mountains, once he got to the top, wasn't so keen on the climbing bit. 'Of course I did,' he said, imagining himself in Lederhosen, beginning to thwat his thighs, a distant oompah, oompah pah pah, which turned out to be Mandy ranting in a tuba sense, 'I wanted her to take an overall role looking at the murder along with the dealings at Cedric James bank; and of course they have it in for Seb, and I need to know just how much.'

'They do? And Seb knew the rhyme?' slowly things were falling into place for her.

He explained further, slapping his thighs more as the oom paa paa band got louder, 'They cannot understand him. For the Met it is something outside of their field of understanding, but if they were briefed on MI5 they would know that there are quite a few Sebs in there. Very valuable they are too, but the Met think Seb is the murderer.' Jack laughed, Mandy didn't, 'I think they think that Seb is running a highly-sophisticated crime unit, can you believe that?' and he laughed some more; Mandy didn't.

Mandy didn't believe, but she could see why the Met might think that, 'Jack, do you know who murdered those people?'

He nodded, 'Well, I can make an educated guess, but I'm not minded to follow it up. Let sleeping, or dead dogs lie; quite apt when you think about it,' and he laughed to himself; thought it was quite a good joke, especially as he had said it in a German accent.

'Jack be serious, speak English, stop slapping your thighs and tell me who you think did the Pall Mall murders?'

Jack looked confused that Mandy had not already realised who it was, or why she would even want to know? It was difficult to tell, it was his dimwit look that he had mastered. 'It was Burial,' he said, 'fancy a hot chocolate?' he thought things were over. She didn't, and

showed her ire. Probably the hot chocolate he thought, he knew she was not overly keen on the beverage.

She tugged his arm, 'No, I don't want a feckin' hot chocolate, I want to know about Beryl and I want to know about the water Jack, and let's take the water first, please. Jackie seems to think this is your emotional key and so does Seb, clearly, as well as his feckin' loony granddad, so please explain it to me, your wife, the woman who loves you, your Mother feckin' Superior.' His face registered a reality moment, he'd made it to the Convent, late, but he was here and just before the Germans.

For Mandy, she knew she had her man and she stopped him pacing and guided him to a seat at the dining table, disappeared and returned with a Jameson's for him and a glass of white wine for herself, thinking that Jonas gave white wine to Della; where did that come from?

'He gave wine to Della because he's in love with her,' Jack said. 'Jonas is a gypsy at heart and Della has clearly struck a note with him, which is all he needed and is what he has waited for, a bit like you, when you saw me,' and he ducked and swayed to dodge the imaginary physical rebuttal that ought to have accompanied Mandy's look, but didn't; now he was really confused and his dimwit look came in handy. 'Christ knows what will happen next but it could be convenient for us...' he thought on, '...depends on how Della feels about the bloke I suppose,' and Jack tapped his finger rhythmically, it was Dr Who, but this didn't concern him at the moment, he carried on, responding to Mandy's look, 'but it looks like she's reciprocating all the way eh? That's my gal; that was Dr Who by the way, what I was tapping.'

Mandy shook her head again, marvelling at how he can flit from one subject to another so quickly and it all seemed coherent to him, 'I know it was Dr Who, but how will it be good for us?'

'Oh shut-up Sweet'art, don't tell me you can't see how valuable she would be down here in our team?' Jack chuckled, then he dreamily projected his thoughts into the future, 'If she was in with Jo Jums then I think we could really step back and do something else.' He paused, saw the penny had yet to drop, 'You see, Della is a doer not an organiser, a tad Maverick actually but that can be good.' Again, he looked quizzically at her, he knew that sometimes she thought he was a bit of a maverick and he wanted to see her reaction, saw none so carried on; safe? Not sure, 'She will think laterally you see, and let Jo Jums run the unit, indeed would prefer that.'

Mandy watched him shape to take a sip of Jameson's and she allowed her heart to flip. She wanted to slow down, and with Jack. She worried about the danger that dogged his heels and knew also that it had a frisson of excitement for him, but it was starting to wear on her nerves. 'That sounds good but worrying Jack.' Mandy decided not to pursue this for the time being, 'Now, the water?' He looked into the tumbler of Jameson's, swirled the whisky and looked at the depth of colour, sniffed but didn't drink. She sometimes wondered if a lot of his things were ritual and not about the consumption. She had seen this before and seen him not even drink the drink. 'Jack?'

He looked up and she could see his resolve; he would tell her, 'When I was twelve I went on holiday with one of my aunts and a cousin. It was a rare treat, my first time away from my family where, as the oldest of the kids, a lot fell on my shoulders. I remember the steam train to the coast from London. I remember the caravan park but most of all I remember the beach and the sea. I got caught in a cross-current and it took me not further out, but across to a deeper bay area; I was out of my depth. Sound familiar?' she nodded and held his hand, he was becoming upset. 'I struggled to get in. I swam as best I could but seemed to get nowhere. I could feel the current like little fish on my legs but tugging me under and away. I called for help. Can you imagine what that is like, to call out for help, from strangers, people who you don't know but need, and desperately; a sense of embarrassment; even though you know you could be dying. Can you imagine that? I could see the faces so clearly on the beach, can even now; people oblivious, and nobody heard. I always loved the Stevie Smith poem, *Not waving, drowning*. I put my feet down, felt rocks and then didn't feel them. I eventually made it to shore, pushing off the rocks when they were there and as a consequence, my feet and legs were being cut to ribbons.

I had drifted a long way across and when I did eventually get ashore, I had to make my way back along the beach to my Aunt who was now frantically looking for me. She hugged me, I remember, it was nice, a first, and we became very close afterwards. She took me to a first aid booth and they looked after my feet and legs. I remember we had a roast lamb dinner in a cafe afterwards, I can still taste it, savour the mint sauce; lamb is still my favourite meat. Nothing was ever said. It rarely was in my family, but I can recall the feeling now and how I relished the hug from my aunt, she touched and hugged me afterwards, subtle, but it was there. I needed it and need it now and always will. I can picture it now, can feel the fear now, and the desire to give up, even now, to let myself slide into the sea and just go, no more responsibility. Just as I did in the Solent off the fort and Fatso's trawler, remember? You dived in and saved me.'

Mandy nodded, she did remember and it explained a lot.

Chapter 20

'Hello Mike.'

'Della,' the Priest replied and sidled up and pecked the DI from the Met on the cheek, she made her cheek available, sort of a peace offering, 'good to see you again.'

'Is it Mike? I'm not sure about that, and I'm certain I've been manipulated by that tart Jack Austin.' Della stretched up to the tall priest and held Mike's shoulders so he could not retreat from her rebuke; she held his eyes while her own sought an answer.

'Yes, you make a fair point, he is a tart. Where's Jonas?' the slippery Priest survived and slipped from her grasp and gaze and pirouetted, to survey the bar.

'Well it doesn't take long for word to get around in the bloody spook world.'

Mike relaxed and returned his gaze to Della, 'Another good point, and don't ask me why I say this, but Jack thinks you and Jonas is a good thing. As I say, don't ask me why, but the eejit does have a feel for these things.'

'Does he?' Della sloped her head and sent her tractor beam out to further discomfort the man of the cloth, 'And I suppose he's steered my career whilst I remained oblivious?' she held her ground, the challenge was out there but would Mike pick up the gauntlet.

Mike's jitters returned; Della may only be a sparrow but she packed a mean verbal punch, 'Well not just Jack, but he has always been interested in what you've been doing.'

Della sat and leaned back in her chair, the same one she sat in last night before quiz started, 'Jonas is getting breakfast. I suppose he's blissfully unaware?'

'He is about a lot of stuff; some he knows because of Seb and of course his dad. I understand you've had your eye on Seb. Very perceptive but it's not what you think.'

'He's one of us? I assumed with the questions last night,' Della said, right on the money.

'Jack had him in a long time ago; nobody really knows and so best to keep a bit schtumm with Jonas for a while. So...' and he rubbed his hands together as if he was about to savour something delightful, '...Jack says you're thinking of coming back into the fold?'

Della gave Mike her old-fashioned look, which he thought she had probably learned from Jack, he knew Jack was a good teacher because Jack had told him so, especially with looks, 'Did I ever leave Mike?'

Mike chuckled and his beetroot nose wobbled, 'Well no, of course not,' and he stopped before he said anymore as they were joined by Barry, looking like he had slept badly, shaved badly, and dressed himself without the help of his mum.

'Father Mike, this is Detective Sergeant Barry Richards,' Della said, gesturing with her head and rolling eyes, which conveyed all Father Mike needed to know. Mike stood and shook Barry's hand, and mimicking Della, gestured with a nod for Barry to take a seat as if Mike controlled what was happening, which of course he usually did.

Barry did not sit down but continued his subliminal hostilities with Della; Mike read this in the man's bloodshot eyes. 'Well this place just gets weirder and weirder, as do you Inspector,' Barry said, 'you are full of surprises,' and Barry drilled his look into Della, the contempt not missed by Mike, but to Della this was normal; she shrugged.

Mike pulled a chair up for Barry, 'Sit Barry,' he said firmly, and Mike brushed the man's leg as he sat; he had his confirmation, but just so Della knew where he was coming from and that he would handle her revenge, 'Barry, you not married then?' Mike spoke to Barry but looked at Della and winked.

Barry looked surprised, but answered, 'No, the job you know.'

'What about the job?' Mike intent, fixing Barry with his Holy Joe Priest look with angelic gobshite, brass knobs added; Barry was dead meat.

'Well, err...' Barry jittered; Mike was used to this reaction and leaned into Barry's personal space, '...it doesn't leave much time, you know?'

'No I don't, an attractive man like you?' Barry blushed; Mike didn't, and pushed the bastard. 'You know Barry, as a priest I get to see and talk about a lot of things; I see all as they say,' and he winked and looked heavenward, then swung back to earth to face this particularly nasty mortal, whose roughly shaved cheeks flushed a deeper crimson.

Della began to enjoy her sergeant's discomfort and she applied a syrupy, southern belle smile, 'Barry, is there something you've not told me?'

Barry was saved further torment, as a beaming Jonas kicked open the door to the bar and delivered full English breakfasts.

Della looked lovingly at him, 'Jonas babes, just some toast for me please lover boy,' and she stroked his bottom. Mike noticed Jonas lean into the touch as he handed out the plates like he was dealing cards, ignoring the protests and indiscreet sexual mannerisms from Della. He leaned over her and she was obscured from view by his huge presence; all Mike could hear was whispers and some Della giggles. Mike put his hand onto Barry's leg as Jonas sat down; both Barry and Della were blushing.

* * *

The weather had not redeemed itself and Jack and Mandy dwelled longer than normal in bed heaven; warm and toasty, snuggling, enjoying listening to the whistling wind and the rain beating at the windows. The sashes rattled, and although she knew this would let the draughts in through the old windows, contrarily, it made Mandy feel warm and cosseted, cuddling close to an affectionate Jack.

She wondered what he was thinking, 'What're you thinking Jack?'

He turned his head so his eye would face her, breathed in the smell of her; he loved her early morning smell. He liked her all dolled up and with her Opium perfume, but nothing beat her natural smell for him, it was this sense he could conjure up in his mind and frequently did when daydreaming. Her face was becoming animated, he noticed these sorts of things, which is what made him such a good lover, or so he thought; excitement or annoyance, it was difficult to tell, he laughed.

'What?' she asked irritably; so it wasn't excitement.

'Sorry sweet'art, I was enjoying your face as it changed from blissful relaxation to early doors annoyance.'

'Do you enjoy winding me up?'

He returned a beatific smile, he was good at them, and nodded, then kissed her and did the things she liked; they felt under no pressure for time these days, so they made love. The rollicking fireworks of the early days of their relationship had not faded but were reserved for their fizzers. This morning, it was a gentle and sensitive love making, shared endearments and reinforcement of the love they felt for each other. Mandy had questions, like what the feck was happening, and she knew he would tell her in time, maybe at breakfast if she nailed his feet to the floor.

* * *

John Sexton kissed Beryl goodbye, leaving for the city on the early train. Seb nonchalantly squashed past them on the threshold of the back door, on the way to his shed, as if completely unaware of their presence. The parents exchanged a glance and some raised eyebrows; all was normal. They had shared some racy sex through the night and reinforced their marriage bonds, if not their vows. Beryl felt good, invigorated, and quite agreeable; she was pretty sure Jonas had found the one he was looking for. Funny how things worked out she thought, as she waved goodbye to John and put the old Mac on and the flowery boots, to head over to see her oldest son and to question this Della more closely. If she was okay with Della, she might wander with her around the cemetery, in particular past the Barnes mausoleum and wind their guests up a bit; least this is what Jack wanted her to do, but she would make her own mind up and resented being told what to do by a decrepit filth tosspot. So she set off; a brief wave to the ghost.

'Erp beit Benrial,' Ghost said.

'Erp Bit,' she called back; Jack had taught her some basic frontier tosspot gibberish.

* * *

Jo Jums was in the community policing unit earlier than usual. This was easier now her husband Tanner was working from home, having acquired a consultancy position with an obscure Government department that miraculously appeared when as a couple, they were desperate. He was due to be made redundant and this coincided at the time MI5 wanted Jo to take over Community Policing from Jack. Tanner could deal with their four kids and get them off to school, but she was not sure if he could deal with knowing his wife was now a spook, not yet anyway. Ordinarily, she liked to see the kids off in the mornings, but today something was brewing and Jack, the so called *nouveau consultant*, was involved, so she needed to have her wary head on; he was not best known for stepping back. Regarding Brian Mayhew she had organised the team last night from her home phone, and was relieved that Alice felt okay about tippy toeing her way back to work.

Jo, hands on her child bearing hips, surveyed her realm. It was still called *Community Policing* (CP) but in effect this unit took on all of the *off-the-wall* incidents. This could range from real community policing, like telling Ada Bailey to take her knickers off the line if they were blocking the neighbours' sunshine, to dealing with terrorist incidents. It was to recognise and admire, the consummate spook cerebral skills of Jack Austin, who had set CP up as a benign front for his MI5 investigations, that nobody seemed in the least bit curious as to how this unit operated, and seemingly, in an autonomous way, sometimes recruiting squads from elsewhere in the City as and when they were needed. The serious crime squad for instance, known as the Sissies by Jack and of course by everyone now, were all but permanently set up in the back half of the huge CP room as a matter of course these days. Jack Austin had installed them behind the wonky old bi-fold screens that offered a semblance of division to the tired, hall like CP room, saying "They will be in nobody's way in that part of the house"; *Lady Catherine de Burgh, Pride and Prejudice* – "brilliant wasn't it?" Least this is what Jack tells everyone, all the time, never ending, ad infinitum or "forever and ever amen", as Father Mike often said, also many times over and over... Aah bleedin' men.

Jo was convinced that both of these elderly spooks were overdue a stay in a loony bin or better still should head straight to the knacker's yard.

* * *

Mike kept his hand on Barry's thigh, Della and Jonas had eyes only for each other, and while Barry shuffled and sorted his feelings, Mike answered his phone. 'Hi Jack, yes she's here,' and Mike passed the phone to Della as Jonas, in a very suggestive manner, picked some HP sauce from the corner of Della's mouth with a sausage and inserted it into her mouth. She whooped to Jack on the phone, like she was a Red Indian, Jonas wobbling the sausage to assist the modulation of tone; she was enjoying life.

Della settled, 'No Jack you can't 'ave me sausage,' Della said, and she spluttered some of the sausage as she laughed, and Mike marvelled at how Della had slipped so easily back into working with Jack. 'Okay Jack; I said okay...' she stopped, looked at Jonas, '...

yeah, he's a prairie 'at, but I like him, so again, okay; ta-ta ugly.' She closed the call on a giggling Jack, passed the phone back to Mike and turned to Jonas, 'Jack says you're a Pratt,' and she stroked his face, 'but you're my Pratt, so you are...' and she pinched and wobbled his cheek, '...are you not little diddums?' Jonas nodded; completely besotted.

Behind them, Beryl nodded, approving some more of Della whilst impressing Mike with her creeping up skills. She was about to speak when Della's phone rang, 'Allo, yes, no, I've been briefed. No, Barry's wiv his priest confessing sumfing about a closet,' and Della giggled like a schoolgirl. Barry silently fumed and Mike smoothed the man's thigh and the bubbling agitation became guttural grumbles that could have been purrs? Della was listening, watching, and smiling, 'Okeydokee mate.' She closed the call and before Barry could rustle up a repost, she swung to Mike. 'That was my Super (Superintendent). Mike, be a darlin' and drop Barry at the train station pretty please, he's going back to town.' She turned to Barry, 'Barry, I'll be staying down 'ere and working with the Yokel Community Policing turnips.' She then cast loving eyes onto her gypsy dreamboat, 'Jonas, would you mind very much if I stayed with you please, pretty, pretty please with brass knobs, gorgeous lover boy,' and she pursed her rosy lips, air kissed and stroked his face and followed this up with a playful cheek slap.

Beryl settled, this woman was more than a match for her Jonas and if she was not much mistaken, she had Jonas hook line and sinker; good. Jonas for his part knew that the upper hand he felt he had yesterday, had firmly been passed to Della and he was strangely okay with that.

* * *

Jack had taken an early morning call from his son Michael, who was at medical school in London with his long standing and looking like, life time partner Colleen. Jack had nicknamed the lovely girl Winders, which indicated to everyone, especially his son, that Jack loved and respected the girl. Winders was the nickname of Jack's window cleaner Dad in Stepney, East London, and Jack had been known there as Winder's Boy.

Winder's Boy looked back at Mandy who was sitting at the breakfast table in a silk nightie that she knew he loved. Jack was in his boxer shorts and a shirt with one misaligned button done up, that he knew she tolerated; just. He finished up the call and came back to the table with a perplexed look, 'Michael says that Winders and he are having Christmas lunch with her Mum and Dad, but they'll be staying with us. Why d'you think he's telling us now, it's only November?'

Mandy thought she needed to educate Jack some more about the moirés of domestic organisation that, to him, just happened, 'Because Jack, I imagine Colleen's mum is asking her daughter so she can prepare, and I also imagine that Colleen has been asking Michael to make his mind up, probably for weeks now, and if my guess is right they have argued last night about it and Michael lost, which is why he rang you this morning.' She looked up and he had moved on, oblivious to the point, probably saw it as irrelevant, certainly not interesting, and was now at the sink emptying, washing and filling his well-used mocha pot for another round of treacle black, robust coffee.

She sighed. 'Did I get the impression that you are coming in with me today Jack?'

He looked back at her from the sink whilst screwing the pot together; she smiled at him again, had he heard? 'What you smiling at love?'

'You, screwing the pot together; think you could screw anything else this morning?' He put the pot down and came over to her and whispered in her ear. His breath caused her to shiver, she wondered what he had said because it was his frontier gibberish, but she didn't care; they went back upstairs.

* * *

Mike gave his seat to Beryl, pressed his hand on Barry's shoulder, leaned in, and with his lips grazing Barry's ear, he whispered so everyone heard, 'Shall I help you pack?'

Such was the presence and subliminal power of Mike O'Brien, that Barry stood unaware of the concealed titters from Della, Jonas and now Beryl. Mike steered the detective sergeant with a firm hand on Barry's lower back, to the door that lead to the stairway, 'I'm gay as well Barry,' Mike said so all could hear. Barry said nothing, just walked in front of Mike and plodded the stairs; Della's revenge achieved.

Beryl put her hands up like a squirrel eating nuts from its paws and said "Ooh err matron", in her very best camp voice. She stood, 'Della will you walk with me?'

'Mum please,' Jonas pleaded, desperately circling his wagons around Della.

'Jonas, do you have work to be getting on with?'

'Yes Mum,' Jonas sighed.

'I'll just get my coat Burial,' Della said as she stood, bending down to kiss Jonas into his laugh, Della had used Jack's familiar name for his Mum, and eventually Beryl laughed as well; this was a younger female version of Jack Austin, and she loved him; so.

* * *

Mandy returned from the shower to see an elephantine arse in very tight shorts, bent over and preventing the daylight from penetrating to the back of the bedroom; Jack was tying the laces of his plimsolls.

'Jack, you're not going to the gym are you?'

He looked up, his face puffed and purple, 'Darlin' you just don't get a body like this...' and he presented her his Mr Atlas pose, '...you 'ave to work at it,' and he feigned a few ballet steps and chuckled. He had forgone his old rugby shirt with paint splashes, and acquired, from God knows where, Hagrid's vest with huge arm holes, but he did still have his old rugby shorts that were so tight they left very little to the imagination in the bits and pieces department.

Mandy sighed as she took in the vision before her, 'Jack, have a shower and come into work with me please, I want to know what is happening. We can knock off early and we'll get you some less obscene gym kit and I will get some too and we can make this a joint effort, okay?' Jack flung his hands out and Mandy got in quickly before he could sing, *the hills are alive*, 'What Jack?'

Jack had inadvertently applied his dimwit face; the game was up, 'I don't know how to say this... I've done some silly things at the gym, but it's only while I adjust to the equipment; it's all modern you see.'

'Is it Jack and the young ladies clad in tight Lycra?' He looked shocked and she let him off her shepherd's crook, 'It's okay, get showered and dressed, I quite fancy some of the aerobic classes anyway, but now, I need to call Jackie and then Beryl.'

'What do you need to call them for, and what's acerbic? I reckon I could do that as well.'

Mandy tapped her nose several times to address the several points he had raised, said it was aerobics, and he knew better than to push. In all honesty he was relieved she now knew about the minor difficulties he'd had at the gym, and was confident she would be impressed when she saw him working out. He was on big girls' weights and should be onto boy's stuff very soon, least that's what the gym instructor had said, but then she was clearly besotted with him, and then he worried about what Mandy would think, but decided he could forget about it for a bit.

'I would if I were you love, no need to distract yourself, and if she really does fancy you I will get her off to Specsavers.'

'Did I...?'

'Yes you did,' and she pointed to the shower as she picked up the phone, still laughing.

He called back, another of his incongruous of the wall, out of the blue, statements, 'What was the name of Sherlock Holmes's bruvver?'

'What?' but he'd gone – so she left it.

Chapter 21

Della had only her flimsy, designer, town raincoat and a scarf Jonas had found her. She wore her jeans from last night, the bottoms tucked into Jonas's thick, *Big Foot* socks, and Angel's lumpy bovver boots. Although the rain seemed to be holding off, there was a stiff breeze.

'I will get you some wellies love, what size feet do you have?' Jonas asked.

She looked at him, questioning, 'Six Jonas, but please don't bother,' and then she recalled Pansy and Angel's flowery wellington boots. 'Jonas,' he looked up, 'if you do get me some Roger Mellies can I have helicopter ones?' He looked confused, 'And if they don't have helicopter, get me plane,' and she and Beryl shared the laugh as they disappeared out of the door, skirted the only slightly receding lake, and headed over the road to the cemetery gate.

Beryl noticed Della looking back at her swamped car, 'Jonas will get that sorted for you today and then you can park it in the cemetery with ours.'

Della nodded her thanks and paced to keep up with Beryl, who appeared to be on a mission. Beryl excused herself for a bit and disappeared into the house while Della kicked her heels, flapped her arms to try and generate some warmth whilst looking across the expanse of tombstones and mausoleums. She reflected that she had not hesitated to run back into Jack Austin's arms, and wondered if it was because she wanted to stay in the arms of Jonas, but the truth was she had liked it when she worked with Jack, and after he returned to Portsmouth she could not settle, railing frequently at some of the stupid spook antics and the pansy arse bureaucrats; at least with Jack it was a tin barf (laugh) and he wasn't a toffee nosed twat; well he was twat but she was sure he didn't have a toffee stuck up his fireman's hose.

Beryl was back, 'Let's walk around the cemetery, there are things I want to talk about and show you.'

Della looked sideways at Beryl, physically and metaphorically, 'I can understand that you would want to talk to me about Jonas, how I will be with Seb, what I might think about Pansy and Angel, but show me?'

Beryl chuckled, 'Jack said I would like you and I have a bigger bonus if you and Jonas can hold it together.'

Della stopped and held onto Beryl's shoulder, deciding they would talk about this face to face, 'Jack told you about me?'

'Yes darling, but even he would not know that you and Jonas might be attracted to each other.' Beryl smiled and pushed home her point, 'Della, you are definitely no angel and you are thankfully not stupid, and all of that is a plus for me as far as Jonas and my family go. You will come to realise, if you haven't already, and if you don't I will tell you, and even then, if you are in any doubt, Jack will reinforce it to you later; to John and me, the family is everything. You have been watching my husband and you will know that he's a philanderer.' Della looked shocked and Beryl was shaking her head, 'It's okay, of course I know, and he knows I know. To be honest love, I'm one to fancy a bit on the side myself, even fancied a bit of left footing if you were interested?' Della blushed, knowing Beryl had a daughter that batted off the left foot. Beryl carried on, apparently unaware of Della's ruminations, 'So, you see all is well in this state of Denmark, as Jack says. At the end of the day I know that to John, and he knows as far as I am concerned, the family is everything and we stick together, will always stick together and fight together, and it's this that comes first. We are having this walk, when we get going that is, because I want to weigh you up a little more than the reports from Jack, which would be pretty unreliable as far as his understanding of you as a woman.' Beryl paused to allow this to sink in.

'You researched me?'

Beryl started walking and Della fell in line, 'Yes, I knew you were coming down here and I knew you were investigating John, Seb and the Pall Mall murders.'

'You did, and you know about the Pall Mall murders?'

Beryl stopped and Della had to walk back to face her. Beryl took Della's face in her hands, 'Those people in the Pall Mall star chamber were going to kill John, or would have done after they learned of his involvement in the national debt rescheduling; so I killed them first,' and she let go of Della's face to flick her hands out to suggest, what else could she have done, then carried on walking.

'Beryl stop!' And Beryl did. This time Della, marginally shorter, looked closely into Beryl's eyes, 'You killed the PM cabinet secretary, the chief whip and the leader of the armed forces? Pomerol?'

'I did, and I would do it again if anyone threatened me and my own, and that includes you now if I am not very much mistaken,' and she stroked Della's face, a motherly, vixen's caress.

Della had to admit it felt nice, but shook herself, 'Beryl, you do know I'm a police officer don't you?'

Beryl laughed volubly, 'No you're not, you're a spook, and Jack said you will be okay with it and understand, you were one of the few real coppers left,' and Beryl crooked her index fingers like arthritic quotation marks. 'Jack said you had already put two and two together, and this was in your summary report to your bosses. They laughed you out of the Superintendent's office; if what Jack says is correct?' Beryl looked at Della's face for a response, saw it and knew she was right.

'It's true, and Jack knew? Knows? My report? Knows you killed those people?'

'He's not asked outright but he knows, so does Mandy now I wouldn't wonder, because she's as sharp as a tack and a good match for Jack, just as you will be for my Jonas. Bless you darling for falling for my lad. I would want nobody less for my boy, but tell me something?'

'What?' Della was still shocked, she was sure she looked daft with her mouth open, and then there were the bovver boots and she was shivering because the Mac was no defence in this weather, out in the wilds of the country; only looked good in the poncy wine bars of London. 'You know he will not leave Sebastian don't you, and you know that Seb will not want to leave his shed?'

'Well Beryl, to be honest wiv yer, I've not fort that far ahead.'

'Don't bullshit me Della, so tell me, as a committed Londoner, will you commit to Jonas and will you, as a consequence, commit to Seb?' Beryl had her stern and serious face on; maternal hackles had risen.

Della thought, and Beryl allowed her the time, 'Yes Beryl I will, and don't ask me how I know, but something happened when I first saw Jonas, and I just knew.'

'He did too, he has told me.'

'He has, he did?'

Beryl offered a warm smile that Della sensed embraced the whole of her heart. Beryl started walking again, 'So, you see that mausoleum,' she pointed and Della looked, 'it is the Barnes family tomb.'

'Yeah, I see it,' Della said, wondering what of it?

'Well that currently has three men down there and they are bugging Seb's shed and our house,' and she pointed to another tomb, 'and that Mausoleum is the Sidney family, and that has weapons stored. They're all useless now, apart from the one I borrowed and put back. It can be found and used as evidence later, and you will have a satisfactory conclusion to your Pall Mall case. Apart from that one machine gun, we have buggered them all and they are blissfully unaware, as they are also blissfully unaware that we have tapped and traced all of their equipment in the Barnes Tomb.'

'How did you do that, and who are they?' Della asked.

'Seb looks after the cemetery, you can see the north-east quadrant now has all the tombstones lined up straight, and all the paths cleared, re-laid, ship shape and Bristol fashion.' Della nodded as Beryl waved her hand pointing over what Della assumed was the north-eastern quadrant. 'At the same time Seb arranged for a labyrinth of tunnels, large storm pipes really, underneath the whole cemetery, and these pipes link the various mausoleums and other things that frankly I do not know or care about, but it did afford Seb and Jack the opportunity to get into the tombs and do what they had to do.' Beryl laughed at the beauty of the idea, 'Seb calls them his catacombs,' and she laughed some more, 'he always wanted some of them,' and she hemmed and smiled.

'Who are they Burial?' And as she asked that Della realised she had passed on from the multi-murder confession, and had also accepted it, as had Jack Austin and Mandy by all accounts.

'Jack thinks they are right wing activists, but John thinks they're a spin-off from the financial world, masquerading as fascists; a bit of revenge and a bit of shite stirring we think; Jack and Seb are still looking into this. One thing is for sure, all of this 6, 57 shite is cock and bull, and I did not like what happened to Snail last night; what the fuck is that all about?'

Beryl put her arm around Della, 'Time to get you back to Jonas, he will be worrying about what I'm telling you; he's very protective you know.'

Della was not sure what to make of that, and what the feck was 6, 57, but let it go, along with the murder confession and the weapons cache. She wanted to go back and fuck the brains out of Jonas, and then she had to go to work she supposed; what a bleedin' fag.

Chapter 22

'What is it Nobby?' Mandy was leaning over Jo's shoulder, watching as Jo sketched a brief for the team meeting at her CP desk, 'Nobby lad, I haven't got all day?' she turned to face Nobby.

'I've just been to the loo and...'

The young detective constable was interrupted to endure some of the famed Mandy impatience. 'Nobby, I am very pleased you are keeping regular, but I'm busy.'

Alice could be heard giggling behind her bandages, enjoying the humour from Mandy, but relishing the prospect of Nobby's reply; her man had an acerbic wit and she loved it, loved him.

'Thankyou Ma'am, I was always told in police training school to keep my senior officers informed of my bowel movements, and also of course, if you think a senior officer is going bonkers in the toilet.' He was a little miffed but took pleasure in the laughter from Alice and he turned and smiled at her, but was brought back to earth by Mandy.

'Nobby, what are you talking about?'

He had her attention now, along with everyone else in the CP room. Paolo, who was just back from a serious injury to lead the Sissies, wheeled his chair to poke his head around the wonky bi-folds, 'Normality resumed then?'

'Yes Paolo, thank you, Nobby please?' Mandy was curious, in an agitated way.

'Ma'am, Jack seems to be in pain, bending his body and his arms and going "Oooh" a lot.'

'Is he in front of the mirror?' Mandy asked, already relaxing.

'Err, Yes.'

Nobby tensed, Mandy relaxed, and then returned to what she was doing with Jo Jums, casually calling back over her shoulder, 'That'll be him practicing his body popping, the Ooohing is *Beyonce*, least that is what he says it is.'

'Oh,' and Nobby whispered to Alice he thought it was *JLS* and sat down waiting for the briefing to start.

Mandy threw him a distracted comment, 'Nobby, be a love and get him out of the bog please, so we can start?'

Nobby stood but sat back down again as Jack came through the door singing an incomprehensible song in frontier gibberish, which compensated for the fact that he knew neither the lyrics nor the tune but, of course, it sounded fine in his head; just not to anyone within earshot.

'Jack shut up and sit down, Jo you ready?' Mandy had asserted her command.

Jo nodded she was ready, stood and looked around the CP room while the serious crime boys scooted their wheelie chairs to take their places. Jed Bailey won; Paolo still had to get back up to speed having been recently "Sliced up a treat", as Jack described it, by a scimitar attack in the confessional box; an attack that had killed his wife, Ting Tong.

The voluminous, hall like, CP room was tatty almost beyond belief. The Commander had offered to "Tart it up a bit" but Jack had refused. While waiting for everyone to settle, Jo smiled to herself as she recalled the scenario; Mandy was the Superintendent in charge and had only found out about the declined offer months after. However, the room was comfortable, clean because it was cleaned and nurtured by Dolly the diminutive ancient cleaner, who Jack paid for himself; she needed the money and he loved her and that was all there was to say, except there was a story back in the mists of time. She especially polished the old plastic tiles and Jack really liked this, the smell reminded him of his Nan and when he was a boy. So the room was full of character, lavender scent from the polish and, some would say, full also of cowboy misfit characters who after a while, found they liked it too. Jo often thought the room was a metaphor for Jack Austin's disfigured face, ugly, sometimes shabby, but loveable all at the same time and she for one liked it as well; maybe not the smell; the geriatric Dolly had more than a hint of lingering urine that the lavender had difficulty in masking.

The CP unit was delineated by zig-zag screens; they zigged and zagged in order to remain upright, having lost the support from the ceiling track many moons ago. The screens formed a part of the perimeter wall for bench desks that held workstations. The desks continued on three sides of the space, both sides of the divide. One of these sides, known as silicone alley, had six flat screens set up in a line. This was the computer specialists that Jo Jums now realised had come courtesy of the intelligence services, well at least one of them, Frankie, who was the lead; a tall woman about forty, slim, fit and dressed in a masculine style, beautiful in her way, serious in her way, extremely good in her way; she was a whizz at the computers - Jack's words not her own, but it was true – she was a marvel.

Jack had brought Frankie in from MI5 and selected an assistant for her, a relative novice police woman, Way Lin, whom he had called Confucius for various non-PC reasons. The PC joke was ignored by many, who assumed that the computer illiterate DCI Austin could not possibly have thought of this, but, as many who got to know Jack Austin realised, what you see is not always what you got – least this is what he tells everyone. So the short, short sighted, slight, deceptively frail appearing, Chinese girl, answered to Connie; Frankie's name for her now very adept computer partner and also her partner at home, both originating from the Isle of Lesbos and apparently left footed, also according to Jack, quoting *Mary Poppins*, so he could not be contested.

The team worked well and the character of Jack Austin had stamped itself on the team as well as the CP room, and taking pride of place was the Jack Austin deck chair, erected beside the meeting table which was affectionately called the chaos table. It was called this not because it was a jumble of ill fitting, mismatched tables, varying in form and colour, a fabrication of uneven heights that had caused a number of coffee and tea spillages over the years, which Jack argued added character, all of which it was; it was called the chaos table because Jack liked to promote his own brand of *Chaos theory*, and this table was therefore known as the chaos table; simples.

The theory could be seen locally at what was left of Jack's own work station, after everybody had plundered it of all the stuff he never used, like the computer and, well, everything except the phone, and he avoided that if he could. Jack's localised chaos theory could be seen as a mass of post-it notes, scraps of paper with no rhyme nor order on his desk. Every now and then, he would pick up bits and shout, "Oh feck, I'd better do that" and then, "Out of chaos comes order", his justification.

The conference table was arguably a more ordered form, mainly because it was monitored by Jo Jums. The general concept was that if anyone had an idea or wanted to talk about something, they wrote it on a scrap of paper and chucked it into the centre of the table. It was then free for anyone to read, think about, and discuss at the next meeting. It was not only efficient and creative, it obviously also had its fun moments, like a note Jo was reading now that said, *Anybody fancy going to a wrapping concert at the Guildhall next Friday?* It could only have been Jack's note, and not because of the misspelling or the fact that she thought it said, *he and some of the girls at the gym are going and Mandy doesn't want to go,* a clear afterthought at the bottom, but mainly because the writing was almost illegible. It was Jack's doctor handwriting, which was a lot like his frontier gibberish.

The crime wall, which took up the fourth flank of the CP Room, usually just chalk and *Chinagraph* board, now boasted projector screening capabilities, a white board and other forms of computer enhanced technology, all sneaked in whilst Jack had been off sick. It was not that Jack was a Luddite or even a dinosaur, he would contest that he embraced modern technology, it was just he didn't know how to work it; that was all. The wall had remained quite clear since the Norafarty / Len affair. Today though, there was posted the picture of Jack sitting with Snail on the promenade edge, and pictures of Snail taken at the hospital last night; Jack avoided looking at these.

Nobby embraced the newly established technology and he ran the wall, ably assisted by Alice now she was back.

Jo Jums impatiently tapped her foot, 'Jack we are ready, are you sitting in your deck chair or a wheelie chair?'

Everyone swung in their seats to look at Jack, seeing him genuinely undecided. Mandy wheeled, then stretched in her chair and toe poked him up his backside, and he plumped down in his deck chair; sorted.

Jo started, 'Okay, the pictures are of one of Jack's best mates,' she paused for a little laugh but the black humour, often associated with the police, rarely manifested itself in this unit; Jack frowned. He always said a copper should empathise with the victim, feel the agony, the pain, get through that and then, "Get the bastards".

Jo shaped to continue when her phone rang. She put one hand up, to signify a pause and lifted the receiver with the other, 'DI Wild', she listened and then, a little exasperated, 'Okay Sid put her on.' She put her hand over the phone's mouthpiece, 'Jack it's someone called Della? Sid said your phone is off the hook, but this Della is insistent.'

She proffered the phone but he did not look like moving. The fact was, he had just got himself comfortable, settled, 'Jo, I took the phone off the hook just so I wouldn't be disturbed, der.'

A female voice could be heard squawking from the phone in Jo's hand, "Jack you tosspot get up and talk to me."

Putting the phone back to her face, 'Could not have put that better myself,' Jo said to the woman she did not know, and proffered the phone again. Jack made to stretch but the chord only had so far to go, so he scooted as best he could in his deck chair to meet Jo; at least an inch. Without thinking, Jo freed a snag from the main cable and the phone eventually reached Jack who had settled back down again, but he took the phone, which he thought was a kindly gesture and would be appreciated by Jo.

'Della sweet'art, you do know I outrank you.' The squawky voice could be heard again, this time a raucous derisory laughter, as Jack held the receiver away from his huge, but largely ineffective ears, and he shouted back to the phone like it was the other side of the playground. 'Della, Jo can hear you and you want to make a good impression!' he looked up to Jo Jums who was now standing dangerously close to the deck chair. Jack cranked his neck and looked around the plump woman to see if any help was coming from Mandy, there wasn't; in fact, Mandy seemed to be enjoying the discomfort of her husband. Jack thought wives were supposed to leap to the defence of their husbands; Mandy frowned at his outspoken thoughts.

Jack drifted off, not unusual in this man who had acquired many defence mechanisms and the questioning look from Jo and equally forceful tone from Della on the end of the phone, the spousal neglect, seemed to pass over him; one of his better Church of Egypt manoeuvres. Jo took the phone back from Jack, 'Hello Della, this is DI Wild; Jack would probably have told you I am called Jo Jums or Maamsey, but he seems to have drifted off. So, who are you again? Oh, hold on, he's back in the land of the living and is signalling for me to walk four miles to give him the phone back.' The cackling laughter on the end of the phone complimented the tittering in the CP room.

Jo handed the phone to Jack, 'Della darlin' you're late for your first day at work, not a good impression. So listen up sweet'art, put Jonas down and go in and see Seb, mention the Glory Hole, and ask him about the lemon beach hut. Then take Jonas and Cabbage for a walk on the beach and have a nosey around, then get into work – okay sweet'art babes?'

Jack handed the phone back to Jo Jums who was then the recipient of the reactive Della tirade; she apparently did not like being told what to do. Jo spoke calmly into the phone, 'Della, your invective is wasted, but please rest assured that I will pass it on in full measure when I put the phone down.' She listened, smiled, said goodbye, put the radioactive phone down and turned to Jack, who seemed quite satisfied with himself. Jo disturbed his relaxed moment, 'Della said to "shove the phone up yer 'arris and ta-ta for now".'

There was general raucous laughter, but Jo was zeroing in and Jack, being an observant sort of chap when life and limb could be at stake, noticed. 'Jo, steady Eddie girl, I've just got the enquiry going. She's going to walk Cabbage with Jonas and see what she can see at the beach hut, okay?'

Jo Jums looked to Mandy, who found it very hard to contain her giggling, 'Well I suppose it was expecting too much to look for your support, Superintendent?' Jo said, stressing the Superintendent.

Mandy gathered herself and stood, 'Okay, I am sorry Jo, Jack consider yourself on a fizzer,' and there were more laughs as this was a joke that had established itself, around Jack of course, when the new Chief Constable, a Big Society volunteer retiree from the army, Colonel Horrocks, informed Jack, frequently, that his behaviour would result in him being on a charge. Jack had said that in the army they would call that a *fizzer*. Nobody knew if he was making it up, but they liked it all the same. Mandy gave Jack a warm smile, as between them both, they had nicknamed their particularly saucy sex as *fizzers*, so much so that I have written it in italics, as Jack is sitting in his deckchair still and it is nearly Italian – *don't look at me, read the other books; I'm not yer Mum (also in Italics, so this is serious, mum says so)*.

Mandy held the floor and indicated with a flappy hand for Jo to sit down, and she addressed the gathering, still with a fixed grin, 'Della is Detective Inspector Delores Lovington, The Met, Fraud and Serious Crime and seconded to murder and working on the Pall Mall murders. So most of you will now recognise the connection with our recent investigation with Len or as we called him Norafarty.' She allowed herself a laugh at the use of one of the many derivations they had used for the name Moriarty, and accepted the admonishment from Jo Jums as fair and reasonable, but still everyone laughed until Jack spoke, in a whisper.

'My-loft,' that was it, and Jack resumed his slumbering posture, not noticing the shrugged shoulders of his wife, who carried on; only mildly curious.

'DI Lovington is seconded to our unit for a while and heaven help us, Jack knows her as do you I think Frankie?' This told Jo Jums all she needed to know as Frankie nodded that she knew Della. Frankie was MI5, as was Jo Jums now, and so she relaxed about the new member of her team being inducted by Jack without her say so, not unusual, and had happened many times before, but she still expressed her displeasure.

Jack knew he had a storm to weather and was determined to do it with good grace, 'Wake me up when it's over,' he said, and again to himself, 'My-loft,' a casual statement as he prepared to get his head down; he was a little sleepy and could do with a ziz.

Mandy continued, 'I will interpret the frontier gibberish for you,' and she looked pointedly at Jack who knew enough to duck a look, even with his eye closed. 'Cabbage is the dog belonging to the landlord of the Gravediggers pub, Jonas Sexton, who is the son of John Sexton, the Chairman of Cedric James bank. Please let me know if you are not keeping up, because it gets more complicated.' She looked around her, 'Okay, so Della and Jonas are going to walk Cabbage, who Jack named as he is a Collie.' There were perplexed looks, so she elucidated for the humorously challenged, 'Collie, cauliflower, cabbage.' There was a sound of "Oh Yeah", and she carried on, 'Snail, one Professor Brian Mayhew,' and she pointed to the pictures, 'was badly beaten beside a lemon beach hut on Eastney beach last night. Della, accompanied by Jonas and Cabbage, will try to see what she can, without raising any suspicions; a sniff around, and then Della will be in. Maybe Jack you can take this on from here please?'

He yawned, looked to all intents and purposes as if he had been rudely awakened but did stand, body popped a bit, went "Oh oh, oh, oh oh, oh oh", and looked at Mandy.

'*Beyonce*?' she asked.

Nobby said '*JLS.*'

Jack told Nobby to fuck off; he would have nothing to do with a pansy arsed boy band, and held his stomach in for all to marvel at.

'You putting weight on Jack?' Jo said, never one to miss a trick.

Jack looked askance but caught the joke as everyone rolled up. The problem was he'd forgotten what he was going to say. He wandered around a bit, stiff legged. People thought it was his Douglas Bader, WW2 Flying Ace impression, and went to do the flight goggles, with upside down hands and looped fingers, and commenced la-laa-ing *633 Squadron,* but Jack left the room; they assumed to turn his spitfire around (a WW2 euphemism for going to the toilet).

After a while he had not returned and Mandy stood, 'Oh Christ, I'd better see what's up with the Turnip.'

She went out, looked in the gents, he was not there. He wasn't in her office, just down the corridor; he was nowhere to be seen. She stood thinking when Jo Jums poked her head around the door, 'Sid's phoned, a Zombie just walked past him and out of the building, what d'you want us to do?' Mandy scratched her head physically and metaphorically, tried to recall if they had mentioned any of his PTSD trigger phrases that Jackie had said to watch out for, but couldn't recall any.

Chapter 23

'Della kissed Jonas deeply, and holding her hands on his face she stepped back and looked at him, he had to bend to follow her, 'I'm just going to talk with Seb; I'd like to do that on my own if you wouldn't mind sweet'art.' Not a question but a loving statement. Jonas was not sure what was happening, but in the few hours they had known each other he had already decided this woman could have anything she wanted, confident she would not take advantage. He watched her tippy toe around the reducing lake, now just a large puddle, which prompted him; he had to collect her car. She seemed oblivious of the lake and her absent car, her thoughts focused, as she disappeared through the gate and turned to Seb's shed. She tapped on the door and heard a muffled, "Sextons Detective Agency."

'Seb it's Della, can I come in please?'

She heard whirring and then several mechanical clicks that she assumed were a series of probably three deadlocks releasing. The door opened and Seb was there, he said nothing, just turned and headed back in. Della took her bovver boots off; Beryl had briefed her, but Seb was back anyway on his hands and knees, following, polishing the floor and her non-existent tracks. He stood after satisfying himself the floor was okay and then, in a very mechanical fashion, he hugged her stiffly and kissed her three times on her cheeks. He stood back and looked pleased with himself, 'Mandy says to do that to anyone I like, and I like you.' That was it; he turned and sat at his desk, his back to her.

Della felt unusually warmed by the gesture as she took stock of the interior of the shed. It was very much a nineteen thirties modelling, posters on the wall that seemed to indicate the carefree nature of life before Hitler had asserted himself onto Europe, chuffing trains through the countryside, charts of the Solent that looked modern, out of context, as was the computer array. The charts had arrows and comments lined up in a regimented fashion around what was annotated as *The Glory Hole* and *Fort Cumberland*. She decided to save that for another time and shuffled her way to a more than substantial brown leather 1930's style armchair. She jumped backwards onto it, allowing her momentum to slide her to the back rest; her legs automatically straightened on the seat and her feet dangled outright in front of her. She wiggled them, feeling physically rather well. Jack had mentioned all of the Seb methodology to her yesterday evening, "Just express your thoughts and allow yourself to go with the flow". The feckin eejit she thought, and then she thought one evening back with that ponce Austin and she's already speaking cod Irish.

'I was wondering about the lemon beach hut where Snail was attacked yesterday. I wondered if I should have a little look, maybe go for a walk with Jonas and Cabbage?' She waited as Jack had also suggested. The computer printer whirred. Seb turned and handed her aerial photos, not Google earth but clearly satellite photos of the military kind. He then produced the same shots but with thermal imaging; it showed ghostly figures manhandling someone beside the beach huts, she presumed it was Snail last night. 'I suppose a little wander around might be okay?' she said into the ether, and waited for Seb's response. This came in the form of a very slow rotation in his huge office chair, whilst the printer behind him whirred some more. Della looked at Seb, almost lost in the girth of the chair; he looked so much like his Mum, she thought. He had some of the facial features of Jonas and his Dad, the nose, eyebrows that were dark, contrasting strangely with his honey blond hair, but really this young man was all Burial.

'Please be careful Della,' Seb said as he spun and addressed the whirring printer. The chair returned and Seb handed more prints to Della, 'Jack will want these; they are prints of the fort, but more importantly The Glory Hole buildings, just in case. I think he should avoid the Glory Hole and stick with the fort. Some of the Glory Hole stuff is *hush-hush* and I've not had time to hack it all; anyway, Jack has been down there many times before. I'm hacking the MOD now but it will take some time, please let him know I guessed the layout; it is important, but I suppose he will not even look at it.'

Seb mused and Della could hardly tell the difference in his visage as he appeared completely unanimated. She tried to not look shocked at the thought of Seb hacking into the MOD computers, and then thought, she had already passed over the Beryl multiple murder confession, and then thought, bugger it, I deserve something like this, and if Jack's involved it might just be fun and then there was Jonas; her tummy and lady bits fluttered.

She took the papers, folded the MOD prints and squashed them into the back pocket of her tight jeans to give to Jack later, shuffled off the chair and went up to Seb, 'Fanks Seb, take care yerself,' and she kissed the back of his neck, slipped and slid her feet on the way back to the door, like she was arse skating, so she could give the floor a bit of an extra polish with Jonas's huge woolly socks on her sparrow's plates of meat (feet). She slipped Angel's bovver boots back on and went out, hearing nothing from Seb, just the locking devices behind her, lyrically, mechanically saying goodbye.

Jonas was outside waiting, he held a vast and thick sheepskin coat like a matador, and Della responded by scratching the toes of Angel's bovver boots on the path, stuck her fingers out from her head like horns, ran and spun as he laughed, and she backed into the coat with her arms out and accepted the sheepskin armholes and masculine embrace with relish. She leaned back into Jonas's muscular frame as he did the coat up for her, feeling her body as he descended with the buttoning. She tilted her head backwards to smile at him upside down; screamed, 'Christ what was that?' She looked down at the immense, lollopy red tongue of Cabbage; the dog was eager to get on with the walk.

Jonas had the broadest of smiles and she melted into the crook of his arm, 'We'll go through the cemetery and keep our guests on their toes shall we?'

Della nodded and watched Cabbage take off, clearly familiar with the route and noticed also as they walked on that Miss Eliza Docherty, spinster of this parish, who had died in nineteen thirty-two, was the unsuspecting recipient of a vast dog poo that both Jonas and Della decided to leave as a parting gift.

'That's good luck I fink?' Della said.

'Is it, then I hope that Miss Docherty appreciates it,' Jonas said with a broad grin, and they giggled and walked off hugging, trying to get as physically close together as they could and still maintain a steady forward momentum.

* * *

'Sid said he may have got a cab, but that's not like him, he would normally scrounge a lift from a patrol car.' Mandy was on the phone to Jackie Philips who was equally concerned. 'We have patrols out but none have reported seeing him.'

'What about Seb?' Jackie mused.

'Jackie, that's brilliant – give me a sec,' Mandy hung up and immediately called Beryl. 'Beryl, its Mandy, Jack has gone on the missing list. Can you ask Seb where he thinks Jack might go? You will, thanks, I'm in the office.'

* * *

Jonas and Della lingered at the Barnes mausoleum, kissed and cuddled. 'This is one of the old mausoleums; I will show you inside one day, I haven't been down for quite a while.' They then wriggled themselves off, Jonas head into the wind, Della sheltering into his huge frame, knowing Jonas's words and their fits of laughter would have been heard by the Barnes men, alerted and wound up by now, which of course was Jonas's aim. They threaded their way through the tight streets of terraced houses that after a short distance opened

150

onto the barren Eastney beach. Jonas released Cabbage and the dog immediately loped off, zigzagging, spoilt for choice in the surfeit of smells that, after some time, ended up with an extended sniff outside the door to the lemon beach hut. The Snail vomit still noticeable to a hound albeit the intermittent rain bursts had all but removed any visible evidence; just the odd bit of carrot.

Jonas and Della approached the lemon bathing hut. Della was not aware of the thought processes of Jack, not yet, but even so they approached with caution. However, there is only so much circumspection that Della could ever manage and she grabbed Jonas in a provocative manner, and he allowed her to push and shove him to the hut and to slam him against the door. She leaned into him and they kissed passionately, 'Jonas I want you now.' He looked perplexed, if not a little worried. 'D'you fink we can get into one of these beach huts; I'm gonna fuck yer brains out.'

Jonas caught on and made a move to the door handle. The door immediately burst open knocking Della flying and clunking Jonas on his forehead, as two brawny skinheads in Pompey Football shirts, followed on and drove home their advantage with a swinging punch to Jonas that struck full on his jaw. Jonas responded with his fists of iron, and plunged them fully into the first man's nose; Della heard it crack, and for her part, she used all of her pedal deftness, learned in the Hendon policewomen's football team, and ably assisted with Angel's bovver boots, she struck home a pearler into the gonads of skinhead number two. She followed this up with a creative side footer to the head that ensured the man stayed down with something additional to think about, other than the pitch of his voice and that he had been bested by a rather attractive, petite woman, albeit in bovver boots and a huge sheepskin coat.

Jonas had his man in a lock, which he slowly released when he became aware of a young woman standing in the beach hut doorway with a levelled gun. Della reacted when she saw the girl and stood rigid, wary, eyes swivelling looking for the main chance. The man at her foot began to stir and rise up when Cabbage, out of nowhere, had the woman's gun hand in his mouth, the gun fired and the stray shot hit the first skinhead in his thigh, as he was rising to get a freebie punch at Jonas. Della looked at him, the man did not look well and may have mentioned the fact, but before she could inflict anymore damage they were all swamped. At first it was the miasma of revolting smells that knocked Della back, then an arm, as she was brushed aside. The wounded man was smothered and was coughing and choking. The young lady was restrained by a woman and the second thug, still with his hand examining his privates and wondering if he could count to two, was held by another of the tramps.

It was the woman tramp who spoke, 'Jonas, Della, do you have a phone?'

Della responded, nodding, but then realised she had left her phone back at the Gravediggers, what was happening to her, but then took her phone from Jonas's outstretched hand and looked to the tramp woman, who seemed to assume control.

'Phone into Jack's team, I take it you have the number?'

She nodded but did nothing, just taking in the scene; four tramps, three men and one woman, reeking to high heaven but fit as the fleas that surely inhabited their bodies and clothes, and, in total command of the situation. Della recovered and rang her last call number.

* * *

Seb had suggested that Jack might visit Snail in hospital.

Mandy put her hand on Jack's shoulder and looked over him to Snail, in his Insensitive Clare bed, as Jack called the ICU (Intensive care Unit), taped up, tubes and wires everywhere. She noticed the moisture in Jack's eye, 'He might not make,' Jack said, 'and the irony is I think his daughter is alive and I have a shrewd idea where she might be.'

There was a flicker of Snail's eyelids, Jack lent in. Snail was more fragrant now following the ministrations of some underestimated nurses; cleaning up Snail was almost beyond the call of duty. 'Try not to speak Snail old son, pull through and I may have some good news for you, come on mate.' The flicker in the eyes stretched to a smile displaying a set of good but neglected and now damaged teeth. In a whisper, directly into Snail's ear, Jack said, 'Power politics Snail my old son; who was Sherlock Holmes bruvver?' and not for the first time wondered about the ragman roll; a reverse strategy? Was he being played at his own game?

A nurse was there, 'I will have to ask you to leave Inspector, the doctors are due but you can come back any time after.'

Jack patted the back of Snail's hand which all of a sudden grabbed, a feeble grip and a pathetic smile, 'Mycroft Jack, but you'll not find him,' Snail said weakly and Jack nodded, then backed away and bumped into the nurse, and that elicited a frail chuckle from Snail.

'My-loft? Yes,' Jack whispered to himself as he stood up from Snail's bed and scratched his nose, and Mandy could hear the cogs of his rusty brain whirring; clanking actually as he kept his cogs in his fireman's hose, or so he often said.

'Come on Bozo,' Mandy said, 'let's get you some gym kit, okay?'

Jack nodded and they walked the very familiar hospital route back to the car park in silence; no shared thoughts but Jack's mind still rattled and she could still hear it; he rarely did anything quietly.

* * *

In the CP Room Jo Jums had organised the teams to begin information gathering, Snail, his background, friends if any beyond Jack, a picture of this sad individual being composed by Nobby and Alice upon the crime wall.

She was watching Nobby at work when her phone went, 'DI Wild.'

'Jo, it's that Della again, do you want to speak to her? She says it's "double dog" urgent,' Sid said, clearly agitated at being dictated to by someone he did not know.

'Yes Sid, put her through please,' Jo replied, allowing her eyes to scan the ceiling while she waited, 'Della how nice to speak to you again, I imagine you might pop in soon?'

'Jo Jums, listen up sweet'art, I need you to intercept a posse of plods on their way to secure a crime scene; I take it Jack told you about the lemon beach hut?'

Jo sensed an impatient woman that she had yet to meet and understood how Sid felt. 'Yes Della,' Jo said impassively.

'Well, I was having a surreptitious poke around the joint, minding my own, know what I mean like, you know, totally innocent like, wiv Jonas and Cabbage and knock me down with a bleedin' fevver darlin' if we were not confronted by two nasty pieces of work and a little bird who came at us with a gun. We've done the business with them of course, but one of the skinheads has a bullet wound in his leg, which I trod on to make sure it hurt, but I need the girl and the bloke not wounded, to go to our, I mean your gaff, err nick. If you can get someone up to casualty pronto tonto as well, to secure the other geezer, I fink you should; wot d'you fink darlin', Yeah, no? Oh and in these circumstances Jack would normally tell Farver Mike, can you do that as well pretty please; do that, there's a luv and I'll be yer best friend.'

Jo naturally slipped into Mrs Efficiency, putting to one side for another time, the fact she was being dictated to and called Luv and sweet'art by someone she did not know, and the fact that it was clearly another cocky cockney type out of the Jack Austin barrow boy mould; it rankled, and through clenched teeth, 'Okay Della, I have that in motion, are you all okay?'

'We're a bit knocked abowt babes but okay, and tell knob'ead I fink the girl may be Snail's daughter, he suspected that, but the old raspberry tart had it spot on. I'll brief the Noddy boys on site when they secure the scene, and then tell Jack I might need a bit of his Teflon coating if he has any to spare. Soon as I can, I'll be off for a bit of tea and tiffin with Jonas, and be in later so, TTFN sweetart, Ta-Ta for now, and fanks.'

Before Jo could say anything, Della had hung up. Jo breathed in through her mouth and out through her nostrils, thankful she did not have the cold that her kids all had. She pressed the telephone speed dial and called up Mandy thinking, how long has Jack been back? Two hours? Mandy picked up. 'Mandy, it's Jo. The feckin' cockney barrow boy brigade has struck again. I take it you have your costermonger now?'

'I do Jo, but what do you mean?'

'I will explain when you get back, but please get back, as Della has been involved in a gun incident and thinks she has found Snail's daughter.' Jo could not disguise her exasperation.

Mandy picked up on Jo's frustration, but had her own plans, 'I was going to take Jack to get some gym kit...' she heard the sigh on the end of the phone, '...but I suppose we can come back for a while,' she said as she glanced over to an oblivious Jack, waiting to get into her car and mumbling to himself, something about his loft, which she supposed was her loft as well now.

'Good, I will see you then and Mandy, can you pump Jack for some info on this Della woman because this might just be Jack in a skirt; they're both tarts anyway.'

Mandy laughed then harrumphed, because she detected that Jo Jums was serious, 'I will see what I can ascertain Jo, we'll be there in twenty minutes. I take it you will organise a press briefing?'

'I've already sent the message up to the Commander; he's out and expected back at about four, I asked his PA to set it for five thirty.' They both hung up. Jo sighed some more then sat back down and tipped her head back to have another look at the cracked ceiling.

Mandy stood by her driver's side door and looked over the roof to Jack who was looking like a space chicken, kicking the toe of his shoes into the tarmac, his brain in neutral, finger up his arse and was whistling an unidentifiable tune, it could have been *Beyonce* or *JLS*, but who knew, 'Jack.'

He leapt into life, 'Oh Christ I'm so sorry love,' and he ran around and held the door for her. This was not what she wanted but noted that it was something he usually did but had forgotten today. One for Jackie she thought and then how strange, she had resented it the first time he did this, holding the door for her and always insisting ladies first and so on, but just then, she missed it.

Chapter 24

'You've not lost him again have you?'

Mandy offered a token chortle, greeting Jo in the corridor as she stepped into her office. Jo followed and Mandy replied over her shoulder as she hung her coat on the back of the door, 'He's getting bacon sarnies from Jean in the canteen; we need to eat. What time is it anyway?'

Jo looked at her watch, 'Two thirty, and please don't tell me to go to the dentist.'

Mandy chortled at what would have been an instant rejoinder from Jack, "tooth hurty – better go to the dentist then". She laughed at the thought but realised it was relief she felt; relief she had found Jack.

'Right, before he gets back, what's the dope on this cockney bird, Della?' Jo asked, breaking Mandy's trance.

'Bird Jo? I take it you mean woman?' Mandy threw the comment back to Jo while she took her seat, leaned back and sensed some of her tension ebb.

'Nope, I mean bird. A cockney sparrow, and one who seems well and truly flighty to me, and please accept this in a friendly way, she is frighteningly like Jack and I haven't even met her.'

Mandy smiled at Jo struggling to be diplomatic and contained the sigh she felt like expelling, 'I can tell you Jack recruited her for MI5, I take it you worked that bit out for yourself?' Jo nodded and Mandy continued, 'Well it seems she was okay when working with Jack, who was on a temporary assignment back in London, which incidentally he tells me got right up Kate's nose'

Jo settled with a smile, 'You know Kate never wanted to leave London don't you?'

'I do now, Jack has fessed all, but not before Michael and Alana had already told me. Della, I am sorry to say, did get into a number of scrapes, which seemed okay when some of the Jack Teflon coating was around, but shortly after he went back to Portsmouth, the pettiness, as she apparently put it, though I rather gather from speaking to Father Mike, it was considerably more than that, made her quit and go into the Met. She was put on a fast track graduate programme, arranged by the spooks I also surmise; bright cookie but well, you know...?' Mandy allowed the explanation to trail off, which said more to Jo than the previous elucidation.

'Troubles, what were they?' Jo threw out into the ether, not really expecting an answer.

'Mike wouldn't say, but it might be that she has the Jack syndrome of not particularly getting on with the, and here I quote *Mary Poppins*, "Martinet up their own arses, wanker bureaucrats".'

Jo Jums laughed, 'Well, I suppose, seen in a prudential light this may make for an exceedingly diverting time.'

As Jo was speaking Jack plunged through the door, 'Ooops, sorry I thought it was shut, *Pride and Prejudice* Jo, Presto cows juice, babes.'

Jo looked to Mandy, perplexed, and mouthed, 'Presto cows juice?'

'He spoke to Milk'O (*see book 2, Irony in the Soul*) on the phone last night.' Mandy explained.

'Oh,' Jo threw out, just for the hell of it, as Jack took his accustomed orange PVC chair beside the far wall, so he could look out of the picture window at Mandy's and his tree. Jo looked comfy in the comfy psychologically challenged seats, relaxed and completely unchallenged on any front.

'I can get you a sandwich if you'd like Jo,' he said un-wrapping a sandwich and handing it to Mandy, like she was a little kid. Mandy liked this loving gesture, except as he passed it to her so he stuck his thumb through it. He giggled; it was something they used to do as kids, pass a cake to someone, see the pleasure in the recipient's face and then stick a big thumbhole in it; "Great times" he had reflected to Mandy, too many times now, and with so many cakes and sandwiches with holes in.

Jo declined any sort of sandwich, 'No thanks plank, I've already eaten, but before I have to listen and watch you eat yours, you should know that your female alter ego, one Della Lovington, has made an arrest of two thugs and what looks like Snail's daughter. Central plod is bringing them into our nick now.'

'Ho ho, well done Della darlin'...' Jack said, then he stopped and looked concerned, and as if to emphasise the extent of his concern, he refrained from biting into his sandwich. This must be serious Mandy thought, to come between Jack and his sandwich and she passed her time, while waiting for him to answer, wondering if she could stick a finger in his sandwich while he was distracted. '...How many hurt?' he finally said, moving his spare hand to cover and protect the sandwich packet.

'Now why would you say that Jack?' It was Mandy, but could easily have been Jo.

Trapped in the headlights, he replied, 'Oh, no reason, just checking,' and he took a big bite out of his sandwich to dcfcr any need for forthcoming immediate responses; a master stroke, up there with one of his better strategies, running away.

Jo looked like she was giving up anyway and stood to leave. Jack muffled something and Jo looked to Mandy.

'He's asking where Della is,' Mandy interpreted for Jo.

'She said she was going for "Tea and Tiffin" with Jonas and then she will be in, said she had plans for you Jack?' and Jo's eyebrows went up and Mandy's jaw dropped, but Jack was trying to laugh and still retain the sandwich, currently half chewed, and only just maintaining to stay within his mouth.

He muffled, 'I might get forty winks in me deck chair,' and he stood and made a run for it before anything more could happen; like a finger hole in his sandwich.

As the door closed behind him, 'How is he Mandy?'

'Not sure, I need to keep a close eye. He said he stood up in the meeting this morning and forgot what he was going to say and then realised he wanted to see Snail. He thought he'd told everybody.'

The two women looked at each other,

'It's time I suppose, it will just take time,' Jo said and left.

* * *

Jack was asleep in his deck chair when Hissing Sid, the desk sergeant, slithered up the stairs with Della following; he showed her to the CP room. There was a flip over notice on the glazed panel of the door that said *QUIET, JANE ASLEEP*. Della looked through the edge of the square glass window and could see him in his deck chair, turned and told Sid he could go, and just so Sid knew she meant it, she gave him the Della stare and followed this up with some of her acerbic wit (she thought), 'You can fuck off now, you lanky streak of snake piss'; a wit and charm, famous in the Met but relatively unknown as yet in Portsmouth. Sid left, hunched and sulking, dragging the backs of his hands along the floor while Della stealthily tippy toed in, went to the water tower, and much to the astonishment of Jo Jums and Nobby, who had watched her progress, she poured the cup of water onto Jack's head.

A resounding "Aaaah, Feckety feck" echoed in the cavernous CP room and likely further afield as Mandy came running in. Jack was up, remarkably sprightly, hopping about, blowing the water running down his face out of his mouth. He stood there like a kid dragged out of the swimming baths by his Mum, with a soggy bonce and hands out in a pleading *What do I do now Mum* look. The whole of the CP room was rolling in the aisles, the sissies scooted their chairs around to join in the mirth, which by now was thoroughly enjoined by Jack, who loved a practical joke, even if it was on him.

'Detective Inspector Della Lovington I presume?' Jo Jums stood, hands on her expansive hips, looking at Della who had the expression that said butter would not melt in her north and south (mouth), which turned to cats and cream as she replied.

'Jo Jums, sweet'art, lubbly Jubbly to meet you,' and Della strode purposefully to Jo and gave her a hug and a raspberry tart on her cheek.

'The Europeans do three raspberries you know,' a soggy Jack informed Della.

'Do they Jack, well the feckin' Europeans know what they can do; for me one raspberry is enough for anyone.'

'Quite agree Della darlin', but you know if you're in France they will certainly frown on one framboise,' he was laughing, enjoying his joke and the heightened afternoon frivolity. Jack sidled up to Della put an arm around her shoulders, his floppy hair stuck down on his forehead and set to opine to the world; he felt good, even if he looked like a soggy potato; the one at the bottom of the bag that had just started to turn. 'Listen up everyone, this is Della,' and pointing, 'Della, you know Nobby, and here with the Indian swami bandage is my daughter Alice, and of course Mrs Austin you know, and all of these from last night in the Gravediggers. Here we have Kettle, Russell Hobbs, Wally, Frankie and Connie.' Frankie gave her trademark casually rolled Yank salute, acknowledged in similar fashion by Della. 'The Sissics here, Paolo, Jed Bailey, Chipmunk, Dai Bach, he's Welsh, and if I'm not mistaken you know Bookshop, so backs to the wall my darlin's.' Della acknowledged them all, even picked up on the Charlie Drake quote, but Jack had not finished, 'You remember Bombalini?' Della said she did. 'Well he'll be here in a few days as well, so happy days eh babes.'

'Happy days Jack,' she replied by rote.

'Jack, when were you going to tell me about Bombalini?' Jo Jums said, irritated that she learned such information as an MI6 agent arriving to join her team by it being announced across a crowded room.

'Just 'ave sweet'art,' Jack replied, and he beamed as the door crashed open and Commander Manners stood there fuming, only just managing to take in the soaked image of Jack, before he burst with his pent-up invective.

Commander Manners, who looked like a tall and bloated

Captain Mainwaring, was known as Good or Bad depending on what mood he was in, he was also Nobby's dad and at the moment it was definitely Bad Manners. 'Who has an old Saab and has it parked in my parking bay?' he shouted to the assembled cowboys, and he included his son in this broadcast.

Della walked up to him and patted him on the cheek, 'Calm down dear, it's only a parking bay, it's not the end of the world. I'm Delores Lovington and you must be Gerald,' and she kissed him, three pecks on the cheek, the last one evolving into a rasping raspberry. 'How's that Jack, feckin' European enough for you?' She casually threw the comment to the whole room as she turned and headed for the crime wall, and looking out of the corner of her eye, she could see Nobby almost having a fit he was laughing so much. She winked at him, 'Nobby is it?' he nodded, 'understand you do the wall, be a good boy and talk your Aunty Della through will you sweetie; spit-spot.'

Nobby stood and was making his way to the wall when his dad blew again, 'Stop there Nobby, err David and you...' he straight arm pointed to Della, '...just who the hell are you and I want you to get your heap of a car out of my parking bay, now!'

Della turned, 'I told you I was Delores Lovington, same first name as your wife so that should be easy to remember...'

The Commander cut her off, 'My wife's name is Dorothy.'

Della tutted, looked like she might get fed up with the children any minute, 'Yes, but Jack calls her Delores does he not?' and she smiled a syrupy smile to reinforce the win she knew she'd just chalked up, and beamed it to all in the room, just to relax the other kids; she always saw herself as a natural mother. The Commander was stunned, here was this stranger, a beautiful petit woman with a striking cockney accent, the same as Jack's, and strutting in his police station the same as Jack does, parking in his car space just as Jack used to lock his bike up there, and he was starting to feel mollified, which was just the sort of reaction Jack could elicit from him. It was almost as if the illogic of their arguments won over the clear facts of the matter.

Looking back from the crime wall, 'So Gerald; or do you prefer to be called Gerry?' Della enquired.

The Commander looked beaten, 'Gerry is fine...' then he countered with some resumed anger, '...actually no, it isn't, its Jamie but you should call me Sir or Commander.'

Della roared a laugh and a set of pearly white Hampstead's (Hampstead Heath – teeth) twinkled in the reflected light off the ceiling, as her head leaned back, and as it returned to fix the gaze of the commander she said, 'Oh Yeah,' wobbling her head, 'like that'll feckin' 'appen,' and she folded into a belly laugh. 'I think not Gerry my old china, now be a love and toodle off will you,' and she held a limp hand out in front of her and wiggled her fingers to indicate walking, 'or, if you want to make yerself useful I could murder a cup of Rosy (Rosy Lea – tea), cow's juice and two sugars in mine please.

The Commander was pale and looked and felt defeated, bluster and puff gone, deflated; he was completely and utterly out of his depth and began to turn, and in a despairing, desperate whisper, 'My parking bay?'

'All property is feft Gerry, that right Jacko?' and Della swung her smug look to Jack.

And Jack, equally smug said, 'It is that Della and if you're making a cup of cha Gerry, I'll have a girl grey.'

The Commander slunk away.

'What's with Gerry Jack, he's lucky I didn't park me fucking combine 'arvester in his space? And where's my cuppa? Evryfing's so bleedin' slow in the countryside.'

* * *

The office settled but it took some time, they hadn't had such a laugh since Jack had done a similar stitch up on Captain Pugwash and Colonel Horrocks with Father Mike O'Brien pretending to be the Bishop of Portsmouth. It was a sight to see and Mandy enjoyed it, but in truth, she felt a little sorry for the Commander; he wasn't a bad old stick. Mandy looked over at Jack looking to settle back in his damp deck chair, feeling to see if the seat was wet, feeling his bum that had a damp patch clearly visible, with a fixed childish grin that looked like it wasn't about to go anywhere. She just loved his beaten-up face when it emanated mirth. Della was ensconced with Jo, all business as if nothing had happened; so like Jack, maybe Jo Jums had a point.

The Sissies were about to scoot back but Jo pulled them up, 'Not so fast children, I think a quick summary before I have to go to the press briefing; I only hope Gerry has recovered enough.' There was a little titter at the mention of Gerry but frankly their stomachs ached and they were feeling a little roman candle that they ought to be getting on with some work.

Jack called from the soggy deck chair, 'Nobby, do me a flavour son, pass me the dog and bone and dial up Jackie for me and I'll be your best friend. Mandy sweet'art what's Jackie's phone number for Nobby?'

Mandy's formerly tingling bonhomie for her husband and her previously relaxed posture, became upright and rigid, 'Nobby under no circumstances are you to get Jack's phone and dial for him; he can get it himself. Here's the number Jack,' and she scribbled it on a bit of paper and handed it to him, at the same time, curious as to why he would be phoning Jackie, and telling him off all in the same sweeping movement; Jack was always impressed by her multi-tasking abilities, as she followed up with a brilliant and creative ending, 'You lazy toe rag,' and clipped him on his ear – see what I mean, women are such accomplished multitaskers.

Jack envied Mandy this skill although in truth he knew he was equally as good; probably better. 'Sweet'art...' and he sighed like he had told her this so many times, and wasn't it obvious, '...it's nothing to do with being lazy, it's the challenge,' and as if to demonstrate, he pulled a walking stick out from under his deck chair, leaned over and hooked the telephone receiver that bounced onto the floor, and remarkably resiliently, remained intact. He then used the rounded handle to pull the phone towards him, flipped the stick around and leaning out the side of the deck chair, he stretched, unaware that he had coincidentally farted (multitasking you see – you just have to watch for it; or listen for it or wait and smell it I suppose) he used the stick's pointy end, with a rubber cover on it, to bounce on the cut off buttons on the telephone's cradle until he got a response. He shouted to the receiver on the floor, 'That you Mrs Jam, can you get me this number please, me Arthur-ritis is playing up,' and the ephemeral voice on the end of the phone acknowledged him with a chuckle.

He waited while Mrs Jam did the business, looked around, confused as to why people were holding their noses, dismissed it as a joke he had missed whilst busy working, 'Jackie babes is that you, it's your favourite patient here, what, no I just went milk-about; Milk'O and I do it all the time it's the Milkman in us you see.' He stopped and listened whilst bathing in the presumed glory of the cleverness of his remarks to his audience, who all restrained their laughs lest they be forced to breathe in through their noses. Jack carried on his conversation, 'I can't do that love; Mandy's here for one, and two, aren't you from the Isle of Lesbos?' There were guffaws all round but Jack shushed them, he was being serious. You have to be vigilant with Jack as the mood swings were a feature of his mid-life crisis he told everyone he was now having. He had assured everyone that he had moved on from PTSD, "So last year" he had said, in his best effeminate voice, accompanied with some accomplished mincing, which apparently is a symptom of a mid-life crisis or was that was a gender crisis; he wasn't sure except it was a crisis, and everyone else could testify to that fact.

He had explained this to Jackie who, indeed, saw this all very much as a symptom, not understanding, as a girl, that after a while a bloke gets fed up with the same illness and needs another one. This now was his explanation for all the daft, and the occasional serious thing, that he had done or had happened to him lately. He also calculated that he would live until he was one hundred and twenty if this was his mid-life crisis, and was quite pleased with that. 'Jackie sweet'art, shut up and listen please, we have a girl brought

in; she must be about twenty-two, old fashioned brain washing I
fink. Would you be a love and talk it over with Jim Samuels for
me and see if he will let you work on her, get her back for us. I
have a special interest in this girl, I know her Dad. You will; fanks.
How's about dinner over at our arse this evening?' he looked back to
Mandy who had her chin in her hands and appeared to be looking
through her eyelids to the ceiling. 'Mandy's already asked you round,
can't fink why, it's not like I've done anything, but okay, see you then
darlin' and maybe get talking to this girl tomorrow eh? Everyone's
a Cadbury's fruit and nut case, and Toodle pip.' Jackie was a trick
cyclist and so he knew she would appreciate the "fruit and nut case"
quip; he just knew these things, he was a consommé where women
and trick cyclists were concerned.

Jack slung the phone along the floor in the general direction of
its home base, following it with his eyes to see either if it jumped up
miraculously onto the desk, or if it managed to get past an imaginary
winning line, but stopping before going over the dead phone area.
He shook his fist, strangled a "Yeah"; it was an imaginary winning
zone he had hit. 'Sweet'art,' and grinning he looked at his wife as he
laid his head back on his deckchair, 'you've got to get me my gym kit
before they shut; you okay on this one Jo, and with Della?'

'Yes Jack, I think I have my hands full with Della,' Jo replied, 'and
if you're off getting your lycra shorts then I think I might be better
able to focus, so yes, bugger off, and toodle pip?'

'Brilliant luv,' and he rubbed his hands together but realised
he could not get out of the deck chair while doing that. He stood,
energised, like he'd just got off homework from his teacher, grabbed
his coat and walked out like a wobbly pigeon and coo'd a few times,
expecting Mandy to follow. He looked back, 'You not coming
babes?'

'Jack,' it was that tone that could give a man a heart attack. Jack
recognised it immediately and followed her directional gaze, and as
a consequence his eye alighted on the phone, still on the floor, 'The
phone Jack?'

'Oh. Nobby, do me a flavour son, pick that up for us. Come on moy lurvly let's go; hear that Della moy lurv, a country accent, you'll be speaking like that soon,' and he disappeared out of the room, more coos and a wobbling head and walking like he should pop into the toilet as soon as.

Nobby got up and gingerly made his way to collect the phone and put it back in its cradle and back on the desk. 'I don't mind Ma'am, honest.'

'Well you should Nobby, where's your self-respect?' she said, noticing that she was chasing after Jack and simultaneously wondering about her own self-respect.

Chapter 25

In the car park Jack and Mandy kissed for the CCTV cameras, imagined the "Oooh err matron" response in the CP room and they both tittered as Jack held the car door for Mandy, 'Thank you Jack,' she said as she brushed by him and slipped into the driver's seat. He took in her scent, a sniff that sounded like he was snorting cocaine. Mandy marvelled at how she was able to filter out the Jack shite, as she noticed him leering at her legs, trying to see up her skirt; she liked that better, probably because there was no noise attached she imagined.

Jack settled himself in the passenger seat and they belted up; a silent ritual that Mandy respected; Jack's first wife Kate had been killed in a car crash, she never wore her seatbelt. Mandy rested her head on the back of the seat, 'Not a bad first day back Jack, one milkabout, a shooting, no sex on the desk but I think Della was the icing on the cake, what d'you think?'

'I think we should have had the sex on the desk sweet'art and don't worry about Della, she's good at what she does. Yeah she can seem a bit brassy, but honestly, she's a lovely woman. Beryl would not have approved of her so quickly for Jonas if she'd not seen it as well.'

'Hmmm, well if a mass murderer thinks she's okay? But seriously, I'm not sure we can take two of you in the unit?'

Jack laughed theatrically, 'Darlin', you plank...' and he turned to her so she could see his good eye, '...I'm a part time consulate,' and he turned back and waited to get going.

'Oh, sorry, I missed that bit; did you mean consultant?' Mandy said, starting the car.

'That's what I said diddli...?'

Mandy drove out of the secure car park, past Della's beaten up old Saab in the Commander's parking bay and out into the dark and the road south to get some gym kit.

'....I love you darlin',' Jack said.

'And I love you...' Mandy responded by rote, she was preoccupied thinking Della has a beaten up old car and so does Jack, when he drives that is. 'Jack, I'm not going to find out that Della is another one of your daughters am I?' He stopped from falling asleep to allow a tight chuckle, but she noticed that he thought seriously for a minute.

* * *

Spotty, the young press relations officer, was anxiously pacing outside the press briefing room, 'What's this about Jo?'

Jo gave a calming look to Spotty, the one she reserves for her husband and kids when they're being eeejits, 'Spotty, I am sorry if you feel in the dark, but things have been a bit hectic; please roll with this for the moment, okay?'

Spotty nodded, okay with the look and the rolling. The Commander, in contrast, was completely unfazed about the press briefing and more focused on talking to Jo confidentially. He tugged her sleeve, preventing her following Spotty into the press room, 'Who's this Della Jo?'

'Met, Jamie,' she replied curtly, and scurried after Spotty's rabbit's arse, looked back at the Commander and it appeared that the answer, Della was from the London Metropolitan Police, had done the trick.

'A law unto themselves the Met, and a feckin' cockney to boot,' he muttered as the press came to attention.

Spotty kicked off, 'I am going to ask Detective Inspector Wild to talk about what has been happening,' and he leaned back in his chair, stretched his arms back to the table and nonchalantly poured himself some water, to cover up the fact that he had not a clue what was going on.

Jo took her time as was her style, 'I know the local paper...' and she paused to look at Bernie (LeBolt) Thompson, the local Evening News crime reporter and more importantly, and worryingly, a drinking buddy of Jack, '...have been reporting the resurrection of the Portsmouth Football club hooligans, the *6.57*. We are aware also that some of the disturbances that have been happening around town are being attributed to said, *6.57*. However, we are not convinced this is necessarily the case, although it is not beyond the realms of possibility that some of the old thugs or their kids are being wound up to get back into action.' She waited for the usual interruptions to subside, before she continued. 'This morning we arrested two men and a young woman, and we are questioning them in connection with a serious assault on a tramp last night. The man attacked was Brian Mayhew, formerly a professor of Politics at the London School of Economics. Some of you may remember that the summer before last, Professor Mayhew's daughter was thought to have drowned in a Jet Ski accident off Langstone Harbour. I say thought, as her body was never recovered,' and Jo allowed for the agitation at this news to defuse.

'It is unfortunate, but the loss of his daughter, or maybe the not knowing, caused the Professor to have a mental breakdown and he has regularly been seen looking out to sea for his daughter off the Eastney end of the promenade. It is sad but true, that the mental and physical health of this man has deteriorated, despite the comfort and lodging offered by the Sexton family in the Eastney Cemetery chapel.' This elicited interruptions, asking for more information on the Sextons and the cemetery. Jo looked and nodded to Bernie.

'Inspector, how is the professor?' Bernie dutifully asked.

'Ah, someone with a grain of humanity and concern,' Jo injected some Mumsey wisdom into the proceedings, 'he is seriously ill in ICU at QA hospital, the prognosis is fifty, fifty...' she fluttered her hand, '... and before you ask, he has not been able to talk as yet,' this was agreed with Jack, so as to take the pressure off contacting whomever, down by the fort; Jack wanted to get his pigeons in a row. She thought he meant ducks, but you never knew with Jack. 'The point we want to labour is that we are not totally convinced the thuggery is football madness, and we are asking for information from the public to be fed to us here at Kingston Police. We have been gathering and filtering all of the other reported incidents, along with the assault on Professor Mayhew, and Community Policing is leading this investigation alongside the Serious Crime Unit.'

Spotty nodded to local BBC TV, 'Inspector are you leading the investigation and is the rumour true that DCI Austin is back?'

'I am leading the team and Detective Chief Inspector Austin was in today and is acting in a consultancy role. As you know he is being treated by police doctors for Post-Traumatic Stress Disorder, although currently he is insisting it is just his mid-life crisis.' She waited for the laughter to fade. 'So, he is around but not, if you know what I mean. I suppose what I am saying is, no change there then,' and the press laughed, knowing very well the reputation of Jack Austin and secretly hoping he was back; things happened around that man, and they had yet to meet Della. Jo signalled to Spotty to wind things up, stood and left.

✦

Chapter 26

When Jo got back to the CP Room it was a hive of activity, the TV was still on and she thought they had probably all watched the briefing, but it did not have the rows of seats that were normally lined up. She knew Jack arranged the seating, not so he could monitor what was discussed with the press, but had been primarily so he could watch Mandy on the telly. She noticed also that Della had nicked Jack's work station, such as it was. She had pushed his pile of chaos notes to one side and already had a computer set up and running. Where did she get that, was all Jo could think; probably nicked it being a cockney, but snapped out of her jaundiced thought process as Della was in front of her and talking.

'Hi Jo, wadda yer know, let's have a wander and get to know each other.'

'Join you in a walk around the room, it can be so refreshing?' Jo replied.

'Jo, *Pride and Prejudice*, brilliant, I'm gonna like it 'ere. No...' and she nudged Jo with her elbow, '...I 'ad in mind a wander and I didn't want to do it lonely as a cloud; go see Gerry. I may have ruffled his fevvers a bit. Okay with that darlin'?'

Jo noticed that Della, like Jack, was not really asking but saying, and was also expecting Jo to follow her, as Della headed for the door. Jo eventually caught up, 'You know where Gerry's office is then, and if you don't, I suggest you follow the trail of feathers, because I'd say you more than ruffled them?'

'Not a bleedin' clue sweet'art but I would have got there in the end, but since you're 'ere maybe you could lead the way?' Jo

172

could not help but be amused, and once again see the likeness in behaviour with Jack. Mandy had told her once how Jack had wandered all around a school because he was too proud to ask the way to the drama studio. Mandy had mentioned something about *Pride and Prejudice*, but ho hum, she dismissed it, they were outside the Commanders side door to his office. Jo stopped to talk to Della, 'This is the side door, it's like Mandy's office below but I think we should go via his PA, this way.'

Jo walked off but heard Della tap the door and walk in and immediately say, 'Gerry, 'ow you diddlin my old China, (china plate – mate)?'

Jo rushed back to fan air into the Commander's face, at the same time wondering if Della got away with a lot of her bare faced cheek because she was so stunningly beautiful, and laughed, as this is what Jack, so erroneously said about himself.

'Well said Jo.'

'Did I just speak...?'

'You did Jo and tolerably well,' the Commander said, seeming to have recovered some humour and poise, so much so, he was able to manage a *Pride and Prejudice* rejoinder himself.

'*Pride and Prejudice* Gerry, you beautiful old sod, come 'ere and Aunty Della will give you a hug and a raspberry.'

Jo could not believe it but the Commander presented himself for the cuddle and a resounding raspberry off his bloated Billy Bunter cheeks.

'Right then, sit your arse down Gerry and let's pow wow. I have no doubt you're wondering what's happening, as is Jo, I suppose?'

The commander and Jo both nodded and took seats as Della strode purposefully around the office, looking like she was wired and ready to bounce off all the walls and not for the first time that day Jo worried if maybe Della was on something, but shelved that thought because Della was rolling again.

'Righto gorgeous; you know I'm talking to Gerry don't you Jo?'

Jo stifled the laugh, 'I was worried for a minute there Della' and looked to a bashful Commander Gerry, who appeared immensely flattered; the Della magic she imagined.

'Yes well, I seem to be surrounded by a multitude of women from the Isle of Lesbos, so less said eh...' and Della fluttered her hand. 'Commander, we have some serious shit going down on your manor and so I fink we need our sensible 'eads on for a bit.'

Jo thought how long had Della worked with Jack? The expressions, the mannerisms, were all the same, and she also recognised the tension she ordinarily felt when Jack was espousing authoritively about something he was making up as he went along.

* * *

'Jack you will look stupid in those shorts and that shirt is far too small. Just how slim did you think you were when you picked that one up?'

He looked back at Mandy, held the shirt up that could have come from the children's department when compared with Jack's body. 'What? I thought this was nice, understated.'

'Undersized is more like it. Come here, try these on.'

He looked at Mandy like she was learning impaired, 'It's alright love, blokes never try things on, they either fit or we make 'em fit,' he said scratching his whiskers, distracted.

'Try them on sweet pie.'

It was the menace behind "sweet pie" that made Jack duck into the tiny changing cubicle, as Mandy shared a laugh with the female assistant. He poked his head around the curtain. 'What?'

'Get back in dopey.'

He did as Mandy told him and there was more laughter as the assistant and Mandy watched Jack struggle in the very small space, his legs and arms intermittently poking the curtain open so you could see Jacks varicose vein riddled legs appear then disappear, then his skinny artist's arms and finally, his bare, furry, spotty bum stuck out as he bent down to pull up the shorts, which made both women guffaw almost uncontrollably.

Jack was of the view that hospitals, and now shop changing rooms, were a female conspiracy against men, but he would show them, and he strutted out of the cubicle, determined to do just that, catwalk fashion, in his Adidas shirt and flappy, baggy shorts. 'I like these shorts love, lots of ball room.' He looked at the girl assistant who was struggling to hold in her hysterics and the obvious rejoinder, 'I'll have three sets all the same please,' he said.

'All the same?'

It was the assistant but clearly Mandy was agreeing with her, and said, 'Give him the black, the blue and the pink set please.'

Jack, who was already heading back to the cubicle, spluttered and turned, 'Pink?' but then, too late, saw their conspiratorial laugh, and conceded; he would wear whatever Mandy chose, he looked good in anything anyway.

'You think so?' It was the shop assistant but could equally have been Mandy responding to Jack's outspoken thoughts. Jack gave in and went to get back into his normal clothes.

'Normal? For the elephant house yes,' now that was Mandy

* * *

Della and Jo walked slowly down the stair together, heading back to the CP Room. Jo stopped on the landing, Della further down, turned and they faced each other. 'Della, you know that was a very good briefing, thankyou – I can now see where Jack's head has been. Is Mandy aware of all this?' Jo asked.

Della retraced her steps, 'Can't be certain but she's a sharp one, and between you me and the gatepost, I'm pleased for Jack; he's fallen on his plates of meat there; was a time when I worried abowt 'im.'

'Well, Mandy would say she has also done well for herself, but I struggle to see that,' Jo answered.

Della laughed and they recommenced walking down the final flight of stairs to the first floor, 'Yes Jo but you know, apart from all of the stupid antics of Jack and the associated stress and worry that goes with the man, he's actually a good and loving person, for a tosspot bloke that is.' Della looked back wondering at the silence and why Jo had stopped in her tracks, 'Jo, you okay?'

'Della, you do realise that you are exactly like Jack, and now I will have double the stress, don't you?'

Della walked back the couple of steps and playfully punched Jo in the shoulder, Jo went reeling, 'Shut-up you dipstick, you know you nearly had me believing you there. Jack said you were good and he was right,' and she skipped off down the steps chuckling and calling over her shoulder, as Jo picked herself up, 'Righteeo Jo, I'm off to the rodeo and a good rogering with my new bloke; see you tomorrow.'

Jo watched Della disappear into the CP room and reappear shortly after wearing a huge sheepskin coat that swamped her delicate frame. 'You still 'ere,' she called as she passed, 'Jonas leant me the sheepskin coat, bleedin' freezing out here in the countryside, not baaa'd eh?' and she skipped off again, bearing the load of the huge coat, as lightly as she patently bore the weight of the world.

Chapter 27

Jack phoned Bernie LeBolt. They discussed how to bring the government down now that the tripartite agreement between the main political parties, following the deal to regularise the country's debt over seventy years, had expired. Jack deliberately spoke haltingly, appearing to want to close the call, and Bernie, the news dog, sensed elicit information may be available.

'Come on Jack spill the proverbial, confidentially of course, and its newshound.'

And so Jack told him, anonymously, of suspicions about a *Real IRA* cell, working out of Portsmouth. He agreed that Bernie could look into it, but to let him know if they found anything that might be useful to the police, save them doing it, what with the cut-backs and everything. So they wound up their stilted, and to the point conversation, that had to be on Jack's mobile phone as Mandy had been talking for the past half hour with Jo Jums on the house phone.

He went into the living room. Mandy was still talking to Jo and he heard her say, "Rigmarole?" and Jack made to beat a retreat to the kitchen; too late. Mandy summoned him with a wobbly bent index finger. He took her hand and smoothed the finger straight for her and she smiled, until he stuck it up his nose.

'No Ragman Roll, cor why you no risten,' it was Jo Jums doing her *Benny Hill* Chinese accent to Mandy over the phone. Mandy looked at her eeejit and could hear in her mind Jack saying just that. 'Can you take a picture of Jack in his gym kit, I'll get Nobby to put it on the crime wall; I'm sure him dressed like that constitutes a crime of some sort, even if it's just the fashion police.'

Mandy flicked another glance at Jack who was now wandering lonely as a cloud, jerking his head in and out, which had her slightly worried. 'I'm inclined to agree but I don't want to embarrass him too much, I'm still unsure where his head is?' Mandy replied, distracted by Jack's jerky movements, as he headed for sanctuary in the kitchen.

Jo responded, 'Well no change there then, except I am worried about you, going soft in your old age Ma'am. Anyway, just push him a bit on the spook talk please Mandy, I tried to press Della but she just said she was off, and I quote, "For a good rogering with her new bloke", heaven help us eh, and what's this shite Jack talking all northern, and cooing?'

'Didn't Jamie push as to what was happening?' Mandy asked, skirting over the fact that Jack had been talking in a northern accent for a while now, and walking like a chicken with tourettes.

'Do you mean Gerry, and I mean the Gerry now so besotted with Della that I fear for him when he gets home to Dorothy if he can't wipe the stupid grin off his, and I quote, "boatrace".'

'Okay Jo, I can't think about that now, you have a good evening and I will see you tomorrow after the gym. I have an aerobics class that Jack says he wants to do as well, but I will strong arm him into the gym while I do the class,' both women chuckled and said their goodbyes.

'Ay-oop luv, thought I could do t'acerbics with yer, you know, something together as a couple, as eck as like.' It was Jack speaking in a northern accent and eavesdropping, which he wasn't that bad at for a deaf twat; the listening that is, his northern English accent was shite, as eck as like.

'D'you even know what aerobics is Jack?' she knew not to press for an explanation of his accent, yet.

'Well nay pet, but if lassies can do it, I'm sure as eck I can hen, or are you worried I would be the star?'

'No Jack that is not what I am worried about. Now, tell me what a Ragman Roll is and then we can talk about the accent.' He'd been caught in the headlamps and she could see he was set to go milkabout; he had that lonely as a cloud look, the one where he picked imaginary daffodils from his fireman's hose. 'Jack, Ragman

Roll?' Mandy pushed, 'Della has just been into the Commander with Jo and spilled a load of tripe, and Jo picked up that Della paused over a light bulb moment, and said to herself, "Ragman Roll". Call me old fashioned but this has the Jack Austin stamp all over it, and Della has just cottoned on, and so I need to, and then I will tell Jo. See how it works? Teamwork, you know the thing you talk about but struggle to do?'

'Did she say Rigmarole lass, cause that is like an elaborate or complicated procedure, or a set of confused and meaningless statements, as eck as like?'

'No Jack, I am sure that all of those things apply equally, but Della definitely said "Ragman Roll". I am also thinking this has something to do with the Sextons', and let me speculate a bit more, the so-called Chapel Club of tramps? Della also mentioned the ghost of the cemetery; a ghost, and then swore in French, saying "Merde", what the feck is that all about?'

Jack sat back with the broadest of grins, seriously impressed with his wife, 'Amanda darlin' you are good, you have it spot on bonnie lass, but won't Jackie be here in a minute pet?'

'She will, but before we go to bed you will tell me all, okay Jack?'

Jack looked like he had been struck by a bolt of lightning, the last thing he needed was to have a, *we must talk, talk, before bed*, but he carried it off magnificently he thought, trusting in divine intervention that she might forget! So you see, Jack thinks he knows women, but... what can I tell yer, d 'yer thinks it's easy?

'Right on darlin', treble cosmic,' he said, to show he was not frightened and had this base well and truly covered.

Mandy let that one go into the trash, along with his pigeon talk and northern accent, none of which she understood, although she was worried as he had been walking funny and moving his head backwards and forwards? She presumed it was pigeon, but hoped he had not developed another affliction, although she thought it could have been his tourettes getting worse.

* * *

Pansy and Angel were looking after the pub. They had never known Jonas take any time off before, except on a family holiday and that would have been to make sure Seb was looked after, while Mum and Dad were having sex. So they felt he deserved this time alone with Della. They liked Della, although Angel felt there was more than met the eye, and was discussing this at the bar when Della appeared behind them; creeping up like mum Pansy thought.

'Angel darlin' you're very perceptive, but I am a filf of course. When d'you go to the Chapel next?'

'When Jonas is down, we will go over then,' Pansy said and looked at Angel quizzically.

'Mind if I come with you?' Della asked, casually.

They were even more perplexed; 'Yes of course; it's not so pleasant over there, are you sure?' and they pinched their noses to indicate what was meant.

'I wanna fank 'em, what they did to help Jonas, Cabbage and me today; you 'eard didn't yer?'

'Yes, we heard. Angel is about to get the soup and bread so if you chivvy up Jonas we can be getting over there,' Pansy said, gesturing with her immense head.

* * *

The CP room had all but emptied. Jo Jums was clearing up a few things and in the whirl of doing this she turned to Nobby and Alice, 'You two get off, Jack's back on the scene so you need to rest while you can...' she paused, '...and then there's this Della, God help us,' and Jo swept out the room, metaphorically slapping her forehead, putting her coat on as she went, a huge Mumsey bag slung over her shoulder that bounced on her hip , just as she used to bounce her kids when they were little, and she bounced down the stairs and bounced past Hissing Sid.

Nobby looked at Alice. 'What is it Alice?'

She returned his stare, a bandaged face that said nothing, or was it she was unsure of what she would say, he couldn't tell, 'Nobby, I love you and I'm sorry.'

He saw a tear, which was rare for Alice. 'It's okay my love,' and he scooted his chair over to sit facing her, and took both her hands and placed them with his in her lap, 'take your time, I'm going nowhere.'

'I know you say that Nobby but I've been afraid you will not want me if I'm scarred. What if they can't make it better?'

She looked distraught and Nobby's heart melted, 'I have said, and will say again, I love you, and if that comes with scars then so be it. You have a spirit and soul that I love with all of my heart,' he smiled at Alice who raised her head to look at him. He dared to reach out and touch her face, and this time she did not stop him. 'And of course, you have a lovely arse,' and he pretended to look around and be scared, 'shit your dad's not around is he?'

'Nobby you feckin' Turnip,' and he made to defend himself with his arms over his head, peeking through defensive fingers; she was smiling. 'Nobby, I love you and I believe you, will you move in with me please; into our house?'

Nobby's beaming face was enough to tell her that he would, and that they will likely be okay, 'Can I come with you tonight?'

'Yes please, I would like that, and anyway it might not be advisable to be at home with Delores when Gerry gets in,' and she laughed at the name her dad called Dorothy, that Della had also used, and Della calling Jamie, Gerry; blimey it gets complicated. 'He's upset about the car space, but your Mum will want to know how to get that dim-wit grin off his face. She's quite something that Della eh?'

'She is, let's go home and go to bed.'

Alice nodded, she was up for that.

* * *

Jimbo and Johno were splashing themselves down with meths and special brew, 'Pansy and Angel will be in with dinner soon,' Jimbo said, as the cans and bottles sprayed their contents. Jimbo was put in mind of the aftershave ads, "Splash it on" he said, his best impression of *Henry Cooper* the boxer, who did the adverts so long ago, when he was a kid.

Marge chuckled knowingly, 'Hmmm Jimbo, you have that *Lynx* effect, would you like to join me on my settee later?'

'Shut it you two, I can hear Pansy.' It was the fourth member of the Ragman Roll, Chas, and they all attuned their ears, heard the iron hoop that lifted the large latch, it grated as it twisted. Jimbo thought Seb needs to oil that, as he watched the heavy timber door swing open.

Pansy stepped in and called, 'Cooeee light refreshments,' and Angel giggled and Della belly laughed.

'Pansy, I 'ave to get you away from Jack's influence,' Della said, knowing the quote was from the monkey adverts for *PG Tips tea,* many years ago.

Jack knew them all and quoted them often, as did Jimbo, who also knew Jack very well, and he responded, 'Avez vous un cuppa,' from the tour de France monkey advert.

Pansy giggled and the soup wobbled. It was the thick beef and Jimbo was ready for it, it was a bitter cold and raw night and they will need something warming in them for when they went out later; they had things to sort for Jack. Jimbo's eyes watched Della follow up the ministering angels, watched as her practiced eyes took in every detail of the inside of the chapel, but not before she had covertly and expertly weighed up the four disgusting individuals.

Angel served and Pansy dipped out of the door, picked up the tray they had left outside and stepped towards the eastern quadrant, and the Catacombs. She returned shortly after with a wall of timber completely covering the top half of her body. Jimbo had remarked several times before that he wished he had Pansy's upper body strength; he did not even want to recall what Jack's response had been.

* * *

Jack was cooking in the kitchen; Mandy liked this about Jack, he loved cooking and she appreciated it, even if it meant more often than not they had fish or seafood. Mandy and Jackie were talking closely and quietly at the dining table when, by contrast, Jack noisily appeared with a bottle of Muscadet and some clinking glasses. Jackie looked at the Muscadet, and looking up from the table to Jack, she said, 'Fish?'

'Aye pet,' and he waved his head in a northerly fashion, "appen 'tis, and it'll be along toute-suite, as 'eck as like,' and he disappeared whistling La Marseillaise in a northern accent.

Jackie whispered to Mandy, 'French? Northern accent?'

Mandy shook her head, 'The northern accent has been going most of the afternoon, a sort of a continuing theme, the French is because of the Muscadet but Allah be praised,' and she bowed to where she thought Mecca was, 'he has stopped singing "How much is zat dawgie in ze vindow" in his Gestapo accent, since the dog fighting lads got their just desserts.'

Jackie squashed her hand to her tight-lipped mouth, stifling a giggling fit, as they heard the end of the French anthem, "marchon, marchon", in a northern English accent, from the depths of the kitchen, stifled more giggles as, "ou est le pouffe célèbre", also in northern, and increasing in volume; Jack was on his way back.

'Arr-reet girls, get yer laughing gear round this chocks,' and he plonked the plates down in his best silver service fashion, that Mandy called cast iron service.

'I 'eard that pet,' and he looked back and Jackie and Mandy pretend whispered.

'Did you hear that?'

'Aye bonnie lass, I did that,' and he made his getaway, returning with the vegetables in serving bowls. He ran his hand over Jackie's shoulders in an affectionate way that Jackie had now gotten used to, and he made his way via Mandy, kissed her, then sat. It was his thing, physicality, he had explained this many times before and they understood; they just wished he would stop explaining it. Jackie had though confided in Mandy that it displayed a form of compensation for something that had probably been missing in his earlier life. Mandy knew it was, and he and she more than adequately made up for it, she liked it as well; felt she needed it as much as he did.

'Aye up, why're yer both looking at me like that; is t' fish off?'

Jackie answered, 'Well, I can only speak for myself in that, apart from the *milkabout* today, because you spoke with Milk'O, I was wondering why the northern accent?'

'Pigeons canny lass, pigeons,' and he stuck his nose close to the fish and Mmm'd.

Mandy banged her cutlery down and Jack jumped up, his hand grabbing his heart, 'Eh oop luv, what's ailing thee?' Mandy said in frustration, which immediately dissipated as she shared the laughter with Jackie. 'Jack, what about feckin' pigeons,' Mandy asked, 'and explain the northern accent, pretty please with injuns on top?'

He flicked his head in obvious pride, 'I'm practicing for being a pigeon fancier. I'm meeting the pigeon lorry early tomorrow morning,' and he looked at the two women as though it should have been obvious. 'They bring the pigeons down from up north and let them go at 7 am, and time the birds as they fly back to their lofts up north, see? I got to know the lads on my morning walks and I wanted to see it, it will also help me to have a discreet look around Fort Cumberland as they let them go nearby the Glory Hole.'

All Mandy and Jackie could do in response was laugh some more and knock back their wine. Jackie picked up the bottle and wobbled it, 'I don't suppose you have another one? This could be a two-bottle problem Jack.'

He got up, 'Aye lass, 'appen I 'ave,' and he went off doing his pigeon walk that looked more like his Swan Lake, pregnant donkey walk, but with a wonky neck.

'There's nowt so queer as folk Mandy love,' Jackie quipped, and Mandy appreciated it as did Jack who had heard as he bent to the fridge and farted. They heard that also, but they were already laughing, so carried it on for a little more; women multi-tasking Jack thought, and secretly admired it.

* * *

'I'll see you back in the pub in a mo Pansy, I wanna fank these people proper,' Della said, and Pansy and Angel smiled at Della, looked around the chapel to make sure everything was ship shape and Bristol fashion, in case of a Seb impromptu inspection. They did think that Della had her work cut out for herself, talking to the tramps with their not particularly well attended noses currently steeped in soup bowls, slurping and sucking on the bread; but left her to it.

The door thudded shut and Della strode around the chapel, the sheepskin coat seeming to follow her, disguising any foot movement below; it was as though she floated, and as she marvelled at some stained glass and then a brass plaque, she spoke as if to herself, 'I 'aven't seen the *Ragman Roll* for a long time. The last time I saw it used, was...' and here she seemed to pause and overtly rub her chin, in order to recall a date or time in history, '...several years ago, in London, and organised by a total dipstick the name of Jane Austin.' She turned and all the dirty faces looked up from their soup bowls as the sheepskin coat moved to circle them; a sheep corralling the sheepdogs. "Ow long you been at it then?' and Della directed her gaze and question to Jimbo, for no reason other than he seemed ready to talk.

'And you are?' Jimbo asked.

'Me? I'm the feckin' eejit that walked a week for a stupid fucking fortnight and still there were no apples in the bunch of feckin' grapes. So, you going to tell me who you are?'

Jimbo flashed a smile that would have been radiant, if he had not dulled down his teeth; tea Della imagined, she'd seen that before as well. 'I'm Jimbo, this is Marge but Jack calls her Flora.'

Della intervened, 'Because of the margarine *Flora* I suppose?'

'We imagine so, but do you ever know with Jack?' Della imagined not, but flicked her head that Jimbo saw as his prompt to continue his introductions. 'This is Chas,' and pointing to a slumped form beside the stove, 'and this slovenly turd is Johno.'

Della gave the appearance that she was taking all of this

information in, floated some more, the sheepskin coat grazing the recently swept stone floor. 'You the Jimbo that was with Jack when he blew up the sports pavilion, and were you in the Downing Street team?' Jimbo nodded he was, and Della offered sympathetic eyes, 'I was sorry to 'ear about Wilf, he was one of my first training officers. Not so sure it's safe for any of you lot, you do know Jack is back in Twatland and I'm not talking reindeers or Laplander muffins 'ere, I 'ad more in mind bozo munchkins. I refer of course to his brain and his propensity to get all and sundry into hot water.' She thought, then continued, 'Some of that hot water I might also suggest, you all could use as well, by the way.'

Marge spoke up, 'Heard you were back in Della, so I suppose it is doubly dangerous for us now, and for the record, I am not particularly happy about your gung-ho style as much as I am about Jack's. This is why we followed you this morning. Jack thinks you did well at the beach hut, but what if that trail is dead now?'

'I was wrong abowt you Marge, it's not Flora margarine; it's probably cause you're slippery and not particularly tasty,' Della accompanied this with some brass knobs, and Jimbo and Johno laughed. Chas was the sullen one, and Della looked at him and thought, I suppose you always have to have one. She looked back at Marge and revised her thoughts, well two I suppose. She turned to Jimbo, preferring him to all of them; Johno seemed okay but a bit too much grimacing for her liking, 'Where you off to tonight? I suppose Jack has some bird-brained idea about seeing what is happening around Fort Cumberland?'

Jimbo laughed.

'Not that funny Jimbo?'

'It is actually Della, because Jack is wheeling in a lorry load of pigeons from the north, to be released early tomorrow morning beside the Fort entrance. You know that pigeon fanciers up north do that down here don't you?'

Della's antenna was alerted, 'Well I do know that Jack said he wanted to get his pigeons in a row, so I guessed it wasn't ducks.' Jimbo, Johno and Della laughed. Marge stared, and Della wondered if Chas was a chapel statue. 'You out tonight, only it's cats and dogs and feckin' freezing.'

Marge answered for them, 'We are Della and it is our business, not yours, and that's the way I would prefer it. I want to stay safe.'

'Oooh err Marge, you've got a flea up your 'arris girl, literally,' and Della laughed at her joke but turned on her heel, floated to exit the chapel and looked back from the door. 'So be it Ragmen, but you know where to find your Auntie Della if you need 'er,' and she went for the drama queen exit but the door wouldn't open, 'feckin countryside, they never have simple doors.'

Jimbo opened it for her and whispered, 'For the record, I am pleased to see you Della, you are good, bloody dangerous, just like your mentor, but good, and don't worry about the capture this morning, that was going nowhere and we were going to recommend they be hauled in after what they did to Snail.' He thought on, a bit melancholic, 'And thank you for your words about Wilf.'

Whispering back, 'I take it Snail is not one of us?' Della gestured with her head, sweeping her eyes across the chapel.

'No, just some poor sap that Jack has connected with; like us all really?' and Jimbo swept his eyes in the same direction, 'but I think Jack sees something,' Jimbo shrugged, 'and he is slowly wheedling, don't ask me what, but he has kept a close eye, so to speak,' and Jimbo laughed as he touched his filthy nose.

Della laughed with Jimbo, 'And the ghost?' and she wooed and groaned her best spectral impression, and made a pretend scared shiver that disguised the fact that Della was thinking she might know who Ghost was.

'No, another Jack Sap – nobody knows much about him, and for the record he is ghostly, here now...' and he clicked his finger and thumb '...then gone.' The girls leave food for him; sometimes it is eaten, sometimes not.'

'Thanks Jimbo,' Della smiled, 'I'd give you a kiss but I never liked Carlsberg aftershave,' and Della dragged herself and the sheepskin out of the chapel.

Outside, Della stood facing into the fine mist of rain, blowing a multitude of pinpricks into her boatrace, she marshalled her thoughts and felt she knew where Jack was heading; laughed to herself, 'The feckin knackers' yard, that's where.'

'Worked that bit out already, well done love. Have a cup of tea with me; Jonas will be okay for a while.' Beryl was dragging the last vestiges out of her a fag, leaning in the back porch of Sexton House; she flicked the dog end into the vegetable patch and then felt a shiver of guilt and thought she would pick that up in the morning lest Seb found it; there could be hell to pay.

'Thankyou Burial, I could murder a cup of splosh,' Della replied, shuffling alongside Beryl under the porch, 'I assume you have some of them weapons in your house, because I'm thinking we may need them soon?' Beryl smiled and tapped her nose. 'Thought so,' Della said, and they went in for a cup of cha and a serious chat.

* * *

Jackie departed in a cab and Jack, leaning back on the front door as he closed it, could see Mandy had that, *We're not going to bed until we have talked*, face on, that probably most men around the world would recognise. 'Time we talked love?' he said knowingly, and this elicited a deceptively benign smile from her.

'Spill the beans Jacko,' she replied, 'and shall we start with the pigeon lorry, how come I only hear about this now?'

'I'm only looking for a chance to dig around the Glory Hole stuff...' Jack kicked off his defence as he walked back and sat at the table, '...the fort and the MOD buildings, to see what I can, and incong.. er incoper.., secret like.' Mandy chuckled, and Jack wasn't sure if the talk was over or he should be offended. 'What is it bonny lass?'

'You, incognito?'

'Aye pet, I'll put on some old clothes, the pigeon lorry is going to swing by tomorrow morning about five and pick me up, and then we park up outside Fort Cumberland and watch and see; simples!

What could go wrong?'

Mandy leaned back in her dining table chair, 'And that is all, is it?'

'Honest injuns.' He wasn't sure she had fully grasped his point, 'Look sweet'art, those thugs are not working alone. Even though we've put out the message that Snail has said nothing, they will be expecting me sometime, but not yet, see?'

She was also aware that Jack's plans can often go awry, and was about to push the point further, when the phone went.

Jack looked at his wrist and Mandy her watch, 'Late for a call Jack?'

'It is love,' the phone rang on.

'Shall I answer it Jack?' she asked with an unfathomable expression.

'Aye bonny lass, I'm part-time don't forget.'

She had to restrain her laugh in order to maintain her fed up look that Jack had not picked up on of course. 'Hello,' as she picked up the phone, blunt and to the point. 'Jamie, what is it?' she listened to the commander, 'Okay, I'll see you there, goodnight.' She hung up and looked at Jack, a quizzical look that he liked; a bit Greta Haribo and he liked those chewy sweets, especially the fried egg ones, and he thought this signalled the end of the conversation and her siren look was the precursor to bedtime, with him; *he didn't want to be alone*.

'That was Jamie,' she said unnecessarily, 'Del Boy is down tomorrow morning and wants a meeting at seven; the General, Jamie, Jo Jums, Del and me, what's that about do you think?'

'Not a clue lover,' Jack said, 'but it has stopped our other conversation, and I feel like rubbing me Alice bands all over your body.'

'Jack you smooth talking bastard, get up those stairs now,' Mandy said in her Swedish, *Greta Garbo* voice; Jack loved his siren trouble and strife, dismissed any thoughts about floundering on the rocks, and made a klaxon sound that he knew Mandy liked.

Chapter 28

The next morning Mandy woke early, disturbed by a thrumming, the vibrations of a diesel engine which rattled the sashes in the bedroom windows, and this irritating phenomenon was blended with an underlying hint of hypnotic cooing noises. The street door closed as near to quiet as Jack could manage, about five on the Richter scale, and he was off. Mandy could just hear an "Arr-reet Tom lad" and she was sure she heard a sigh that had to be the driver, Tom, before Jack slammed the lorry cab door. She had called him mad last night and he saw this as a compliment as it confirmed his self-diagnosis of a mid-life crisis. Mandy drifted but could not return to sleep and so got herself up, abluted, and went into the police station.

* * *

The General, Jamie, Jo Jums and Mandy had been in for some fifteen minutes, exchanging small talk and abysmal banter, when Del entered and quipped, 'Jack asleep in the deck chair?'

Mandy thought that sometimes Del Boy, their MI5 operations director, *Minternational man of mystery,* was as bad as Jack, but she kept her counsel, pre-occupied as to what this early bird meeting could be about, and what Jack was up to, so she replied in an automaton manner, 'Nah, he's pigeon fancying pet,' and pulled her chair closer to the conference table, and wondered, did she just speak in a northern accent?

The Chief Constable, Colonel Horrocks, known as the General, kicked off, 'Ahemm...' paused, and looked like he was trying to understand about the pigeons, but the "Ahemm" was how he started any discourse. He was an old school, Blimp-like, army officer, guaranteed to rub Jack up the wrong way and so he did at first, but in true Jack style, he had found a chink in the martinet armour and there was now a good relationship growing in that particular chalk and cheese department. The General, looking to Del for reassurance, was still a little out of his depth and also erroneously thought Del was from the Gnome Office; well he was in a way. 'Did you see the Evening News, late edition, last night Mandy?' the general finally said.

Mandy was circumspect in her reply, a little of the *Jack* trepidation seeping into her body language, 'Err, no General, I presume there was something interesting or the Gnome Office would not send Del Boy down, and his Mum must be worried, having to get him up this early, and I bet he didn't wash behind his ears.' She covered her nerves well and Del, the master at subterfuge, gave her an approving smile, appreciating her banter.

The General continued, presenting Mandy with a copy of the newspaper that looked like he had just ironed it. She did not look, choosing to lay it flat on her lap, her folded hands on top as she leaned into the conversation, preferring to be told what it is the General wanted her to know; she would look at the paper later to make her own mind up on whatever it was that had got them so hot under the collar, and whether she should be equally agitated. She never liked to be rushed into an immediate opinion.

'Yes well, Ahemm...' the General stutter started again and Del Boy, known to be the epitome of patience, unusually got fed up with waiting and took over.

'The paper reports an anonymous source saying that there may be a *Real IRA* cell active in this city.' He left it there, knew Mandy would cogitate for a bit and come back with the subsequent required response.

A curious look on Del's face Mandy thought and flicked a glance to Jo Jums who shrugged; she hadn't a clue either. 'Can I ask who the journalist was please?' she had cogitated and sensed where this was heading, and it was likely at this very moment, covered in pigeon feathers.

'Bingo Mandy, one Bernie Le feckin' Bolt!'

Del Boy had a smug smile that disguised the fact that he was annoyed, worried, or was it just his time of the month Mandy thought, allowing herself a Jack, naughty girl chuckle; Jack did the naughty girl chuckle really well, well he would being a tart, she also thought, and struggled to contain an all-out guffaw.

Mandy looked up from the perfectly folded newspaper, and with a tight grin said, 'And you think Jack slipped the story in?'

'Well that is not what we are immediately concerned about, although we no doubt will come back to that at some time. No, the problem is that we know nothing of this activity but learned yesterday evening that a police sergeant, Paddy Mulligan, has gone missing.' Del left that in the air, observing Mandy's inadequately disguised body language; Mandy had jolted at the news. Del continued with a childish smile on his baby face, 'As Jack would say, what d'you make of them apples sister?' Mandy laughed, it is exactly what Jack would have said, whilst thinking, Paddy Mulligan, the desk sergeant who had it in for Seb, the penny slowly dropping for Mandy; Mulligan, the dogs, Brian Pinchfist; all of this musing was missed by Jamie Manners and the General, but Jo Jums and Del noticed. 'So where actually is the man himself?' Del asked, in cod Irish.

Mandy smiled, a watery grin, which feebly masked the inner turmoil of her incomprehension of what the hell Jack was up to, besides his feckin' pigeons. 'Del, he is pigeon fancying,' she answered, and left it at that, in order to give herself time to marshal her thoughts.

Del went to retort but the phone rang. Jamie picked it up to save the General getting his tin legs into action. 'Commander Manners,' he said, and paused to listen and looked more than a bit dumbstruck, 'Err its Jamie not Gerry,' the dumbstruck bozo slowly applied an unctuous grin to his corpulent chops, '... I...I'll pass you over; pardon? Well I love you too... Err.'

He gestured with the receiver to Mandy; she'd already guessed who it was and raised her eyebrows accordingly to admonish the naughty boy commander, 'Della?' He nodded as she took the phone, 'Della,' she said and listened, moved almost imperceptibly to the edge of her chair and slowly rose; a half crouch and the newspaper creased as it fell to the floor. The General looked at the paper then scanned his office, probably looking for an iron; he was perturbed as Mandy continued her conversation in the crouch. 'Seb has another copy of the plans does he; can you bring them?'

Della was reporting that Jimbo had fed back to her that there was activity brewing at Fort Cumberland, and it was coinciding with Jack arriving with his pigeon lorry. Jimbo was concerned Jack would stumble into something. Mandy was truly worried and now fully erect, the newspaper trampled, and with an accompanying despairing lilt, Mandy concluded the call, 'I'll see you there; you've told Mike?' She hung up and looked at Del but thought, did Della just say that she and Burial had Jack's bottle and glass?

'Della?' Del asked unnecessarily.

Mandy nodded.

'God help us,' Del Boy and Jo Jums said in unison.

Jamie grinned, and Jo Jums remarked behind her hand to Mandy, 'It's the same inane grin he had yesterday evening.'

* * *

Aye opp, trouble at t'mill, or fort as eck as like...

'To you, t' me, t' me, t' you...' Jack was having great fun with his *Chuckle Brothers* repartee, though it looked like Tom was not particularly enjoying Jack's northern accent, as he guided the reversing pigeon transporter onto the tarmac apron outside the gate to Fort Cumberland. "*Vehicle reversing; vehicle reversing*", the lorry's mechanical voice, discordant and alien in the peaceful dawn, alerting Jack, who was standing and guiding, 'Eh oop Tom lad, thy machinery should 'av a northern accent, as eck as like.'

Tom sighed, parked and switched the engine off and the cooing became more distinct, harmonious even, as the tranquillity of the early morning reasserted itself, still, dark, dawn just poking its nose over the eastern grassy ramparts of the Fort. Fort Cumberland was an old brick fort set into grassed earth ramparts and stood to defend England against Napoleon, who never turned up in the end because it was raining; least this is what Jack told Mandy and Jackie last night, laughing his holey socks off; Jack called the holes spuds (potatoes) and Mandy thought she would discuss this with him sometime, probably just before bed time, and then he will have had his chips.

Amid the cacophony of cooing and fluttering feathers, Tom mustered a reply, 'A, meeester, hadaway wiv yer an stop thy piss taking or i'll bang thee on thy ed. Why I ever agreed tee this, I'll never ken.'

'Oh brilliant accent that Tom, now get thee out then we can mash thy a brew, ave thee got t' girl grey lad?'

Tom, who had volunteered as driver looked like he might give up, he Psssst to Jack who came to the driver's door.

'Wot be it lad?'

Whispering, Tom told Jack just what was being it, 'Jack man, there's nobody around why do thee have to talk in thy northern accent, what you are shite at?'

Not really whispering, Jack replied, 'Because Tom lad, they are here; somewhere...?' he looked around him, not seeing anything, '...they are here, my eye is twitching – see,' and Jack wobbled the puckered eye socket skin with his finger, which was conveniently placed as he had just been picking his nose, and he was sure this had proved his point. Tom looked at Jacks dodgy eye, that now had a bogey stuck on the wrinkled skin, and felt a shiver; he really was not sure why he agreed to this and then remembered, Jack had offered him a Pony (£25). He had always wanted a horse but still wondered how he would get it home. (*And they say there is no difference between the south and the north of England!*).

'And how on earth will they hear us with the noise of thy birds,' Tom tried to explain, giving up before he had even finished.

But they had heard, and two thugs in Pompey Football shirts, appeared at the cab and were currently standing behind the deaf aidless, and totally unaware, Jack. 'Oi mush what you up to?'

Jack jumped, turned and faced the taller one with two front teeth missing and a broken nose. They were both fat and Jack immediately knew he could out run them both, especially as he had his new gym plimsolls on, 'Eeh up canny lads, thee made me joomp then; this be pigeons lad, wots it to you, as eck as like?'

'Fuck off,' the male model said; obviously the brains of the outfit Jack thought.

Tom opened the door but the other thug, a full set of teeth but all rotten, put his boot up and slammed it back. 'He told you to fuck off.'

Both men were clearly testosteroned to the brim and unaware of how funny they looked to Jack; wobbly fat, buzz cut hair and really ugly. Jack wondered, were there women that fancied blokes like this? He supposed there were and he could recommend them to *Specsavers,* and then he thought, if they couldn't have him they likely had to settle for something like this he supposed.

'Wot you mean mush, I got meself a bird,' the male model retorted.

'Wi eeh, did I joost spake me finking loike?' Jack said with accompanying pigeon neck movements. The fat thugs nodded, looked at each other as if for the first time realising they might not actually be attractive, and Jack carried on, making a mental note to recommend, with a certain amount of irony, *Weightwatchers* as well as a dentist. 'We'll be on our way bonny lads; just as soon as we let thee birds go.'

'Well let them fucking go, and do it now,' Brains with missing teeth said.

Jack looked at his wrist and his nonexistent watch, 'No can do until seven lad, that's when thee birds are clocked like, it's a race see;

we do this alt t' time.'

It looked like the bozos could not understand and were irritated by that fact, but they enquired almost politely, 'How much longer then?'

Jack looked at his wrist again and thought, then said, 'Half an hour.'

Rotten teeth grabbed the lapels of Jacks thick fleece that Mandy had recently bought for him, and he panicked that it might get spoiled, 'You ain't got no watch, fuck face.'

Jack was immediately concerned that his face might look like a fuck, and then was perplexed as to what that might look like, and reasonably assuming it was something attractive, said, unruffled by the thugs but definitely concerned for his Mandy fleece, 'Its half past six, check thee watch.' Thug boy let the Mandy fleece lapels go and looked at his watch, 'What time you got bonny lad?' Jack was in wind up mode and Tom, peeking from the cab window, was looking worried. It looked like rotten teeth was trying to think of an answer. Jack tapped the toe of his plimsolls into the tarmac, twisted a pose and thought he looked quite good in them, a bit like *Seb Coe*; only a lot younger and certainly better looking than the Tory Toff. 'Time then?' he wound some more.

Reluctantly, 'Half past six,' brainy teeth replied.

'Good, you got that right, I thought you were going to say a hair past a pimple, cause that's what I got,' Jack answered, laughing and pointing to a hairy red spot on his wrist. Jack then moved to the back of the lorry and both thugs followed; Tom jumped out of the cab.

'What you doin?' shite teeth asked.

'Mashing thee a brew lad, I take it you lads want one, it's a wee braw morn and we all could do with some warming up eh?' Jack realised he'd slipped into Scottish but the thugs hadn't noticed; maybe he could have some porridge? Jack liked porridge but ate it sparingly, well sparingly for the renowned Portsmouth Gannet, he was always afraid it would make him ginger, and to be honest, he liked wearing underpants and even more so when he wore a skirt; it could get drafty living by the sea. Jack got the primus stove out and was turning on the gas and flicked his fingers at the thugs, 'Light; come on or you can't 'ave any splosh.' They produced a lighter and with a thump the gas exploded into life, singing the hairs on the back of Jack's hand. He blew the small brush fire out and smelt it, 'Cor blimey that pen and inks and bugger goes my timepiece,' and laughed to himself and brought an old whistle kettle out of nowhere, and plonked it on the gas, making a mental note to avoid cockney as well as the Scottish.

He went around to the lorry's passenger side, took the opportunity for a look around, and then produced two-fold out camp chairs and dragged them back to his improvised camp fire, sat on one to make himself comfortable and then took the *Sun* newspaper from his back pocket and settled down for a read. Even though it was still relatively dark he could look at the pictures and turned to page three, cawed, and showed the picture of the scantily clad model to the two thugs, 'That's my Mum,' Jack said.

The ugly thugs looked at the picture, they couldn't resist, and one of them, clearly the thicker of the two short planks said, 'That your Mum?'

Tom splurged out a laugh that all in all, and he would reflect upon later, Jack considered a mistake. Tom risked a glance from his own camp chair and the thugs were looking around. 'Company Jack lad,' Tom said and Jack looked up, and sure enough no teeth and a load of bad teeth had been joined by three more Pompey shirts, but these were wire brush merchants, skinny, in a powerful looking way, a blur all over their skin that Jack assumed were stupid tattoos.

Jack ordinarily would mention his observations about sartorial delegance and shite tattyoos, and enquire if their kids had been drawing on them while they'd been asleep, but thought it would be wasted, especially as they carried machine guns. He thought he knew the name of the guns but couldn't recall. As previously mentioned, Jack was not a gun man, though he did think he looked hard, so to speak. 'What are those guns called?' Jack asked. The wire brush merchants looked confused, and that reassured Jack that they were just as dozy as no teeth and shite teeth.

'Kalashnikovs,' one of them said, clicking the gun as he said it, and standing like he desperately needed a poo.

'Kalashnikovs eh, you communists then' Jack asked, thinking his question was obvious and wondered if now would be a good time to open up the conversation to the wider aspects of stoicism?

Tom wondered if Jack meant socialism, and may have mumbled this under his breath, as Jack looked like he said diddli, under his own breath that steamed into the frigid morning air.

This under breath exchange of views produced more confused looks from the ugly thugs, and eventually the intellectual one spoke, 'Fuck off wanker.'

'Look, I will fuck off just as soon as I've had me cup of splosh, and how did you know I had a wank this morning; was it cause me eyesight's a bit wonky?' Jack instinctively knew it was likely too late for him to change back to northern or even Scottish, even these thickos had cottoned on, so Jack thought he might try a bit of Scouser; he instinctively knew he could blend into Liverpool if ever he went there, but the clicks of the guns told him he'd been rumbled.

Just then a number of things happened, and Della reported that it was because Jack farted that it kicked off, and absolutely nothing to do with her; she said "Honest injuns" and crossed her fingers in the air, stood on one leg and spat into the wind, so it must have been true, although Jack said she should have spun around three times before she'd spat, for it to be really true; Jack was an expert interrogator and it was this in-depth knowledge of excuses that made him, he thought, so expert.

However, Jack did indeed fart, he said it was because he was scared and considered himself lucky he'd not followed through, which probably would have been okay except he had lifted his leg as Kipper does, and the jet of foul air, invisibly whizzed past the primus stove and ignited, causing a blue flame, that Jack later recalled was a bit like Apollo thingy taking off, but this flame, of dubious pedigree, actually ignited some loose feathers that began to flare and burn. The whistle on the kettle blew and Jack jumped up and shouted Feck, then police, then banged the lever to release the birds as boiling water spilled over his nice new plimsolls and scalded his foot. He bent down to check his foot, which saved his life as a burst of communist machine gun fire zinged past where his head had been, missing his bonce but hitting the pigeons as they made their bid for freedom into the Southsea skies, bound for the north, the sky now clearly showing that daytime was imminent.

The previously hushed and tranquil Southsea air was now shattered by echoing gunfire and thick with spraying blood and a cloud of feathers, like a ticker-tape parade, as Jack and Tom dived under the lorry and the wire brush and fat ugly dodgy teeth crew opened up a coordinated salvo.

'Eeh oop Tom lad, time to feck off I think,' Jack said.

The noise was deafening and Tom had not heard as he was preoccupied with screaming, in pain; Jack had observed before to Mandy, that if you get hit with bullets, it can make you temporarily deaf and therefore, as he had been hit several times with bullets and even blown up, which some would argue is worse than bullets, he did not actually need deaf aids, but tea and symphony. Jack noticed the wounded and temporarily deaf, not death, Tom, was looking like he might grab forty winks and so he dragged the man to the other side of the lorry and stacked him by the large rear wheels and, in another moment of pure genius, he released the second side of the bird cages. Not many birds flew away; the wire brushes had fired indiscriminately, and although Jack had gotten away unscathed, many of the birds and Tom, did not.

Jack's hearing, now being finely attuned, picked up continued firing, but it seemed to be coming from the nearby bushes; momentarily he did think it was lucky that he had not been shot or he might have missed this, so Jack sneaked a look, and from around the giant lorry wheels, whose tyres were now deflated, he could see Burial and Della walking and spraying bullets as they approached the scene. Shite teeth and no teeth were lying down and did not look very well at all, a wire brush had clearly taken a number of hits, another brush was dragging a third wounded brush back through the gates and into the fort, and a tramp, who looked like Chas, was dragging Marge, and all assisted by what looked like a Portsmouth Ranger. Jack could hear approaching sirens and allowed himself a little relax as he looked across to Della and Burial as they dived for cover behind the lorry.

Della squashed with Jack behind his wheel. 'Budge up Jack.'

'Oi, get your own wheel,' Jack said, not unreasonably in the circumstances, after all, he'd got there first.

Chapter 29

Mandy and Del Boy were in a patrol car speeding to Fort Cumberland; Jo Jums had stayed back to set up a command base and had already summoned her team and arranged for tactical support to go to the Fort.

'Mandy, Del,' Jo called over the patrol car radio, 'we've had a report of automatic gun fire from the fort. Take care as you approach, Tactical are on their way, I've arranged for ambulances and paramedics and we have a medevac helicopter also on stand-by.'

'Oh God, here we go again,' Mandy said, metaphorically slapping her forehead, then actually slapping her forehead as she said to Del, 'he was just going to let some pigeons off!' and she felt a combination of exasperation and anger, but oddly, a sense of elation also. Only then did she think, Christ I hope Jack's okay – strange that; maybe she was not quite ready for retirement?

* * *

'Nerty bleck fuern weel.'

'Ghost, where the hell did you pop up from?' Jack said, a tad scared, he was generally uncomfortable around ghosts, which was why he avoided mortuaries and post mortems; shed loads of ghosts there, it stood to reason.

And then in a rare moment of eloquence, Ghost spoke firmly to Della, 'You, do you have crime scene gloves?' and flicked his bony fingers, guaranteed to get right up Della's nose and, if he wasn't already a ghost, then he could very well soon be.

Della looked askance, 'Who me?'

Burial said, 'I think you're the only copper here.'

'What about me?' Jack said, offended.

'Oh shut up Jack,' both Della and Burial said, as Della handed the Ghost some latex rubber gloves, just before Jack could pass on his scenes of crime Marigolds.

'Marigolds Jack?' Della said.

'You never know when you will have to wash up Della,' Jack smirked, knowing he had won that one. Any form of repost or laughter was forgotten as amazingly they watched Ghost rip the clothes from Tom's torso, tear some of his own rags and pad some of the wounds. Tom was choking, blood filling his mouth and he was struggling to breath.

'Biro,' and Ghost flicked his fingers again, and Jack was stumped; he thought he knew frontier gibberish but miraculously Burial proffered a Bic, which Ghost took apart. 'Your Swiss knife Jack,' and flicked his fingers again.

Jack rummaged in his round the houses and couldn't find it, then felt some warm fumbling in another pocket, one he'd completely forgotten he had, and had a passing concern for the onset of Old Timers. 'Oi Della, Mandy could be here any minute!'

'Shut it Jack you dozy old bastard, here Ghost,' and she passed Ghost the knife, and they watched as the skin and bone tramp took the blade out, felt around Toms throat, and then shocked them all as he stuck the knife into Toms gullet.

'Feck me Ghost.' Della said.

'Gerd enny jep not.'

'Righto Ghost,' Jack said, recognising that the moment for eloquence was over, as he watched Ghost fit the biro tube into Tom's throat. Ghost leaned down, listened and felt comfortable that Tom's breathing was working, and went to work on the rest of the bloody pulp that were Tom's limbs.

'Nobody move,' a shouted command from the tactical unit who had fanned the lorry and fort entrance.

'Is that you Cisco, only I need to move my foot or I'll get camp and walk funny, and I may need a poo in a minute?' Jack shouted back.

'Jane?'

'Yeah Cisco, and can we get this sorted before Mandy finds out mate? Be your best friend.'

'I've already found out Dinlo,' Mandy shouted; a detached voice, as dawn rose, whatever time she got up, not that you would recognise her or call out hallelujah, as it was looking like being a miserable day, and not just because there was now a frigid fine mist of rain; Mandy had caught him, he had blood and feathers on his new plimsolls and his fleece was not so sartorially becoming as it had been.

Jack looked around, scared, 'Is that you love? I fink I've got a bit of a cold coming on.' It was all he could think of in the time, and he hoped it might defuse some of the anticipated anger and get a bit of symphony going. He waited for a response to see how the strategy had played out. He heard laughing and thought, it may just have worked.

'Jack is it clear for the paramedics, and do you need a hanky?' Cisco called, chuckling.

'Yeah Cisco and call in a Medivacuum helicopter,' Jack replied in a commanding manner; he was a natural, and he knew this, just needed to convince everyone else.

'On its way,' Cisco called back, stifling a laugh at Jack's malacopperism.

'Who's hurt?' It was Mandy.

Jack relaxed; Tom was looking at Jack and thankfully smiling with his eyes. He tried to remember what it was Tom had said to him before Ghost stuck the biro in; something about this had better be a good horse? Mind you he had just been shot by a communist machine gun.

* * *

Tom was taken off by the helicopter, the paramedics saying to Jack that he had done a good job, and had probably saved the man's life. 'I did nothing it was...' and he looked around and Ghost had disappeared and then Jack thought, how had Ghost got to them through that hail of bullets unharmed, but relaxed when he realised the tramp was so skinny that probably all the bullets had missed, laughed a bit to himself, but still he wondered, and then thought, gerdy ferkin' nerd; cod Irish frontier gibberish.

He stopped that thinking as Mandy cuddled and kissed him and then wiped his nose with her beautifully smelling handkerchief, 'How's the cold love?' a stunning smile that had Jack instantly melting.

'It's alright love; I've got my own hanky you know, though yours smells nicer.'

'Don't you dare get that snot rag out and embarrass me.'

He sighed, a sense of relief; things were normal, a man knows he has to test these things.

'Yes they are normal Jack but only until we get home,' and she enjoyed the look of dread on her husband's ugly boatrace.

The paramedics had moved onto the skinheads but they were all dead, which disappointed Jack because he wanted to kick them for luck. He figured he might need all the luck he could get when he eventually got back home; Jack was notoriously superstitious, as well as ugly.

* * *

Things settled, and Del Boy began briefing Della, Mandy, the tramps and the tactical guys.

Mandy recognised Jimbo, 'Hi Mandy.'

'Jimbo,' she acknowledged but maintained a fragrant distance and held her handkerchief to her not insubstantial nose; it had some accumulated Jack snot, so this required her to summon super human efforts, and fortunately he had not quite sniffed out all of her perfume. She muffled a query; 'Ragman Roll Jimbo?' and Jimbo smiled his tea stained grin.

The uniforms secured the scene, and Jack directed a squad to the coastal side of the fort. He also suggested that they get some harbour police to trail the shoreline, aware that it was not so long ago that there had been a bloody skirmish on this beach, and the reasons for that were now becoming clear.

Del approached, 'Good skills that Jack, you just may have saved that man's life.'

Jack looked confused, looked to Della, and noticed that Burial had disappeared, which was just as well he thought. 'But I didn't do...'

'Shut it Jack, you were a bleedin' whizz,' Della said with a broad grin and then "Whooo-eeh-woo" waving her arms about, phantom like.

'Did you not see...?' Jack felt an involuntary shiver.

'What Jack, see what?' Della pushed.

'A ghost?'

And they all laughed. Mandy felt his head to see if he had any bumps, which he did, but they were old ones.

He decided to let it go.

'You can take your marigolds off now Jack; I think we can let him off the washing up, eh Del?' Mandy said smiling at him. Del laughed and nodded, walked up to Jack and took the bloodied rubber washing up gloves off his hands. A uniform bagged them. Jack let that go as well; he felt a bit scared, was he the only one who saw Ghost?

'Jack can we focus please,' Del said, 'they've taken Flora, and Della said something about the Lone Ranger?'

'Did I Tonto...?' Della giggled. '...Yeah we need to get to him pronto Tonto and Marge as well I suppose, if we must,' and she wobbled her head like it was no skin of her nose if they did or didn't.

'Back door...' Jack almost said to himself as he blew air that vaporised in the chill damp morning, and he looked at the sky that now threatened heavier rain; at least it was daytime, and then he cried.

'Oh No,' Mandy said, and went to cuddle him, looked back to Del, then Della, who was shrugging with her face. She let him sob into her shoulder and when the tears began to subside, 'What is it Jack?' He looked at her, sniffed and went to his pocket for his hanky. She shoved hers at him, just in time. 'Jack?' a little of the famed Mandy impatience showing; she was a lovely and generally empathetic woman, but had only so much patience and it got used up a lot living with a wimp.

'Do you think I'm a wimp love?'

'Did I...? No I don't think you're a wimp Jack' and she looked at Della and said behind her hand, 'a girl's blouse,' and shared a titter with Della.

He nodded but looked to the ground and cried again. Oh Christ she thought as she followed his gaze and saw a blood soaked concrete apron, covered in sticky feathers and then all of the dead pigeons and some not quite dead; she now knew why he was crying.

Del Boy was at their side, he knew Jack well, 'We have someone from the nearby bird sanctuary coming and he will help those poor birds, okay?' Jack nodded but couldn't help feeling guilty, but knew it would pass, and probably sooner than it should, and Mandy relaxed, because when he spoke his thoughts in *Pride and Prejudice* speak, she always knew he was on his way back.

'Did I...?' and Del confirmed with a grunting nod; he was still a tad fed up, so Jack swung his gaze to his plates of meat, twitched his toes, and Mandy worried if he had been shot in the foot again; they were blood soaked. 'Oh, look at me feckin' plimsolls, I'll have to get some new ones now and I was just getting some juice into these.'

'I know love, that was why I was putting them in the garden at night,' Mandy said reassuringly.

'That was you?'

'Yeah, why, did you think it was a ghost?' and they all laughed except Jack, he was definitely scared of ghosts and Mandy told him she had his tan brogues in the car; she didn't have the heart to tell him they were stinking her boot out, because he was so excited; they were his favourite footwear and as Mandy could testify, they definitely had juice.

Chapter 30

'Jack, you mentioned a secret back door?' It was Della, and she confirmed Seb was getting Jonas to bring down some plans of the fort. 'Back door?' She repeated, letting him know she had not forgotten, which was just as well, as Jack had forgotten; he was putting on his tan brogues and stopping Mandy from throwing away his bloodied plimsolls.

'Yeah, all old forts have them, and often they lie undiscovered for centuries. They won't be on Seb's plans otherwise they wouldn't be secret, would they?' and Jack allowed himself a chortle, then saw the pigeons and sniffed; Mandy thrust her hanky at him, just in cases.

Della showed some of her own impatience, equally a match for Mandy's, 'Well that was a brilliant idea Brains, so all we have to do is find the secret back door that has remained a secret for centuries. Mandy, I don't know how you put up with him?' Mandy was about to mention the papal blessing, and the fact that Father Mike had promised her a sainthood if she married him, when Jack said, "I know where it is".

'You do? You bleedin' turnip, why d'you not say?' Della said threateningly.

'I was keeping it a secret,' and Jack tittered, which everyone seemed to agree was better than crying.

Della derred, 'Mandy you need a bleedin' sainthood living with this tosser,' she said, resisting giving Jack a slap, settling on a finger flick to his ear. Mandy looked around to see if she had spoken her thoughts, but assumed that Della had super human powers of thought transference, similar to her own; it's a feminine trait, whereas men are just super human, occasionally wearing their Y fronts outside their trousers after a few beers.

'Right then, tell us where it is and Della and I can get going,' Jimbo said, heading off World War Three.

'Know your way when you get in then do you Jimbo?' Jack asked, wobbling his head.

'Well no, but you can tell me,' Jimbo was also a little irritated, and wobbled his head back and added some brass knobs, which secretly Jack admired, but he needed to square away Jimbo.

'And when you're inside the inner sanctum?' and Jack hummed, it was *The old rugged crawse* apparently, a hymn his Nan used to like. Mandy had no way of knowing if the tune or even the words were right; she needed to concentrate, because it seemed to her that it was different every time.

'Jack you are not going in,' it was Del but equally could have been Mandy or Della, Jimbo however seemed resigned; he'd worked with Jack before.

'Jack you are definitely not going in, you know you're a bleedin' Dennis the Menace don't you?' this was Della, and everyone looked at her, admiring her effrontery, 'What?' she said, flicking her head, affronted.

Jack had moved on from *The old rugged crawse* and was stirring himself with *Onward Christian soldiers*, this time the tune was right but Mandy was pretty sure he had the words wrong, *Marching to the rubbadub*?

'Okay Jack, you can show the way but stay back and out of it,' it was Della and both Mandy and Del Boy looked at her. 'What? Why the bleedin ell d'yer keep lookin at me?'

Del Boy answered, 'I'm in charge Della.'

Della pulled a funny shape with her mouth while her eyes disappeared into her skull, and then she guffawed, 'Oh Yeah, in your dreams Blondie,' and she ruffled his hair which, seen in a prudential light, could be considered as affectionate. 'Right then Jimbo, gather up what's left your motley ragman roll and let' s follow the turnip,' and she kicked Jack up his arse and picked up the machine gun she had recently used to mow down some skin heads. She laughed to herself, mowing, here she was a town girl and never expected to go anywhere near a lawn mower, although she was not averse to a puff of grass every now and then, but that was the extent she was prepared to tolerate the countryside.

'Is that an M 275 Della?' Jack asked looking at Della's machine gun.

They all laughed and Della came back, 'No plank that's a motorway, this is an M 60 – I think that goes in and out Leeds, but that's up north so what do I know?' she thought a bit, then said, 'and what do I care, as eck as like?' laughed again and grabbed Jack's hand, 'Coming for tats tosspot?'

Jack resisted being dragged away by Della, and leaning over, he kissed Mandy's ear and whispered some frontier gibberish that thankfully she understood, and she watched him go off for tats, with Jimbo and Johno following; he called back as he was being dragged.

'Mandy, set up a base just off the fort approach road and contact Jo. Get all the support we need...' he added, not so whispery, as Della dragged him further away '...brief Father Mike, he will know what to do,' and after his issuing of orders, that could have had him manalised at any moment, Del Boy started to follow Jack, Della and the ragman roll, what was left of them.

'Del,' Mandy called.

'I'll take care of him Mandy.'

'Don't just take care of him, make sure he goes nowhere near the danger zone...' and she watched Del disappear chasing Jack's crazy gang and she felt a pang, was that fear or excitement. Was this what she signed up for with Jack? She knew it was and that there would be no way to change it until he was in his nursing home; she then had a minor flutter at the thought of what disruption he would cause as a geriatric; so she phoned Fatso and Maisie as he had asked and then father Mike.

* * *

'It's here somewhere,' Jack was kicking the ground with his newly acquired, ancient, tan brogues, his favourite footwear after his ballet plimsoles; he tried not to notice the snorting from Della; she was so like Mandy he thought, ironically, just as Della was thinking Jack was a dozy bastard. In the meantime, Jimbo had uncovered the 'Back door' which was an old outfall pipe and grate. What Jack was looking for was the key to the padlock, which he was sure he had put by a tuft of grass. They had all looked at the surrounding multitude of tufts of grass, in this wasteland full of grass tufts, responding to his outspoken thoughts with derision.

'Fuckin' 'ell Jack,' and Della let off several rounds that not only eased the lock but the whole end of the sewer pipe.

'Might need to get maintenance onto that Della,' Jack said.

Della laughed at Jack's remarks as Jimbo's radio squawked, 'What was that Jimbo?'

Jimbo squared Mandy; 'If I said Della was easing the back door open would that be good enough for you Mandy?' and they heard a very large sigh and then radio silence.

Jack looked and Della was gone, 'Like a rat up a drainpipe Del; you'll need to watch 'er.'

Del grimaced, but it was wasted as Jack had dived into the pipe to follow the cockney sparrow, or was it a rat, and he heard the echoing, laughing exchange back down the drain, 'I can see your 'arris Della.'

She wiggled her bum for him, 'Just look Jack, no touching or you'll be sucking fish stew and gravediggers through a straw.'

'Shut up you two and get on,' Del Boy had caught up to Jack's backside, not an enviable position; I know who I'd rather be following.

'Oooh, who's a grumpy sod?'

'Della please,' Jack could hear Della giggling to herself as she dropped into a small chamber, remarkably trusting that there was a floor, as any light seepage had disappeared; just a faint residue from an old vent shaft; Jack followed.

'Get orf you dirty bugger,' Della said to Jack with a giggle in the back of her throat.

'I'm looking for the goggles,' Jack said.

'Well you won't find 'em up me bottle and glass,' and Jack laughed; he loved working with this girl.

'Jack, I'm a woman.'

'Did I...? Anyway, you're a bird and you'll 'ave to lump it.' Jack said giggling.

'What now Jack?' Del asked as he joined them.

'Well there are some night vision goggles here somewhere and I need to find them, I've determined that they're not up Della's bum, so I imagine they're on this shelf.' Jack could hear Della still giggling and Del, Jimbo and Johno sighing as he handed out the goggles.

'How did you know there were goggles here?' Del enquired, wondering if he should just leave it.

'Have you never played cowboys and Indians Del?' Jack answered, and Del had his answer, which confused everyone except Della; she often made shite up like that herself.

'Well you must have been the bleedin' Indian, 'cause you're covered in fevvers,' Della said, and she laughed raucously at her own joke.

Jack slumped, he thought of the poor birds, 'Oh Jack, I'm sorry, look, you can have the really nice goggles,' the closest Della came to compassion.

'Can I?'

'Can you buggery, you can have them old ones,' and they both tittered as they were looking at each other with their goggles on, and then the three blind mice, Del, Jimbo and Johno.

'Goggles please Jack,' Del said, his hand out, and Jack handed out more goggles, but not before checking to see if they were better than the ones he already had.

* * *

Mandy sat with father Mike in his old Volvo, Mike looking out of the window at the dead pigeons and skinheads, humming *Ave Maria*, although it could have been *Bob the Builder* he was so tuneless. In the meantime, Mandy was coordinating the operation with Jo Jums. Maisie and Fatso had said that they could have their trawler off station in about an hour. Mandy told them that Jack had said to tell them that he wanted to catch the next train, and they all groaned a minuscule titter, Maisie and Fatso because they liked Jack's crap jokes, but Mandy because she loved the twat and was scared for him.

Chapter 31

Goggles on, the giggling was mainly from Della because Jack was being serious, which she found truly funny; they followed him down a tight concrete corridor, which twisted and turned. After a while they came upon a bright key-pad beside a door and Jack tapped in a code. They heard the mechanical chimes of well-maintained and oiled locks reacting, and after a short while the steel door swung open towards them.

Jack dodged the swing and bumped into Della, 'I suppose you fink that's funny,' she said, holding her nose and chuckling.

Jack joined her laughing whilst moving into the ante chamber, beckoning the team to follow, after which, the door closed automatically and a light came on. They lifted their goggles as Jack tapped a code into another pad, and they eventually passed through into a voluminous control room where bright lights also came on automatically.

'I'm not even going to ask how you knew those codes Jack, but it probably has something to do with your cowboy outfit?'

'Indian Del,' Della said, and they all looked at the ugly, half blind cockney eejit, covered in drying blood and stuck on feathers.

'So what can I tell yer, d'yer think it's easy,' Jack said, just for them, confident they would appreciate it.

'Yes we did appreciate it Jack, now what?'

'Okay Del, I need you to be serious for a minute,' Della appreciated that one, as they followed Jack to the other side of the room. 'Right now, this is the command security centre, and he tapped another code and opened a door in a steel cupboard and handed out some motorway machine guns to everyone except Della.

'Oi mush what about me?'

'You've already got one,' Jack said, trying not to be childish as Del had requested, hoping he noticed that it wasn't him, but Della being silly.

'Yeah but it's used and it's messy?' Della explained, holding her machine gun out, further explaining it was a northern one, and she would prefer another motorway, "pretty please with some injuns on top" she said; Jack noticed that she had left off the brass knobs. 'I didn't think brass knobs were appropriate Jack, we're being serious,' Della replied to Jack's outspoken thoughts, but took the opportunity to go "Ner" to Del Boy.

Jack understood Della's point, being an expert on knobs various himself, and he threw Della a nice new machine gun from the south, which she caught and all in one movement she slung the old one on a bench, grinning, and began doing the business with the new weapon, patent glee on her boatrace. Jack exhaled noisily and said, "Kids" and not for the first time wondered if maybe Della was a little bit of a cycle-path.

Before Della could argue she was not about to cycle anywhere, Del stepped in to do a bit of commanding, 'Jack, that's it now, you don't know how to use one of these guns and I cannot let you go any farther.'

Jack sloped his head, and everyone knew some bullshit was coming; it did, 'Oh, is that right Del, and d'you know where you're going, do you? Do you even know where you are? I know this place like the back of me hand,' Jack said showing everyone his palm, which also involved straightening his head shortly afterwards; he was buggered if he could do both at the same time. As a kid he had struggled with patting his head and rubbing his belly in a circular fashion, but he was not about to tell this lot.

Della flung him her motorway gun and said, 'There you go sunshine, already to go, just let the safety off when you need to, and don't try to fire it while patting yer crust of bread or rubbing yer Aunt Nelly,' and she grabbed another for herself from the cabinet;

she was a like a kid in a sweet shop.

Jack grinned at Del, which magnificently covered up his embarrassment for his lack of coordinating skills as a kid, as he whispered to Della, 'Where's the safety?' and unsubtly, she showed him.

'Okay Brains, where are we?' Jack rattled his gun and made like a fierce soldier, shaped a pose with the motorway gun and just knew he looked the part, and if he didn't already know, there it was staring back at him in a mirror on the wall; he admired himself.

'Yes Jack you look good, I'm going to regret this I know. So where are we?'

'We're in the Glory Hole.' Jack answered Del.

'The where?'

'The Glory Hole Del, it's what the locals call this part of the old military establishment. It's actually a full nuclear command base in case the navy dockyard to the west of Portsea Island is targeted, which it would be of course,' and he derred to himself whilst wobbling his head, wondered if should show them that he can pat his head and rub his belly?

Del looked confused, 'Jack, please, concentrate, are we not trying to get into Fort Cumberland?'

In an exasperated tone Jack answered Del, 'Yes Del, all in good time, and obviously this what the skinhead bozos in Fort Cumberland wanted me for, to get them in here...der, but I thought you might like to see this first. D'you want to see the command rooms, they're brilliant, loads of little twinkling lights and things, and as it's nearly Christmas?'

Della hooted with joy, 'Yeah Jack, I'd like to see 'em,' then she looked at Del, and in a voice, considerably deeper in tone, 'maybe on the way back, what d'yer fink?' a serious voice; she didn't want Del Boy to think she was a turnip.

'That's what I was suggesting dinlo, on the way back, now, come on,' and Jack, having superbly face saved, led them through another labyrinth of tunnels, some requiring the goggles as Jack was not sure where the light switches were, and sometimes the bulbs had gone and what with the cut backs and everything; he stopped talking when he got the *Cut the political diatribe* look from a goggled Del, and eventually he stopped in front of another steel door and electronic key pad. He turned to address his men, 'Right men...' Della was annoyed at that, but let it go in a mature manner, '...just beyond here is another lobby, and then the Fort. It is an alternative means of escape from the command centre and links into the old secret escape tunnel from the Fort.'

'Where do we go after that?' Jimbo asked.

'I don't know it's a secret,' Jack replied and doubled up laughing with Della, he loved it when he could repeat a really good joke. He eased back on the mirth and after having applied his serious head, Jack explained further, 'Well, that is what they call a lottery and you know what I think about that? It's just a greed wagon. Now if they broke it down into loads of prizes at say a hundred grand, a lot more at say ten thousand pounds, then that will make a huge difference to the lives of lots of people.' Jack looked around him, it was stunned silence, 'Right...' he took a deep breath, '...when we get to the other side, we will have to go down a runnel. It is steep and probably slippery with slime as we've had a lot of rain, so be careful. At the bottom of that slope will be a chamber that opens into some cellular rooms, and my guess is that they will be there. It is the farthest point if you are coming from the main entrance, and it's hard to find. But coming this way; ipso facto,' and Jack beamed, loved it when he could use Italian, and accompanied his deckchair talk with wavy hands. 'Also, as it's an escape route, they will likely be thinking of using it, escaping, you know?'

They did. 'So we need to be quiet then?'

'Exactamondo Jimbo, and of course we do not know how many are down there.' Jack said.

* * *

Mandy had arranged and coordinated the operation on the ground, and this had been fed back up the line by Jo Jums. She had agreed that the tactical guys would approach from the front of the fort, having been briefed to look out for Jack and his entourage. They had a senior Portsmouth Ranger on site now, and after a minor Mexican stand-off, he'd given the fort keys to Cisco. Mandy thought it was the mention of the machine gun terrorists that did the trick, that and he had to go and attend to his sudden bout of diarrhoea.

Cisco had the main gates in the screen wall unlocked without any reaction, and his men fanned out over the grassed ramparts and stealthily approached the entrance to the fort buildings, a pair of robust looking timber doors. They had been made aware that these doors had solid locks, for which they had keys but the doors would more than likely also be barred from the inside. Cisco had agreed with Ops on some plastic, with just a mewed response from the English Heritage man, who had turned up in his tweed jacket with leather patched elbows, a waxed raincoat and, incongruously, bicycle clips on his corduroy trousers, that nobody could stop looking at; wondering where his bike was.

Mandy told him to fuck off, but she did it really nicely. She gave the historian his due as he removed his Barbour coat and stood his ground, resolute in his mission to protect a listed English monument, and Mandy was sure he cried as Cisco blew the front doors off their hinges; there was just the main fort doors to go. 'Mr Merrydew, can you please go to that command van and sit in there please. We need to keep you safe,' he looked like he might protest but moved rapidly to the van when automatic gunfire was heard and bits and pieces of debris could be seen flying into the air. Mandy watched him running to the van and thought that maybe he will need the cycle clips after all, and she smiled at Mike; she was actually enjoying herself, now how could that be?

'Because you're a natural Mandy, Jack has known it for years, which is why he recommended you a long time before you two were even an item.'

'He did, and I am, and did I...?'

'He did, and yes you are and yes you did,' Mike answered.

'Well what do we do now?' Mandy asked Mike.

'I don't know, I thought you were the natural, the one in control; Jack always said you would know what to do.'

'He did?'

'He did.'

'Well, let's go to the command vehicle and have a cup of tea then.'

'There you go girl; that's what I call taking command,' Mike said.

Chapter 32

'Jack you follow after we've all gone down, okay.

'Why Jimbo?'

'Well for one, you said it would be slippery and two because I said so.'

'And three?'

'I never said three, but now you mention it, I don't want to face Mandy if you get hurt.'

'You're a cowardy custard Jimbo, frightened of a girl.'

'Jack do as he says.'

'Righto Della, just sayin' that's all,' and Jack pressed the code and the steel door opened silently and a foul-smelling draft immediately hit their nostrils.

'You were right Jack it is slimy and really pen and inks,' Della said, nasally, gripping her fireman's hose.

Jack poked his head into the steep sloping tunnel, 'Yeah it is slimy but I just farted, I think that could be what you can smell?'

'Oh righto Jack,' Della said, as she followed Jimbo and Johno, pushing past Del Boy.

Del looked at Jack, 'Why did I allow you to persuade me to take Della back on?'

'Because Del, she's good.'

'Yeah, keep reminding me will you,' and Del lifted his leg over the rim of the door and gingerly made his way into the tunnel, testing his footing and holding his nose as he went.

Jimbo and Johno had made it to the bottom and they could hear a heated discussion taking place just a short distance from where the tunnel discharged. They stepped onto the concrete floor that was also green and slick. There was a half open doorway to another chamber and they could hear the men preparing to make an escape up the tunnel, which made its way, eventually, to the seafront; they could hear the waves crashing.

'I think that's far enough,' a rather better spoken skinhead was pointing a machine gun at them; Della, Jimbo, Johno and then Del Boy were ensnared, then disarmed. The posh skinhead looked up the tunnel to make sure nobody else was following, and satisfied, he nodded for his prisoners to make their way into the adjacent room when a scream was heard and a lot of machine gun fire. Jack slid down the tunnel with his gun firing automatically, spraying bullets everywhere as he slid into the chamber, like a fully armed flailing monkey on a flume at the swimming baths.

Del, Della and Jimbo dived for cover but Johno was hit in his leg, as Jack splurged through the tunnel mouth, rolled and consequently sprayed the room, killing all the skinheads present and splintering the door, as another skinhead crew tried to close it; they made a run to somewhere else in the fort.

Della crawled to Jack, 'Fuckin' Ada Jack, what you doing, and where the bleedin' 'ell 'ave you been?' she helped him up. He managed with a lot of oomphing and howling to get himself stood upright, everyone trying to avoid the dangerous end of his machine gun.

'Put the gun down Jack,' Jimbo took command, which rather riled Jack; he was the leader wasn't he?

'Alright Jimbo, keep your girdle on,' Jack said, and he placed the gun down on the floor and it spat a bullet out that just missed Johno, who was leaning against the wall holding the wound in his thigh.

'For feck's sake Jack, you've already shot me once.'

'That means good luck Johno,' Jack replied waving crossed fingers.

'Does it?' Johno asked.

'Yeah, don't it Della?' Jack said, not so confident, not accustomed to being questioned on matters of good luck.

'It does Johno, but there's only so much luck you can take before you're brown bread. So Jack, what you doing and where've yer been?' Della tapped her foot.

Was she irritated, it was hard for Jack to tell, but Jack did have a brilliant answer, 'Well I'm rescuing you...' and he smiled his best victory grin, '...and I had to go for a tom tit, you remember I farted, well I nearly followed frew.'

Della laughed and pretty soon after, Del, Jimbo and even Johno laughed but that ceased when a skinhead appeared brandishing a pistol. Jack, still laughing, walked up to the bloke, 'Oh shut up mate, I've got a bleedin' 'edache and more than a touch of diarrhoea,' and he knee'd him in the nuts. The skinhead folded and Jack relieved him of his gun as he went down. Jack turned to Johno, 'Now this is what you do for good luck,' and he kicked the bloke again, 'see, I'm gonna be really lucky now.'

Della kicked the man in the face, 'I could do wiv some of that luck Jack.'

"Elp yerself Della,' Jack said being obliging, 'I'm always magnum...errmeger... 'appy to oblige in victory Della darlin'.'

Del stopped anyone else looking to get lucky and Jimbo snapped a cable tie on the man's wrists before the man knew what was happening, apart from he was aware his luck had run out, and it had been passed to a one eyed ugly fat old bastard and a beautiful petit woman, who seemed more than capable of handling a motorway machine gun.

* * *

In the meantime, Cisco had pressed on at the fort entrance, and despite the intense fire fight, they had secured a hold on the gate, but now they faced crossing what was called, in the olden days before it rained and Napoleon didn't turn up, the killing zone. This was a wide-open space that any invading army, with raincoats so as not to get into trouble from their mums, would have to cross to get to the next bastion, and this area was defended by strategically placed arrow loops that clearly had various communist and motorway machine guns, and not bows and arrows, sticking out of them. Cisco's men holed up and waited while they had an idea – he radioed Mandy for an idea, so she put her cup of tea down to think of one.

'Hmmm, what do you think Mike?' she said.

'You're the brains of the outfit, I'm the just the eye candy...' Mike said, '...but if I was pushed, I would try to think like Jack.'

They both laughed like drains at the thought, which was appropriate, as Mike was an MI5 conduit, but then they quietened and it was clear they were both trying to think like Jack and this was interspersed with the occasional giggle, and a brief, "no", "surely not", and a look at each other. "Really, do you think that would work?"

'Well it is probably what Jack would think of, I think.' Mike said.

So they settled on the plan of action, radioed this to Cisco, who said, "Really, do you think that could work?" and Mandy telephoned the motorway traffic police and set about it.

* * *

Deep in the bowels of the fortress there were just ominous intermittent rumbles to suggest violent activity at the fort entrance and Jack wasn't joking when he said he had a dickey tummy.

Jimbo had applied a field dressing to Johno's wound, a temporary fix, 'Okay, where to now Jack?'

Jack looked affronted, 'Please?'

'Oh God Jack, you juvenile,' Della's famed impatience, 'where to now pretty please with brass knobs?'

'Well Della, first of all, that should have been honest injuns, not brass knobs, and I suggest we have a shufty around.'

'A shufty around?' Della mimicked Jack, but added some of her own facial gurneying accompaniment and a bit of pansy arsed mincing with floaty arms, 'Bit scientific for you Brains, and I fort you knew this place like the back of yer Alice bands?'

Jack ignored the barbed comments from Della, he put it down to jealousy; he'd had this all of his life, and decided this required a flounce in response, so he minced off in the direction of the runaway skinheads, whilst pretending he knew where he was going. He stopped and they all bumped into him, Jack had just realised he was multitasking and was quite pleased with himself.

Della pushed past him muttering, 'You feckin' twat,' then stopped in her tracks.

Just in the next room they saw Marge, no spring chicken, trussed up like a Christmas Turkey, but smelling decidedly rougher.

'Well Flora,' Della smarmed, 'bit of a turn up this, me rescuing you?' and Marge reflected the embarrassment in her eyes as Della circled and delayed the actual rescue until she had fully milked the situation. In the end Jimbo stepped past her and cut the cable ties and Marge stretched her limbs, rubbed her wrists and then pulled the duct tape from her mouth in order to hurl invective at Della. 'Stop Marge,' and Della put her hand up, 'you wouldn't wanna 'urt the feelings of Auntie Della now would you?' and Della tilted her head to one side and grinned.

Marge bit her tongue, mainly because Del and Jimbo were telling her to do so with their eyes.

'Get yourself a weapon Marge and follow us,' Del commanded.

Marge did this and as she was scrabbling on the floor for a discarded machine gun, she informed Del that Chas and the Ranger Jet Norris were in on the plot.

Del's shoulders sagged as he sighed, 'Well,' he said 'it does offer an explanation as to how this mob were able to get access to the fort, and how they were ready and waiting for Jack and his pigeons...' he paused, thinking on, '...presumably, as Jack surmised, to gain access into the Glory Hole; then what?' Jack looked like he was ready to provide a thoroughly reasoned explanation that he had just thought of on the spur of the moment, but Del stopped him, 'Okay Jack, save it for later, let's go and get the rest and see what we have afterwards, eh?'

'What, go with Diabolical Jack and Calamity Della?' Marge said.

Del looked despairingly at Marge, 'Yes Flora, I mean just that; now please.'

Chapter 33

'You cannot be serious?' a squawky voice on the phone said, and Father Mike and Mandy looked at each other in poorly disguised mirth.

'Listen Top Gun, all we are asking is for you to drop into the Marine barracks, they will give you a couple of bombs and you just drop them into the fort courtyard, trying not to hit Cisco on the head of course; easy peasy Japanesey,' Mandy said quite reasonably, looking at Mike, responding to his priestly chuckle.

'You could be Jack, you know that Mandy.'

'Yeah, God help me,' she said despairing.

'He will Mandy, you have a papal blessing!'

So Mike cleared that one up. Mandy looked at Father Mike and grimaced, that showed the feckin' priest and she went back onto the blower to browbeat Top Gun again. 'Listen Top Gun, we need a really good helicopter pilot and we could only think of you,' magnificent female thinking; you have to hand it to them because I would never have thought of that (well of course I did, I'm writing it, but in context...).

Top Gun preened in his reply, 'Really, well, why didn't you say so in the first place,' they could imagine him wobbling his head, 'where do I get the bombs again?'

See what I mean, up against a woman, Top Gun didn't stand a chance.

Mandy, with her *God save me from little boy's* face on, looked to the sky but only saw the roof of the incident van, and she returned her eyes to the ground where they assessed a corduroy trousered eejit, smelling ever so slightly of soiled underwear. She looked further down, he still had his cycle clips on, which she was relieved about; she needed to walk on this floor.

'Top Gun,' Mandy spoke into the phone, trying to sound energetically pleased that the helicopter pilot had agreed to the plan, 'get down to Eastney beach, by the pastel beach huts, and you will see a bomb disposal land rover. Drop onto the beach or something, and Major Laugh will give you the bombs and a quick lesson on how to use them; hang on,' Mike was tugging her sleeve, 'What is it Mike? She was irritated.

'I was going to suggest that Major Laugh go with Top Gun and he can do the bombing,' Mike said leaning back, in a defensive manner.

'Did you hear that Top Gun?' Mandy moved on, 'Good, well I will speak to Laugh and arrange it, now put some petrol in your helicopter and jump to it, there's a good boy, spit-spot.' And Mandy blew him a kiss down the phone; confident that Top Gun would appreciate it.

She hung up and before Mike could get in a rejoinder to suggest she sounded like Della now, she immediately telephoned bomb disposal at the marine barracks, 'Major Laugh please.'

The girl on the end of the phone laughed, 'What, are you having a laugh?'

Oh no Mandy thought, this is what you get for taking Jack literally, but Mike snatched the phone from her, 'Hallo love, this is Father Mike O'Brien and you should punch this code into your little box of tricks please, he quoted some numbers, a few letters, and in a matter of seconds a Major Jim Thompson was on the phone.

'Mike you old bugger, I hear you need some flash bangs, is this for Sunday Mass?' it turned out that Major Laugh was a friend of Mike, as well as Jack, and, coincidentally, liked a laugh.

'Jim, I'm passing the phone to Detective Superintendent Amanda Bruce, she will tell you where to go and what to do.'

'Is that Jack's new wife, because I hear she tells Jack where to go and what to do, poor old sod; got his come uppance there then,' and he laughed but stopped when Mandy said that Mike had already passed the phone to her. Major Laugh harrumphed, but in a manly, nutter, bomb disposal fashion, she imagined, and then he picked up the instructions from her and jumped to it, just a little confused by the "spit spot"; "that was *Mary Poppins* wasn't it?" he had asked. It was a film which he liked, like everyone, but not the penguins, but then Jack had assured him before that nobody liked the penguins, although he also knew Jack thought that this was a shame, because everyone liked "*It's a jolly 'oliday with Mary*", and he did too.

Mandy told him to shut-up, and to Foxtrot Oscar and get his bombs.

You see, to know Jack is to be Jane, as Major Laugh realised he'd spoken his thoughts, and so he fox-trotted off, stepping in time to get some bombs, whistling "*It's a jolly 'oliday with Mary*" like Julie feckin' Andrews on top of a mountain.

* * *

Jack and his team, now lead by Della (she was insisting) was making a systematic sweep of the inner belly accommodation of the fort, steered by Jack and his photographic memory of the plans.

'Jack this is the second time we've been past this room.'

'Is it?' Jack queried the look on Della's face.

'Yeah, now, d'you actually know where the bleedin' 'ell you're going and d'you really 'ave a photographic memory?'

'When you say photographic memory Della, d'you mean like, can I remember some pictures of me Mum and Dad and some holiday snaps? I remember one at Carisbrooke Castle which was a good one of me sitting on a cannon, I think I was about ten; I think I was sitting on a cannon, I think it was Carisbrooke?'

Della's shoulders shrank, 'Del, you can be leader.'

'I don't want to be leader, what about you Jimbo?' Del said.

'Fuck off, we're lost aren't we?' Jimbo said despairingly.

Jack had an answer, 'No Jimbo, we are not lost. We are in Fort Cumberland,' and he applied a smug grin and scored himself 500 points, but mainly kept it to himself for later.

'I know exactly where you are and here is where you are going to stay.' It was Chas, and he had five gross skinheads as back-up, each with machine guns levelled at them.

Jack turned, and being Mutt and Jeff had not heard, of course, 'Hi Chas, look it's a bit embarrassing, but I'm a tad lost and I want to find my way out; I 'ave to take me library books back.'

'What?'

'Library books Chas; do you not go to the library? Well if you did, you will know that the Tory bastards have put these Big Society volunteer Twats in, and all they can do is charge poor people like me a fortune, just because I forgot to return my books that might only be a month or two overdue; I ask you?' Jack sat back and waited for a reply, but just saw a stunned Chas and five thickos in Pompey football shirts, all of whom had probably never passed over the threshold of a library in their lives.

'I have,' one of the thickos spoke up in response to Jack's spoken thoughts.

'Did I...?' everyone nodded, Jack fumbled a reply 'Have you...?'

The literary thug replied, 'Yeah, and you 'ave a point, all these Big Society knob heads what know nuffing, in it?'

'It is mate, in it,' Jack said in a passable street conversation style. 'What authors d'you like?' Jack was starting to enjoy the conversation now, settling in you might say.

The skinhead walked past Chas and was approaching Jack, talking, 'Well, I like the classics, Tolstoy, Dickens and Jane Austen.'

'You like Jane Austen?'

'Yeah, what of it?'

'Oh no, just he's one of my favourites,' Jack said mincing around a bit, mainly because he sensed a diahoerea moment and as everyone knows, mincing can be as good as a cork up yer backside, 'and your family they are all well?'

'Tolerably well thank you,' the skinhead replied, enjoying himself.

'What about modern day writers? I hear that Pete Adams is a good; *Kind Hearts and Martinets*, you read that? It's feckin' brilliant.'

'Not sure I've heard of him?' the Pompey Tolstoy replied.

'Well you bleedin' wouldn't 'ave, cause he's probably struggling to find a feckin' publisher, so there you 'ave it, a sorry state of literary affairs; in it.' The skinhead supposed it was, but without realising, Jack had relieved him of his gun and sprayed it around a bit, and supposed that at least that bloke wouldn't need to worry about getting his library books back now.

In the confusion, Jimbo had seized Chas and turned him as a shield and he went down, hit by Jack's indiscriminate firing; Della managed to grab a weapon and finished the others off.

As the echoing of the firing dissipated they noticed Jack looked distressed, 'What is it Jack?' Del asked.

Jack swung his puppy dog face to Del, 'It's just, I hate it when you have to kill a reader. If someone reads, then there is always hope, and he liked Jane Austen and I've always liked him.'

'Yeah, I can see where you're coming from there Jack but then, seen in a providential light, the fucking bastards were just about to kill us!' Della said in her poncy Liza Bonnet Doolittle, the mad hatter out of Stepney, East London, voice.

'You make a fair point Della, so whose leader now, I sort of lost track.'

* * *

Top Gun circled above Eastney beach. He could see the pastel coloured beach huts lined up, sentinel, as if to repel sea bathers or nudists. He manoeuvred his helicopter to circle, noticing a land rover pull up and a chap get out and wave. Nose down, he dropped and hovered over the road, it would be too dangerous to land on the shingle beach. Startled motorists eventually pulled over, and he touched down.

'Major Laugh?' and Jim Thompson nodded, 'hardly saw you there what with your camouflage gear,' and Top Gun, who was also a comedian, obviously, waited while Major Laugh rolled in a couple of the bomb canisters, and then leapt up into the helicopter. As he jumped in, Jim Thompson pulled on some headphones and activated the radio. Top Gun confirmed they were on Mandy's frequency, 'If that is possible for a man; on a woman's frequency,' he went on to say and then blanched, frightened that he may have relayed that comment while Mandy was listening; she wasn't, he needed to press the button. He pressed the button, 'We're about to take off Mandy, we will approach the fort killing ground from the seaward side so they will not be able to see us, and will only hear us when it's too late. You'd better warn Cisco, out.'

'Wilco Major Laugh, roger you and out.' Mandy replied.

Mike's eyebrows shot up and Mandy coloured, 'I'm sorry Mike; it is what Jack would have said,' and she knew it was a very poor defence even before she said it.

'I know, but from you...' Mike answered with his understanding, holier than though angelic gobshite look.

Mandy agreed, but from the window of the incident van they could see, over the top of the fort, the helicopter positioning itself for a run, and so she decided to park that for a bit; then frowned and looked to Mike.

'Park?' Mike said.

'Should I leave him Mike?'

They both laughed and then put their serious heads on, things were about to happen and they watched as the helicopter skipped over the seaward ramparts and then hovered just before the killing ground and then tipped forward and they could see Major Laugh hurl his bombs with deadly accuracy. Top Gun swung his craft and he skit scooted and skedaddled, as he said over the radio; was that in Top Gun? Jack always said it was, "I feel the need, the need for a sandwich", but it changes every time.

Cisco, under cover of the smoke and the blinding flashes, ran to the fort doors and planted his plastic and retreated a safe distance and crouched, hugging the base of the wall. The doors blew and they waited a few seconds for the debris to settle and smoke to clear before they charged the gap.

Chapter 34

'Oh alright I'll lead,' Della said.

'Well I'm not going if she's leading,' Flora said.

'What? That's not particularly nice considering I just rescued you.'

Jack sighed and walked on, he'd remembered the way now, up a sloping tunnel that Della mentioned they had passed several times, but refrained from saying more, as an immense blast shook the structure, hurting their ears as the sound wave resonated down the tunnel.

'Christ what was that?' Marge screamed.

There was a second blast and a flame seared into the top of the corridor, and white smoke and floating ash and debris was visible in a halo of light, which pierced violently into the previous gloom.

'This way' Jack said.

'What?' The others said.

'I said this way! I'm leader,' and Jack began running and rubbing his eye, irritated by the smoke and the now blinding light, his ears hurting as they replayed the boom round and around his largely defective ear drums. Crossing the tunnel they were knocked over as a crowd of skin heads appeared from out of the smoke, charging down the corridor, away from the machine gun fire that strafed the massive gap that had appeared.

'Oi, careful! Oops Feckety Feck – this way,' Jack called and rushed into an adjacent corridor and up a short flight of steps, into another corridor that went off at right angles, into another corridor.

He could hear Della behind him, cursing his sense of direction, which he ignored and assumed the others were close on her heels and probably grateful that he was guiding them to safety; he didn't need to look, he just knew these things. At the end of the latest corridor their passage was blocked by a locked, solid oak door. Jack stood back and fired at the lock, missed and hit the wall with about seven hundred bullets and those behind him hit the deck to avoid the ricochets.

'Ow, Ow Ow' Jack was jumping up and down; one of the ricochets had hit his left upper arm.

'Shove over wimp,' Della took control, instinctively knowing she should have been leader.

'Della, I am wounded you know,' Jack said, hurt more emotionally than physically.

'Yeah, so shove over yer girl's blouse,' and Della fired and hit the lock with just one bullet, followed up with a kick from Angel's bovver boots, and the door swung open to reveal a cavernous room, and Jack was immediately struck by the brilliance of daylight as it reflected off whitewashed walls, instantly aware that, one, it must have stopped raining and the sun was out, and two, this room had windows, or was that three, if the sun was two. But, if he had been thinking straight, he would have noticed that the room was an infirmary, and that would have been four, or maybe five. However, there were six beds in line and half of them had occupants, one of whom was Johno, stripped down with a drip in his arm.

'How'd he get here?' Jack said.

Johno was out of it and could not answer for himself, but had it not been for Della sitting on and poking the other two wounded men, in turn, they would have been trying to get out of their beds to repel the intruders. As it was, they moaned as their wounds barked at them. A door opened and a nurse appeared to shush everybody, and then disappeared again through a door with an obscure, white glass, porthole. Jimbo snapped ties onto the wrists of the naughty patients, as Jack went to the door, 'I'll have a look as I'm leader. Della 'ave butchers 'ook out the window and see what's happening outside,' Jack said.

'You bloody look out the window,' Della replied petulantly.

But Jack had already passed through the porthole door, and as a consequence, Della and Jimbo were forced to pick Jack up, who'd farted then fainted. They dragged Jack back into the infirmary and dropped him to the floor with a thump, which amused Della, and then Jimbo peeked into the room and could not contain his amazement. This new bright white room, artificially lit, with no windows, was clearly an anteroom to an operating theatre; they could see it through the glazed wall at the end. The nurse was triaging three men lying on stretchers, all had gunshot wounds. On the far side, of what was also a big white painted room, were more stretchers, seven in all, and they had corpses, some draped with blood stained white sheets. Through the fully glazed screen, at the end of the room, Jimbo could see an operating theatre with someone being operated upon by just one gowned and masked surgeon; a skeletal shell of a man of indeterminate age, a stubbly black beard, partially covering an emaciated skull that accentuated very creepy features, deep shadowy eye sockets, protruding cheekbones, knotted long hair; Dr Death?

The surgeon looked up, noticed Jimbo as he kicked at a bucket that overflowed with body parts, and in one sweep of the same leg, his foot hooked a drip stand and it was pulled to him. The surgeon continued his work, which looked to Jimbo like it amounted to keeping as many surgical balls in the air at one time, the anaesthetic, the suction and Jimbo supposed the repair work on what was clearly a uniformed man and, if he had to guess, was Jet Norris, the Portsmouth Ranger.

Jack had recovered but was looking pale and Della told him so; she knew he didn't like to look like a bucket. He unsteadily stood behind Jimbo, Jack explained that it wasn't him being a girl's blouse; he was carrying a serious gunshot wound to his upper arm. 'Just a scratch,' Jimbo said, looking back to the juggling surgeon, barely able to contain his amazement.

'It's not just a scratch! It's a bloody great big bullet 'ole, and is quite painful, don't you know.'

Della looked at Jack, shook her head, wondering why he'd become Uncle Josh all of a sudden, then said, 'Shut-it Jack you big baby,' then mimicking his uncle josh, 'don't you know,' and picked her nose and flicked it at him; she knew how to get to a man when he was down.

'Did you hear what she called me Jimbo?' Jack said, he had a few retaliatory weapons as well, principally telling on people and getting them into serious trouble, '...and, she flicked a bogy at me.'

'Yes I did hear and see, now shut-up.' Jimbo said, 'Della what's happening outside?' and Jack wobbled his head as if to say, told you to look outside.

Della went to the window, tipped her toes to see out, 'There's a bunch of inflatable dinghies dragged up onto the shore,' she reported, and further observed, '...and spilling out of what is probably Jack's not very secret tunnel, is a load of Pompey shirted skinheads getting into the boats.' Della scanned the horizon, 'There's a pretty nifty looking boat off-shore waiting to collect them by the looks of it,' she added.

'Oh blimey,' Jack said.

'My thoughts precisely, so what do we do Oh illustrious leader,' and Della mock bowed to Jack.

'Have another look outside and see if you can see Fatso and Maisie's trawler yet?'

Della looked a little pissed off at Jack ordering her around, but reluctantly went back to the window, 'I can see a trawler, but it's still a distance away and if they get that boat going, I'm pretty sure no other craft will catch 'em.'

'Okay so we have to delay them. Where's Del with that radio?' Jack reacted.

At that moment, Del and Marge came in, both nursing wounds. Jack went up to Del, 'Just a scratch that Del, look at mine, and I want you to note I 'aven't cried yet.'

Marge definitely had more than a scratch, she'd taken a hit in the leg but it was the wound in the side of her chest that worried Della.

Just then the surgeon, in bloody scrubs, appeared and went

straight to Marge, 'ferty wern esten able.'

The nurse acknowledged and said she would clear the table.

'Vertnet bon pet,' Jack said in northern frontier gibberish. The surgeon looked at Jack, nodded, and Jack made a grab for Del's radio, punched a number of buttons and the radio resisted him, squawking back loud static, so he shouted at it, which didn't seem to work either.

'Give it 'ere,' and Della grabbed the radio, tapped gently and then spoke, 'Mandy darlin', you there sweet'art; over.'

Static, clearly Mandy was not there but then she was, 'Yes I'm here, is that you Della, what's happening; over?'

'We'll need paramedics and medevac helicopters,' Jack nudged Della, 'what is it Jack?'

'It's medivacuum'

'It's okay Mandy, it's just Jack being Jack.' They could hear the sigh of patent relief from Mandy, but Jack was nudging Della again, 'Tell 'er I'm seriously wounded but I'm not crying – go on, and you forgot to say "over",' he flicked his hands out, quite remarkable when you consider he was seriously wounded, 'just sayin', that's all; you 'ave to say "over" or "10-4" I fink?' then nudged Della not to forget to tell Mandy about his wounds.

'No Jack, I will not do that to her, she seems nice, learning impaired most likely, ending up with you, but nice,' Della impatiently replied.

Through the static Mandy was trying to make contact, Della intercepted, 'Mandy, listen, I'm sure you have a squad seaward side, but you need to reinforce that, they're escaping and it looks like they're heading for a powerful boat stationed off shore,' Della said, but clearly Jack wanted to say that.

Mandy replied, 'Della, we have that sorted. We are trying to round up as many as we can as they come out of the tunnel, some have already reached the boat and others are in the dinghies.'

Della walked to the window and could now see all of this happening on the narrow strip of shoreline, 'Okay Mandy, we'll need back up ASAP and if you have the plans from Seb, we are located in the infirmary, over and out.'

'You said nothing about me!' Jack was further ignored as Del and Jimbo were carrying Marge into the operating theatre; Della protested that this cannot be happening, and we do not know who this surgeon is.

'Cretessen fink bat,' the surgeon said.

Della looked at Jack, 'What did he say?'

'He said if he does not operate on her chest now she will die for certain,' Jack said.

Della ignored her natural instinct to question the veracity of Jacks translation, and pointed to the bodies stacked to one side, which now also included Jet Norris, 'And what about this lot? not a bloody good track record, I'd say!'

'Feck bird.'

'What did he say?'

Jack translated, 'He said "bloody women".' Della's back was up but she was halted by Jack as he conversed with the doctor, 'fer bit en saus ipple?'

'Dent bon ach,' The Doc replied.

Jimbo returned from having deposited Marge on the operating table.

'Well?' Della said.

'Well what?' Jack said.

Della's reserves of patience had expired; further exacerbated as Jack was looking out of the window, mentioning that it had turned out nice. 'Yes Jack it has turned out nice hasn't it; what did Dr Blood say?'

'He said, shut yer trap and he knows what he's doing,' Jack answered. Dr Blood in the meantime had torn Del's shirt sleeve off and applied a field dressing to the wound which, if Jack was any judge, was only a scratch compared to his great big bullet hole. He did consider pressing it with his finger to see if Del would cry, but dismissed that as childish.

'Semp itten git.'

'What did he say?' Della asked again.

'He said, yes it would be childish, did I...?'

'Give me your radio Del,' Jack said.

'Why, what you going to do?' Del said.

'Oh nothing I was going to go onto five live, I think its prime monsters question time and I always like to listen to a consommé bozo. Shut up Del, I'm gonna call out the life boat of course.'

'What?' Della said.

'You 'eard Della,'

Del held the radio away from Jack, and so Jack poked his finger on Del's dressing.

'Ouch.'

Jack snatched the radio, hit loads of buttons and then shouted at it.

Della took it from him politely, 'Hello Mandy, do us a flavour babes, call out the lifeboat and tell them that Jack and I will meet them there – there's a love, and Jack says to ask for Sponge Bob, Okeydokee, and I'll be your best friend. Oh and tell the cavalry not to shoot us as we come out, okay.'

Mandy sighed into the radio, 'Will do Della, how's Jack, I thought I heard him crying?'

'No, although if he doesn't do as he's told, he soon will be – see you at the lifeboat station; out.' She turned to Jack, 'Right, where the feck's this lifeboat then?'

'I thought you knew? And you forgot to say "over" again.'

Della looked dumbstruck and was even more so when Jack called "April Fool" and marked up an extra 623 points, which he declared had him as leader for the day, if you added the 500 just now, and before Della could say anything, he took off and she followed in hot pursuit, Jimbo on her heels.

Chapter 35

'They reached the main tunnel, Jack holding his nose; it smelled of smoke and bombs, and as the smoke cleared they could see the entrance, and Jack mentioned, in passing, that it seemed considerably larger than he remembered it, and this did elicit a giggle from Della. Jack poked his head around the corner to look out from where he knew the main door used to be.

'You're guessing that's where the main door was aren't you?' Della remarked.

'Oh Yee of little faith Della...' and Jack poked his head out again.

"Friend or Foe?" A shout from outside.

'Foe,' Jack shouted and then turned back to have a giggle with Della, which was just as well, as a well-aimed fusillade of automatic fire crashed and splintered into the wall beside Jack's head. 'Oi mush watch it, it's me, Jack Austin,' he shouted his indignant repost.

'Is that you Jack,' Cisco called back.

'No it's bleedin Atilla the Hun!' and he went to giggle with Della again, which was just as well again, as he was just missed by another salvo.

'Fuckin' 'ell Cisco, what's your game?'

'Is that you Jack?' a distant voice.

Never let it be said that after about fifty goes, Jack Austin never learned his lessons, 'Yes Cisco, it is me, and yes, I am a friend, so why are you trying to kill me?' Jack said.

'You said you were a foe,' Cisco said.

'I was using dramatic irony dipstick, to demonstrate the furtivity of your de...bolical question,' Jack said, looking back to Della who was giggling, 'what?' Jack said. Another salvo, clearly not aimed at Jack but close enough for him to remember he had a bit of Delhi Belly, hit the back wall.

'Cisco, what are you about?' Jack shouted.

'Just having a tin bath Jack, and did you mean futility?' Cisco shouted.

Della laughed behind Jack, 'I thought Cisco was a country yokel, how come he knows cockney?'

'I think I must have taught him, that and dramatic irony,' and he called out to Cisco, 'Cisco, I'm coming out now with Della and Jimbo, any chance we can do this without getting our Swedes blown off?'

They could hear Cisco having a tin bath with some of his team, 'Okay Jack, come out with your jokes in the air,' and the tactical mobsters all guffawed at that one.

Jack looked back at Della and she shook her head, 'Bloody kids and their guns' Della said.

'Spot on, Della.' Jack said as they left with Jimbo trudging a prudent safe distance behind.

* * *

'Hello, are you Sponge Bob?' Mandy enquired of what was obviously the booted and suited lifeboat driver.

'Robert yes, but Jack thinks I look like *Sponge Bob Square Pants* when I have my life jacket and stuff on,' Sponge Bob said, clearly irritated.

Mandy sniggered; she could see where Jack was coming from, 'Listen Bob, this is going to be dangerous, so just a minimal crew and if any of you don't want go, then say so.'

'First of all, it is Robert, and I will go; apparently I owe Jack one,' the posh sea sponge said.

'You do?' Mandy asked, intrigued.

'I don't, but he says I do!' Bob replied shirtily, and Mandy chuckled to herself, was about to ask why, but was distracted by the sight of Jimbo, armed to the teeth, jogging comfortably towards them, followed closely by a squabbling Della and Jack, each carrying automatic weapons that may or may not be related to some motorway near Leeds.

'Come on Jack, they'll be in France by the time you get there.'

'I am wounded you know Della,' Jack replied with ragged breath, 'and this machine gun is fucking heavy, it must have more bullets in it than yours.'

'That Jack is just a scratch, and shut yer trap and concentrate on running,' Della said, struggling to disguise her laughter.

'You do know I 'ave a dodgy knee,' and Jack saw Mandy giggling at him approaching, so he shouted to her, 'tell her love, tell her about my dodgy knee.'

Mandy said nothing but looked to Father Mike for heavenly guidance, as he arrived after miraculously managing to placate a bicycle clipped English Heritage nerd, and now had joined her for a bit of *Minternational Rescue*. He was apparently insisting he be Virgil, but if Mandy knew anything about the price of fish, and she did, Jack would want to be Virgil.

Della and Jack reached the lifeboat station and Jack immediately bent himself double, sucking air from wherever he could get it; it was not a pretty sight and an even worse sound. It had gone quiet, except for Jack, and Jack looked up and saw an audience all trying desperately not to fold into hysterics; he ignored them, there was serious stuff to do, 'Sponge Bob, have you not got Thunderbird 4 out yet?'

'It's Robert Jack and it's a lifeboat.' Sponge Bob replied, trying very hard to be seriously pissed off.

'It's not Jack, its Virgil, so shut up Spongey and get number 4 out of the pod will you.'

'I'm Virgil, you can be Scott,' Mike said.

'Snott Tracy, feck off, I'm never going to be Snott Tracey. Mandy, tell him it's my turn to be Virgil, tell Mike he can be Snott, but I'm definitely Virgil.' In the meantime, as Mike and Jack testiculated, the others were into the lifeboat shed, sorry Thunderbird Two pod, and were climbing aboard Thunderbird Four and trying to get away before Snott and Virgil arrived. Jack shouted after them, 'Oi, you can't go without me, Sponge Bob, hold up,' and Jack leapt onto the sliding boat and they left Mike behind. 'He'll just have to be the one up in space,' Jack said, 'what's his name?'

'Pratt?' Della offered up.

Jack was convinced she had that wrong and that could mean serious points for him, but he had to defer this as the boat hit the water and he felt a little bit tom and dick, so he put his best Captain Mayhap face on, then realised he was Virgil, and had to change it; it's a tough life being an eejit.

* * *

In the meantime, Fatso and Maisie's trawler was bearing down on the patrol boat. They could see in the near distance the black inflatable dinghies in the water, outboards buzzing, pushing the little boats toward the mother ship, slow progress in the choppy seas; the wind picked up the crackling sound of the tactical forces firing salvos from the shore and the occasional return fire.

Fatso reckoned it would be another twenty minutes before they would reach the patrol boat, suggesting to Maisie that hopefully, they will just think we are out fishing. 'Oh Yeah, you feckin' dipstick, like a normal fishing boat would head towards a load of gun toting thugs if they had the chance,' Maisie replied, pre-occupied at the front of the boat making bombs and other things; probably knitting some nets while she was at it; she was good at multitasking.

'Good point babes, how're the bombs coming on?' Fatso shouted back, a call barely audible over the high pitched whine of the engines as they responded to full throttle.

Maisie, clearly revelling in the excitement, called back, 'Nearly there, Little Jack is just finishing the last of the explosives, a few more Molotov cocktails and we're done.'

'Good, then let's get to it, spit spot,' Fatso called back.

Neither had really heard each other but they both grinned having picked up the use of *Mary Poppins*, these were two people who loved Jack, always will regardless; they had loved him ever since he had saved their daughter Dottie from the serial rapist, who went on to gouge out Jack's eye with a boat hook. They owed Jack big time, and if that meant laughing at his jokes, well; they loved him anyway.

* * *

'Whooooah!' Jack screamed as the lifeboat slewed at the bottom of the ramp and Sponge Bob threw the throttle and the twin screws went immediately to full power, the bow rising as the boat took off, and spray hit their faces. Bob steered the boat into the channel and powered through the narrow harbour straits. It was not such fast going, the rip tide was running inward, 'Come on Spongey,' Virgil said.

'It's Robert Jack,' Sponge Bob shouted back.

'Spongey, it's Virgil,' Virgil said.

'Okay if I call you Virgil will you call me Robert?'

'Oh Yeah, like I can see that happening,' Della shouted laughing her head off, thoroughly enjoying herself.

Mandy looked at Jack and then Della, and was now even more convinced that Della had to be another of Jack's stray love children, and she determined to discuss this with Alan on the radio, in his bloody space station; Mike had given in and Jack had confided to Mandy that he had no staying power; it was all the wanking that Priests did, he'd said. Mandy was still trying to get over the shock of all that, when the lifeboat broke free of the tidal tow and lurched forward, into less agitated water in front of the fort and the Glory Hole.

'Down everyone, here we go, I feel the need, the need for speed – aah haah,' Sponge Bob called; ironically Top Gun had called out something dissimilar when he dropped off Major Laugh.

'Sponge Bob are you enjoying this?' It was Mandy admonishing Robert, and she had just managed that, when she ducked down as they heard the boat hit by sporadic bursts of machine gun fire from the shore.

'Its *Top Gun* talk Mandy,' as if this was all the explanation that was needed, as they all held on for dear life as Sponge Bob began swinging the powerful boat too and fro, zig zagging toward the first rubber dinghy, and taking an occasional sneak peek, Mandy could see the faces of the skinheads and their look of horror as Sponge Bob ploughed into and over the first rubber dinghy. The lifeboat veered and headed for the next target; this one not going down so easily, the skinheads aboard firing consistently at the lifeboat. They could hear thud after staccato thud as the bullets hit the reinforced plastic hull. Sponge Bob reassured them that none of this would affect the buoyancy and Jack popped out from behind his hideaway, to say this was why he had opted for Thunderbird 4, that, and Sponge Bob owed him one.

'I do not owe you one Virgil, and it's Robert.'

'For crying out loud Bob, can we concentrate please, and watch out for Fatso's trawler will you,' Mandy shouted, now truly fed-up. They did not hear Robert's repost to Mandy as Thunderbird 4 swung again, three sixty degrees and as a consequence, flooded one of the dinghies with water, soaking the occupants and forcing them overboard into the sea with the sheer force of the tidal wave.

Chapter 36

'Bring 'er about Little Jack,' Fatso called; he had switched the helm with his youngest son and joined Maisie at the prow. The trawler responded sprightly, 'Give it all we have,' and little Jack reacted to his dad's command and pushed the levers so that both diesel engines, that had idled while they prepared the nets, steel ropes and bombs, throbbed a return to full power, and the fishing boat thrust into a hail of bullets face on. The metal hull sparked, pinged and panged, and Maisie and Fatso crouched behind the cowl, where the seamless hull folded over to form a small shelter. Little Jack steered almost blind as he was hidden behind his own steel shield in the wheel house, an instinctive sense of where he was going and when he would get there. He guessed he would be there now and chanced a look; the baddy boat had a scrambling net over the side and naughty skinheads were clambering aboard.

His peek was greeted with a salvo of pings and sparks, but he managed to call to his Mum and Dad that they were there and, as pre-agreed, he ploughed on and rammed into the side of the patrol boat. Clunk, crunch, pow! The steel prow ground and chewed into the side of a craft, twice the size of the trawler but built for speed, not robust seas or resisting substantial trawlers. Little Jack eased off the power and the trawler receded and bobbed, the patrol boat rocked violently as it was released from the side on thrust of the fishing vessel. This allowed Fatso and Maisie to stand and lob their homemade bombs, a mixture of fused biscuit tins, old wine and beer bottles, which burst into life with booms and whooshes. Flame and explosive force tore into the temporarily stranded vessel. The patrol boat swung in response and powered up to pass the trawler, so it could manoeuvre into a better position to return some fire, to where Maisie and Fatso were concealed.

Little Jack read the move and spun the wheel and kicked the engines into life; the trawler turned into the path of the nimble vessel and then little Jack shoved it into reverse and backed into the baddy boat. The lurch was traumatic, but Little Jack maintained full reverse throttle and the two boats were locked up again, this time the swinging jibs and mechanical arms on the rear of the fishing boat, began wreaking havoc with the patrol boat superstructure. Fatso broke cover while the occupants of the patrol boat were thrown into disarray, some into the sea, and he released the winch locks with a swing of a hammer, and the nets and their hawsers wanged and ran free, onto and over the patrol boat. They hooked onto antennae and a couple of mounted guns, winches and rope locks. Fatso, satisfied they had it secure, shouted to little Jack, "Full ahead" as he locked the net's hawsers. Immediately Little Jack flung the levers and the waters churned as the trawler began to gather some purchase and move away, pulling the now listing patrol boat with it, snagged in the nets.

Thunderbird 4 pulled alongside and Jack and Jimbo could see the chaos on the 6,57 craft as they both jumped onto the side running deck, Jimbo un-shouldering his machine gun and firing almost simultaneously into the large control cabin, and then swinging to the back of the boat and firing at spare fuel drums. Immediately the rear of the patrol boat exploded into a ball of flame, the power of which knocked Jack off the boat and into the sea. Jimbo pushed home his advantage as the 6,57 boat, being pulled along by the trawler, listed to at least thirty degrees and any stability to enable a fight back was gone, the remaining skinheads on the deck jumped ship.

Little Jack saw this and signalled Fatso to release the nets again, and with another swing of the hammer, the hawsers snapped, wanged and began to unwind. The patrol boat bobbed back and forth like a cork in a storm, and went into another list, as little Jack manoeuvred the trawler and Fatso clunked the hawser locks again.

Jimbo, having read what was about to happen, fixed his grip and with one hand, was able to fire again, the superstructure of the boat was clear and Jimbo edged forward to the patrol boat control cabin and fired deep inside. Jimbo took a hit in his shoulder from a pistol shot but managed to stay aboard and release a final salvo; this did the trick and after a very short while silence reigned, except for the throaty roar from the burning at the back of the boat.

'Get off Jimbo, it's gonna blow,' Fatso's detached voice from the prow of the now rapidly retreating trawler. Jimbo dived at the very moment the boat exploded, and he felt the full force of the blast pick him up mid-air and hurl him at the water, which he hit with such force it knocked him out. Jack was spluttering around, panicking, but by good fortune Jimbo came to the surface nearby, and Jack's resolve overcame all of his fear of the water, and he struck out towards Jimbo.

He reached the MI5 man and was able to flip him so his head was out of the water, and kicking furiously he tried to pull clear of the sinking patrol boat. The sea though was engulfed in flame from the spilled and ignited fuel; Jack could not see where to go. He could hear nothing other than the roar of fire sucking in the oxygen, when all of a sudden he felt his kicking legs become entangled. He looked, he had a foot and then an arm trapped in Fatso's nets; he was being tugged and dragged. Coughing and spluttering Jack managed to keep himself on the surface and to hold onto Jimbo as they cleared the fireball, and then the nets were released and he felt the weight of them tugging him down and under the surface. Jack dug in, pounding his legs to keep both his and Jimbo's heads above water, but the freezing cold of the sea and his reducing energy levels, were causing him to succumb. He recalled Hastings and rallied; a brief moment when he found some super human strength, but it soon expired when he felt no rocks beneath his feet, and that feeling of euphoria and the release of responsibility was upon him.

'Don't give up Jack, please don't give up.' Jimbo called, but it was no good, Jack had given up. All he could think was this was his density... 'It's destiny...' Jimbo managed to say, but Jack did not hear, just felt he should welcome his fate. In fact, the sensation was not that bad. He went under and Jimbo went with him. He surfaced again, 'Please don't give up Jack,' Jimbo cried faintly. Jack went under again, his thoughts, how many times do you go under and that will be the last, the one you don't come up from. Please make it three; I've had enough, he said to himself as he went under for the third time and stayed under. The noise of the bubbles he found remarkably relaxing, the suffocating pain of his last breath was thrust in front of his mind, and he thought he should just let it go, suck in some water and then the static air was fierce and hot in his throat and the grip on his chin hurt, but he could breathe; he felt Jimbo go and heard thrashing around him. It was then he thought he would open his eye. Mandy and Della had him under his chin and armpits, Fatso had Jimbo.

'Don't you dare fucking give up Jack Austin, just don't you dare, do you hear me you deaf twatting gobshite.' Mandy shouted continual sweet nothings into Jack's largely ineffective ears and then there was a lot of loud splashing and bubbles and he recovered his senses. Jack choked and spluttered and the pain returned, the responsibility returned, the pressure returned, and finally, at last, the hope returned, incongruously accompanied by the neverending thought of despair and disappointment; and then, what would Mandy say and, Christ, was that Della?

Chapter 37

Slap, slap, 'Oi Virgil wakey, wakey - some bloody *International Rescue* he is; come on Jack mate, wake up 'cause you owe me one.'

Jack coughed and spluttered, his one eye opened and he croaked, 'Call it even, eh Sponge Bob.'

'It's Robert, Snott.'

'It's not Snott its Virgil.' Jack coughed.

'He's alright, come on Bob let's get back home I'm soaked and it's feckin' freezing,' Mandy said, but it equally could have been Della, a shivering sparrow at the back of the lifeboat.

'It's Robert,' Sponge Bob said.

'Whatever Spongey, please get me home,' Mandy replied.

The rescue helicopter had winched Jimbo out of the water and he was on his way to QA hospital. The rescue man in the sea had determined that Jack was okay, even though Jack was claiming he was seriously wounded, but the doc on the winch wire said it was only a scratch and he could go to the walk-in centre when he got ashore. That was when Jack had farted, Mandy knew because she saw the bubbles in the water, and then he fainted like a true drama queen; attention seeking. So Mandy relaxed and settled down to enjoy a short spell of tormenting her husband, enjoined equally by Della, when they got on board the lifeboat; albeit they had to do it through chattering teeth.

'Thunderbird 4 Mandy,' a weedy response from a wet weed; a drip really.

She swivelled her eyes to the sky, thick black cloud was gathering again and she wasn't thinking metaphorically; or was she?

* * *

They left Sponge Bob winching his Thunderbird 4 back into the shed and complaining about how he would have to explain all the bullet holes to the RNLI (*Royal National Lifeboat Institute*). Mandy reassured him that it will be alright and Father Mike, who was there to greet the returning mariners, said he would make a call; probably from his space station.

'How's Del and Marge Mike?' Jack asked.

'Del is fine, they operated and removed the bullet and he will be okay. What is intriguing is that the surgeons at QA said that whoever did the field work on Marge had probably saved her life; they had not seen such good trauma work in ages. They also said it had been quite a remarkable day, so many gunshot wounds, most of which had now been triaged and then shipped off to overflow hospitals in Southampton and Winchester. They singled out the driver of the pigeon lorry, who was almost certainly saved by the field tracheotomy performed, not by you Jack of course, but by that tramp with the Bic biro and, although it was thought that Johno's was just a leg wound, the bullet had in fact grazed an artery and it was about to explode. The surgeon in the fort, who incidentally has disappeared, almost certainly saved his life as well. He was probably part of the Pompey 6, 57 set up. So, what d'you think of them apples sister?'

Mandy looked at Mike and all she could think of to say was, 'Inky pinky thet dot.'

'Do what?' Mike said.

'No apples in that bunch of grapes, is what she meant Mike,' Jack said smiling.

'Oh, well I'll take your word for that.'

They clambered out of Mike's old Volvo, Mike complaining that he now had wet seats, and they ducked under the police crime scene tape and headed to the fort entrance. Cisco was there trying to placate the English Heritage man, saying it was only a little flash bang and it would be easy to fix.

Mandy saw the look in Jack's soggy eye, he was shivering, but he found some energy from somewhere, 'No Jack Please' but she let him go, he had steam to let off she imagined, but frankly she needed dry clothing and warmed herself with the crazy revolting thought of a bath with Jack.

Jack pushed Cisco to one side and went to speak to the bicycle clipped nerd, but then looked back to Cisco, 'If you call out friend or foe, just what sort of answer are you expecting Cisco?' Cisco looked like he had an answer but Jack continued, 'If I was a foe, I would hardly shout out foe would I?'

'But you did call out foe,' Cisco said in his defence.

'Yes, and that my philistine Rambo, is what they call dramatic bleedin' irony my old son, listen and learn, or I'll take your nickname away and then where will you be. Right!' and he turned to have a go at the English Heritage man but he'd gone, 'Oh Feck where'd he go?' and Jack looked to the fort approach road and saw the nerd cycling away. 'Where did he keep that bike Amanda?'

'Well you two are a pretty mess considering you were just releasing some pigeons Jack,' and Jack looked at the Commander and then to where Tom's lorry stood, and the bodies of the dead pigeons still laying where they had dropped early this morning. Jack felt a tug at his heart strings.

'As long as it's not your fart strings,' Mandy said chuckling.

'Did I just...?'

'You did sweetheart and come here,' and Jack walked into Amanda's sopping embrace, and it felt good as they squelched together.

'Ouch, my arm,' he went for full on symphony, more in hope than any anticipated success.

'Oh you wimp, it's only a scratch,' see what I mean; it's tough being a bloke.

'It's not a scratch it's a great big bullet hole,' he explained, as if he needed to.

Mandy smiled her Nightingale smile, he was mollified, 'Okay, we'll get you up to the walk-in centre and they can put a little plaster on it. Jack, I'm shivering, shall we go and have a hot bath; has your cold come back?' Jack was sniffing.

'No, I was checking for gangrene,' he said craning his neck examining the wound and smelling for putrefaction.

Mandy rolled her eyes, 'Jamie, have you seen Della?'

The grin returned to the Commander's face, 'Well she said something about someone had some plans for her, and tea and tiffin? Do you know, I'm not sure I understand that woman, but she's good isn't she?'

'Yes,' Jack said.

'No,' Mandy said, but then her phone went. 'Hello,' and she listened. 'Okay Beryl, do nothing yourself, please, Jack and I will be there in a minute, have Della and Jonas arrived back?' She listened some more then hung up and shouted, 'Cisco.'

'What?' he was just behind her and Mandy jumped.

'I think you mean what Ma'am? But forget that, Incident Van now, and Jamie you had better come along.' She said on the move.

'Barnes mausoleum is it sweet'art?' Jack asked.

'How did you know?' she stopped in her tracks and Jack bumped into her.

'I should've thought about it, but what with being seriously wounded...'

'It's just a scratch Jack, but what should you have thought about?' Mandy asked.

'The command for this bloody lot was from the Barnes Mausoleum, or at least via the mausoleum, and of course they will have known what was happening, and I have no doubt they have taken Seb, am I right, and Della and Jonas?' Jack said to himself as he watched Mandy's bum bounce as she trotted to the incident van and call back, "yes"; he liked her bum, especially when it bounced and he especially liked steadying it, so he went after her to see what he could do to help; he was so considerate when you remember he was cold, wet, shivering and seriously wounded.

Chapter 38

'When you said you'd take me down 'ere I was rather expecting it to be more frivolous,' Della said, looking up into Jonas's eyes, concerned for him, as he had been shot in his thigh and arm; both of which she was thinking might impair his bedroom performance for a while, and she was right royally pissed off about that. Jonas looked at Della and wondered what on earth he had gotten himself into; Della looked completely unfazed by the men and their machine guns, and seemed more worried about his wounds, which comforted him somewhat (the crazy fool).

She appeared also to be even more concerned about cuddling Seb, and reassuring him. 'S'alright Seb luv, the cavalry'll be 'ere in a minute.'

'I wouldn't be so sure of that,' one of the Pompey shirted gang said, one with a moderately intelligent look, quite young, and Della, looking around at the array of electronic equipment, realised that the whole operation had been controlled from the bowels of this mausoleum.

Della looked at the serious turnip and wondered if he knew what he was up against, 'Look sunshine, you're way out of your depth 'ere, and I wouldn't be at all surprised if your Mum'll be pissed off wiv you, if you get home; the naughty step just ain't in this.' She looked at the football turnip, allowed this to sink in and then she continued, 'D'you notice I said "if you get home"?'

Pompey shirt seemed unimpressed and smiled a thug ugly grin, 'Jack Austin,' he said in reply, 'I hope you are not relying on him, because he's dead.'

Della did allow a deep intake of breath, but reassured herself that Jack was a difficult bugger to finish off, and she would know; she'd tried often enough.

'You have Della?' Jonas remarked, in pain.

Della looked stunned and realised that two days with Jack, she not only was speaking cod Irish, she was also speaking her thoughts and was about to think some more things, but other things happened, and really fast. First of all a coffin lid burst open and a shout of 'nerd bit bollix' reverberated in the cave like space, as Ghost rolled out and knocked the legs away from the three men who were pole-axed out of fear and then, of course, no legs. Jonas reacted swiftly and with his good leg kicked away the guns, fell over, but collected one of them and threw it to Della who did the business with the mechanical clicks and knocks, indicating to the men on the floor, and to everyone else, she knew exactly what she was doing.

Jonas, standing again but leaning on a coffin, ushered the men to the wall at the back of the mausoleum as Jack poked his head out of the coffin, 'Anyone seen a ghost?' he said, and Della folded and belly laughed which gave one of the pompey lads a chance to run at her. She had of course released the safety and the gun spat bullets, hitting two of the Pompey guys, and Jonas, pushing himself off a nearby coffin, grabbed the third, and held him in a neck lock and was pounding his face, shouting, 'You fucking bastard, nobody does that to my woman.' Jonas had the man more than subdued; in fact it was only Jonas holding him by his neck that kept the man off the floor and that was with just one hand, and standing on one leg, the other hand, after completing the punching, was on the end of a wounded arm of course; keep up.

Della pecked Jonas's cheek, 'Ah Darlin' that's such a sweet fing to say, you can consider yourself on a definite promise after we've killed this lot; I'll put a plaster on those bullet 'oles and you'll ave no brains left after I've finished wiv yer.'

Jonas smiled as Jack popped his head up from the coffin again, 'All over?'

'Yeah Jack, you heroic toerag,' Della said.

'I am wounded you know,' Jack said and Jonas asked how he was feeling.

'Don't be a daft bugger Jonas he only has a scratch, just like you, now shove over,' and Jonas put the thug down and limped out of the way as Mandy's head popped over the coffin side and she stepped out, rapidly followed by Burial; rather aptly Jack said.

'Okay let's get this last Herbert out,' Mandy said, 'and Della, I think you should ring the Met and call this in, get the guns sorted in the Stanley mausoleum and, in due course, they can identify the Pall Mall weapon. Your nick I think, and as Jack and you would say, a right Brahma?' Mandy mimicked Jack's accent.

Della acknowledged Mandy, stepped past a grinning Jack, and headed for the steps outside and ducked back as machine gun fire chewed bits of brick, and sparked off the decorative wrought iron gate.

'Oh feck me,' Jack said and shouted, 'Cisco you turnip it's just us foes.'

'Oh, right-eo Jack; sorry,' a distant cry.

Jack went over to Seb who looked like he was about to go into serious shock, whispered to the autistic lad, who all of a sudden became galvanised and pushed past all of them and disappeared into the coffin; a lad on a mission. Jack phewed, then tripped over Ghost who was working on the bastards on the floor.

'Ferken 'ell Jak'

'Ferk ern yerself Ghost, they're scum, leave em,' Jack replied.

And then in another rare moment of eloquence from the Ghost, 'Treat the body in front of you Jack.'

Jack was moved by the skeletal surgeon who, through all of the commotion, had not stopped working on the wounded men, regardless of the fact that they did not deserve to live, in Jack's opinion. He knew Ghost's story and it was not a happy one.

'Siggy, I'm sorry, you're right and you are better man than anyone, Ghunga Din.' This was an Indian fella and not frontier gibberish, Jack pointed out to Mandy, who poked him in his wound to shut him up, 'Ouch!'

Ghost did look up for a moment and the frail looking corpse of a man had tears in his eyes, almost as if his life passed before him, and Jack broke down, fell to the floor and hugged and wept with the Ghost, sharing all of Ghosts travails, all of his misery and woes, his constant and undying belief in mankind and the responsibility they both felt for it, in their own personal ways.

Della and Mandy looked at each other and together they shrugged and headed for the entrance to the Banks mausoleum, just as the paramedics were entering.

'Hi Bazzer.'

'Hello superintendent; busy day.'

'Yeah – you can call me Mandy you know?'

'Yes Mandy, thank you, and there was one of your lot over the far side of the cemetery, he was dazed and seemed to be making a run for it. We have a team with him now but I heard one of your chaps say he was IRA.'

'Paddy Mulligan?' Jack asked from the bottom of the mausoleum steps.

'Yeah Jack; that was it,' Jack nodded and decided to ignore Mandy's old fashioned look, even though he liked that one; he needed to get his massive bullet wound sorted before his arm fell off.

'It's just a scratch and we need to have a talk you and me, and before we go to bed,' she said, scaring the bajeezers out of Jack who was outside now, which he thought was convenient because he needed to look to heaven and illicit a bit of support that he fully expected to get, otherwise what was the point in having a papal blessing.

'I'm not sure a papal blessing can be considered as a get out of jail free card?' Mandy said.

'Did I ...? and Mandy nodded, he did, and held her man tight. She sensed her adrenaline levels plummet and sobbed into his shoulder, and of course he joined her, because she was squashing his bullet wound and it hurt. They both felt bony, but strong arms around them. Mandy looked up, it was Ghost.

'Erp bit; lit et ert lerv.'

'Tak Sig." Jack said tearfully, in his best Danish frontier gibberish; he'd been watching Borgen on the telly Mandy recalled, so that explained that...

Chapter 39

The press had not caught up with the action at the cemetery, 'They're too busy getting their noses into the trough of carnage at Fort Cumberland,' Jo said, talking to Mandy on the phone.

'Jo, set up a press briefing for 5.30. This will give us a couple of hours to get something sorted,' and she closed the call and munched her bellyache burger, bought for her by Jack from the caravan vendor beside the lifeboat station; she knew she would regret it, and that was after Jack had argued with the vendor that his soaking wet fiver was legal tender, and all the vendor had to do was put it on the line to dry. "In the rain?" he'd replied unreasonably in Jack's view. Mandy thought he would be lucky to get a bank to take that note, but they got the burgers all the same and quite remarkably she enjoyed it; she was starving. They returned to clear up some issues at the Fort and then at the Lifeboat station, as the incident vans were being shut down.

'Press conference?' Jack asked.

'Yes Jack,' Mandy said.

'Well, I suppose it has to be done. Call Jo back, tell her you, me and the Commander on this one; okay?'

Mandy looked shocked and then thought that maybe he was winding her up, you never knew with him, 'No Jack, you've not done one since, err, since...?' her stomach churned and it was a combination of bellyache burger and recollections of a traumatic time.

'Since you were shot at outside the station?' (Book 1, *Cause and Effect*) he said. She looked at him with watery loving eyes, recalling how he had saved her from embarrassment when she was about to choke in front of the national media, following the shooting incident outside the police station.

'Yes Jack, though the Commander will not allow you in front of the cameras; you know that.'

'I do, but I need to speak out. There is something that needs saying and after that, maybe I will call it a day? I want you to call the briefing with the Commander and I will join you improm... err partoo...okay?'

Mandy did not know what to think, he looked so serious and she knew that look, and she also knew that she would follow him and his bloody looks, 'What is it Jack; what are you thinking, please tell me.' And he did tell her and she decided to go along with him, but only if it was impromptu.

* * *

Jo Jums seemed only slightly put out that Mandy was taking the press conference. Frankly she was relieved, acknowledging to herself that she was only marginally up to speed with what had happened at the fort, not at all at the cemetery, and she was also busy processing prisoners; those that were still walking that was. Apparently, someone had given Jack a gun and she sighed, picturing Jane Austin; a monkey with a machine gun. Spotty, in contrast, was agitated. He'd had a fifteen-minute briefing with Mandy, the Commander and the Chief Constable, and was rattled that Jack Austin sat in and even more unnerving, he had said nothing and had blood splatters on the arm of his shirt, and even more unusual, Jack walked with them to the door of the press conference room and whispered something to the superintendent, just before they went into the room.

Not unusually, the press were excited, though this seemed even more manic than normal. They'd had only a whiff of what had been happening as they tried desperately to catch up the detail of a shootout at Fort Cumberland and, as they had gathered and set up their distant positions, they had had a grandstand view from the shore of a sea battle, which was already being described as rivalling the Battle of Trafalgar – Jack of course appreciated the exaggeration, and Mandy was not sure if he had not even slipped the suggestion to Bernie.

Spotty, now very much an experienced and consummate professional PR man for such a young chap, opened up and there was immediate silence; an air of expectancy, tantalisingly drawn out by the growing theatrical expertise of Spotty.

'As you are aware there has been a lot happening in Portsmouth today.' He allowed the nervous tittering to die down, 'I will ask you to please keep your questions until after the briefing as we have a lot to get through; Commander,' and he nodded to Jamie to take the ball.

* * *

Back in the CP room, the Telly was on and the team stood and watched; no pretence of working. The chaos that was the custody suite downstairs was a minor distraction, as the team used this as an opportunity to find out themselves, just what had happened, and all apparently out of the blue. Jo Jums did however remind them that she had said to the team, only last night that Jack was back, and of course there was now Della!

"Oh Yeah", being a breathy collective response.

* * *

The Commander started up, not overly confident and sure they'd agreed with Spotty that Mandy was going to start. 'In the past few weeks, we have been briefing about the almost overtly and obvious resurgence of the 6, 57 crews, and how we were not convinced, and counselled that this appeared more than just mindless football thuggery. We have had a number of discreet surveillance operations in place over this period and one of these directed us to Fort Cumberland this morning.' Mandy looked to the Commander to see if his nose grew, it didn't but it should have. 'I am going to pass you over to Detective Superintendent Bruce and she will now brief on the detail.' The Commander looked rather pleased with his hospital pass.

Mandy was ready, and waited for the hubbub to settle. It had been a while since she had briefed from this podium, and the press were clearly excited. She kicked off by summarising the events that led up to what she had heard Jack telling Bernie was the battle of Waterloo, just prior to Trafalgar. She had to concede that the fort was built to defend against Napoleon, who had not turned up, according to Jack, because it was raining. She looked out and the press were laughing and scribbling notes; she realised too late she had spoken her thoughts and this explained later why it was thought she had named the battles and also, according to the press, because it had stopped raining at least for the duration.

She could not explain or discuss Jack's conspiracy theory as she was already under strict orders to keep secret the existence of the underground MOD bunkers. So it was allowed that the fort had been taken over by thugs, for reasons as yet unknown. The press of course pressed, and she knew also that tomorrow's papers or even the late evening news, would be full of pundits expounding ridiculous theories and she knew also that one at least would be right, if the 'D'- Notice was not issued pronto tonto (a 'D'- Notice is a government order for press secrecy in the national interest).

At Portsmouth University there was a professor of strategic warfare studies, and he was a mate of Jack, of course, and a source of a lot of Jack's information, of course, and also drank at Jack's local pub, C&A's, of course. And, if that were not enough, he was also one of Jack's team that conspired to bring down the government, of course. None of this was as sinister as it sounds, of course, as to date, all they had done was to talk about it and get slowly inebriated. Despite all of his boisterous revolutionary buffoonery, Jack had still not even arranged the demonstrations in London; his excuse being that he had to arrange for a good pub to be kettled into!

So, almost in her stride, she carried on to talk about the sequence of events, the covert surveillance, the pigeon lorry, and eventually the battle and how it had all panned out. She made special reference to Tom, from up North, and she pulled herself up as she slipped into a northern accent, much to the amusement of the press and horror of the Commander and Spotty. She mentioned that a cache of arms had been found and these were thought to link back to the Pall Mall murders. She paid tribute to the support received from the Met and Tactical Support Unit, and was about to talk about the process they were now embarking upon when there was uproar. Jack appeared from within the standing and clambering press, and he walked to the dais.

The Commander was fighting an apoplectic fit, but the consummate Spotty, imitating Jack's stopping the traffic hand, calmly said, 'You all know Detective Chief Inspector Jack Austin, I think he may have come to inform us of developments in his mid-life crisis, or to describe his latest fashion modes,' Jack was drying, but not by much, and he looked a lot like a wet rag; which he was of course. Mandy however had changed, she always kept a change of clothing in her office and this had, as you would expect, amazed Jack who never thought of things like that.

The thought of how wonderful his wife looked brought a smile to Jack, as he climbed the dais and whispered into Spotty's ear, 'Good man yerself Spots lad.' Cod Irish; he was settling in for his address to the nation and so needed to be serious.

The press corps sat and very quickly came to attention, the old-fashioned reporters like Bernie, pencils at the ready. Jack left Spotty's ear to pay some overt attention to Mandy's, and she batted him away with a smile, and all of this frivolity was warmly received as Jack stood erect and presented his ugly, scarred, exhausted and soggy face to the Nation's press.

'Recently, the nation's debt, that had so saturated and crippled the people of this country, was rescheduled over a long term at low interest. This relieved the pressure on all of us, and as the Prime Monster hinted...' he stopped as there was a guffaw and he looked at Mandy, 'What?' she just smiled at her eejit husband, and that was all he needed of course. '...As I was saying, there was the hint of a conspiracy and we announced that those responsible would be brought to book; least that is what we had hoped, I hoped, and I will not give up on, I suppose.' He gave a look into the cameras, shrugged, a shrug clearly meant for Mackeroon and his sidekick Blogg. 'We have to be vigilant, we cannot let any bad apples remain however integral a cog they may appear to be, in whatever machine appears to be feckin' flavour of the month...' there was a giggle from the press and a grumble from the Commander. 'Today, I also warn, as did Abraham Lincoln apparently but I was first and he copied me, there is no grievance that is a fit object of redress by mob law, but then again, what did he know about the price of fish?' he looked around.

Mandy looked up in horror, and if she was any judge of fish prices, he was now a fart in a trance; she was worried, but he was continuing.

'We need to take this opportunity to rebuild a world where people can focus on what they're good at, and not just imitating the so called successful phoneys on the television? We must not recklessly abandon the care for our fellow man in the name of personal wealth and power, or even personal survival. We cannot prosper off the broken back of the ordinary working man and woman; it is just plain wrong. We must look out for, and root out those that do this, those who care not if they in the process crush humankind into the dirt, grind to pulp the human spirit? The fucking bastards...and this is what has been happening,' he wobbled and Mandy took his hand; he calmed.

'I say Jack...' the Commander whispered, 'keep it down old man.'

Water, not inappropriately, of a duck's back to Jack, as he continued, 'Our best defence against anything like this happening again, is for us to not be selfish, to look to our fellow man and help where it is needed, and I don't mean the bleedin' Big feckin'

Society.' There was a wave of chuckles that Jack ignored. 'It is not a sign of success to be wealthier than your neighbour, and it certainly is nothing to be proud of to flaunt that wealth. There is more to humanity than wealth, and it most certainly is not a symbol of success or, more importantly, fulfilment.' There was a gentle ripple of applause that looked like gathering momentum, but Jack was stopping traffic with his hand, 'This brings me onto my final and principle point. You have all been writing about him, the Ghost of Eastney cemetery.'

This did illicit a furore of shouts and calls, but Spotty stepped in, curious himself as he had been continually batting away questions about the Ghost, primarily because he didn't know about the Ghost.

Jack continued, 'The Ghost is...' and it was clear he was emotional, Mandy saw his eye begin to well up, '...is, Sigmund Merde.' He waited for the clamber to again die down, 'If the name is not familiar to you, I will refresh your memories, for this is a man whose name has literally become shit. He is a man who, unjustly, has been aggressively abused, denigrated and isolated by a prejudiced and a thoughtless and callous society, even deserted by his wife, child and his family, and I make this stand today to redress the balance, to redress a gross wrong, and to insist that this man be allowed to stand back in society and take his rightful place beside the greatest of our national heroes, but more importantly, the greatest of this nation's humanitarians.'

There was silence and not surprisingly to those who knew Jack, his emotions were on Fred alert; he was tearful and Mandy stood and wrapped her arm around his shoulder, no intention of stopping him talking, but to support him, to give him the physical contact that she knew he always needed. He looked deep into her eyes. He felt like stopping, but was committed, if only for Siggy's sake, but he still mentioned for her not to squeeze too hard, as he was seriously wounded; well what did you expect.

'Sigmund Merde was, is, a trauma surgeon of the absolute first order. There are many involved in today's chaos who owe their lives to him, for he was there in amongst the bullets, the explosions and carnage and with not a thought for his own safety; he treated policemen, villains and civilians alike, and I quote Dr Merde, "You treat the body in front of you", The Hypocritical Oath all doctors take.'

There was gentle laughter and he looked to Mandy again, she pulled him tighter but was riveted because she was only just learning about Ghost herself.

'What...?' but he carried on after a brief wince, that he thought might come in handy before bedtime, and the "talk". 'In the terrorist bombings in London, many years ago, Sigmund was the principle trauma surgeon and saved many lives, at the scenes and back in the trauma centre. This included the terrorists, and later that day, a wounded terrorist called at his home and he treated the man. This act of humanity brought down his world. He was vilified, because he treated and saved the life of the man who had bombed a coach full of children. The terrorist is still alive today and at large, and I remind you, Dr Merde "Treated the body in front of him".'

Those of you who can recall, Dr Merde was subjected to the most horrendous abuse by you the Press, the State, and worse his wife who left him taking his beloved only daughter, and he has not seen or heard from them since. He was barred from being a surgeon, later reinstated as it was pointed out by a sympathetic barrister, that he was only doing what a doctor should do, and I repeat, "Treating the body in front of him". However, and tragically, he never learned of that. He disappeared.'

Jack breathed deeply, composed himself to reveal more facts, 'I can tell you now that the so-called Legend of Beirut, Libya, Afghanistan and most recently Syria, and many other conflicts, is none other than Sigmund Merde. He was the doctor who, regardless of his own safety, was at any and every front line, there to treat civilians, friends and foe alike. It was he who arranged, via *Medicine Sans Frontiere*, to get vital medical supplies into the war zones. Nobody knows how he did this, but he did, and today at Fort Cumberland, he was there; aware that something tragic was going to happen and again, regardless of his own welfare. And now he has gone; again – where? Who the feck knows?' Jack was despairing, throwing his arms out.

'How did I know that this was going to happen? I will tell you; it was not because we are super sleuths, it was because Ghost told me. He knew, and those that had the power to stop it happening also knew, were told, but did nothing, and that is the question I will leave with you today. Why was that? Why was it that the people who could act, who knew, did nothing? Is it happening again, and we need to look very closely at the governance of this country, the Politicians, the Whitehall Mandarins, the Financial System, who knows? And, who is still in place and looking for revenge, a misplaced sense of reparation or redress?'

He calmed, looked into the BBC camera, he pointed, 'My-loft, I know about you, you are the one and I know,' he tapped his nose; this could mean he knew who My-loft was or someone could be shagging on a sack of rice (Book one – *Cause and Effect*, the start of it); with Jack you just never knew. But Jack knew, and he stared with his mad, red rimmed eye into the camera and mouthed the word, "My-loft" and tapped his nose again.

He stopped and there was a raucous clamour, the Commander was trying to get past Mandy to usher Jack out. He had overstepped the mark again but Jack stood his ground, reinforced by his wife who stood four square with him, as he remained staring directly into the BBC camera.

'We need to find Dr Merde and we need to give him the recognition he deserves, and we need to grovel at his feet and beg his apology; if it's not too late? As for me, I've had enough of this shite; watching my front, sides and especially my back, and especially from all of you Whitehall Mandarin shysters that crawl up my trouser legs to bite me feckin' arse.'

He looked at Mandy and spoke to her, 'I'm officially retired,' and he kissed her and she helped him from the room as he sobbed into her shoulder; the hub-bub from the room, a distant echo.

* * *

Ghost and Ragman Roll

Jack and Mandy return in

Merde and Mandarins – Divine Breath

Autumn 2017

Author Note

Redress - setting an injustice right; the term may imply retaliation or punishment

Ragman Roll - I first learned of the term Ragman Roll as the origination of the modern day expression of rigmarole, by Albert Jacks in his book Red Herrings and White Elephants. Jacks says the expression dates back over 700 years, and was used to describe a deed of loyalty to Edward I that was signed by Scottish noblemen that eventually became a shambles of dishevelled documents that when unrolled was forty feet long. I liked the sound of Ragman Roll and so used it completely out of context. The modern derivative is thought to be 'rigmarole', now used to describe anything or anyone, of a troublesome, time consuming, awkward nature.

Ghost – A Spectre or a Spook?

About the author

Pete Adams is an architect and designs and builds projects around the UK when he's not writing up a storm. Pete describes himself as an inveterate daydreamer, escaping into those dreams by writing funny stories that contain a thoughtful dash of social commentary. With a writing style inspired and shaped by his formative years on an estate that re-housed London families shortly after WWII, Pete's Kind Hearts and Martinets series of books have been likened to the writing of Tom Sharpe.

Pete says that the best feedback he's had on his work was that "it made me laugh, made me cry and made me think." People have said they laugh out loud reading his books, and if he can continue to get that reaction from his readers then he says he would be very content indeed. Pete lives in Southsea with his partner, the Irish nana, and Charlie the star-struck Border terrier, the children having now flown the coop.

Pete Adams

ISBN - 978-1-909273-96-2

£8.99

Out now!

A Barrow Boy's Cadenza is book 3 in the Kind Hearts and Martinets series

DCI Jack Austin – Jane to his friends and the not so friendly – knew he shouldn't have come in to work. Following a terrorist bomb, an incident with a tutu and a hangover that would fell an elephant,

270

investigating dead dogs, dodging bullets and being pulled sopping wet from a naval harbour is not conducive to a sunny disposition. But when the Head of Armed Forces and a City Banker are brutally murdered what's a dashing DCI to do?

FORCE, a powerful Star Chamber, is under threat and Jack will need to go deep undercover to get to the bottom of the sinister plot. As revelations and rocket attacks threaten to turn his world upside down (and ruin his best pair of trousers), Jack will need courage, skill and a huge dose of lady luck if he is to bring the perpetrators of a nefarious plot that goes all the way to the Prime Minister's office to justice.

As the trail leads to a showdown at the Albert Hall, Jack Austin, quintessential jumped up barrow boy and Portsmouth's very own self-styled national icon, must fight to save his reputation, the country, and the lives of those who matter most. And work out just what a dead dog has to do with it all......

Pete Adams

Urbane Publications is dedicated to
developing new author voices, and publishing
fiction and non-fiction that challenges, thrills and
fascinates. From page-turning novels to innovative
reference books, our goal is to publish what
YOU want to read.

Find out more at

urbanepublications.com